VIKING KISS

"What is this that you do with the mouth?" Nama muttered against his lips.

"It is a kiss," Garrick replied. "Have you never been kissed before?"

"No, my people know nothing of this. But," she paused, "it creates a pleasant feeling."

"Pleasant?" He frowned down at her as though he were displeased. "That is not the feeling I wish to convey."

"Would you like to try again?" Nama asked innocently.

"Indeed I would." His mouth claimed hers again. Nama felt a stirring in her belly that spread downward. She felt breathless, excited, wanting something more, yet unable to determine what it was.

He lifted his head and gazed down at her. "Still only pleasant?"

"My heart beats so . . ." Nama took his hand and lifted it to her breast. "My heart beats like thunder."

"Do you want me to stop?" Garrick asked, tilting her chin to look at her closely.

Stop? She widened her eyes and shook her head. Her action caused a smile to twitch at the corner of his lips.

"Then, let us continue."

BETTY BROOKS

VIKING MISTRESS

ZEBRA BOOKS
KENSINGTON PUBLISHING CORP.

ZEBRA BOOKS are published by

Kensington Publishing Corp.
850 Third Avenue
New York, NY 10022

Zebra and the Z logo Reg. U.S. Pat. & TM Off.

First Printing: September, 1994

Printed in the United States of America

Prologue

1213 A.D.
Spring

"Nama!" The name struck the mountains, then bounced away, striking the cliff opposite before the sound reverberated back again. *Nama, Nama, Nama!*

She swallowed against the rising horror as she fell, knowing with a certainty that only death could await her below. She would either be crushed by the jagged rocks on the canyon floor or drowned in the turbulent river that, even now, reached for her with white-tipped fingers.

Those thoughts flashed through her mind as she fell, falling as swiftly and as straight as a spear thrown by a skilled hunter, and although her mouth was wide with horror and her eyes so round the whites could be seen all around, she was unable to make a sound, unable to express the terror she was feeling.

Then she reached the bottom.

Immediately, rushing water enveloped her, cold and icy water that swallowed her in one gulp, sucking her under and twisting her over and around into a maelstrom of fury. She was propelled to the surface for one short moment, just the barest instant, but it was long enough for her to gasp a single breath of air before she was forced under again.

A cold, hard knot formed in her stomach, spreading quickly through her body, sweeping over her legs and chest where it mingled with an odd burning sensation that was forming in her lungs.

Nama felt these things and acknowledged them as the Spirits reached out to her, beckoning with warm smiles, urging her to leave that useless body and join them.

She felt herself turning loose, rising up, with no more substance than smoke, then hovering there to gaze down upon her own body. She felt pity for the useless, fear-ridden shell. It continued to fight, twisting and turning, arms and feet working frantically against the pressures of the angry water that bucked and roiled, threatening to rip the limbs from their sockets.

Why did her body continue to fight so hard? she wondered. Did it not know the end had come? There was a journey to be made now. A journey that led to eternal peace and happiness.

Disembodied, she continued to watch her body kick furiously, clawing at the heavy walls of water above. *Give up,* she urged silently. But the foolish girl would not. The empty husk that was herself broke surface again, hung there for one long moment before another wave crashed down and sent her plummeting downward again.

Let go! she told her struggling body. *You cannot survive this. Embrace the death that awaits you and allow me to find peace.*

But her foolish body would not yield. The desire to live was too strong. Nama found herself floating downward again, entering the body that continued to struggle, even though those struggles were useless.

Then, suddenly, amazing though it seemed, something solid struck her arm. Reacting swiftly, she wrapped her cold fingers around it and clung with every ounce of strength she possessed.

$\mathcal{O}n\varepsilon$

Fall

The limestone sides of the ravine provided respite from Wind Woman's hot, stinging breath. It whistled across barren, broken land, churning up dirt and sand as it went, covering everything in its path with gritty dust.

A young woman, with tangled dark hair tumbling past her shoulders, knelt at the bottom of the gully, sheltered at last from the whip of Wind Woman's constant lashing, and yet, she was barely conscious of that fact. Her attention was focused instead on the elk that lay shivering on the ground unable to even attempt escape because of the slender white bones protruding from its broken hind leg.

The girl—Nama, formerly of the Eagle Clan—looked into the animal's wide dark eyes. "Forgive this woman for taking your flesh, Sister Elk." Her throat was parched and dry, thickening her voice to a husky sound. "For six moons I have lived alone and my body is weak, deprived of nourishment that you will provide. But I promise to make your death as painless as possible and when you have departed the land of the living I will sing your soul to the Blessed Star People."

Nama imagined she saw acceptance—and perhaps forgiveness as well—in the eyes of the elk; but the animal continued to stare at her with unfaltering gaze and Nama, coward that she was, found herself unable to use the crude knife she had made from a sharp-edged stone to cut the elk's throat.

Suddenly, the elk jerked, its legs kicking out rapidly while it swung its head back, extending a long, slender neck to its fullest length.

Nama understood immediately. The animal—knowing how badly she needed meat to survive—was offering itself to her and making the kill easier by avoiding her eyes.

"Thank you," she whispered tenderly.

Then, realizing that if her hand faltered the animal would suffer more, she pressed her knife hard against its neck, digging through hide and flesh until beads of blood began to seep through.

Nama's hands trembled and she grunted with the effort needed to cut around the elk's throat. As she did so, Nama kept her eyes fastened to that area where she worked, unwilling to look higher lest she see the animal's pain. She pressed harder with the crude knife, slicing through the jugular vein with a feeling of relief. "Your suffering will soon be over," she murmured, settling back on her heels to wait for the animal's spirit to depart.

Hunting was a new experience for Nama. It was a task reserved for the men in her clan. But now, since becoming an outcast, she must fend for herself.

A quick look at the elk's glazed brown eyes told her its life was almost over. Raising her arms skyward, Nama began the death chant that would send its spirit to the Star People.

Singing a soul to its eternal journey should never be done with undue haste, but surely, Nama consoled herself, she would be forgiven this one time. Her body was lean and weary, her limbs weak and thin because her belly had been empty for too long a time.

In the past she had been fortunate to find enough small animals willing to give up their lives for her nourishment, thus granting her continued survival, but it had been several days now since her last meal, and even that one had been meager at best.

Nama knew how lucky she had been to find the elk, for starvation had already showed its ugly face to her. Now she could send it away, for, although the animal was lean, its size was enough to ensure that, if carefully conserved, the meat would last her for several weeks.

A quick glance at the elk told her it was lifeless. Nama gutted the animal quickly, then dug her hands into the moist warm cavern and removed the liver. With a sigh of anticipation, she lifted the warm meat to her mouth and eagerly consumed it. Then, with hunger satisfied, she sat back on her heels and considered the problem of carrying the meat home. She was still worrying the matter over in her mind when the fine hairs on the base of her neck suddenly raised and icy fingers slid down her spine.

Someone—or some *thing*—was watching her!

Her heart beat a crazy rhythm as Nama snatched up the crudely made spear left close at hand, leapt to her feet, and spread her legs in a fighting stance. Although Nama presented a fierce appearance on the outside, inwardly she was quivering like a hunted rabbit.

Her wary gaze swept the gully, moving swiftly over the gray-and-rose-colored flats where clumps of bushes bristled. She saw the dead, sun-blackened tumbleweeds that were piled atop each other, blown there by Wind Woman's breath, but paid them no mind for they were of no consequence; they could offer no hiding place to an enemy.

Where was he? she wondered fearfully. Where was this enemy that sent shivers down her spine?

Unable to spot another living soul, Nama tilted her head back and sent her gaze sweeping up the limestone sides of the gorge, farther even, until she could see the top.

For a brief moment her gaze fastened on a dust devil that whirled and danced above the ground, hiding what lay beyond from her probing eyes.

Suddenly, with quickening speed, Wind Woman swept the dust devil away, carrying it in a northerly direction, then whipping the dust into a hazy cloud. Nama, who had been following it with her gaze, was about to turn away when she detected movement within the haze.

Her eyes narrowed on the spot and she waited breathlessly as the air slowly cleared until, finally, a human form was revealed. Silhouetted against a sky that was already growing purple and red with the onset of twilight, he seemed larger than life.

Who was he? she wondered, her heart giving a crazy jerk of fear. Why did he stand there so motionless, watching her so intently? Could he be from the Wolf Clan? Maybe, but considering the arid country around them, it was more likely he was from the Desert Clan. Desert or Wolf, what did it matter? Both clans represented danger to her. The thought of her fate if captured by either clan chilled her soul and coiled her belly into a tight knot of fear.

"Ho-yah!" the stranger called in greeting. Then, as though he had only been waiting for her to see him before he came closer, he began to descend the limestone slope, dislodging a shower of dirt and pebbles as he went.

"Hold!" she shouted, surprised that her voice sounded so fierce and bold when she was so frightened. "If you wish to survive this moment, then come no closer!"

The stranger skidded to a stop halfway down the slope and spread his arms wide as though to assure her of his good intentions. "Allow me to approach, woman. I mean you no harm." Although he spoke the words of assurance, he held something long and narrow in his right hand. It was shorter and thicker than any lance she had ever seen, but the object could be a weapon of some kind, she reasoned.

Her heart jerked, thumping like a rabbit caught in a trap, as she stared at the man, taking note of his height—a good double-hand-span taller than she. Although he wore a loose elk-hide shirt and trousers, she could still see he was well built and would easily be able to subdue her in hand-to-hand combat.

"Come, woman," he coaxed. "You have no need to fear me."

Nama wanted desperately to trust him, and yet, did she dare? She was all alone, with no protection except that which she could provide herself. But if he spoke true and really meant her no harm, she might make an enemy of him if she drove him away.

She hesitated, afraid to allow him closer, yet fearing she could not make him leave. But a decision must be made. "What do you want?" she asked, wondering if he would leave if she offered him food.

Instead of answering her question, he said, "Put down your spear woman. You can trust me."

Did she dare? She continued her silent appraisal. He was almost as lean as she. Perhaps he had only approached her because he was hungry.

She swallowed around a lump of fear. Clan courtesy demanded she offer him a portion of her meat since there was plenty. But that courtesy belonged to the life she had left behind. She was no longer

Eagle Clan. She was an outcast, had obtained that lowly status by her own actions.

Feeling a quick stab of self-pity, she shrugged it away. She was an outcast by her own choice.

Realizing the stranger was still balanced precariously on the slope waiting for her decision, Nama focused her attention on the slender object he carried. One end dug into the limestone slope and was obviously helping the man retain his balance. It was that fact alone that helped her identify the object. It was not a weapon, but a staff—a walking stick with a ring of white, barely discernible at this distance, painted around the top, exactly like those used by the traders who traveled among the clans.

Relief washed over Nama, replacing her fear. Her stomach unknotted and her tense muscles slowly relaxed. He must be a trader, she reasoned. Why else would he carry the staff that identified him as such? Nama lowered her spear.

Fool! an inner voice chided. *He could be anyone. He could have stolen the staff. Make him identify himself.*

Nama jerked the spear up again, hoping the need to hurl it would not arise. "Who are you?" she called, watching him closely, ready to scramble to safety should the occasion warrant it. "Are you a trader?"

"That I am," he replied. "May I approach now?" Without waiting for permission to do so, he clambered down the sides of the arroyo, obviously taking it for granted that she would no longer object. When he stood beside her, his full lips curled into a grin. "I should have identified myself in the be-

ginning. Black Crow's the name. And who might you be?" His black eyes burned dark and impenetrable as she studied him. His skin, dark and leathery from constant exposure to the wind and sun was especially red on his straight nose and high cheekbones. He carried nothing in his hands except the crooked walking stick, but there was a bulging pack on his back that, until now, had been hidden from her view.

Her gaze dwelt greedily on the pack and excitement coursed through her at the mere thought of all the treasures it must contain. Did the trader carry seashells from the clan living near the big salt water? Or perhaps some of those brightly colored feathers taken from the large birds that made their home in the rain forests in the southern lands? The memory of those very treasures, displayed by the last trader who came to her home among the cliffs brought an almost overwhelming sense of homesickness to Nama.

Realizing that Black Crow still waited patiently to hear her name, Nama wondered how she could give it to him? Traders went everywhere. They traveled easily through all the lands, visited and were welcomed within every clan they encountered. But Nama's name—and her whereabouts—must not be known, lest her enemies learn where she was and come for her.

As though sensing her hesitation, Black Crow said, "Traders do not reveal what others wish to keep secret; but if revealing your name causes you fear, then you may keep it to yourself."

He looked with hungry eyes at the elk on the ground, his gaze dwelling on the broken leg. "The Spirits have seen fit to bless you." His dark gaze lifted to hers again. "You have enough meat to last for some time, but you need help carrying it. It appears I arrived just in time."

Nama felt her hesitation leave her, swept away as though it had never been with no more assurance of his honesty than the kindness reflected in his dark eyes. "I would be grateful for your help, Black Crow."

"There is no need for gratitude. The deed benefits both of us." He shrugged off his pack, dropping it to the ground. "Is it far to your home?"

She tensed momentarily, then chided herself for doing so and pointed toward the limestone cliffs that rose in the distance. "I live in a cave up there."

"You are from the Eagle Clan."

It was not a question, merely a statement, but it caught her unawares, halting her movement in mid-stride as she was bending over the slaughtered animal. She straightened immediately, looking at him with newborn fear.

He smiled at her. "I do not tell secrets," he reminded quietly. "Your home will not be revealed through any word or deed of mine."

Tensely, Nama searched his expression, but found nothing there but concern. Slowly, the tension drained away.

The trader's full lips spread into a wide smile. "Now that we have dealt with your fears, you must help me lift the elk to my back, Woman of the

Eagle Clan." He bent over the carcass and grasped the hindquarters. "You may carry my pack," he added, as though bestowing a great favor on her.

Nama wasted no time with useless protestations about the elk being too heavy for him. Ofttimes hunters were forced to carry a greater weight than their own. Knowing that, she hurried to help him lift the slain animal; and when it was safely installed across his shoulders, she picked up his pack and her lance and led the way back to her home in the cliffs.

Two

The stars were glimmering brightly in the darkened sky by the time Black Crow finished dressing out the elk. As was the custom, he saved the hide and intestines, which would be used later for various purposes, then disposed of the remains away from the camp. When he returned, the pot of stew Nama had prepared was ready to eat.

After filling two wooden bowls with the savory stew, Nama handed one to Black Crow and bade him eat.

"When you are ready," he said politely.

Seating herself across the firepit from him, she scooped a generous portion onto a bone spoon and carried it to her mouth. "It is good," she said, heaving a sigh of contentment.

"My feelings exactly," Black Crow agreed. "There is nothing more satisfying to my belly than elk stew flavored with onions and prairie turnips."

"I have not thanked you properly for the vegetables," Nama said. "The stew would not have been as tasty without them."

"Your gratitude is not necessary," he said, the formality of his tone tempered by his wide grin.

"Consider it an even exchange. The vegetables for the meat." He settled back against the rocky wall and examined her boldly. "You must either be the bravest of women or one of the most foolish ones."

"Why do you think that?" she asked, raising dark brows questioningly. "Is it because you find me here alone? That is not so unusual. I know many women who live alone."

"Old women," he said shortly. "Women who are no longer attractive to men. Women who are past the age of childbearing and have nothing to offer except a sharp tongue."

"Perhaps my tongue is also sharp."

"Perhaps. But there are many men who would disregard a sharp tongue when confronted with a woman such as yourself."

Nama knew she had been given a compliment and it made her feel uncomfortable.

"You are not only alone," he continued, "but you apparently wish to remain that way."

"That is so." She moved restlessly, having no wish to continue the conversation. Perhaps it would be best if she retired for the night.

"Have you heard the story of Rattlesnake Woman?" he asked suddenly.

She shook her head. "Who is she?"

"A woman who lives with the Round Hoof Clan. The story is old, as is the woman, and the tale has been told many times over. But it is not a happy tale."

"Tell me."

As though he had only been waiting for her response, he took up the tale of Rattlesnake Woman, speaking of her at length, repeating what he had heard of the child she had been and of the count-less beatings she had endured at the hands of her father. Long before she reached womanhood, she had taught herself to wield a knife in a manner that would have done honor to the strongest warrior.

Nama was puzzled. "Have you told me the story because you find a resemblance between Rattle-snake Woman and me?" she asked, when he had finished speaking.

"No," he answered gruffly. "You have not yet separated yourself from the rest of humanity. But you may yet attain that goal. Given enough time you could become very much like her."

"My childhood was not miserable!" Nama said abruptly, unwilling to leave that impression with him even though they might never meet again in this life.

"I did not mean to imply it was," he said softly. "Nor am I attempting to discover things that you would hold secret. It was only my wish to make conversation."

"Then please do so," she said, relaxing some-what. "I would like to hear of the places you've traveled and the people you have met."

"What interests you most? Do you wish to hear about the people who live near the great salt water? Or perhaps you would be interested in the great longboat that was stranded for a time on a muddy shoal."

"Longboat?" she questioned huskily.

"Yes." He seemed not to notice her interest. "I am told the boat was of massive proportions. Huge, the natives said, large enough to carry many warriors, perhaps ten times all my fingers. The men who occupied the boat were strangers to this land. They were unaware of the shoal that reached far out into the Great Muddy River until it was too late."

"I would hear more of the boat and its occupants," Nama said.

The trader spoke at length about the longboat; but although there was much speculation, there was little fact, for the tribe who lived near the river kept their distance from the boat, fearful of the carved beast head that reared above its prow.

Nama listened intently, wondering if the boat the trader described had belonged to Eric, the golden-haired Viking who had traveled to the mesa where the Eagle Clan lived and stolen the heart of her friend Shala.

The mere thought of Shala caused a sweeping sadness that bent Nama's head lower. Was Shala dead or alive? The question tormented Nama for, without her interference, Shala would never have left the cliff dwellings, would never have found herself a prisoner of the Wolf Clan.

The trader, seeming to become aware of her lack of interest in his latest story, said, "Something troubles you, Woman of the Eagle Clan. It is not my wish to pry in matters that do not concern me, but perhaps you would be less troubled if you spoke your thoughts to another."

"My conscience is sorely troubled," she said huskily, surprising herself with her words. "But revealing my thoughts cannot make it less so."

"Perhaps your conscience is too easily troubled," Black Crow said gently. "You are little more than a child. Surely your sins cannot be so great."

"You think not?" Her gaze slid past him. He had no idea what she had done. And yet, if the past were hers to live over, how could she react any other way? "I have no remorse for the deed," she said quietly, "only for the result."

"Would it help to speak of it?"

"No," she said quickly, then just as swiftly changed her mind. "Yes. I would speak of it . . ." Her cheeks flushed as she added, ". . . if you will not betray my trust."

He spread his arms wide and said, "I am a trader, Woman of the Eagle Clan."

"Nama," she softly corrected. "My name is Nama. You may call me that." She waited quietly for some kind of response, some sense of recognition from him, but there was nothing in his face to show that he had ever heard of her. "You guessed right, Black Crow. I *am* a woman from the Eagle Clan." He made no comment, merely waited quietly for her to continue. "You obviously know that my clan—that is," she corrected swiftly, "my former clan—build their homes among the cliffs. There is safety there, high above the canyon floor. It is a place where no enemy can reach without warning. Even so, we—they—are constantly under attack from others who wish to steal not only their hunting grounds, but the crops they work so hard to grow. One such clan, the people from the desert, coveted our . . ." Nama knew that she had included herself in the clan again, but it was so hard to speak as though she were an outsider. " . . . lands and our homes. In order to protect us from constantly being under attack, a bargain was struck with the desert people. Their chief, Standing Wolf, would be given a bride, one who would be chosen from among us so that our people would be bound together. Each of us was aware that, with the combined strength of both clans, we could easily chase away those brave enough to attack us."

"A good plan," he murmured.

"Yes." She lowered her dark lashes, unwilling to see his reaction to her confession. "But the maiden chosen refused to put the good of her people before her own selfish needs. Her cowardly heart was revealed when she ran away."

His hand covered hers. "You were the maiden that was chosen to sacrifice herself."

"Yes." She bowed her head, unable to face him. "Now you know part of my shame."

"Part of it?"

"I was . . . afraid to go alone." The words would not come easily. "I had a good friend. She went with me and, although I cannot say for sure, I fear she may have perished."

There was a long, thoughtful silence. Then, "Did you force your friend to go with you?"

"No!" Her head jerked up. "I would not! She left for reasons of her own."

"Then how can you blame yourself? Whatever happened to your friend was not the result of your actions."

"Not so," she said huskily, looking past his shoulder where the firelight cast dancing shadows on the walls. "The story is yet untold. We had only gone a short way when we were taken prisoner by Wolf Clan warriors. We managed to escape from them, but were eventually caught." Her gaze turned inward as the memory of that time surged forth in her mind. She remembered the way Hooked Nose had looked with lustful eyes upon Shala, remembered the way her friend had fought so hard to save them both and felt shamed that she alone had escaped his clutches, leaving her friend behind to face the consequences. "It was my own cowardice that caused our downfall," she whispered. "Shala's lance was beyond her reach. She looked to me for help; but I knew nothing of weapons, knew nothing of courage, and when I threw the spear, my hand trembled and my aim was not true." When she remembered how Shala had looked the last time Nama had seen her, weaponless, sprawled on the ground where her tormentor's blows had sent her, the tears Nama had been holding at bay brimmed over and slid down her face.

"How did she die?" he prompted gently.

"I have no way of knowing," she replied huskily,

bowing her head with shame. "I never saw her again."

"You threw the spear then ran away?" he asked.

"I did not run away!" she snapped, jerking her head up, and glaring indignantly at him. "He picked me up as though I were nothing more than a stick and threw me over a cliff. I barely survived the fall. I would not have lived through it had there not been a river below that was swollen bank to bank from the spring thaw."

Another long silence, then, "Why do you torment yourself this way? You did not run away and leave your friend alone. You said so yourself. Why, then, do you continue to blame yourself for what happened?"

Her face crumpled and her shoulders sagged with despair. "Because it was my fault we were captured by the Wolf Clan. If I had not been such a coward, had done my duty, Shala would have stayed with her husband."

"Shala?" His gaze narrowed sharply on her face.

"Yes." She sniffed and wiped the tears from her face with the backs of her hands, barely aware of the childish action. "You have heard of her?" For some reason, unknown to herself, Nama was not surprised.

"We had occasion to meet," he said, recalling that incident with a smile. "And, from what I observed, her nature appeared such that she would attach no blame for her circumstances to you. But . . ." He frowned at her. "When did all this take place? Surely she was not taken by the Wolf

Clan a second time? I expected her Viking to take better care of her."

"You know of Eric?" How could that be? Eric had only arrived at the mesa during the past long, white, cold season; and he was only there for a few short moons.

"I know him," the trader replied. "They were together when we met near the long river flowing beside the tall mountains located a moon's cycle from here."

"But, how—" She broke off, her confusion deepening. "When did you see them?"

"When the land was fresh with new spring grass," he replied, watching her with dawning comprehension. "After Shala's escape from the Wolf Clan."

"She escaped from the Wolf Clan," Nama breathed, feeling a heavy weight leave her shoulders. It was a good feeling, one that she had thought never to know. She had carried the guilt for so long, always burdened by the knowledge that she was responsible for Shala's death.

But I am not guilty! her heart cried. *Shala is not dead.*

"Do you know how she managed to escape? Did Hooked Nose harm her?"

"Hooked Nose? The name is unfamiliar," the trader replied. "But the people of the Wolf Clan spoke at length of Bull Elk, the man Shala killed by tearing his neck apart with her teeth." His full lips stretched into the wide smile that came and went so easily. "Most of those who knew him said he deserved such a death."

Nama's heart was light as she returned his smile. "It is good you came, Black Crow. You have eased my mind. Now the only load I must carry is my shame for being such a coward when duty demanded that I help my people."

"Then you have no guilt to carry at all," he said gently. "Although a trader belongs to no clan when he chooses to travel, there was a time when all of us did belong to one or another of them. When I was a clan member it was our custom to allow our maidens to choose their own husbands. No one had the right to choose for them."

"The same holds true for the Eagle Clan, unless the shaman—or the council of elders—deems it otherwise," Nama told him.

"Then forget it, Nama," he said gravely. "It is time you put blame behind you and looked toward the future."

While she turned his words over in her mind, she noted his gaze, sweeping around him, apparently taking in the sparseness of her home that was empty of the usual comforts—the rugs made of hide or woven rushes, painted clay jugs and pottery that were valued by her people—and she felt his sympathy, felt it and was angered by it. There had been no time to make such luxuries. It was all she could do to keep herself alive these past moons. When she found herself alone for the first time in her life, Nama had known nothing of hunting, known nothing of fending for

herself. With so much to learn, there had been
no time for the weaving of rugs, no time to make
pottery or to tan hides as she had done when she
lived among the Eagle Clan. Instead, her time
had been spent on learning to track game, on
finding the right flint rock to use for spear-points,
on finding wood for a shaft that would move swift
and straight through the air.

"Leave this place with me," he urged, unaware
of her growing anger. "This is no life for a young
woman such as you. You should not be forced to
live in this manner, with no companion to ease
your loneliness and no man to stand beside you,
to protect you from scavengers and men who might
claim you for their own."

She raised her chin a degree higher, and her
words, when she spoke them, were tinged with defiance. "I have no need of protection, Black Crow.
I have changed. This woman is not the one who
fled her People. She has taken control of her destiny."

"And that destiny is to live alone?" He swept his
hand around the emptiness. "With no comforts
whatsoever? With no other voice to break the silence around you?"

"There are times when I miss those things," she
admitted. "But there is much to be gained from
solitude. My wants and needs are not the same as
they were. I am stronger now, more sure of myself.
And I like being independent." She smiled at him.
"Men do not like those traits in a woman."

He frowned at her. "No. But perhaps if you worked hard to subdue them, then—"

"I cannot change what I have become," she interrupted.

"Cannot, or will not?" Black Crow questioned.

She uttered a soft laugh. "Does it matter? Either way I remain the same woman."

"You should not remain here alone, Nama. The long cold season comes soon; and if you do not leave this mountain before it arrives, you may never leave it."

"I will consider your words carefully, Black Crow."

"And you may go with me?"

She smiled at him. "No. Your path leads north. I have no wish to go there."

"You will not reconsider?"

"No," she said firmly. "But I wish to thank you for your kindness. The news about Shala's survival was greatly appreciated."

"I am thankful I could relieve your mind about the matter. It would have distressed me to confirm your belief about her death," he said gravely. Then, expelling a heavy sigh, he added, "I have traveled a great distance without enough rest of late. With your permission I will stay awhile. Just a few days until my sore feet heal and my body regains its strength."

"You have my permission, Black Crow," she said, holding his gaze steadily. "I will be grateful for your company. It is true my days are lonely. But there are worse things in life than loneliness."

"Yes. Who would know that better than a trader? Perhaps I could return your kindness by offering help of some kind. We might even make a trade."

"I have nothing of value to trade," she said regretfully.

"You wear a turquoise necklace and bracelet," he reminded.

"Yes." She fingered the necklace. "Do you like them?"

"A trader likes most things." He noticed her eyelids drooping heavily. "You are tired."

Nodding wearily, Nama said, "Yes. Very tired." She longed to stretch out on her sleeping mat, but knew courtesy demanded she offer it to her guest.

Black Crow forestalled the offer by settling down against the farthest wall. "You keep your sleeping mat," he said, yawning widely. "My bones would not rest well there since I usually sleep on the ground."

Needing no further urging, Nama settled down on the bed of rushes carried from a distant river and closed her eyes. But, although her aching body appreciated the softness of the mat, she could not rest. Had she seen a flare of passion in the trader's dark eyes? It was only a momentary thing, gone almost the instant it appeared, yet it made her aware of his wish to possess her.

Having learned much about him while he talked, Nama felt sure he would not force himself on her. Instead, he would wait—like Nampeyo from the Eagle Clan, who had loved her for years—until she was ready to accept him. But that would never happen. The man she would voluntarily allow to possess her—the man who must first claim her heart—had not yet entered her life. And she doubted that he ever would.

Three

The full moon glimmered softly, shedding its pale light over the wide, muddy river, illuminating the billowing sails of the great longship moving slowly upstream.

On both sides of the water were dense forests where Spanish moss, ivy-draped live oaks, and water sycamores grew in abundance.

Although Garrick Nordstrom was aware of the wild beauty of this new land, he had no time to waste in admiration. Instead, he stood erect, rudder in hand, his attention focused on navigating the river that had already proven itself treacherous.

Garrick was a brawny man of a score and seven years; and although he was not tall by Viking standards, he stood well over six feet. His massive shoulders and muscular chest, coupled with his indomitable courage, made him a man to be feared by those who displeased him.

A howl sounding in the distance caught his attention. His green eyes swept the banks of the distant shore, searching for the creature that had uttered the sound, but there was no discernible movement there.

Even as he watched, the howl rose in volume: A high-pitched, undulating sound that was taken up by another voice, echoed by another, then still another, until there was a veritable chorus resounding across the water.

The howls slowly died away and, although Garrick strained his ears, listening intently for something out of the ordinary, there was nothing. No other sound except that of water lapping softly against the boat and oars dipping into the water as the brawny crew rowed the Viking ship forward.

Even the nightbirds had ceased their call the instant the canine chorus sounded and they remained silent, as though danger lurked among them and to sound their cries would only serve to alert predators of their presence.

Garrick wondered momentarily what creatures had uttered the mournful cries. They sounded very much like those made by the wolves that occupied Norway, his own native land so far away.

Footsteps, thudding across the plank deck, caught Garrick's attention and he flicked a quick glance at the man who approached. Karl Nordenskiold. He was not only a good friend, he was also the only man among them who had traveled this watery passage before. And, when they reached the appointed place, it would be his finger that pointed the way the previous party had gone.

"How much farther?" Garrick asked.

"We are close now," Karl replied quietly, searching for landmarks on the distant shore. His dark eyes met those of the man he had called friend since early childhood. "If memory serves me right, there are only two more curves in the river before we reach that stretch of water."

"Good." Garrick sighed and rolled his head on the stem of his neck to release the tension.

"You are tired."

"A little," Garrick admitted.

"You should have let me guide the boat."

Garrick's smile was grim. "Allow someone else to captain my ship? You know me better than that." His gaze swept the nearest bank. The forest was not as dense there. "This looks like a good place to drop anchor, Karl. We could travel upstream by horse."

"There is a better place around the next bend of the river," Karl replied. "The banks are wider at that point and the *skraelings* who occupy this land will find it difficult to surprise us should they be of a mind to attack."

Garrick's copper-colored eyebrows drew downward in a frown. "Do you think they might? You said none attacked you before, and you were trapped on the shoal for the whole of winter."

"That is so," Karl agreed. "We *were* left alone. Nevertheless, we were made aware that we were always under observation. All the time we were here. They never once relaxed their guard. Nor did they ever allow us the peace of knowing their intentions. We tried on numerous occasions to make contact with them, but each time we went ashore we could find no sign of them. They seemed to disappear into thin air."

"Do you think they were afraid?" Garrick asked.

Karl fell silent for a long moment before replying. "No. They were not afraid. Each and every one of us sensed that fact. We felt they were just being cautious because our kind was unknown to them. No," he said again. "It was definitely not fear that made them keep their distance. Just caution. And possibly curiosity. We felt they wanted to know about us—about our habits—but were unwilling to make contact with us. Instead, they watched."

"And you never search for their villages?"

"We explored an area around the river, always keeping in mind that we must return to the longboat before nightfall, but we found no villages within that boundary."

"And you felt no need to go farther?"

"We could not. Eric left orders for us to remain on the longboat and keep it safe. Since our numbers were only six we could not spare the manpower needed for a search party. Nevertheless, when Eric and the others failed to return, we attempted to follow their path." Karl's expression was grim. "It was useless though. Too much time had passed. Time and the elements had erased all trace of them."

"Since Eric was afoot, he would have followed the river," Garrick mused. "The need for water would have been uppermost in his mind."

"His plans were to follow one of the tributaries. We searched all along its banks for weeks. But there was no sign of him." He gripped Garrick's shoulder to emphasize a point. "Eric was a powerful man, Garrick, as were all the men who followed him. And yet, despite that, despite their strength and courage, they failed to return."

"That fact has never left my mind for one moment since you brought the news home," Garrick said grimly.

"I would never have left without them had Eric not left orders for me to do so," Karl said. "Even so, we waited long beyond the date set for sailing, hoping all the time they would return."

"You carry no blame, my friend," Garrick consoled gruffly. "I know you did everything possible to find my brother."

"Yet it was not enough."

"Perhaps the gods will be kinder now and allow me to find them . . . or at least to know their fate."

"Olaf goes with you?"

Garrick answered the question with one of his own. "Do you think he would be content to stay behind? Although he has a gentleness inherited from our mother that keeps him happy with only his sheep for company, he also has our father's blood running strong in his veins."

Karl smiled widely, showing white teeth in a sun-browned face. "There has never been a more courageous man than your father, Fergus Nordstrom. Nor could there ever be. And yes, you are right. Olaf may be a farmer, but he has the courage of his father and his brothers, who have all proved themselves in battle."

"As have you, old friend," Garrick said. "No one has ever doubted your courage."

"Courage matters little if not coupled with good sense," Karl said. "See that you use some on your journey. Be extremely careful. It would pain me greatly to carry news of your death home. Your parents have already lost one son. Take care you do not join him in death."

"Do not accept his death so readily. You may well be proved wrong."

"I pray it will be so. Nevertheless, heed my warning and see to your own well being."

Garrick gave a short laugh. "You will not rid yourself of me so easily, old friend. I have no intention of dying and leaving Brunhilde to your care." It was an old joke between them, concerning a woman they had both known since childhood and, at one time, had both wished to possess. But that time was long since past. Both men had gone on to other women, other pursuits. Now nothing but a pretense of rivalry remained between them.

"Eric had no intention of dying either," Karl said morosely. "How do you expect to locate him when I could not?"

"You were hampered by the great distance he traveled," Garrick said. "I will not be. Midnight will carry me swiftly through this land."

Garrick's gaze swept midship where the horses were stabled. The black stallion would prove a great asset. His strength and endurance was unmatched, and would speed up the process of searching for Eric.

"Almost a year has passed since Eric began that journey and yet you think to make short work of following a trail gone cold long ago."

They had gone over all this many times before they left Norway, but Garrick remained adamant about searching for his brother. He would not rest until he brought Eric back, or at least satisfied himself that Eric was dead. If that were the case, then Garrick would find his bones and give his brother a decent burial.

He turned his attention to the job at hand, maneuvering the long boat around the great bend of the river, then paused to study the layout of the land.

Karl had remembered well. The river was considerably wider at this point, the shores so distant they were barely discernible in the light of the moon. It was a good place to anchor the boat.

He gave the orders to drop the anchor; then, after telling Karl to set the guards to watch, Garrick sought his bed, knowing that after he left the longboat little rest would be found for a long time to come.

Wind Woman flattened Nama's rabbit-skin dress against her body as she stood on a rocky knoll above the treeline, watching the tiny speck that was Black Crow move slowly across the desert. She would miss his company, and felt a small measure of regret that she had refused to accompany him.

But that regret was fleeting. Gone in the blink of an eye.

Lifting her gaze skyward, she saw the storm clouds gathering over the mountain. Did the clouds contain rain, or would cold white flakes soon cover the ground? Perhaps Black Crow was right. Staying on this mountain might mean death.

But where could she go?

North and west contained mountains where enemies of the People lived. She had no notion what lay to the east—her mountain blocked that path anyway. That left the south. She turned her face in that direction and considered the dry, arid land that would take many days to cross. But beyond that point, the trader said, lay forests and streams that knew nothing of the cold white season. Game and roots would be in plentiful supply.

Although it sounded too good to be true, Nama made the decision to go there.

Four

Nama had not overestimated the distance. She traveled for five days across dry, arid land where there was no shelter to be found from Father Sun's hot gaze. Nor could she hide from Wind Woman's raw, scorching breath that blew continuously, flinging sand and grit across her face and into her stinging eyes.

Time seemed to drag on endlessly as Nama made her stumbling way across the immense, inhospitable desert. She dug roots to eat when she chanced to find them, breaking open cactus and sucking the moisture out of the water-heavy pulp at the core of the plant to keep going.

For the most part she walked with head down, plodding endlessly forward, pausing to rest only when her weary legs refused to carry her one step farther.

On one such time, when Father Sun was hovering just above the western horizon, Nama slumped down against a slanted rock to rest, then looked back the way she had come. Only then did she realize she had left the plains behind.

Swiveling her head on the stem of her neck, she

looked forward again, taking in the huge rock formation in the distance thrusting out of the desert floor like an outstretched hand pleading to the Great Creator for moisture. And farther on, beyond the rocky upheaval, was the forest she had been trying so hard to reach.

Relief flowed through her as she realized it was no longer just a blue haze, but could be seen with a distinctness that meant she was only a short distance from it. That knowledge, added to the fact that darkness would soon cover the land, lent strength to her body and wings to her feet. She hurried forward, limping past the rocky upheaval and continuing on her way.

She stumbled on, even after Sky Man had donned his purple-and-red cloak, intent on reaching the forest, quietly whispering her gratitude to the Spirits who watched over her for guiding her this way.

Darkness covered the land by the time she reached the river. Nama stretched full-length on the ground, lowering her head until her mouth was against the water. Then, drawing in long sips, she filled her mouth, cooling her dry, parched throat as the water slid past and entered her stomach. Even though her thirst was great, she forced herself to drink slowly, knowing too much water would make her sick. Nama was on the point of turning away when something across the shimmering water caught her eye. Some movement that was barely perceptible.

Gripping her knife with one hand, she shifted

the spear, readying it for a throw if danger suddenly appeared.

"Whooooo." The loud cry came as a night owl swept from the forest and circled the pond before entering the dense growth again.

Uttering a deep sigh of relief, Nama felt some of her tenseness flow away. She was too jumpy, too easily scared. Imagine, she thought; being frightened by an owl.

Her gaze swept over the water again and she felt a sudden longing to bathe herself before retiring.

No sooner had the thought occurred then she laid aside her weapons, stripped away her clothing, and waded into the water.

The cold, shimmering liquid slid up her legs, soothing the scratches there, then crept up her hips as she waded deeper. Soon it was lapping against her waist, her midriff, then caressing her breasts.

When Nama was neck-deep in the water, she arched her back and swam in slow, graceful movements, covering the length of the pond then swimming to the bank again, blissfully unaware of the man, clad only in a loincloth, who stood watching.

Garrick and his brother Olaf had been searching the wild, untamed land for what seemed an endless time, avoiding the *skraelings,* the savages who occupied the area, whenever they could, fighting when they were forced to do so—which seemed much too often.

As days turned into weeks and still there was no sign of their older brother or any sign of what had happened to him, despair for his fate became their constant companion. But rising above that despair was a growing admiration for this land where game was plentiful.

One day, as the sky was growing purple and red with the onset of twilight, they crossed a river that ran wide and clear, washing downstream over high, limestone falls.

The black stallion Garrick rode had only reached the farthest bank when they saw a white-tail deer grazing in a clearing that was bordered on three sides by spruce, ponderosa pine, and aspen. Grass grew in abundance there, along with a bright array of flowers. The deer, upwind of them, continued to browse, seemingly unaware of their presence.

"Look!" Olaf whispered, his finger pointing out the animal.

Even as the words left his brother's lips, Garrick was already removing his crossbow and fitting it with an arrow.

The arrow made a shushing sound as it flew through the air, straight toward its target. It struck the deer and the animal jumped straight up, landed on all fours, and attempted to run. But it could not. The arrow had found its mark and the deer, although unaware of that fact, was dead on its feet. Its legs suddenly buckled and it fell to the ground and lay still.

"Good shot," Olaf congratulated. "Looks as

though there will be fresh meat in our camp tonight." The blond giant urged his mount forward until he was beside the fallen animal, then, dismounting, he knelt to examine the deer. "It was a clean kill," he said, sparing a quick glance for his brother, who had followed him. "Look! Your arrow penetrated its heart."

Garrick's lips quirked in a grin. "Did you expect otherwise?"

Olaf had no need to answer. Garrick's skill with the crossbow was legendary to all who knew him.

Hunting and trapping played a much larger part in the Norwegian economy than merely satisfying a wish for a varied diet. Bearskin and reindeer hides were valuable articles for trade; as were walrus hides and sealskins, walrus ivory, train-oil, whalebone, feathers, live falcons, and dried fish. But the value Garrick received from those items was not the only reason for his occupation. By trapping the wild beasts he made the uplands safer for their sheep and cattle.

"Why not make camp here?" Olaf asked, sweeping his gaze over the meadow. "There are enough trees to shelter us should it happen to rain." He flicked a glance at the cloudless sky. "Although it should not do so. There is grass aplenty here for the horses as well as water."

Garrick turned his considering gaze to the west. The sun was already sinking below the horizon. Dusk would soon turn into night. "This place suits me well enough," he replied. "It will be dark by the time you get that deer dressed out."

"By the time *I* get it dressed out?" Olaf questioned with a lift of his eyebrow. "You offer me no help? The animal is *your* kill, Brother."

"For that reason you have the privilege of cleaning the deer," Garrick said, dismounting with fluid grace, then unbuckling his stallion's reins so the horse could graze.

Although Garrick's horse, Midnight, had been trained to stay near his master, Olaf's steed, Thunder, could not be trusted to remain without first being hobbled. It was for that reason alone that Garrick, after removing the saddles from both horses, attached a short length of rope to Thunder's front legs.

Leaving the horses to graze, Garrick gathered an armload of firewood. Then he ringed a small depression with stones, ever mindful that a fire could spread and grow out of control in a matter of moments.

After sparking flint to kindling, he blew at the resulting flame, then added larger pieces of wood to it. "Cut me some strips off that deer," he told Olaf, "while I prepare some sticks to skewer it on."

"I am ahead of you," Olaf said, pointing out several choice strips of meat already laid aside.

"So you are," Garrick said, peeling the bark away from a thick stick he had cut from the nearest pine tree.

After the venison had been skewered and placed over the fire to cook, Garrick poured ale into two silver-rimmed mugs and handed one to Olaf. Then he sat back on his heels and watched the flames leap and dance as they ate hungrily at the wood. Even though his eyes were on the flames, his thoughts were not. Instead, they had wandered back in time. He thought of his brother Eric, remembering him as a child in baggy trousers, the leader of the three brothers, always the one to choose their latest game.

Garrick smiled as he remembered Eric running ahead of them, urging them to hurry along to their favorite swimming hole where they would test their skills against one another.

It was a game enjoyed by most Vikings, a game where speed was less prized than the ability to drag one's opponent down and hold him under until he collapsed.

Of course there were those who called the Viking games barbaric, and yet these pastimes taught skills that were useful in battle on land or sea.

"What do you think of, Brother?" Olaf asked, returning from the creek where he had washed up. He picked up his cup of ale and squatted across the fire from his brother.

"My thoughts were of Eric," Garrick replied. "A year is a long time, Olaf. Three seasons have swept away all trace of his passing. I fear our journey is for naught. If he had been capable of returning to the longboat, he would have done so long ago."

"He might have returned after the longboat departed."

"Had he done so, he would have waited there, knowing we would return for him."

"Yes," Olaf agreed. "And since he did not return, it must mean he *could* not do so."

They fell silent, each brother busy with his own thoughts. Even the forest was still, as though those creatures occupying it were paused in waiting.

"He is dead," Olaf finally said. "I have known it all along. But it is hard to accept that he will never return to us." He bent his head and studied the flames intently. "Do you think we should return to the longboat?"

"Not yet," Garrick said. "We will search a few more days. Perhaps another week. But then we must return." He sighed deeply. "There has been no rain to speak of and the water level in the river may be dropping. If we stay much longer, the longboat could become stuck on a shoal as Eric's boat did." He sighed again. "It will be hard to go back, hard to take word of his death home."

Garrick's thoughts turned to his parents, dwelling for a moment on the heartache they would surely feel when informed of Eric's demise. As was the way with all Vikings, family ties were of the utmost importance to them. They had taught their children to stand by one another in all difficulties, taught them to combine their strengths so they might avenge any injury inflicted on any one of them.

"I think Mother and Father have already accepted the loss of their eldest son," Olaf said gruffly. "But what about Brynna? How will she cope with the loss of her favorite brother?"

"Perhaps we are mistaken," Garrick replied.

"Even though we found no trace of Eric and his party, there are two more directions that are being searched this very moment. Perhaps Eric has been found even as we speak together."

That thought cheered the brothers somewhat and, after checking the meat and finding it done to a turn, they ate hungrily, putting aside words about their brother's fate and speaking instead of times past, of days when the three brothers had competed for the hand of the same girl, of boyhood days when they had played together and roamed the family lands carrying stick swords into battle against a pretend enemy.

The last remnants of day were just a memory and the stars twinkled in a night-dark blanket with only the full moon to light the land when Garrick rose, arched his back, and grimaced with pain.

"A long walk should ease the ache in my back," he said. "Do you want to come?"

When Olaf shook his head, Garrick left him. He had only gone a short distance when a scream cut through the night like a lightning bolt ripping through the darkened sky.

Five

The scream froze Garrick mid-stride.

Although his every instinct told him to hurry forward, to render aid to whoever was in need, he realized he must exercise extreme caution. This land contained many dangerous surprises, not the least of which were the fierce *skraelings*.

"Aaiieeeeeee!"

The scream came again, piercing, terrified, easily recognizable as a woman's cry of utter panic. For that reason alone, Garrick could not ignore the sound.

Guessing the scream had come from just beyond the bend in the river, he dashed forward, using the trees growing along the riverbank for cover. As he drew nearer, he became aware of loud splashing. He rounded the curve, his gaze sliding back and forth, skimming quickly across the shimmering water that was bathed in the moonlight.

Then he saw her: A young girl standing in waist-deep water, illuminated by the pale light.

She stood with her back to Garrick, a vision of budding womanhood, staring at the opposite bank where there was a thick growth of willows.

What had frightened her? he wondered, watching as she plunged deeper into the water.

Fear clutched at Nama as she waded deeper into the water, desperate to escape the warrior that had thought to capture her.

Where was he? she wondered frantically.

She wasted no time on another scream, knowing there was no hope of anyone coming to her rescue. Instead, her cry was more likely to bring aid to her attacker.

That thought had her plunging deeper into the river.

Splash! The sound came from across the river; Nama ignored it, keeping her attention fixed on the nearest bank. There was no way her enemy could have reached the other side without her noticing.

Where was he? Had he retreated so quickly because of her scream or because she had gone deeper into the water and the man could not swim? Hoping that possibility was a fact, Nama plunged even deeper into the river, keeping her gaze focused on the riverbank where she had been attacked.

Had her weapons been discovered? If they had not, then perhaps she could swim beneath the surface to a place downstream where she could leave the river in safety.

Suddenly, the water surged around her, making her aware she was no longer alone. Before she could react, her enemy shot upward, grinning in triumph as he captured her and dragged her out of the river.

Terrified, Nama struck out with her fists, but her efforts were in vain. He struck her a hard blow against the side of her face that sent her tumbling toward the ground. Then he stood over her, breathing heavily, a look of lust in his dark eyes that sent a new thrill of fear sweeping over her.

She scrambled to all fours, trying to scuttle away from him, but he followed, kicking out with his foot and connecting with her stomach, driving the air from her body.

Nama coughed, trying to ignore the pain as she sucked at the life-giving air. Before she could recover though, his doubled-up fist landed her another hard blow and the stars fell around her as everything faded to black.

Garrick swept out of the river just as the *skraeling* sent another kick toward the unconscious girl. It landed with a heavy thud against the girl's hip; and the act was so cowardly, so vile, that Garrick could not have stopped the roar of rage that erupted from him even had he tried.

He turned on the savage, drawing his fist back and driving it hard against the other man's chin. Smack! The sound of fist striking flesh gave Garrick a feeling of satisfaction. As did the fact that the blow swept his opponent stumbling backwards.

Smack! Garrick landed another blow to the chin.

The *skraeling* staggered, then fell, striking the ground with a hard thud.

Garrick ignored him then, leaning over the girl to see how badly she had been injured.

A soft sound alerted him to danger and he spun around . . . just in time.

The *skraeling*, having quickly recovered, leapt toward Garrick, moonlight glinting off the tip of the wicked blade that was already curving downward.

Flinging himself sideways, Garrick threw up an arm to deflect the blade. He felt a sharp pain as it sliced into his flesh and a warm spurt of blood gushed from the wound.

Wrapping his fingers around the *skraeling's* wrist, Garrick squeezed tightly, increasing pressure until the knife dropped to the ground with a clatter.

The man's eyes glared his hatred at Garrick. He lashed out with his foot, connecting with the Viking's shin. Whack! Garrick ignored the pain, concentrating instead on vanquishing his enemy.

Rage held Garrick captive. Blind, consuming rage for the man who had misused the girl so badly and now thought to slay him.

Reaching out, Garrick wrapped his fingers around the other man's throat and he squeezed hard, continued squeezing until the *skraeling's* eyes glazed over and his body became limp and he knew the flesh he held was lifeless. Only then did he release his hold.

Turning from the dead man, Garrick moved to the girl who lay among the reeds with such absolute stillness.

Was she dead?

Fearing the worst, he bent over her, searching for the pulse point at the base of her neck, heaving a sigh of relief when he found it beating steadily.

She was even more beautiful than he had imagined. Her dark hair spread around her head and shoulders like the petals of a moonflower that opened only at night to reveal a perfect center . . . in this instance, her perfect features.

Garrick had known many women in his time, but there was something about this woman that set her apart from the others. There was a look about her, something so totally different; and yet, if asked to explain, he would not have been able to do so.

Why did he feel so drawn to her? he wondered. What was there about her that made her so appealing?

He bent closer, sweeping his gaze over her features again.

What was that darker spot over her brow? A bruise?

He touched the place gently and saw her long, thick lashes quiver slightly at the contact.

Was she waking?

Apparently not, he decided, for her eyes remained closed. His gaze lowered to her mouth. Her lips were full, perfectly formed to tempt a man's. And he was tempted, he realized, then chided himself for doing so. Thor's teeth! The girl was badly injured. How badly he had not yet determined.

His breath quickened as he visually examined
her naked body. It was even more desirable seen
up close. Her hips were nicely rounded and her
high breasts, so firm and full, rose gently like
miniature, pale half-moons above a waist no bigger
than a handspan.

Garrick's lower body tensed, his manhood pressing tightly against his breeches, and he curbed the
urge that was so powerful within him . . . the urge
to strip away his clothing and mount her.

Realizing he was behaving like some untried boy,
he ran his hands lightly over her limbs, assuring
himself she had broken no bones. Then, bending
closer, he slid one hand beneath her shoulders and
the other beneath her knees, intent on carrying
her back to his camp. But at the first contact the
woman's eyelids jerked up and, even as he recognized her fear, he became aware of moonlight
glinting against something shiny.

A knife! With disbelief, Garrick watched the
blade swing up, then arc down toward him.

When Nama wakened to find her attacker bending over her, she managed to control the shudder
of fear that streaked through her and the scream
that threatened to erupt. Instead, she lay passively,
staring at him through slitted eyes, her scrutiny
hidden by the dark fringe of lashes.

His appearance was strange, his hair resembling
flames in the pale moonlight, an image that had
gone completely unnoticed when he had made his

attack on her. Perhaps, though, her fright had been so great that the color of his hair had simply not registered.

Forcing herself to remain still, Nama endured his touch, feeling it soft against the flesh that he had so recently abused. Somehow she managed to continue to breathe evenly, hoping to give the illusion of sleep as the stranger's hands moved along her arms, then ran down the length of her legs.

Whether his purpose was to seek out her injuries or merely to satisfy himself that she still lived remained a mystery. But Nama had no doubt that she would soon know.

An icy chill settled over her as her attacker continued his examination.

Becoming aware of something hard pressing into the flesh of her back, Nama considered the possibility of using the object—hopefully a rock—for defense.

Suddenly the stranger slid one of his hands beneath her shoulders and the other beneath her legs. As he lifted her, she reached for the object beneath her, felt the curve of a blade and realized she had found her knife. She groped higher, curving her hand around the handle and gripping tightly.

Then, with a speed that surprised even herself, she swung the knife in an arc and brought it down.

Nama knew she would have killed him had the blow landed as she had intended. Instead, it struck the man high, entering his left shoulder.

If she had not been so frightened, Nama might

have found his expression humorous. He had been placid at first, almost expressionless; but when the blade entered his flesh, the stranger expressed astonishment that quickly turned to disbelief. However, those emotions immediately gave way to fury and, with a roar of rage, he released her.

Nama struck the ground hard, knocking the breath from her body. Whoosh! She lay there . . . stunned, watching incredulously as he jerked the knife from his shoulder and contemptuously flung it away. Then, before she could react, he bent over her, wound his fingers through her hair, and yanked her toward him until her face was only inches from his own.

Six

"Thor's teeth! Have you no gratitude, woman?" Garrick demanded, glaring at her with burning, reproachful eyes. "Is this the way you reward me for saving your life?"

Although he knew the *skraeling* woman could not possibly understand his words, speaking them aloud served to express the fury Garrick felt inside. He seethed with it, barely controlling the desire to wrap his fingers around her slim throat and strangle the life from her body.

The woman struggled against his hold, jerking her head this way and that, causing him to tighten the fingers that wound through her hair.

Tears of pain welled in her eyes, and she spewed out her rage in a guttural language that was completely unknown to his ears. Then, curling her fingers into talons, she raked them across his left cheek.

Garrick felt the warmth of fresh blood flowing from the wound she had inflicted. Enraged that she would treat him in such a manner after he had saved her life, he shook her into gasping silence.

"Desist, woman!" he snarled. "You cause yourself unnecessary pain. Your efforts are puny against my strength, unworthy of mention."

Instead of ceasing her struggles, she continued to fight furiously; and unwilling to bear the abuse, Garrick wrapped his arms around her and secured her against his chest. Her eyes widened then and she uttered a scream that must surely have carried for miles around them.

Garrick had no way of knowing whether it was fear or anger that drove her, and he had no time to consider the matter. The shriek had barely erupted from her lips before she pulled one hand free and struck him a blow on his wounded shoulder with one balled-up fist.

"Damnation!" he howled. The blow sent pain shuddering through him, and he fought against wave after wave as he shook her hard again, taking extreme pleasure in watching her head bob on the slender stem of her neck.

Even as he punished her, she punched him again, managing somehow to strike the exact same spot.

Tears of pain stung his eyes, and that enraged him even more. She was only a *skraeling* wench, only half his size, and yet she had managed to bring tears to his eyes, a feat that was completely unheard of.

Viking men did not cry.

Almost overcome with fury, Garrick released her shoulders and wrapped his big hands around her smaller ones, capturing them as surely as he would a butterfly and, with anger still driving him, he

tightened his fists around them, squeezing . . .
tightly . . . watching her face, wondering how she
could be so fierce, so savage, and still have such
an innocent look about her.

Even as he asked himself that question, her chin
lifted, her pain-filled eyes met his and she moaned
low in her throat.

Immediately, he loosened his grip.

Thor's teeth! He silently cursed himself for a fool.
Had his anger driven him senseless enough that
he had used his greater strength to crush the fragile bones in her hands?

Another moan escaped her lips and he was on
the point of releasing her, certain she had learned
her lesson, when she leaned her head into his good
shoulder.

He felt her breath against his neck and realized
she was on the point of swooning. Guilt flooded
through him. No sooner had that feeling surfaced
than he felt her lips against his throat. Then, to
his utter astonishment, her teeth fastened against
the side of his neck and she bit down hard.

Pain sliced through him as her jaws locked on
his flesh. He had never been bitten before and was
startled that it hurt so much—and infuriated as
well. He was angered that the woman he had saved
from being attacked by another should be the one
to bite him now.

"Ungrateful bitch!" he snapped, loosening her
fists and wrapping his hands around her head to
yank her loose from his flesh.

But she would not be so easily dispatched. She

hung there like a leech, intent on doing as much harm as possible while she had the chance. Even so, she was no match for his greater strength.

Digging his fingers into the softness beneath her chin, and his thumbs into the tender flesh of her lower jaws, Garrick jerked her away from him.

Immediately, she curled her fingers into talons again and struck for his eyes as though it were her intention to blind him. Had her nails struck as she intended, she would surely have accomplished her goal, but Garrick, realizing his danger, reacted quickly, jerking his head to the side, causing her nails to slice through the flesh of his cheek instead.

"Desist, woman!" he snarled for the second time.

Wrapping his fingers around both wrists, he managed to keep her head at a safe distance from his body.

Just when he thought he had her subdued, her knee came up sharply, striking him in the groin.

"Unghhh!" he grunted, sweat popping out on his forehead as pain washed over him in waves, like an incoming tide swept against the shore by a hurricane.

She turned to run, but he reached out and snared her wrist with his right hand, stopping her in mid-flight. She kicked out with her feet, aiming at his groin again; but he dodged the move, then yanked her forward.

Throwing her on her back, he flung himself atop her. Holding her arms in a spread-eagle manner, he secured her body and legs with his own.

The action brought his body hard against hers and, as her frantic movements finally ceased because his weight was so great that she was held firmly in place, he realized something that he had completely forgotten in the heat of battle.

She was completely naked.

He had no more realized that fact when she began to shake convulsively. He spared a brief moment to wonder if it were from fear or because of the cold night air and the fact that her body was still damp from the time she had spent in the cold water.

Her dark eyes were huge and round and she held them wide open, staring at him as though fearful of what would happen should she look away.

"Do you give in, woman?" he growled, noticing his voice sounded ragged and harsh. It was a wonder he could speak at all, with his breath coming so quick and uneven.

They continued to stare at each other, neither one blinking, as he held her beneath him with the weight of his body. Her breath, like his, was harsh and ragged, and her fear suddenly became recognizable . . . almost a tangible thing.

She *did* fear him. That was obvious now. And so she should, he told himself. He had gone out of his way to try to help her, and she had rewarded him by trying to kill him. Even now he could feel blood flowing from the wounds she had inflicted.

His lips tightened grimly as he considered the woman beneath him. Her looks were deceiving. Although she appeared innocent, almost child-like, he had learned that appearance was deceptive. If he allowed the woman freedom, she would most likely renew her efforts to kill him.

Slowly, Garrick became aware of her hard, taut nipples—he could feel them through the fabric of his upper garment—pressed tightly against his chest. He felt a sudden urge to cup them within his palms, and the thought caused a stirring in his lower body and brought a sudden ache to his groin.

Garrick knew the instant she became aware of his maleness. Even in the pale light of the moon he recognized the sudden awareness, the flicker of a different kind of fear that suddenly sparked in her eyes.

Yes. He recognized that fear and felt angered by it as well.

What need had she to fear him? He had done naught to her, had only tried to defend himself from her wrath.

Nevertheless, whatever the reason, the woman obviously *did* fear him. He knew that for a fact, could smell the fear surrounding her like a thick, early-morning fog that could only be dissipated by the heat of the rising sun.

"Have no fear, woman," he said gruffly, knowing she would not understand, yet hoping to allay her fears by injecting a small measure of kindness into his voice. "It was never my intention to harm you."

Realizing her fear had not decreased, he knew he must show her by his actions that he was harmless. With that in mind, he released her.

She moved with the swiftness of a cat, rolling out from under him and scrambling to her knees. But he reacted with equal swiftness, reaching out and snaring an ankle with his fingers. She tried to kick her leg free and he yanked her toward him, sending her off-balance, crashing heavily to the ground.

The woman lay still, unmoving.

Was she merely waiting to catch him unaware or had she injured herself with the fall?

He crawled forward, making certain to stay over her, expecting her to spring to her feet at any given moment. Instead, she continued to lie there, motionless, her eyes closed, her lids a pale shadow against her cheek. When he saw the dark stain spreading down her face he knew the reason why. She had obviously struck a stone. A quick inspection told him she was not badly injured; the blow had only rendered her unconscious.

Without a second thought, he picked her up and slung her across his good shoulder. Then, scooping up her hide garment, he tossed it over her naked body, sent a contemptuous look toward the primitive weapons that lay on the ground, nudged the limp body of her attacker to make certain it was lifeless, then strode swiftly downstream, retracing the path he had trod earlier.

Soon he saw the flames of the campfire in the distance and recognized the shape of his brother outlined beside it. Olaf was still seated on the fallen log where Garrick had left him, as though only a short time had passed.

With his gaze pinned on his brother, Garrick

missed the brush on the ground that he had previously avoided. It crackled beneath his boots and Olaf jerked his head around, probing the darkness with his gaze.

"Garrick?" Olaf called. "Is that you?"

Garrick hurried forward at a ground-eating pace, intent on reaching his brother before he called out again. "You are lucky it is I, Brother. Had I been one of the *skraelings* instead, then you would surely be dead now."

"It has been days since we saw sign of the *skraelings*," Olaf said calmly.

"Not anymore."

"You saw sign of them? Fresh sign?" Suddenly, Olaf jerked to his feet. "What are you carrying?"

"A woman."

"A *skraeling* woman?" Olaf asked.

"What other kind would there be around here?" Garrick asked dryly. "Of course she is a *skraeling* woman."

"Then her people must be somewhere nearby." It was a statement, not a question. "Thor's teeth, Garrick! Why did you bring her with you? When she turns up missing, they will look for her. Take her back where you found her."

"No," Garrick said. "She would warn others of our presence."

A heavy sigh escaped his lips. "I suppose you are right." Olaf's eyes widened, as his brother was suddenly illuminated by the campfire. "Damnation, Garrick! The wench is as naked as the day she was born!" His gaze dwelt on the rounded bottom beneath his brother's hand, then dropped to the slender legs and bare feet. "I am surprised at you, Garrick. The night air is cold. You should have dressed the wench once you finished coupling with her."

"You take too much for granted," Garrick said wryly. "We have not coupled." He laid the girl on the ground, taking care to do it gently. "She is without clothing because she was swimming, Olaf. I have done her no harm. She fell and struck her head against a stone."

"You should have left her for others to find," Olaf said grumpily. "Surely you realize the danger of bringing her—" He broke off, staring at his brother with something like consternation. "What happened to your face?" His gaze dropped lower, became fixed on the blood seeping from the wound on Garrick's shoulder. "Thor's teeth, Garrick! Did you tangle with a bear?"

"Not a bear," Garrick replied. "Only the woman. She stabbed me."

"Stabbed you?" Olaf's voice was incredulous. "A little thing like her? I have trouble believing that."

"Believe me, Brother," Garrick said grimly, looking down upon the young woman who appeared so young and vulnerable, completely exposed in all her naked glory with the moonlight trapped in her glorious hair. "This woman has more courage than most men. And she fights like a she-cat protecting her cubs."

Olaf's gaze was locked on the naked girl, a fact which caused Garrick much annoyance.

"She is stronger than she looks," he said gruffly. "My wounds are proof of that." His irritation increased as Olaf continued to stare at the girl, his expression akin to awe.

Garrick bent over and picked up the hide garment that had fallen to the ground and spread it over her, covering her naked breasts and thighs with it.

Olaf looked at Garrick then. "Her legs and arms are covered with scratches. How did she come by them?"

"I have no idea," Garrick looked at his brother's sympathetic face. "Save your sympathy, Brother. She is not badly hurt, only unconscious."

"She was alone when you found her?"

"No. There was another with her. A man. He attacked her and I killed him."

"Perhaps you should have left them alone," Olaf said. "We have sought to avoid the *skraelings* so far. Why interfere with them at this point?"

"She would be dead had I not interfered," Garrick said, wondering why he had thought it necessary to save her life. He explained what had happened, feeling the need to stop Olaf's questions. The wench had occupied enough of his time already.

"Perhaps we should leave this place before others come to seek revenge for their kin," Olaf said.

"My thoughts exactly," replied Garrick. "Saddle the horses while I tend to the woman."

"Tend to her?" Olaf's gaze narrowed on his brother. "What do you intend, Brother?"

"Thor's teeth, Olaf! I only mean to dress the wench. Would you have her travel in this state of undress?"

"I would rather not travel with her at all," Olaf replied shortly. "But we seem to have no choice. If we leave her she will alert others to our presence." He considered his brother's wounds. "You are still bleeding. Mayhap you should dress your wound after you finish with the maid."

Garrick ran his fingers over the scratches on his face. "These are of little consequence." Touching his shoulder, he felt the sticky wetness of blood. "I suppose this must be dressed though."

"Would you have me do it?" Olaf asked.

"Later," Garrick replied. "We should not linger here."

"Neither should you lose more blood."

Realizing Olaf was right, Garrick stanched the wound with a soft cloth, then turned to the task of dressing the woman while Olaf went about the business of saddling the horses and loading their supplies on them. Both of the brothers were conscious of how open the camp was, how easy it would be to attack if the natives were of that mind.

They already had one brother missing, perhaps dead, and Garrick was not prepared to suffer the same fate.

Nama woke slowly to the sound of drumbeats. They throbbed in time with her head. *Thrum, thrum, thrum.* She groaned softly, turned her head, and felt her stomach twist with nausea. Instinctively, she tried to press her hands against her belly and found she could not. She had been sleeping on that part of her body.

Sleeping? Something about that thought did not ring true.

Her eyelashes fluttered open and she found herself gazing into a thick, black nothingness.

Blinking her eyes rapidly, Nama tried to dispel the blackness, but was unable to see through the shadowy darkness. The throbbing in her temples increased, causing a curious surging, a motion that was hard to define; and the throbbing was odd, sounding curiously different than she had imagined upon waking.

What caused the difference? The sound was not the musical *thrum, thrum, thrum,* that was usually produced by drums; instead, it had a slightly smothered sound, more like *clop, clop, clop,* as though the hide covering the hollowed-out-log base of the drum had not been stretched tight enough.

Nama swiveled her head again and blinked her eyes several times, trying to bring her vision into focus. The blackness had given way to dark shadows that resembled trees, yet they had a curious upside-down look about them.

That cannot be, her mind protested. *Trees do not grow upside down. You must be dreaming.* She strained her eyes, demanding that the world right itself. But it refused to cooperate. What is happening? she wondered.

Even as she worried over the problem, the throbbing in her temples worsened. *Thrum, thrum, thrum,* She winced with pain and closed her stinging eyes, then quickly opened them again. The world, instead of righting itself, remained firmly fixed in the same upside-down position.

Why?

She rolled her head to one side and looked at the shadowy trees. They were firmly rooted in the ground as they should be, but they were rooted upside-down.

Finding herself unable to sustain such an awkward position, Nama relaxed her head, allowing it to return to its original resting place. That was when she realized her bed was moving beneath her.

She gave a sudden jerk of fear, then her heart picked up speed, beating like that of a rabbit with a fox close on its tail. What was this thing that she lay upon? she wondered. Whatever it was, it was definitely alive. And it was big enough to carry her across its shoulders.

Holding her breath, hardly daring to breathe, she ran her palm lightly over the thing. Although it was smooth, it had the feel of soft fur. Not thick, she decided, but fur, nevertheless.

Nama knew of nothing that was large enough to carry her, except a bear. And Brother Bear would never think to carry her across its shoulders.

What then?

Suddenly, a human voice spoke somewhere nearby. If she were not mistaken, the sound came from above, and behind her. And, although the words were vaguely familiar, she was unable to comprehend their meaning.

Cautiously, she lifted her head, hoping the thing—or person—that carried her would not detect the movement, else it would know that she was conscious. She swiveled her head and stared up at the speaker.

Her eyes widened. He sat astride the thing that carried her; and even in the moonlight, she could see the man was enormous. Fear was born anew. The stranger who confronted her was the man who had attacked her.

Seeming to sense her conscious state, he looked down upon her, meeting her wide, fearful eyes. ". . . you . . . wake."

It was not her language, although some of the words were familiar to her.

Instead, the man used words she had learned from Shala, words learned originally from her friend's Viking lover.

Even while the man spoke, he was pulling back on two thin strips of hide held in his right hand. Immediately, the movement stopped, as did the incessant drumming that, she was certain now, was the cause of her throbbing temples.

Nama held her silence and the stranger—Nama's captor—hooked his fingers beneath her waist and plucked her from her uncomfortable position and settled her before him, atop the beast that carried them.

For it was a beast, the like of which she had never seen before.

Even as she reached that conclusion, Nama knew she could not look away from the stranger, dared not, even to see what manner of animal carried them so easily, for seen this close up, and outlined by the full moon, the man looked even more formidable than before.

He was tall, like the Viking Eric had been; and the clothing he wore seemed to be fashioned from the same material, a fabric that Eric had called linen. The upper garment fit close against the man's body, and the trousers fit snugly, outlining his muscular legs and thighs.

Could this stranger be related to Eric? she wondered. It was possible, for they spoke the same language; yet there was definitely a difference in their appearance. This man's hair was the color of fire while Eric possessed hair of a golden color. And this man did not have Eric's gentle ways. Eric would never have attacked her as this man had done, would never have struck her in such a cruel manner.

Remembrance of that moment caused Nama to remain perfectly still, to appear subdued when she was not.

She had learned much during her fight for survival, had learned that perhaps, she was not such a coward as she had thought. Had she not fought like a she-cat when attacked by the stranger? And she would continue to fight . . . with every fiber of her being. He would not find her the biddable child she had been only a short while ago. No! She was Nama. Woman of the Eagle Clan. This night marked the end of her innocence. She had fought like a warrior; therefore, she would become a warrior. But there was more than one way to fight. At the moment it behooved her to remain silent, to appear subdued in the face of her enemy.

But he would learn soon enough that she was a woman to be reckoned with!

Since he seemed uninclined to present an immediate danger to her, she looked away from him, her gaze dropping to the beast that carried them. It was enormous. Seen by the pale light of Sister Moon, the animal resembled an enormous elk. But it was no elk. There were no horns to grace its head and its neck was much too long, ridged with coarse hair, quite unlike any animal she had ever known.

Suddenly, she heard a strange sound coming from her captor's mouth. It was a curious clucking sound and it was no more than uttered when the beast resumed its forward march.

Curiouser and curiouser. The man had apparently given a signal to the animal to let it know what he wanted. No. It was certainly no elk. An elk could never be trained in such a manner.

A sudden thought struck her. A dog could be trained. Nama had seen it done. She looked hard at the creature. It looked nothing like a dog; and yet, what else could it be? But if it were a dog, how could it grow so big that it could carry their combined weights with such incredible ease?

Perhaps the animal came from the same place as did the man? Perhaps they both came from the land Eric called Norway. What other answer could there be? she silently questioned. The men who came from that faraway place were bigger than normal. Did the animals also grow bigger there?

Yes. They must be, she decided. And the animal must surely be a dog.

She had no more than come to that conclusion when the big black dog snorted suddenly. The sound made her shudder. Was the great beast angry because she sat astride its back? Would that large head swivel without warning and the long, canine teeth—they must surely be long and sharp to belong to such an animal—suddenly bite off her leg?

The thought caused another shudder to shake her small frame.

The stranger seemed to take the shudder for cold because his arms tightened around her. "No," she protested in her language, even while she realized he could not understand her. "You are hurting me." She tugged at his hands, trying to free herself from his grip.

Another voice spoke suddenly and she jerked around. The stranger was not alone! He had a companion who looked as fierce as he himself did. She renewed her struggles until her captor's sharp voice brought them to a halt.

Fearful of his wrath, she forced herself to remain still, hoping she could make him believe she had accepted her fate.

But she would not, could not. She would hold

her silence, pretend acquiescence until she found a chance to escape.

Her gaze dropped to the big dog that carried her. Was she being too optimistic? The dogs were so big, standing even higher than her head, and she knew they must move swiftly on their four legs.

Remembering the way the camp dogs could sniff out their prey, Nama realized it would be almost impossible to elude such creatures. Yet she must try, for she had made a firm resolution: She would either regain her freedom or die in the attempt.

Seven

They rode throughout the night in a northwesterly direction, following beside the river where it was possible, detouring whenever it was necessary, but always returning to the river again as though the men were using it for a landmark.

Nama's shoulders slumped wearily and she could barely hold herself erect; yet she realized she must, for it was apparent the strangers had no intention of stopping to rest. In fact, they seemed intent on putting as much distance as possible between themselves and the place where they had made camp.

But, Nama consoled herself, as long as they continued to travel she would remain unmolested. There was no way her captors could abuse her while they rode atop the strange creatures.

She felt a sudden surge of dread as she contemplated the journey's end. What waited for her there? Something too horrible to be borne? Perhaps she should leap from the beast and make a run for it. She bunched her muscles, looked down at the ground that seemed so far away, and quickly dismissed the idea. It would never work. The crea-

ture was too big . . . too fast. As were the men.
She would surely be captured before she went very
far and would probably find herself bound hand
and foot.

That realization caused a throbbing pain in
Nama's temples. She tried hard to ignore the discomfort, but she could not, for the pulsing ache
became more intense with each passing moment,
seeming to match the rhythm of the creature she
rode.

Bending her head slightly, Nama pressed her
fingers against her temples, trying to alleviate the
pain; but it did no good.

As though noticing her discomfort, the man riding behind her spoke softly, words that had no
meaning to her. When she made no response, he
spoke again, pulling her closer against the length
of his body.

Instantly, Nama froze and her pulse skittered
with alarm. She could feel the heat from his body,
was totally aware of the lean male strength of
him . . . a fact that caused a curious feeling in her
belly.

Nama leaned forward slightly, trying to evade
his touch, realizing at the same moment that it was
impossible. She must, of necessity, endure his
touch; but she would not allow herself to rest
against him.

Time passed and they encountered rough, broken country that made riding more difficult.
Nama's leg and back muscles ached from the strain
and she found herself wishing the journey would

end. She had no idea how far they had traveled, only knew that it seemed like they had been riding for many moons. The strangers seemed tireless, unlike Nama whose head continued to throb, pounding in rhythm with the animal's large feet.

She tried to rise above the pain, to empty herself of all thought, but it seemed impossible. Nevertheless, she persisted, closing her eyes and willing her mind to leave her aching body, to rise above it . . . rise . . . rise . . .

Her tense muscles relaxed and the pain in her temples eased . . . slowly . . . slowly . . . seeping away until it had completely disappeared. A slight tug was exerted and she felt heat against her back. Without a second thought, she snuggled against it and fell into an exhausted sleep.

Nama had no idea how long she slept, only knew it was the cessation of movement that finally woke her. Lifting heavy eyelids, she peered through sleep-dazed eyes to see the face of Father Sun peeping over the eastern horizon.

Feeling the warmth of her captor's body, Nama realized she had slept in the arms of her enemy. That knowledge caused a rising bile to sting the back of her throat and she swallowed around the nausea.

Why had they stopped? she wondered anxiously, searching the limestone bluffs between which a narrow creek—obviously a tributary branching off the wider river—flowed. Did her captors intend to make camp? Her heart gave a sudden leap of fear at the thought.

Perhaps, though, she consoled herself, they had only stopped so the large dogs could quench their thirst.

The golden-haired giant suddenly broke the silence, speaking unfamiliar words and pointing toward the cliff overhang at the base of the farthest bluff.

Instead of responding verbally, the flame-haired man who sat behind Nama made the clucking sound that sent the beast they rode forward. Without the slightest hesitation, it entered the water, waded through the shallows and splashed across the creek to the farthest bank, coming to a stop beside the overhang.

The beast had barely ceased moving when Nama's captor slid to the ground and turned away from her. *Oh, Great Creator,* she exulted silently. *Escape is at hand!*

Reacting with a swiftness that startled them as well as herself, Nama dug her heels into the creature's side and made the clucking sound that seemed to control its movements. But, although the big dog shuddered slightly, it refused to obey her command.

"Go!" she shrieked, kicking the animal's sides again and beating at it with her fists. "Run! Flee! Take me away from here!"

But it was already too late! The flame-haired giant had realized her intentions and, with a thunderous expression, he reached up and yanked her down, holding her slightly above the ground as though to remind her of his greater strength.

Immediately, fear swept over her, racing down her spine and spreading outward until it coiled into a tight knot in the pit of her stomach.

"Release me, please," she whispered, staring fearfully at the big man who continued to hold her above the ground.

He shook her hard, then spoke harshly, uttering a long string of words—none of which she could understand—and all the while his grass-green eyes raked her with withering scorn.

Nama felt dizzy from the rough shaking and she shook her head to clear it. The action obviously angered him because he shook her again.

"Stop!" Nama demanded, feeling a spark of anger at his rough treatment. "Let me down!"

Instead of complying with her demand, he shook her again.

Cold black rage swept over Nama, sending her fear into hiding, and she loosed her emotions on her captor, swinging her foot upward with every ounce of strength she could summon and landing a hard blow against his belly.

"Oooomph!" he exclaimed, the breath whooshing out of his body.

He released her, clutching at his midsection with both hands. Freed from his strong grip, Nama struck the ground with a hard jolt. Her knees seemed to have no substance for they crumpled beneath her, and she stretched her arms wide to break her fall. But something went wrong. Her left elbow gave way and she uttered a cry as pain sliced through her wrist.

"Thor's teeth!" exclaimed the man with golden hair.

The words were familiar to Nama and she looked quickly at the man who had spoken them, wondering again if he were related to Eric. He continued to speak sharply to the flame-haired man as though chastising him, but the words he spoke now were unfamiliar.

The flame-haired man spoke at length, his voice gruff, his expression unrepenting. The golden-haired giant listened to the other man's words, then uttered more of his own.

"Damnation!" the fiery-haired man exclaimed. He uttered a few more words, each of them spoken harshly, then gathered up the straps that controlled his mount and strode away.

The golden-haired giant watched him leave then knelt beside Nama, speaking softly to her, obviously expressing his concern for her welfare. Although her fingers curled into talons, preparatory to attack, Nama curbed the impulse. This man had done her no harm. And he appeared sympathetic to her plight. Perhaps he might be persuaded to help her.

But how would she find the words to use when she remembered so few of them? She could not. Instead she must bide her time, must listen and learn until she could converse with the golden-haired man.

Her mind worked furiously as she considered the words they had used more than one time. They had used the words Garrick and Olaf over and over again, used them in such a way that she felt they must be names. She decided to test her theory.

"Nama." She pointed a finger at her chest, then repeated. "Nama."

He smiled at her, seeming to understand, and said, "Nama."

Feeling encouraged, she pointed at him. "Olaf?" she questioned.

A smile spread across his face, lighting his sky-blue eyes. "Yes," he said, nodding his head eagerly. "I am Olaf. Olaf Nordstrom."

Nama felt exultant. She had understood every word he had said; and although she had never before heard the name *Olaf*, the other name he used, *Nordstrom*, was very familiar to her. It was the same as that used by Shala's Viking lover, who called himself Eric Nordstrom.

She looked past the man who knelt before her, toward the man with flaming hair. "Garrick?" she questioned, pointing toward him.

"Yes," Olaf said, his eyes crinkling at the corner. "My brother, Garrick Nordstrom."

"Brother," she repeated, considering the word. "You . . . uh . . ." She searched through her memory. Brother. Eric had said he had two brothers. "Brothers," she repeated, looking into his eyes as she attempted to communicate with him. "Mothers . . . same?"

He nodded his head. "We have the same mothers, Garrick and I . Where . . ." He spoke some unfamiliar words, then she heard two more that she recognized. They were *learn* and *language*. He was asking her where she had learned their language.

Nama threw a quick look at Garrick, wondering momentarily if she would receive better treatment if she told them about Eric. Probably not, she decided, for the flame-haired man had been unrepentant when chastised by his brother. She decided to keep her knowledge of Eric to herself for the moment.

Nama searched her memory for the words Eric used when referring to the dogs, feeling a small measure of triumph when it surfaced. "Dog?" she inquired, pointing at the creature.

Olaf laughed abruptly. "No," he said, shaking his head. "Horse. Midnight."

She frowned at him, wondering if he had understood her. "No dog?" she inquired. "Horse Midnight?"

"Horse," he said again, pointing to the creature. Then, turning to his own animal, he repeated the word. "Horse. It is called a horse."

"Midnight?" she questioned, hoping he would explain the word.

"Horse's name," he said. "Thunder." Then, pointing toward the other animal, he said, "Horse's name Midnight."

"Thunder and Midnight. Horses," she said, beaming up at him.

His smile broadened in approval. He was obviously pleased with her. "Garrick," he shouted, "She is learning our language."

Garrick sent a speaking glance toward his

brother then resumed his work, tugging at some straps that held a peculiar seat across the creature's midsection. When the straps were unfastened, he lifted the seat from the horse's back and laid it on the ground. Then, striding to the animal's head, he pulled at the straps fastened there and released its mouth.

Nama shuddered as she watched the animal, half-expecting it to seek her out since its large teeth were now free to chew.

Chew what? she wondered, fearing the answer was herself. When the horse lowered its head to the long grass growing near the edge of the creek, she realized it was a grass-eater and expelled a huge sigh of relief.

Even so, she took comfort in Olaf's presence beside her as his brother released the animals. Then, apparently finished with his task, the flame-haired Viking strode toward them, idly beating a leather strap against his thigh.

Nama's gaze fixed on the strap. Was it his intention to beat her?

"Come here," he rasped harshly.

Shaking her head, she backed slowly away.

A puzzled expression crossed his face and he spoke swiftly to his brother, using words Nama could not understand.

Even so, Nama listened intently, her gaze darting back and forth between the two men, hoping to understand what they were saying. But she could not. They spoke too swiftly.

Would Olaf help her if she revealed her knowledge of Eric? She opened her mouth to speak; but before she could form the words, Garrick's right hand streaked forward with lightning speed and fastened around her left forearm.

Her scream was piercing as she fought to wrest her arm free; but try as she would, her struggles were useless. Moments later she lay on the ground, her wrists secured, then linked by a narrow strip of hide that bound her ankles together.

"Son of a dog!" she spat in her own tongue, glaring her hatred at him, wanting nothing more than to kick his teeth down his throat, to send the bits of bone streaking toward his stomach in the hopes they would give him an enormous bellyache.

Unmoved by her rage, Garrick squatted in front of her and gripped her chin with hard fingers.

"Loose me!" she snarled, flinching away from his touch.

He twisted her head toward him, forcing her to look at him. Then, with a menacing grin, he ran the palm of his hand down her cheek, not in a caressing way but in a manner that was entirely possessive.

Screeching her fury, Nama struck at him with her bound hands, but the leather thong that tethered her wrists to her ankles prevented her from reaching him.

Olaf protested mightily, some of his words familiar to her ears while others were not. Even so, she knew he rebelled against the treatment she received.

"She belongs to me!" Garrick said harshly, his gaze roaming over his prize.

Nama's courage faltered beneath his look. It spoke volumes, leaving no doubt in her mind about his intentions where she was concerned.

She turned her gaze upon Olaf, silently pleading with him to come to her aid; but he turned away from her, his face flushing with color, apparently unable to meet her eyes.

Nama realized then that she had been right in her assessment of Olaf. Although the blond giant expressed sympathy for her plight, he would not interfere with his brother's plans.

Even as she wallowed in self-pity, Nama would not allow Garrick to know it. She glared at him and spewed out her hatred, calling him every foul name she could remember, although she knew he could not possibly understand her words.

Her rage only served to widen his lips, but it was not a humorous smile he gave her. Instead, she imagined it was his way of promising retribution at a later time.

When he tired of playing with her, Garrick left her alone and joined his brother. They spoke together at length, words she was unable to understand because they uttered them with a quickness that was hard to follow.

"Damnation, Garrick!"

The exclamation, coming from Olaf, jerked her attention back to them. Garrick had stripped away his upper garment and exposed the wound where her blade had punctured his flesh.

Olaf's expression was one of deep concern. Had her blade dealt his brother a mortal wound? she wondered. The golden-haired giant threw her a condemning look.

What had he expected? she asked herself. Did he think she would allow them to do what they would with her without the slightest effort on her part to stop them?

Nama turned away from the censorious gaze and pretended interest in her surroundings. Immediately her gaze fell on the horses that lingered nearby. They were still grazing on the long green grass. She studied their long legs, knowing with such legs beneath them they might very well have the speed of the pronghorn antelope. And if their long noses had the ability of camp dogs, they would be formidable indeed.

Her gaze returned to the two men. They spoke quietly together now as Olaf washed and dressed the wound on his brother's shoulder.

Nama's lips thinned with anger and she glared at Garrick again. It would serve him right if the wound became infected, would be what he deserved if it festered and poisoned the man.

Her hatred had chased away her fear and, had she been able, she would have done him another injury. But she could not. She could do nothing while bound hand and foot.

Seething inside, Nama turned away from the sight of him. She needed rest in order to gather her strength.

With that in mind, she leaned back against the

hard ground and closed her eyes and forced her tense muscles to relax as she courted a sleep that seemed bent on eluding her.

But eventually sleep did come, creeping up on her like a shadow and taking her to another time, another place. In her dreams Nama went once again to the place of the eagles . . . to the great mesa where she was born and where she had lived until tribal custom had forced her to flee . . . to the home of the Eagle Clan.

Eight

Walks With Thunder left her village at daybreak, carrying her empty root basket over one arm as though filling it was her main concern. But it was not. What she really sought was solitude, time alone to sort her troubled thoughts and, perhaps, ease the burning hatred eating away at her soul.

Her husband, Gray Wolf, was the cause of her hatred. His cruelty had changed her outlook on life, leaving her innocence a thing of the past. She saw everything through a clear, hard outline now . . . realized her future held no hope, no trust or sentiment.

Where was Gray Wolf? she wondered. It was unlike him to remain away from the lodge overnight. Perhaps he had met with an accident. That possibility caused a surge of hope that vanished as quickly as it appeared. Not only was her husband clever, he was also a man of great strength, a man to be feared.

Becoming aware of the moisture beading her face, Walks With Thunder lifted her hand to wipe it away and her gaze caught on the dark bruise that marred her forearm.

Gray Wolf was responsible for the bruise and for the others that were hidden beneath her garment. But the bruises inflicted on her flesh were nothing compared to those left deep inside. His cruelty had shriveled her heart until it had become as small and cold and heavy as a stone.

She pushed thoughts of her husband from her mind, unwilling to dwell on what she could not change, and turned her thoughts instead to finding the trail that would lead to the river, intent on quenching her thirst which had become noticeably stronger with each passing moment.

When she came across the abandoned camp, it was quite unexpected. She was passing through it when something about the way the stones ringed the dead coals caught her attention. She studied the ground and found, deeply embedded in the earth, several unfamiliar prints.

Who, or what, made the tracks? she wondered.

Fearful of watching eyes, Walks With Thunder slid quietly behind the nearest tree. There, she waited for long, heart-stopping moments before deeming it safe enough to venture forth again. After a quick examination of the firepit to determine how long the camp had been vacant, she began a systematic search of the area and discovered her missing husband.

The salt of tears scoured her vision as she looked down at his dead face, but it was not sadness that caused her tears; instead she felt a grim satisfaction that he was gone.

Whoever killed Gray Wolf had done her a great service. She, who had once been known as Desert Flower and was now known as Walks With Thunder because of the scowl that never left her face, exulted in his death.

She was glad he was dead and, if it were possible, would allow those who slew him to go unpunished. But she dared not. Outsiders had killed him and if they were allowed to live might slay more of her clan.

With that fear uppermost in her mind, she hurried back the way she had come. The men who slew her husband would have a considerable head start, but the desert warriors were trained from childhood to cover ground swiftly. There was no way the outsiders could outrun them. No. They would surely be captured before nightfall.

Far to the northwest on a plateau that rose thousands of feet into the air was the village of the Eagle Clan.

Built beneath a cliff overhang halfway up the steep slope where no enemy could reach them from above or below, the three stories of walls and towers that comprised the cliff city squeezed under the cantilevered sandstone ceiling, reaching back deep into the cave.

In front, with ladders jutting from their entrances, were kivas, ceremonial pit rooms, whose stone roofs saw further duty as village plaza.

Across the canyon from the cliff city, located high on the opposite cliff wall, was a small cave. It was to that place that Eric Nordstrom made his way, carrying the haunch of a deer across his back. He entered the shadowy interior and gazed at the woman who sat near the fire nursing their child. Shala's head was bowed as though in sadness.

The babe, as though sensing her mother's grief, released the nipple, screwed her face into a grimace, and wailed.

"Hush, little one," Shala said gently, pressing her nipple into the babe's mouth again. "There is nothing to cause you grief. Your mother dwells too much on what is past and cannot be changed."

"It is a failing that must be overcome," a deep voice said from behind her.

Shala knew that voice, knew it well, and it brought her head around and set a smile on her face.

"Eric," she said, hearing the gladness in her voice as she recognized the massive body of her Viking husband. "You came back early. I did not hear you come in." Her gaze dwelt lovingly on the halo of golden hair framing his face before meeting his grass-green eyes, so like those of their daughter.

"No," he agreed, laying aside the crossbow that he carried and unsheathing his sword before joining her. "Your thoughts were elsewhere." There was an accusatory note in his voice; and yet, she heard kindness there as well. "What past do you dwell upon, my love?"

"My thoughts were upon my own foolishness. It

was that same foolishness that caused my friend to lose her life. If only I could live those days over . . ."

"Do not torment yourself, love," he said, squatting beside her and taking her free hand. "Your friend would not want you to blame yourself."

"No. But I cannot stop doing so. She looked to me for protection, Eric." Her eyes filled with tears. "She was so innocent. Like the babe I hold in my arms. The world will be cruel to our babe if that innocence remains within her." She tightened her arms around her baby and the child looked up at her again; then the infant's eyes moved to her father and her mouth tilted upward into a grin. The nipple, released from the small mouth, exuded droplets of milk that were quickly absorbed by a soft hide garment.

"We will teach our child, Shala," Eric said gruffly. "She will have the courage that dwells in her mother. She will learn how to be a woman; but more importantly, she will also be taught the skills that will make her able to take care of herself if that need should ever arise."

"Yes," Shala agreed. "We will teach her well. She will grow into a strong-willed woman, as skilled with weapons as with pottery and basket weaving. My friend—" She could not speak her name. "—could make the best of pottery, could weave the finest of baskets, but she knew nothing of weapons. Had she been taught such things, she might still dwell among the living. But she did not. The innocence that was so appealing in her was also her greatest weakness."

"Yes. And you must always remember that, love. She was raised to keep her innocence since childhood and would more than likely have remained that way for the rest of her days."

Nama's fury knew no bounds as she used her teeth to chew through the hide straps binding her wrists. And all the while she kept her glittering gaze on the man who was responsible for her captivity.

He would regret treating her in such a manner. She would make certain of that. In her mind's eye she could see him, staring up at her with horrified eyes . . . just before she sliced into his flesh and cut out his heart. Even as the thought occurred, Nama felt horror streak through her. How could she even consider such a violent act? Was this what living alone had done to her?

Granted, the man had treated her cruelly; but did that justify slaying him? And suppose her suspicions were correct and he was Eric's brother? She would never voluntarily hurt Eric, but the hurt would be there if she slew his brother.

No, she decided, expelling a heavy sigh. She would have to put aside her own feelings, would have to leave quietly, taking the chance Garrick would not follow after her.

She realized her actions were quite unlike the girl she had once been—the innocent child who had lived with the Eagle Clan—but the change caused her no displeasure. Instead, she felt a certain amount of pride that a coward such as she could still find the strength of mind she needed to escape.

She continued to chew at the leather straps, pausing occasionally to judge the progress she had made, then putting them to her mouth again, determined to continue until she was free. An eternity seemed to pass before her efforts were finally rewarded. The hide strap broke, releasing her.

Turning her attention to her feet, she worked furiously at the straps there, worrying all the time that the men would wake before she had finished. But good luck continued to favor her, and moments later she stood on her feet.

Nama was on the point of leaving when her gaze was caught by sunlight glinting off metal.

Focusing on the spot, she saw a wide-bladed knife on the ground. It was a good weapon to have, one that she coveted mightily. Did she dare take it?

Her gaze jerked to the hand that lay only a handspan from the knife. It was a large hand. A strong hand. She stared at the long fingers sprinkled with fine curling hair and felt a fascination that caused her a great sense of unease.

She glanced quickly at his face, satisfied herself that he still slept, then bent to retrieve the knife.

Garrick woke abruptly from a sound sleep, wondering what had wakened him. With senses completely alert, he opened his eyelids a mere slit and saw the *skraeling* woman creeping toward him, her gaze directed toward his hand.

Not his hand, he realized suddenly. It was his knife that held her attention! She was reaching for it when he stretched his arm outward to retrieve his blade.

But he was too late!

Before he could close his fingers around the weapon, the girl snatched it up and moved out of his reach.

"Drop it!" Garrick said harshly.

Hearing Olaf's sleepy grumble behind him, Garrick said, "Watch her, Olaf! She has my blade!"

"What?" Olaf roared.

From the corner of his eyes, Garrick saw Olaf circle around the firepit as though intent on taking the girl from behind. "Leave her alone," Garrick said, enjoying the deadly game.

The girl's feet were spread wide and she held the knife before her in a threatening manner. Her eyes darted fearfully, reminding Garrick of an animal held at bay by hungry wolves.

"Drop the knife." His voice was calm, his gaze steady. Garrick was sure of himself, certain of his strength and his ability to defeat the woman. Yet he would not strike out. He wanted her to concede, to obey his command. Even she, savage that she was, must know she could accomplish nothing by continued resistance.

Suddenly, even while he watched, the fight drained away from her. Her fingers opened and she dropped the knife. Then, with lowered head and drooping shoulders, she dropped to her knees, assuming a position of meek acceptance.

Garrick felt a grim satisfaction as he watched her; and yet, there was a sense of disappointment, too. He had not suspected she would so easily accept his demands.

"Watch out!"

Olaf's shouted warning came too late. Garrick had been too intent on the girl's face to see what her hands were doing. The sand struck him full in the face, stinging his eyes and blurring his vision.

Garrick swept his hands across his face, brushing away the grains of sand, aware of the flurry of movement as the woman spun around and, quick as the wind, took flight.

Nama splashed through the silvery creek and dashed toward the willows growing along its banks, cursing herself for her carelessness as she ran.

She had delayed her flight, hoping to steal her enemy's weapon. It was a bad mistake, might result in the loss of her freedom.

Foolish girl, an inner voice chided. But there was no time to consider the foolishness of her actions. Instead, her every thought must be directed toward escape.

Nama's heart pounded with exertion as she left the water. She imagined she could feel the hot breath of her pursuers against the back of her neck as she climbed the steep bank farthest from the Vikings' camp.

Fear lent wings to her feet and she dashed into the willows. Feeling the sting of their branches, she lifted her arms, bending them in front of her to shield her face from the backlash.

Then she was through the growth of willows, racing for the cover of the forest that was only a short distance away, scattering a covey of quail as she ran, leaving them beating their wings furiously as they sought to escape from the mad intruder who had discovered their nesting place.

Heavy footsteps crashed through the underbrush behind her and the sound sent an icy chill sweeping down her spine. Birds flew out of her path; and a rabbit, startled by the noise she was making, fled before her, seeking refuge finally in a hole in the ground.

Nama's gaze darted back and forth as she ran, searching for a way out, a way to elude the men who sought to take her captive again.

The forest was thick with ponderosa pines, aspens, and blue spruce, but they would not hide her long from the men who continued to pursue her. And the path she took became harder to travel, the dense forest slowing her down considerably for, although the largest trees were widely spaced, saplings grew thick and unchecked between them and ivy twined here and there with the bare strings of grapevines.

Thud, thud, thud went her heartbeat.

Crash, crack, pop! went the brush behind her.

Nama realized the Vikings must be gaining on her.

Help me, Great Creator! she cried silently.

Even as she uttered the plea, hard fingers wrapped around her back-swinging wrist, jerking her to a sudden halt. Then Garrick lifted her off her feet as though she weighed no more than a feather and swung her around, slamming her hard against his chest.

"Oooomph!" The breath whooshed from her body, leaving her chest tightly constricted.

Nama sucked greedily at the life-giving air, trying to relieve her tortured lungs that felt on fire from lack of oxygen.

Drawing back her foot, she delivered a quick, hard blow that connected with his shinbone. Nama knew her attempts at resistance had not arisen from courage as much as from sheer terror, knew as well that she must not give in to it.

Her fear doubled as his lips lowered to within an inch of hers and his hot breath washed over her face. She found herself unable to look away from his grass-green eyes . . . eyes that were completely devoid of all mercy or compassion. She knew that if all the worst of human savagery from the beginning of time could be condensed into one individual, if all the violence and raw power could be embodied in one monstrous figure, it would have looked the way Garrick Nordstrom looked at that very moment.

She was so intimidated by him that she could do nothing but stare at him through dilated pupils, waiting with quivering lips for what was to come. The moments passed, long endless moments of time when her thoughts conjured up every torture her mind could possibly imagine.

Something flickered in his eyes, undefinable, but it gave her hope. Had there been an imperceptible softening in their depths?

If she begged for mercy, perhaps he would listen. But how, when her thoughts were so scattered, would she find words to beg? She searched her memory, then uttered the only Viking words she could recall. "P-please," she whispered shakily. "Unhand me."

Instead of releasing her, his grip tightened, his fingers digging into the flesh of her shoulders. In the back of her mind she was aware of the sound of approaching footsteps, but her attention was totally on this man who had frozen at her first pleading word.

Still holding her aloft, he uttered a long string of harsh words, spoken so swiftly that she caught only a few of them. Even so, she realized he was questioning her knowledge of his language.

"I—I—"

"How do you know?" he roared, punctuating each word with a hard shake that rattled her teeth.

"Thor's teeth!" The oath came from somewhere behind them and Nama realized that Olaf had arrived on the scene. He spoke other words, and seemed to be questioning Garrick's treatment of her.

Turning her head, she appealed to him. "Olaf!" she cried. "Make him stop!" Then, realizing she had spoken in her own language, she sought for Viking words that might help. When none came to mind, she said "Eric teach."

Surprise flitted across Garrick's face, but his grip on her did not relax. "Eric?" he repeated. "Speak, woman." Before she could respond, he uttered several other words, none of which she understood.

She shook her head. "Nama . . ." She struck her chest with her fist, then continued. " . . . not know words Garrick speaks."

His look was disbelieving. "You spoke of a man . . . Eric. Eric Nordstrom?"

She nodded her head. "Eric Nordstrom," she repeated.

"Where is he?" Olaf questioned. "Where is Eric? Tell us where to find him."

"Find?" she queried, frowning in concentration. The man spoke too fast. How could she possibly know what he was saying?

"Yes. Eric! We must find Eric."

"No understand," she said. "Speak slow."

"We . . . must . . . find . . . Eric," Olaf said, immediately complying with her request. "Where is he?"

Realizing they wanted to find Eric, she lifted her chin and turned a hard stare on Garrick. "Gone!" she said. "Long gone. Here no more." She found the words coming easier now.

Surprisingly, the big Viking loosened his hold on her. His anger seemed to drain away, leaving nothing behind to sustain it.

"When did it happen?" Olaf questioned.

"Happen?" she repeated, confused.

"When . . . did . . . Eric . . . die?"

Die? Nama recognized that word, and shock coursed through her. They had misunderstood her words and thought their brother dead. She opened her mouth to correct them, then closed it again. Perhaps the Spirits had guided her choice of words, for if the Vikings believed their brother dead, they would not continue to search, would return to their own land.

Nama hoped they *would* leave. And quickly.

Realizing they were waiting for her answer, Nama spoke softly. "Long ago. Eric d-die . . ." She was unable to control the stutter as she spoke the lie. " . . . at time of long, white cold."

"How?" Garrick growled.

She bent her head, unable to meet his eyes. "Eric fall." Raising her hand, she allowed it to drop. "Long way . . . long, long way."

She waited in trembling silence for them to digest her words, wondering what fate they intended for her. She was not left to wonder long, though. When Olaf turned to retrace his path, Garrick followed him, dragging her along behind.

Nine

The flame-haired Viking's ground-eating pace was ruthless, allowing Nama no time to catch her breath as he dragged her along behind him. By the time they reached the cliff overhang where they had made camp, her heart was hammering, her breathing ragged, and the blood pounding in her temples.

Garrick's countenance was grim as he flung her on the ground and, while she sucked in huge gulps of air, squatted beside her.

"Now talk," he said harshly.

His green eyes had darkened remarkably. No longer did they sparkle with brilliance. Instead, they reminded her of Cloud Man, roiling and boiling, just before he released his turbulence upon those below.

Nama licked her dry lips and swallowed around the lump in her throat. Where was her courage now? she wondered. Had it disappeared completely, leaving her with nothing but her coward's heart?

"Speak." Garrick commanded.

"Speak?" she repeated fearfully, wondering what he wanted from her.

"Your name." Although his curt voice lashed at her, he enunciated each word carefully. "What do they call you?"

"Nama," she whispered huskily.

"We already knew her name," Olaf said in an injured voice.

Garrick ignored him. "Where do you live?" he asked her.

"Here." She indicated her surroundings.

"Garrick!" Olaf's voice was a sudden intrusion, his words swift, yet decisive, spoken so quickly that Nama understood only a few of them. But she had no need to follow each word to know he was urging his brother to leave this place.

Shaking his head, Garrick said, "No. Not yet." He looked at Nama again. "Tell me about Eric."

Nama's stomach coiled into a tight knot of fear. Did he suspect she had deceived him? What was the punishment among the Vikings for the telling of falsehoods?

I did not speak falsely, she reminded herself. *Is the blame mine if he misunderstood the meaning of my words?*

"This . . . woman does not understand," she muttered.

"We must learn more of our brother Eric!" Although the tone was clipped, his voice was less harsh. "How long did you know him?"

Nama's stomach slowly unknotted. Perhaps her situation was not so desperate after all. Perhaps

Garrick might even consent to releasing her after
she had divulged the information he desired. "Two
moons," she said. "He . . . Eric . . . stayed . . .
Eagle Clan . . . two moons."

"Eagle Clan?" Garrick frowned down at her.
"You are from the Eagle Clan?"

She felt fear again. What did he know of her
people? When she spoke again, her tone was cautious. "The Eagle Clan . . . my People . . . but no
more." The moment the words were uttered, she
wished them unsaid. What would he make of
them? Would he make her speak of her cowardice?

Her jaw tightened. No matter what he did to
her, she would not utter a word about the circumstances that led up to her being homeless, an outcast from her clan. He could not make her do so,
no matter what he did.

Apparently he had no interest in her. Instead,
he asked about his brother again.

"You spoke of the long cold."

She nodded her head.

"Winter?"

Remembering Eric had used that word for the
season, she nodded again.

"You knew him well?" His gaze was penetrating,
seeming to see into her very soul.

"Well?" She repeated the word, her gaze uncom-
prehending. "This woman does not understand."
She looked at Olaf, hoping he would explain.

"Garrick means . . ." Olaf stopped, looked at
his brother, and shrugged his shoulders. "You explain."

"Was he important to you?" Garrick asked.

Important. She knew the word, had heard Eric use it often. Now she considered it carefully. *Was* Eric important to her? Yes, she supposed he was. But only because he had been so important to her friend Shala.

Nama nodded her head, lowering her lashes to hide her eyes from his searching eyes. "Eric *was* . . . important."

A quick upward sweep of her lashes made her aware of the scowl that had darkened his brow. Why? Was it because he was angry again?

"You said Eric fell. . . . Was that what killed him?" he asked gruffly.

"Fell? Killed?"

"Fall," he said, lifting his arms and dropping them down again.

"Yes," she agreed. "Eric fall." She must convince him of that, else he might think the people of the Eagle Clan had caused his brother's death and seek retribution. He must be persuaded that his brother died of natural causes. "He d-die. Eric die!" Did her hesitation over the word that branded her a liar cause suspicion?

"From the fall?"

Her mind whirled furiously. What had she told him before. Oh, Great Creator, she could not remember every word she had uttered in her terrified state. But she must say something . . . must allay his suspicions; and yet, what words could she say when there were so few at her disposal?

Nama had never been one to speak falsely and

was certain that, at this very moment, the spirit world looked down upon her with disfavor. Yet surely they would understand her reasons. Surely she would be forgiven since there was no other way to protect her people from these Vikings and others who might seek to follow them.

Perhaps, though, she told herself, the story would be more believable if she spoke truthfully whenever that was possible.

Realizing Garrick was still waiting for a reply to his question, she whispered, "Eric fall and die."

"My brother was a strong man."

"Fall far," she said hastily.

"A cliff perhaps?"

Cliff. She knew that word. And that was exactly how it had happened. She beamed at Garrick. "Yes. Eric . . . fall . . . cliff." Even as the words were spoken, Nama's gaze turned inward with remembrance of the time when Shala had found her Viking lover. When he had been confronted by a mountain lion at the edge of a cliff, Eric, weaponless, had tried to evade the animal by leaping for a limb hanging out over the canyon at the same instant the animal made its attack.

The plan had worked. The lion, intent on its prey, had been unaware of the danger. It had fallen to the rocks far below while Eric had been saved by the overhanging limb. But before he could reach safety, the limb had broken, sending him plunging after the animal.

Shala, having heard the mountain lion, had arrived at the moment Eric plunged into the canyon.

Believing him dead and meaning only to obtain the lion's hide, Shala had descended the cliff and discovered that the man's spirit still dwelled within his body.

Knowing she could not move him alone, Shala had hurried to the cliff city across the canyon and asked Nama for help in moving him to her cave.

It was that story which Nama now told the two Vikings who stood above her. She spoke the truth whenever it was possible, but reversed her role with Shala's. Until she came to the end of her story. Then, instead of having Eric survive the ordeal, she told them he had expired from internal injuries.

"So now we know," Olaf said gruffly. "Thank you for telling us, Nama."

Would Garrick thank her as well, she wondered, sweeping her thick lashes so that she might read his expression. But she could not. The smooth planes of his face gave no indication of his feelings.

"Did you love my brother?" Garrick asked suddenly.

Love. Another word Nama knew. She looked curiously at Garrick, wondering why he asked the question, wondering as well how to answer it. But the hesitation was only slight. Shala had cared deeply for her Viking lover, and Nama had chosen to switch roles with her friend.

"Yes," she whispered, feeling a slight flush color her cheeks. "Nama was joined with Eric."

Something undefinable flickered in the depths of Garrick's eyes, and she wondered what he was feeling. For some reason, other than fear, she found his nearness disturbing.

"Bless you," Olaf said softly, breaking the long silence. "Eric must have been happy."

"How long were you together?" Garrick asked, apparently still not satisfied with her explanation.

"Together?" Nama questioned.

He rephrased his question. "Joined. How long were you joined?"

"Two moons," Nama said, looking beyond Garrick's left shoulder as she spoke the lie. Had she not done so she would have missed the barely perceptible, movement near the base of a distant tree.

Instantly, Nama narrowed her eyes on the spot, focusing all her attention there as she waited, knowing eyes were upon them, be it man or beast who watched.

"What is it?" Olaf asked, seeming to sense her unease. "What are you looking at?" He started to turn around, but she stopped him quickly.

"No! Be silent, Olaf!" she said softly. "An enemy watches."

"An enemy?" Garrick asked, keeping his voice low. "My enemy or yours?"

"The Desert Clan is enemy to all except Desert Clan!" she said sharply, keeping her attention on the tree.

Had she made a mistake, she wondered. Should she have kept quiet about the watcher? Perhaps had she done so, she could have escaped from the Vikings while they were under attack. No sooner had that thought occurred then she felt ashamed of herself. These men had not really harmed her. If truth be told, Olaf had exhibited nothing but kindness. And more importantly, they were both brothers to the Viking Eric, who was her best friend's husband. For that reason alone, she could not allow them to be harmed.

Suddenly she saw the watcher and relaxed somewhat. "The enemy is only a woman," she said softly.

"A woman?" questioned Olaf.

"A woman," Nama repeated. "Desert Clan."

Although Garrick's gaze slid sideways, he remained unmoving. "The woman is alone?"

Nama hesitated. "This woman sees no other."

He noticed her hesitation and grasped his sword in his right hand. "You stay here!" The words had barely left his mouth before he spun on his heel and raced toward the pine thicket.

"Wait!" Olaf shouted, hurrying after his brother, blade in hand.

Nama started after them, unwilling to be left alone when they might be racing headlong into the enemy's path, then quickly stopped again. She could never match their speed, so she might as well save her energy. But suppose they never returned?

Somehow, she found that thought unsettling—and not just because of Eric, either. In those last few moments—before the woman had appeared—Nama had felt something new in Garrick's manner toward her. A softening, perhaps? Whatever it was, she wished to explore it further.

And she would . . . if they returned . . .
. . . if *Garrick* returned.

Walks With Thunder moved quietly between the trees, hurrying away from the camp of the outsiders. Fear caused her heart to beat faster as she concentrated on putting as much distance as possible between herself and her enemy.

They must be enemies of the People, she told herself. Men of such formidable size could be nothing else.

It had been pure chance that she had come across their camp. She had not been following their trail, had thought them long gone; but they must have followed the river which wound through the mountains in such a way that their paths could have crossed several times. She had been returning to her people when she'd heard their voices, speaking in a language that was completely unknown to her ears. Her spirit guide must have been with her, else she would have stumbled upon them and would surely have been captured.

Perhaps finding them was a good thing. If they had continued traveling northward, they would surely have found her village and taken her people by surprise. Now, since they had obviously made camp, she would have time enough to warn her people of their progress, to prepare them for the coming battle.

Cra-a-ack!

Hearing the crackle of brush behind her, she

whirled around just in time to see the two giant men closing in on her. She uttered a high-pitched scream and fled deeper into the forest, knowing the strangers continued to draw closer with each passing moment.

But she would not stop. No! Even though she admitted to herself that her flight was useless. Why, oh, why had she not left sooner? she cried silently. Why had her curiosity kept her near the camp until it was too late to escape from the giant monsters? Walks With Thunder's heart beat with the fury of a thousand drums as she ran through the forest, trying to escape from the fate that awaited her . . . trying in vain, she knew. A sense of fatality enveloped her as hard fingers wrapped around her arm and pulled her to a stumbling halt. Then, knowing she was well and truly captured, her trembling legs gave way and she tumbled against the forest floor, hoping death would come quickly for her, yet fearing it would not.

Ten

Only a short time had passed before Garrick and Olaf returned to their camp, the former dragging a struggling woman behind him. Nama could sympathize with the frightened woman since it was only a short time since she herself had been handled in a like manner.

The woman—who could have only been a few summers older than Nama—had cropped black hair. The hairstyle, and the beaded headband she wore, identified her as a woman from the Desert Clan.

Having reached the campsite, Garrick pushed the woman toward his brother. "This one is for you," he growled.

Olaf uttered words of protest so swiftly that Nama was unable to sort enough of them out to make sense. When he had finished speaking, Garrick replied with equal swiftness, ending with, "Do not allow her to escape."

The woman trembled with fear and her eyes fastened on Nama as though afraid to look at her male captor; and yet beyond the fear, Nama could easily detect a glimmer of cold, icy rage glittering in the depths of the woman's eyes. "Who are these big men?" she asked Nama. "And what do they want with me?"

Her words were easy for Nama to understand because the language of all the peoples of the area were very similar. "They are from a place far across the big water. They call themselves Vikings. And they chased you because you spied upon us. Why did you do so?"

"They killed my mate, Gray Wolf. Tell them they must release me at once. They cannot hold me prisoner."

"It would do no good. They pay me little heed; my circumstance is little better than your own."

"Will they kill me?"

"I do not think so," Nama answered truthfully after a moment's consideration. "If that were their intention, it would have been better to do so as soon as they captured you." She realized with a shimmer of gratitude that by reassuring the frightened woman, she was also allaying her own fears.

"They cannot run far enough to escape my people," the woman said defiantly. "They will look for me and they will not stop until they find me."

"Are you a person of importance then?" Nama asked, her eyes narrowing on the other woman, wondering what set her apart from other females of her tribe.

The woman's dark head lifted proudly. "I am much desired by the men of my tribe. My lineage is pure. I am from the seed of Rushing Elk and Sweet Willow. I am Walks With Thunder. Since my husband is dead, there will be many warriors seeking to have me for a mate."

"What does she say?" Garrick asked, suddenly at Nama's elbow. "Is her people nearby?"

"She has not spoken of them," Nama answered, switching almost effortlessly into the Viking language.

"Well, ask her then!" the fiery Viking scolded.

"The man with flaming hair wants to know if your people are nearby," Nama told the woman.

Walks With Thunder lifted her chin and met the Viking's eyes when she gave her answer. "If they were, I would not tell him so."

"She refuses to answer," Nama told the man who watched her so intently.

"What does she speak of then, Nama?" Garrick asked.

"Only that she is Walks With Thunder, a woman of importance in her clan."

Garrick's mouth thinned, becoming ruthlessly set, causing slashing grooves that seemed to be carved on either side of his jaw. A dark stubble of coppery beard accented the strong powerful lines of his jaw and chin; and his grass-green eyes, outlined by thick, spiky lashes, moved restlessly over the area around them, probing the shadows in the dense forest.

"Perhaps we would do well to leave here," he said. "Come." He took Nama's arm and led her toward the horses. "You will ride with me again."

Once again Nama found herself seated before Garrick on the great beast he called *horse*. She was aware of the hardness of his warm body against her back as he gathered up the strips of leather that controlled his mount. Then, resting his hand lightly against her hip, he urged the horse forward.

Weariness settled over her like a heavy blanket and, despite her efforts to keep her backbone straight, she found herself slumping against Garrick, supported by his arms and chest.

She was aware of Olaf's mount with its double load following close behind, but she was so caught up in her own thoughts, so full of questions about these Vikings—Garrick in particular—that she spared no thought for the golden-haired giant and his captive.

They traveled throughout the day, riding in a southeasterly direction; and although the fiery-haired giant spoke no word to Nama, giving her no indication of his thoughts, his stony countenance had softened somewhat. That fact and his strong hand resting against her hip gave her a sense of protection that was new to her. She liked the feeling, even wished, for a fleeting moment, that this man was hers.

How would this man behave with a woman he loved? she wondered. His brother Eric was kind to Shala. Most of the time he allowed her to do anything, to go anywhere that she wished.

Would Garrick allow his woman the same freedom?

That question quickly led to another. Did Garrick Nordstrom leave a woman behind in that faraway land from which he came?

She felt unsettled at the thought and wondered curiously why it was so. This Viking's life had nothing to do with her.

No? a silent voice asked. *Your life was your own until he took you captive. You are no longer free. little better than a slave. Everything you have done to control your own fate has been for nothing.*

Who did this Viking think he was anyway? He had come to this land, a stranger, uninvited, and he had made her his prisoner, striking her with such a blow that she had been rendered unconscious. The mere thought was enough to stoke the fires of anger. They continued to burn until she was fairly seething with rage, yet she could do nothing to assuage her fury, must content herself by straightening her back and leaning forward as much as possible to keep her body from brushing against his.

Yet he would not allow her even that small show of temper, for he pulled her back against him, adjusting her position until it was the same as before, with her shoulder tucked into the hollow under his left arm and her head resting against the solidness of his left shoulder.

The gait of the horse was such that his body rubbed against hers constantly, making her continually aware of his masculinity. Was that the reason she felt so disturbed? she wondered. Was that the reason her heart hammered so violently . . . the reason her insides jangled with excitement . . . the reason for the peculiar stirring she was experiencing in her lower belly, for the heat that began to radiate between her thighs? Was Garrick responsible for all those things?

The thought was, of course, ridiculous, and yet . . . Shala had mentioned similar feelings, speaking of a peculiar stirring that made her wonder if she were sickening for something.

A movement in her peripheral vision caught her attention, and she turned her head to see Olaf urging his mount forward until he was keeping pace beside them. She studied the expression on his face. His lips curled slightly as though he were enjoying himself.

Enjoying himself?

Nama's attention shifted to the woman riding in front of the golden-haired Viking, just in time to see her drop a small strip of hide—torn from the bottom of her skirt—to the ground.

Could Walks With Thunder be marking a trail for her people to follow?

Seeming to sense Nama's attention, Walks With Thunder met her gaze and something flickered in the woman's flat, black eyes. Was it fear? Or was it more a challenge—an invitation to Nama to conspire with her so their efforts might be combined to defeat the Vikings.

What should she do? Nama wondered. She could maintain her silence, allowing the woman to leave a marked trail leading her people to them. Or she could speak now, warning the Vikings of the woman's trickery, perhaps thus insuring a measure of security for herself in the doing.

Whatever her decision, it must be made soon,

for out of the corner of her eye she could see that
Walks With Thunder was tearing yet another piece
of material from her garment. Should she continue
much longer without being detected, there would
be no way the Vikings could escape the wrath of
the Desert Clan.

To Garrick, the ride had become a trial of endurance, and all because of the *skraeling* wench
who refused to sit still. Her constant movements
were a source of deep irritation, were responsible
for the stirrings in his lower body which made him
keenly aware of how long it had been since he had
bedded a woman.

The sweet thought of bedding this one caused
him an immense amount of pleasure, albeit she
was no more than a *skraeling*, a pathetic wretch in
his Nordic eyes. But alas, she was a beautiful
woman, wretch or not. And yet beyond the pleasant
daydreams pressing forward from the recesses of
his innermost thoughts, the feeling was accompanied by something else. An odd sense, he supposed, of something amiss. Something far greater
than their differences. Indeed, for some odd reason far too puzzling for his mind to conjure, he
felt as if bedding this woman would be in some
way wrong. As if—such a ridiculous thought!—he
and the *skraeling* were in some manner akin.

Was it because she and Eric had been lovers? he
pondered.

Yes! Perhaps that was it.

Had his brother cared very much for her? he pondered then. That was entirely possible, he supposed, for Nama was a beauty even by Viking standards. But setting that thought aside, Garrick had to question how a man—ill and unable to care for himself—could become so easily enamored of his caretaker before departing from this world. And if Nama had made his brother's last days happy ones, then he supposed he owed her something for her trouble.

Guilt's sharp sting soon curbed the more lustful thoughts arising in his mind; and he vowed, for the sake of his brother's memory and for any kindnesses she might have disposed in Eric's final days, he would from this moment forward not allow his mind and body to long for her. In fact, he would make every effort to avoid her, keeping himself apart from her so that the feelings of his body might be more easily denied.

Nama moved again, trying for a more comfortable seat on the great black steed; and his hand, circling her waist, was inadvertently brought into sharp contact with her full breasts.

"Thor's teeth, woman! Must you keep moving around like that?" he exclaimed harshly, exasperated by the immediate twinge of lust arising from his loins.

She turned to face him with flashing eyes. "Your animal is not comfortable to ride," she snapped. "It was not designed for a woman."

Her words, coupled with her body pressed against his, made him acutely aware of her femi-

ninity and he felt his maleness stir even more. He
gave Walks With Thunder an assessing look. She
held no sexual appeal for him, so why did he feel
desire for the wench seated before him?

Midnight lurched suddenly, climbing over a
large hillock, throwing Nama backward, closer
against Garrick's aching loins.

Spewing oaths into the air, he reined Midnight
to a stop and bounded over his rump to the
ground, landing with a jarring thump. He stalked
to the horse's side, gripped Nama around the
waist, and dragged her to the ground.

Olaf stopped his horse beside them and looked
curiously at his brother. "What are you about, Garrick?" he asked.

"This fool woman will not keep still!" Garrick
snapped, swinging her into his arms and carrying
her to Olaf. "You take her."

A pained look crossed Olaf's features. "Are you
crazy? Thunder cannot carry three riders!"

"He need not do so," Garrick said grimly. "I
will relieve you of the other one."

Pulling Walks With Thunder from Olaf's
mount, he plunked her atop his horse. Then,
mounting Midnight again, he put his heel to his
steed.

As the black stallion leaped forward, Garrick
threw a quick glance at Nama. Her face, which
had reflected confusion only moments ago, was
now completely devoid of expression. Why? he
wondered, guiding his mount toward a path that
wound up a steep mountain slope.

Unable to find an answer to his question, he tried to push thoughts of Nama from his mind. But try as he would, even though he now felt the rigid, ungiving contours of another beneath his grasp, he could not rid himself of the memory of Nama's body rubbing against his, of the subtle way her hair brushed against his face as they rode, of the feel of that womanly breast beneath his palm.

It was late afternoon when runners from the Desert Clan who searched for Walks With Thunder and her husband found the useless husk that had once been a man. And they found sign that another had been there as well.

"These prints belong to Walks With Thunder," said Gray Eagle, the eldest and leader of the group.

"Yes, they are hers," confirmed Squats By The River. He had long coveted the woman and had occasion to know her moccasin tracks. "She follows the trail of those who slew her husband."

"She is a foolish woman then," Gray Eagle growled. "Why did she not come to the village and seek help? She has no weapons with which to defend herself. How could she possibly hope to extract revenge against Gray Wolf's killers? Have her senses totally left her, do you suppose?"

"She is not so foolish," argued Squats By The River, pointing toward a bush where a small hide strip was caught. "See there, beneath the shrub. She leaves a trail for us to follow."

"Let us hope that she has sense enough to keep out of their sight," Gray Eagle said. "Otherwise we may find the buzzards picking at her bones, too."

They picked up the trail left behind and set off at a steady lope, secure in the knowledge that the enemy could not escape from them.

Eleven

Sky Man's cloak was shaded with pink and purple when they entered the dappled evening of the great trees, making Nama aware that darkness would soon cover the land. As they rode through the gathering shadows, penetrating deeper and deeper into the forest, she listened intently to the sounds around her. Above all other sounds was the muffled clip-clop of the horses' hooves; but below that, on a lower level, she heard the brushing of a branch against a tree and, barely a fraction of a moment later, heard the thud of a falling nut striking the ground.

Startled, her gaze swooped in that direction and she caught a glimpse of a bushy tail disappearing around a limb and realized it was no more than a darting squirrel frightened by the intruders.

The shadows thickened, and chill fingers trailed along Nama's spine. She shuddered slightly and Olaf's hand tightened around her midriff.

"Cold?" he asked.

"No." She hesitated, wondering if she should speak of her unease. "But—"

"What?"

He pulled back on the reins and Thunder stopped immediately. Olaf's body, which had been easy and relaxed, was now straight and stiff as though he, too, sensed some unnamed danger.

"I—I . . . something is not as it should be." She was conscious that Garrick brought his mount to a halt beside them. Conscious as well of Walks With Thunder's hard, accusing, stare.

"What is not right?" Garrick growled, looking at her curiously.

"Listen," she whispered.

"I hear nothing," he replied.

"That is why this woman is wary," she said. "The forest should not be so silent." She tilted her head slightly and listened to the unnatural quiet. "Listen. There is no sound. The squirrels are quiet. The catbirds do not whistle. All the creatures of the forest are watchful. They know that—"

She broke off as her sweeping gaze caught a bare movement high in the uppermost branches.

"There!" she whispered around the knot of fear that suddenly filled her throat. "Located among the topmost leaves is our enemies."

Garrick's narrowed gaze followed hers and he immediately focused on the spot.

Although the war-painted warrior attempted to conceal himself among the leaves which covered the gnarled and stunted limbs, only half his body was hidden by the trunk of the tree. The rest of him was exposed to their view.

Was he alone? she wondered.

No sooner had the thought occurred to her, then

the warrior made his move. With his right hand reaching for his knife, he gave a bloodcurdling yell and attacked.

"A-a-a-iii-eee!" cried the warrior, dropping to the ground in front of them.

The cry was taken up by others, shrieks designed to curdle the blood and send terror through all that chanced to hear them.

Swift currents of blood coursed into the fountains of Nama's heart and her head began to spin around, whirling like a dust-devil as she tried to pinpoint the location of the sounds.

But to do so was impossible. The sounds seemed to come from everywhere. From the ground, from the darkening sky, even from the trees. It was as though all the demons who occupied the third world had finally broken through the barrier designed to keep them at bay and were now in possession of the very air she breathed.

"Get off!" Garrick shouted at Walks With Thunder, almost pushing her from the stallion.

Nama was vaguely aware of the other woman sliding from the saddle while she herself needed no prompting. She leapt to the ground, hurling herself near a spreading bush, hoping it would offer safety.

"Oooofff!" She struck the earth with a hard thud, then rolled quickly aside and pushed herself to her knees in time to see Garrick racing toward the painted warriors.

Bows twanged; arrows whooshed; but Garrick rode on, sending Midnight crashing through the human barrier, and the men of the Desert Clan scattered like autumn leaves before a brisk wind.

Nama crawled beneath the bush, her heart pounding in time with Midnight's hooves as Garrick reined the stallion around and prepared to send the animal through the web of warriors once more.

Drawing his huge blade from its scabbard, he urged the animal toward the enemy, who were still scrambling to regain their weapons.

One of them, a man of broader stature than the rest, wore a beaded headband with a single eagle feather that told of his position among the tribe. Nama knew him for a leader.

Even while she watched, he turned to face Garrick, hatchet in hand, prepared to do battle despite the fierceness of the giant enemy he faced.

"Whoosh!" The hatchet flew across the space separating the two men and Garrick, finding himself unable to avoid the flying missile effectively, slid off his mount and launched himself at the *skraeling*. He struck the smaller man with a blow that sent them both sprawling.

Quick as a wink, the warrior rolled over and dashed toward his hatchet. His fingers connected with, curled and tightened around the handle. Then he leapt lightly to his feet, swinging it toward Garrick with every ounce of strength he possessed.

Garrick felt the air displaced as the weapon missed him by a mere half-inch. He sent a kick toward the other man that struck him in the mid-section.

"Oooofff!" The breath whooshed out of the *skraeling*, sending him sprawling again.

Immediately, the Indian righted himself, leaping to his feet and spreading his legs in a fighting stance, prepared to meet his opponent again.

Garrick realized he and Olaf would soon be overcome by the sheer numbers and spared a moment's thought for the women. Nama had warned him about the ambush, referring to them as "our" enemies. He met her eyes and saw the fear reflected there.

"Run, Nama!" His voice thundered above the fighting. "Flee from this place! I will find you later!"

The words were barely uttered when two warriors attacked him from the side. He felt their knives slice into his flesh, but where was the accompanying pain? he wondered, feeling warm blood spurting from the wound.

From the corner of his eye, he watched Nama wrap her fingers around Walks With Thunder's wrist and jerk her into the shadows.

He wanted to shout at her, wanted to warn her that the woman was dangerous, but he could find no breath to utter the warning. Nor could he go after her. Not with the sounds of fighting all around him, not when he saw another *skraeling* straddling Olaf's back, lifting his knife hand into the air, readying himself to bring it down and claim Garrick's brother's life.

With a roar of rage, Garrick waded through the warriors, surging forward to his brother's aid.

Run! Flee! I will find you later, later, later . . .
The words echoed over and over again in Nama's mind as she pulled Walks With Thunder along behind her, hoping to escape in the shadowy darkness. "Hurry, Walks With Thunder," she commanded. "Do you want them to catch us?"

"Stop!" Walks With Thunder cried, tugging at her wrist. "There is no reason to run! The men you call Vikings are outnumbered by my people. There is no way they can win this battle."

"We must get away from this place!"

"Why?" the other woman asked stubbornly, tugging at her wrists. "I told you they are my people. They will not harm us."

"Have you no sense, woman? Many lives may be lost in the heat of battle. Who can be sure who delivered the killing blows when so many are fighting in such close quarters," Nama countered. "Could you, yourself, identify each of the warriors that you say are your people?" She answered for the other girl. "No, you could not. The shadows are too thick. Now stop fighting me and come along or I will leave you to your own fate!"

Walks With Thunder, seeming to see the reason behind Nama's words, complied.

Even as the two women fled through the forest, Nama's thoughts were on the scene she had left behind. Was the woman from the Desert Clan right? Would sheer numbers conquer the Vikings? She found that thought disturbing.

The sound of battle could still be heard in the distance when Walks With Thunder came to an abrupt stop. When Nama opened her mouth to object, the woman spoke quickly.

"I can go no farther without rest," she protested. "My breath is coming too fast and my heart beats like a butterfly trapped in Grandmother Spider's web."

"We will stop a moment then," Nama said. "But no more." Although she would not admit it, she was grateful for the rest herself.

A low moan to the left jerked her head upright, sending her gaze to probe the shadows. The sound was repeated and she realized it was only Wind Woman playing a trick on them.

"Come," she urged after a moment. "We must go on."

Reluctantly, Walks With Thunder fell in line behind her. Nama set a pace that soon had her heart beating fast again and her breath rasping harshly in her throat.

"Stop!" Walks With Thunder cried suddenly. "I must rest again!"

"No!" Nama said. "We dare not stop again!"

The words were no more than uttered before Walks With Thunder fell to her knees and refused to go farther, no matter how hard Nama pulled at her, how insistent she was that they go on.

"I can go no farther," the woman said, her

breath rasping harshly, her head dropping. "Do what you will, but I cannot continue on this way."

Realizing she would have to stop and allow the woman to rest or go on alone, Nama, reluctant to leave the other woman, sank to the ground beside her. "Perhaps it is safe enough now."

"Whooooo!"

Walks With Thunder jerked upright at the sound and Nama hurried to assure her that all was well. "It is nothing. Just a night owl."

The two women remained where they were as the moon appeared in the night sky. It shed its pale light through the forest, finding them huddled near each other to share their body warmth.

Nama knew she could not allow herself the luxury of sleep although her body cried out for it. She must stay awake, must stay alert at all times.

She sighed deeply, drinking in the cool night air, pulling her knees up, and resting her weary head on them.

Nama was unaware of the moment when she lost consciousness, realizing only that she was growing drowsy.

Then, her eyes closed, her pulse slowed down, and her body went into a restful state of sleep. She was completely unaware of figures moving stealthily along the forest floor.

Each footstep the intruders took gobbled up the fragile space that lingered between them as they came nearer and nearer.

Twelve

"Just look at them, Garrick," Olaf said, staring down at the two women slumbering near each other. "They sleep like the dead while we have been fighting for our lives."

"I imagine they are exhausted," Garrick replied, his eyes drinking in the lovely sight of Nama, dark hair spread across her breasts, highlighted by the moonlight.

"I do not understand your reasoning," Olaf complained. "Why did we have to follow them? it was different when we had our steeds; but now, since we are afoot, the women will only prove burdensome."

"We cannot, in all good conscience, abandon them, Brother."

"Abandon them?" Olaf lifted blond eyebrows. "We are not their keepers. They should be familiar enough with this forest to find their way back to their village."

"You have not been listening well, Olaf. The two women did not know each other before we brought them together. Walks With Thunder belongs to the Desert Clan while Nama belongs to the Eagle

Clan. Their people are enemies. That is why Nama warned us of the ambush. Had she not done so we might not be standing here now."

"You credit her with more than her due," Olaf grunted. "She was only trying to save her own hide."

Garrick speared the other man with a hard glare. "Where is your conscience, Olaf? The wench stood by our brother when he needed her. We would demean ourselves if we deserted her in her need."

"You argue her case well, Garrick. I have no objection to taking her if that is her wish. But she must decide for herself. To take a wench that is forever trying to escape would never do. Especially now, when we have lost our steeds."

"That is the second time you have mentioned our lack of horses. But you need not worry on that score. Midnight will not roam far."

"I realize you trained the stallion to stay close by, but the beast was fearful when he fled, having never before been confronted by the like of these *skraelings*."

"Nevertheless, my steed will not long remain absent," Garrick said firmly.

"Surely you plan to rest before traveling farther."

"Yes. We do not know the area and dare not continue in the darkness. We could easily walk into a trap. We will stay here until first light."

"Good," said Olaf. "Do you want me to stand watch?"

"No. I might as well since I would have trouble sleeping right now."

Olaf eyed the bloodstains on Garrick's clothing and frowned. "You are certain your wounds are only superficial?"

"I have already said they are nothing," Garrick replied. "Only flesh wounds. Nothing to concern yourself with."

"I will take your word for it, Garrick."

Stretching himself out on a thick mat of pine needles, Olaf used his arm to pillow his head and closed his eyes.

Garrick knew from past experience that his brother would be asleep in mere moments. His green eyes probed the shadows around them, searching for sign of the enemy. His anxiety for their position was relieved only slightly by the knowledge that the sleepers were protected by rocks from any missiles the natives might think to hurl at them. He was confident the only way to the others was through himself, and he had every intention of staying alert through the dark hours of the night.

A sharp snap woke Nama and she sat up abruptly, feeling totally disoriented, fighting the fear of the nightmare that still lingered in her mind.

Moonlight filtered through the pines, only slightly dispelling the dark shadows of night. She searched for the source of the noise, uttering a sharp gasp as the dark shape of a large man stepped into view.

"Be not afraid, little one."

Garrick's husky voice had a surprisingly calming effect on her. The fear disappeared and relief took its place. But there was no emotion in her voice when she spoke. "So you found us."

He squatted beside her. "As I said I would." He brushed the hair from her face with a gentle hand, and his touch sent a warming shiver through her. "You were not harmed in the attack?"

"No," she whispered. "And you?"

"My wounds are shallow. Not worth mentioning." He cupped her chin and looked deep into her eyes, and her whole being seemed to be filled with waiting. "Why did you warn us of the attack, Nama?"

"The—the Desert Clan are m-my enemies, too," she stuttered. "They would not treat me well if they captured me."

"You need not have warned us, though. You could have escaped in the heat of battle."

"Yes," she agreed. "But you are Eric's brother."

At the mention of his brother, Garrick released her and drew back slightly. "Yes," he agreed. "I am Eric's brother. And you were his chosen mate."

His smile seemed forced to Nama when he leaned over and touched his lips to her forehead. "Be at ease, little one, and go back to sleep. There will be time enough to talk later."

Straightening himself to his full height, Garrick strode to a large rock that afforded him a view of the surrounding area and resumed his watch.

Although Nama tried to sleep again, her efforts

proved futile. She lay awake through the dark night, wishing she could relive those few moments before she'd mentioned Eric's name.

Garrick was a vigilant protector, seeming neither weary nor sleepy. He was as immovable as the rock upon which he sat—of which he appeared to form a part. His eyes roved without intermission along the dark margin of trees that surrounded them.

Not a sound escaped him; the most subtle examination could not have told he breathed. It was evident his excess of caution came from an experience that no subtlety on the part of his enemies could deceive. It was, however, continued without any apparent consequences, until the moon had set and a pale streak above the treetops, at the bend of the river a little below, announced the approach of day.

Then, for the first time, Garrick stirred. He crawled along the rock and shook Olaf from his slumber.

"Now is the time to journey onward," he whispered. "Wake the women and be ready to go at any moment."

"Have you seen any sign of the *skraelings?*" asked Olaf.

"Not yet," Garrick replied. "But they may have stopped as we did through the darkest hours. Even now they may have taken up our trail. We cannot take that chance. We must find a safer place to conceal ourselves from them."

Nama sat up before Olaf reached her. "I am awake."

"We must be silent," he cautioned. "Other ears might be listening."

Reaching past Nama, he shook Walks With Thunder, startling her out of sleep. Her lashes flew open, and she uttered a fearful shriek.

Nama made a shushing sound and spoke sharply. "Quiet, woman. You have no need to fear these men. They mean you no harm."

"How can you know that?" Walks With Thunder asked. "We should have escaped while we had the chance."

"I have no wish to escape from them," Nama said, feeling surprise that it was true. "They are—"

Olaf finally interrupted them. "You can speak together later. Right now we must hurry along."

Nama watched Garrick plunge into the forest ahead of them, intent on finding a place that would conceal them from the men who would surely be searching the trail behind them.

"Where are the horses?" Nama asked Garrick.

"They ran off, but that is of little consequence."

She wondered if she had misunderstood his words. "You do not care that they are gone?"

"It is of no consequence," he repeated.

"But if we had the animals we could flee this place. Without them we are doomed. The desert people will find us wherever we go." She looked at Walks With Thunder, knowing the woman only remained because she was fearful of severe punishment if she were caught trying to escape. She wondered if she should warn Olaf, then saw there was no need. The blond Viking was watchful, his gaze continually on the woman from the Desert Clan.

They had only traveled a short time when Nama heard a distant roaring. Was it the river, a waterfall, perhaps? If so, it must be a large one. The sound became louder as they approached. When they reached the shore, they found Garrick waiting for them.

The two men conversed in low voices while Nama studied the high, craggy rocks between which the river flowed.

The water seemed piled between those rocks where it tumbled into caverns out of which came sullen, moaning sounds that raised goose bumps on her arms and made her think of evil spirits hovering over the canyon.

"It is a place of evil," muttered Walks With Thunder.

"You have been here before?" asked Nama.

"No. We are Desert Clan. This area is unknown to us." She shivered slightly and wrapped her arms around her upper body. "But do you not hear the Spirits, Nama? They are quarreling, troublesome. It would be best to avoid this place."

"What is she saying?" Garrick asked, coming to stand beside Nama. "Does she know where we are?"

"No. She has no knowledge of this mountain. But she believes it to be a place of evil."

"Then we stay here," he said.

"Where?" she asked.

"There!" He pointed to a place where the water

boiled around the rocks. "That is a cave. We will wait there until we can be certain the *skraelings* have passed us by."

"Could we not return to your boat?" Nama asked quickly, fearful of entering the caverns. "If we stay here, they might find us."

"The longboat is too far away," he said, answering her first question. "And if Walks With Thunder believes this place inhabited by evil spirits, then her people might be of the same mind. They will certainly lose our trail at the river's edge. Come." He took her hand and stepped into the water.

Although troubled, she allowed herself to be led toward the rocks a short distance away, forcing herself to stay calm as the water became deeper and deeper until, finally, she could no longer reach the bottom. Garrick, noticing her predicament, curled an arm around her waist and lifted her against him to keep her head above water.

Olaf was not having as much success, for Walks With Thunder struggled with him, fighting to escape.

Nama could not really blame the other woman; she was frightened, too. Several times she thought the whirling eddies would sweep them away to destruction, but each time Garrick was able to withstand the pull of the current. He continued his slow but steady pace toward the dubious safety of the rocks.

Finally, they were at the rocks; but instead of stopping, Garrick continued on around the stony promontory until he was on the opposite side. There, Nama saw the river eddied into a place where the rock was in a half-moon shape. The waters were calmer, easier to traverse to the dark shadowy cavern that was now exposed to their view while remaining hidden from the opposite side.

Soon they were inside the cavern which proved, upon closer inspection, to be a series of chambers. Nama, too tired to explore, slumped down against the cool rocky floor and stared, wide-eyed, around her.

"It is so big," she whispered.

"Big enough so we will not be crowded," Garrick replied, choosing a spot nearby and stretching out on the floor. "You stand watch, Olaf. I intend to sleep." His gaze went to Walks With Thunder and he added, "Keep that wench under your eyes. She may be trouble yet."

"No," Olaf replied. "She was only fighting because she was frightened of the water. I think she knows nothing of swimming."

"Good," Garrick growled. "Then she will be afraid to leave here without us."

He turned over until his back was presented to them and, almost instantly, he fell asleep.

"It is cold," Nama said, shivering slightly.

"Yes," Olaf agreed. "We need wood for a fire."

"Will the smoke not give away our presence?" she asked.

"Not with the water boiling at the opening like that, " he explained. "The smoke will be dispersed by the spray that lingers around the opening." He

moved farther into the cavern. "Explain to her—"
He nodded his head towards Walks With Thunder.
"—what we are about."

Nama told the other woman that they would only
remain in the cave overnight but they would need
a fire to warm them. Grudgingly, Walks With
Thunder agreed to help Nama search for wood.

They found some tangled roots that were dry
and dragged them to the center of the cavern, then
went deeper into the darkened recesses to search
for more. When both women had their arms
loaded, they returned to find Olaf squatting beside
a stack of wood holding a blazing knot of pine.

The strong glare of firelight fell full upon his
sturdy, weather-beaten features, lending an aura of
wildness about the man, who seemed so quiet and
serene by any other light.

Nama noticed the way Walks With Thunder's
eyes fixed on the blond Viking and stayed there as
though she could not look away. Why did the
woman from the Desert Clan flush when Olaf
looked at her, Nama wondered. Had the rage she
felt at becoming a captive turned into another,
softer feeling?

Nama's gaze found Garrick, sleeping motion-
lessly on the far side of the cavern. Her feet
seemed to move of their own accord, taking her
closer to him. Somehow, she felt more secure just
knowing he was nearby, even though he was unaware of her presence.

She seated herself on the rocky ground beside
the stranger from a faraway land, watching while

he slept and wondering all the while why she felt
it was necessary.

Gray Eagle, one of the surviving members of the
war party, pointed toward a broken limb. "Look!"
he cried. "They came this way." He searched for
another sign and was soon rewarded for his efforts.
"There! A footprint! A sign from the Spirits. We
must pursue the intruders, must drive them from
our land!"

"The beasts they rode are too fast," said
Squats By The River.

"The creatures ran away," Gray Eagle reminded,
sending his gaze over the ragged group of warriors. "Are you rabbits to cringe in hiding from your
enemies," he taunted. "Or are you warriors of the
Desert Clan?"

"We are warriors," replied Squats By The River.
"But we are not stupid warriors. We know the enemy's strength. We would be foolish to go against
Brother Bear with nothing more than sticks with
which to defend ourselves."

"Our enemies are not bears," Gray Eagle
growled. "And we are not without weapons with
which to defend ourselves. Look." He pointed
around the group. "I see hatchets among you.
Bows and arrows. Knives and spears. We are
armed, Brothers. Together, we can defeat the intruders."

"They are giants!" muttered a man. "Perhaps

made that way by the Spirits so they may defeat us."

"Will you let your brother's death go unavenged?" the leader asked, trying to whip them into a fury of passion. "Will you let Walks With Thunder be their victim?"

"See our brothers who thought to stop them!" cried Leaping Elk, sweeping his hand around the area where several of their party lay dead. "They thought to conquer. Instead, they were conquered."

"We were taken by surprise."

"But we thought to surprise them."

"They were not surprised," muttered another man.

"We know their strength now," the leader reminded. "We can do it next time! We cannot stop now. We must go on. Must follow them."

"Everyone knows you want Walks With Thunder," muttered a man.

"Yes?"

"You would profit by catching them, but what about us? How would we profit? Certainly not in death?"

And so it went, round and round, while the leader tried to convince them to follow him onward and another tried to make them turn around. But Gray Eagle's arguments were too strong, his voice too loud. Finally, it was decided. They would go on.

Gray Eagle took the lead to show the others he had no fear of the unknown while the ones who shook with trepidation came behind, expecting attack at any moment. When it did not come, they began to relax and soon all were moving forward at a swifter pace, each one eager for their next contact with the Vikings, certain now they would win out.

Olaf whiled away his time by seeking answers to his many questions about the new land. Nama could respond easily to most of his queries; but when she could not, she looked to Walks With Thunder for the solution.

As they talked, Nama's eyes often sought the sleeping man across the cavern. Finally, she began to feel anxious. "Olaf," she said softly. "Garrick has slept the morning away. I fear his wounds may have a sickness in them."

Olaf sent a quick look at his brother, then said, "He looks to be all right. And he would not thank me for waking him."

Nama could not leave it at that. She crossed the cavern and knelt beside Garrick, feeling an urgent need to examine his wounds, to satisfy herself they were not serious. The bloodstains on his upper garment did nothing to calm her fears.

Carefully, she unfastened the garment and pulled it aside, exposing his upper body to her gaze. She was fascinated by the fine golden hair covering his muscular chest and remembered that Eric's chest had looked the same. Bending closer, she examined the wounds and discovered Olaf had

been right. The cuts were shallow, of little consequence.

Breathing a sigh of relief, she sat back on her
heels and allowed her gaze to travel up his body,
over the muscular chest, the thick neck, his square
chin, and even higher . . . to his brilliant green
eyes that were open and staring at her.

A wild shock coursed through her, a tremor that
worked its way from her eyes to the tips of her toes
and her heart jerked spasmodically, then began to
race madly.

A hard knot lodged in her throat, constricting
her breathing as the smile that had been forming
on Garrick's lips slowly faded.

His nostrils flared and his eyes narrowed, taking
on a look that caused a deep flush to rise up her
neck and spread across her cheeks.

"Why do you look at me so?" she murmured.

Instead of answering, he reached out and took
her hand in his. His fingers probed, easing between hers, moving slowly. His touch was warm,
wildly disturbing, especially when she felt his
thumb moving slowly, sensuously, against her moist
palm.

She was caught in a whirlpool of emotions that
she had never before felt, excited in a way that she
had never imagined possible.

Garrick's hand locked on hers and he pulled her
closer, closer, until her face was only inches above
his own. She could feel his breath, warm against
her flesh, and her lips parted of their own accord.

He tilted his head slightly, drawing her closer . . . ever closer, until her lips were almost against his.

"Garrick!" Olaf exclaimed suddenly. "About time you woke up."

Nama jerked away from Garrick, her eyes wide with shock. What had she been thinking of? she wondered. And what had Garrick been doing to her?

The question lingered in her mind as she joined Walks With Thunder across the wide cavern, leaving the two brothers to discuss their next move. And it continued to haunt her the rest of the day.

Thirteen

The sun was sinking low on the western horizon when Olaf left the cavern to hunt. Within the hour he returned to the others with a deer slung across his shoulders.

"That was quick," Garrick said.

Olaf tossed the deer on the cavern floor. "The animal had come to water," he explained.

An hour later, having filled their bellies with roasted venison, the two men sat beside a fire that was slowly dying out from lack of wood and spoke softly together.

Nama, sitting in the shadows across from them, watched the ever-changing reflections on Garrick's face. For some reason her feelings for him had changed. if asked to explain those feelings, she could not have done so, for, although recognizable, they were totally unfamiliar.

Beside her, Walks With Thunder stirred and rubbed her arms as though experiencing a sudden chill.

"Are you cold?" Nama asked in a low voice, unwilling to disturb the men.

"Yes," the woman answered. "My garments are

damp." She looked at the dwindling supply of wood. "The warmth of a fire would be welcome tonight, but the firewood is almost gone. I fear the night ahead will be long and cold."

"We should have gathered more firewood," Nama said. "But it is not too late. We can still do so."

"There was no more to be found," Walks With Thunder reminded.

"We did not explore the whole cavern," Nama said, getting to her feet. "Come with me now."

Before the woman could react, Garrick looked their way. "Where are you going, Nama?" he asked.

"Walks With Thunder's garments are damp," she replied. "The flames will dry them, but we need more wood to keep the fire burning. it is my intent to gather more."

Garrick uncurled his long legs and rose to his feet. "I will accompany you."

"Do not leave me alone with the other one," Walks With Thunder whispered frantically. "I do not trust him."

"What is she saying?" Garrick asked.

"She wants to come with me."

"She will stay with Olaf," he said gruffly. He pointed to the floor beneath Walks With Thunder's feet. "Stay," he commanded, as if giving orders to a dog.

Nama felt resentment on the other woman's behalf, but held her silence. "Olaf will not hurt you," Nama said to the woman. "He is the gentler of the two."

"Yes. He may be that, but I still do not trust him."

"You are bidden to stay here and you would do well to obey. Give them no reason for complaint and you may yet win your freedom. Olaf will not hurt you," Nama repeated. " 'Just pretend he does not exist."

Having heard his name spoken twice, Olaf asked, "What are you telling her?"

"I said you would not hurt her."

"Did she think I would?" A pained expression crossed his brow, and he looked at Walks With Thunder. "Be at ease, woman," he said gruffly, stretching out a hand toward her.

She gave a small yelp and cringed away from him, her eyes darting this way and that as though she sought a place to hide.

He looked at Nama with confusion. "Why is she so fearful?" he asked. "I have done nothing to her."

"Nothing?" she questioned, arching her dark brows. "Are you not holding her prisoner?"

"Well, yes," he admitted slowly. "But that cannot be helped. If we freed her, she would most likely return to her people and reveal our position."

"Of course she would. Is that not the way you would react if you had been taken from your people?"

"Enough!" Garrick ordered. "Assure the woman

that Olaf will do her no harm if she does not cause him undue misery."

Nama chose her own words to reassure the other woman. "Olaf will not harm you," she said for the third time. "Just keep silent and perhaps he might forget you are here. I will only be gone a short time."

Picking up a stout stick, Garrick rolled it around in the ashes where deer fat had dripped, then he jammed it into the fire and waited until the torch was flaming before leading the way into the dark interior of the cave. Nama followed closely behind him, unwilling to be left alone in the darkness.

A few twisted roots could be seen, but not enough to keep a fire burning throughout the night if they burned as quickly as the ones the two women had gathered before.

They entered a tunnel that wound deep into the mountain. To Nama's weary surprise, it seemed endless. At times the walls widened drastically, then suddenly became so narrow that it could only be traversed in single file.

"Perhaps we have found another way out," Garrick said suddenly.

Soon they came to a deep narrow chasm in the rocks which ran at right angles to the passage they were in but which, unlike the first passage, was open to the heavens.

"Look! You were right," Nama cried, pointing to the crack. She could see the faces of the Star People twinkling against Sky Man's blackest cloak. "There *is* another way out!"

"Yes. But it might prove to be a disadvantage," Garrick said.

"How could the split in the rock be a disadvantage?" She looked at him with a puzzled frown.

"Because the *skraelings* who search for us may discover its existence, and guess we have taken refuge down here. One armed man, situated there—" He pointed at one particular spot. "—could hold us at his mercy."

"Why do you always refer to us as savages?" she asked. "Do you consider yourself otherwise?"

He laughed abruptly. "Yes. I do."

"Why are we more savage than you? We have not invaded your land. It is you who have invaded ours." She was vaguely aware the air had become musty, stale, yet she paid it no attention, desiring to learn more about this man who occupied so much of her thoughts now.

"We must discuss this in length when there is more time," Garrick said, pulling her close enough to slide a hand around her waist. "Right now we need to hurry and gather the wood. And I want you close enough that you will come to no harm."

His breath tickled her ear and she shivered, but the action was not caused by fear. Instead, it came from a feeling deep within her, a feeling that started where Garrick's palm rested just beneath her breast, then continued to spread throughout her most secret body parts.

"Who will protect me from you?" she muttered, unable to hold the words back.

"You need no protection from me." He turned

her around until her taut nipples were pressed hard against his muscular chest. "How could you think otherwise? I would never see you harmed, Nama."

Her name on his lips seemed almost like a caress, and a thrill of excitement swept over her, creating a sudden longing to be held closer, to be absorbed in his strength.

"How could I think otherwise when you struck me," she asked, trying to keep her senses about her.

"I never struck you!" he denied.

"While I was bathing, you attacked me—"

"No, not I, Nama. I rescued you from the man who hurt you—"

Nama remembered Walks With Thunder's mate. "You killed him."

"He was hurting you and would have killed the both of us. I would never hurt you," Garrick explained.

Nama ran her hand over her head, memories of her headache coming back clearly. "What about our struggle . . . ?"

"No! Never!" he repeated. "What happened was an accident. When I flung you aside it was only to keep you from biting me again. I was unaware of the rocks around us."

"Rocks?"

"Yes," he replied softly. "Rocks. You struck your head against one."

"Oh!" The word was a breathy whisper. "Why did you not explain?"

"You asked for no explanations, little one," he reminded. "You wanted to lay the blame at my feet."

"But the blame was not yours," she said softly, gazing up at him with glittering eyes. "if you only thought to help me, then why do you hold me captive?"

"Captive?" he questioned. "You are no captive. You may go if you wish."

Amazing though it seemed, she felt hurt stab through her. "You would have me leave?"

"No. But if it is your wish . . ."

"And Walks With Thunder? She can go, too?"

"The woman would return with warriors," he said gruffly. "She cannot be allowed to leave."

"How long will you keep her?" Nama asked.

"She must stay with us until we reach our ship. Only then will she be allowed to leave."

"She will be afraid."

"Not if you stay with her," he said quickly.

"I *am* in your debt," she said slowly. "Perhaps I could repay that debt by remaining . . . for a while anyway. Just until we reach your ship."

"In some lands, when a man saves a life, that life becomes his to command," Garrick said huskily.

"What would you command of me?" she whispered provocatively.

"Only that you remain like this. Here in my arms."

"You would ask so little?" Nama asked softly.

"And perhaps this." His lips brushed her own

and the touch was like wildfire racing through her veins.

"You . . ." She stopped, wondering how she could explain her feelings, if she should even try. "Why do you do this to me?" she asked, her voice a breathless whisper.

"Because it makes me feel good."

"I—I think we must gather what wood can be found and return to the others," she said huskily. "The desert warriors might have discovered the cave. They may need our help."

The reminder of their situation seemed to pull him from the mood he was in and he set her aside. "You are right, of course," he said abruptly, making her wish she had remained silent. "There will be time for things of this nature at another time."

The words were almost a threat and she shuddered, not from fear but from something else that was yet unnamed, perhaps even unknown.

But the learning would of necessity have to wait until another time, she thought, following his lead and gathering what roots could be found. They had already been gone a long time. Longer than she had intended. And if they did not return soon, they would surely find Walks With Thunder faint with fear at being left alone so long with Olaf.

Garrick and Olaf took turns watching through out the night while the women slept. Since the cavern was dark except for the campfire and since there was no sky to tell them when daylight ar rived, they slept later than would have been their usual practice.

Nama, upon waking, found Garrick just entering the cavern. Finding her awake, he laid aside his sword and knelt beside her. Curling his fingers beneath her chin, he looked into her eyes. "It is past time we left here, little one."

Sensing the urgency behind his words, she said, "Have they found our hiding place?"

"Not yet," he said huskily. His free hand smoothed back her tangled hair. "But we must not delay. They have left the gorge, and if I am not mistaken, they intend to search the cliffs above us. There is every chance they will find the other entrance to this cave."

"Then we must be away," she said, wishing it were not so and wondering why.

"Yes, we must. But remember what I told you last night. There is no reason to fear. Stay close beside me and you will come to no harm."

She smiled despite herself. "I remember," was all she said, but she knew in her heart of hearts that she would obey his every command. Somehow, even in so short a time, this man had become important to her.

Perhaps it was only his strength that gave him such importance, but Nama, who had no one to call her own, knew that she could not leave him. Not now. Nor in the foreseeable future.

Nama wasted no time wondering why it was so, only accepted it for a fact. And, she knew, someday soon would come a day of reckoning, a day when she could no longer put off what was between them. She suspected, that day would not be long in coming.

They traveled throughout the day; and although Garrick continually left them to watch their back-trail, he found no sign of the war party following them. It was on one such occasion that he returned astride Midnight. Behind them galloped Olaf's horse, Thunder.

"How did you find the horses?" Nama questioned when he dismounted.

"I did not," he replied. "They found me."

"I thought they were lost to us."

Although his fingers were busy removing food from the saddlepack, he favored her with a grin. "Had you asked me, I would have told you they would return."

"How could you know such a thing?"

"Because Midnight has been trained to stay with me. He could not find us while we were in the cave, but probably took up our trail shortly after we surfaced."

Nama cautiously approached the stallion. When Midnight showed no reaction to her presence, she became brave enough to stroke his long, velvety neck.

Suddenly, the stallion snorted and shook his head, and with a squeal of fright, Nama jerked away from him.

"He will not harm you." Garrick laughed, taking

her hand in his. "Stroke his nose. Feel how soft it is."

"No." She backed away slowly.

"Come," he commanded. "I will stand beside you while you caress him."

Midnight turned his head and rolled his eyes at her, but he did not appear menacing. Cautiously, she stretched out her hand and touched his nose. Garrick was right. It *was* soft. "Like the skin of a mink," she breathed softly.

"The strange beast allows your touch." Walks With Thunder's voice was filled with awe as she spoke in their tongue. "How does it feel against your skin?"

"Like a mink," Nama repeated, but this time she spoke in the language of the People. "Would you like to feel him yourself?"

"No," Walks With Thunder muttered, taking a quick step backward.

As it happened, Olaf was standing just behind her and she tripped over the foot he had extended in order to reach Thunder's side. She would have fallen had he not caught her in his arms.

"Son of a dog!" she spat, jerking away from his touch. "Release me!"

"I wish you would teach her to speak our language," Olaf complained, turning to Nama. "How can I know what she is saying to me when she uses words I cannot understand."

Nama uttered a short laugh. "Sometimes it is best that you not know."

"Why?" he asked curiously. "What did she say?"

"She called you a son of a dog."

A flush crept up his cheeks. "Why? I was only trying to help her."

"Perhaps she sees things differently, Brother," Garrick said, apparently finding amusement in the situation. "If you had not tripped her with your big foot, then she would not have needed help."

Although Olaf took the teasing with good nature, he seemed bothered by the incident. That night, after they had finished eating their evening meal, he approached Nama and made a request.

"Would you teach me your language?" he asked.

"If you wish," she agreed. "But you cannot learn overnight."

He shrugged his wide shoulders. "I know. But we have time to spare. Especially if we begin now."

"Now?"

"Of course." He smiled widely at her. "There is plenty of time."

He appeared to believe he could learn the language before retiring, a fact which secretly amused Nama. She began with simple words. Words like food, water, and sleep.

Walks With Thunder immediately objected to the lessons. "If you teach him our language, then he will always know what we say," she cried.

"He wishes to converse with you," Nama replied. "And there is no other way he can do so since you will not learn his language."

"Why should he wish to converse with me?" Walks With Thunder asked sullenly.

"How should I know?" Nama asked. "Would you have me ask his reasons?"

"No," the other woman said quickly, turning away from Nama. "Do not ask him. I imagine in time I will learn his reasons."

Nama smiled a secret smile and continued with her lessons until Garrick suddenly rose to his feet, stretched his arms wide and announced, "I am going for a walk. Anyone care to join me?"

He looked at Nama and she, realizing the invitation had been directed toward her, looked away quickly, aware of a flush rising up her cheeks.

"Very well, then," he said, shrugging his shoulders. A moment later he disappeared into the shadowy darkness.

Nama found she could not sit quietly beside the fire and continue with the lessons. There was something tangible in the air, something that caused her to feel a breathless yearning.

"We will continue the lessons at another time," she said abruptly.

Although Olaf was disappointed, he uttered no objection. He seemed not to notice when she rose to her feet and, without a word, walked into the shadowy darkness.

Nama told herself she had no destination in mind, that she had only left the others to seek solace among the shadows; but even as she tried to convince herself of that fact, she realized it was not so.

Nama did not seek peace. instead, she sought the man who was the source of her unrest.

She sought Garrick.

* * *

Shala shifted the baby in her arms as she admired the treasures Black Crow had spread out in the courtyard for all to see. Several of her clansmen had already bargained for goods, but she remained undecided. The necklace, fashioned from tiny seashells, would look pretty around the baby's neck. And yet, Shala herself favored the turquoise bracelet.

Should she bargain for the necklace or the bracelet?

Remaining undecided, she favored her husband with a frown. "Eric. Help me, please."

"What is it you wish, my love?" he laughed. "Just say the word and you shall have it."

"I cannot decide," she told him. "Please help me."

"What are your preferences?" he asked, looking over the goods before her. "The knife?" He picked it up and ran his thumb over the obsidian blade. "It is sharp enough."

She knew he was teasing her, yet she did not mind. "Look at the necklace," she said. "And tell me if you favor it over the turquoise bracelet."

He scooped up the bracelet and fastened it around her wrist. "Comfortable?"

She nodded.

"Then the choice is made."

"No," she said, sliding it from her wrist and replacing it in its original position. "You have not yet examined the shell necklace."

"There is no need, my love. It is too small for you."

"It was meant for a child," Black Crow said, having watched the exchange between them. "See how fine the shells are." He scooped it up and handed it to Eric. "And see how carefully they are fastened together. It is a necklace worth having."

"Then perhaps we should bargain for both," Eric said, flashing a grin at his wife. "What do you say, love? Would you like the necklace *and* the bracelet?"

"Yes," she said breathlessly. "But perhaps we should not. I do not need the bracelet, although it is very beautiful. But the necklace would make a very fine gift for our daughter."

"Wait!" Black Crow commanded. "If you are interested in the turquoise bracelet, then I have another item that might interest you as well." He bent over his bag of goods and pulled out a smaller bag.

Wondering what treasure Black Crow had withheld, Eric stepped in front of Shala, unaware that he was blocking her view.

"It is a treasure," Eric muttered. "Worthy of gracing the loveliest of necks."

"Let me see," Shala demanded, trying to peer around him.

Immediately, he held his hand behind his back. "Turn around first," he said. "It must be a surprise."

Impatiently, she turned around and allowed him to place the object over her head. It fell against the folds of her soft hide dress and she looked down at the turquoise necklace.

She felt the color leaving her face as she uttered a startled gasp.

"What is it, Shala?" Eric asked quickly.

"The necklace!" she whispered unsteadily. "it is hers! The one who's name I must not speak. Remove it please."

Eric lifted the necklace off and examined it closely.

"Where did you get it?" Shala demanded harshly, pinning Black Crow with her dark gaze.

"I traded for it," he said, his black eyes suddenly uneasy.

"You took it from one who was no longer living!" she accused. Clan law forbade the use of her friend's name now that she was no longer in the land of the living. What he had done was unforgivable. He had robbed the dead. "Where is the bracelet she wore?" asked Shala. "Have you already traded it away."

"The bracelet is still around her arm," Black Crow said. "I did not steal the necklace. We traded. The necklace for an obsidian-blade knife." He hung his head as though shamed. "My tongue should be torn out by the roots for breaking my promise to her, but I could not allow you to believe I would rob the dead."

"Your promise to her? She lives?" Shala breathed. "But she could not! I saw her fall to her death."

"She did not perish," Black Crow admitted. "She fell into a river and was swept downstream."

"Nama lives," Shala repeated breathlessly. "The impossible has happened, and my friend lives."

"I speak the truth," Black Crow muttered, "although should not have said so. I was honor-bound to hold my tongue."

"You bear no fault," Shala assured him. "Tell us. Where is she? We must bring her home."

He spread his hands wide. "How can I tell you when I promised not to mention her name?"

"Then do not mention it," Shala commanded. "Just tell us where to find her."

Black Crow sighed. "Since you will have it no other way, then I will tell you." His gaze probed Eric's. "I suppose you will go for her."

"Yes. My wife will not rest easy until her friend is safe among her people again." He met Shala's eyes. "It pleasures me to do this for you, my love."

"I would like to go with you," Shala said. "But there is our babe . . ."

"You must stay here, love," Eric said. "Have no fear about your friend. You will be together soon." He looked at the trader. "Do not worry yourself overmuch. Nama cannot fend for herself long. She will thank you for revealing her whereabouts."

Black Crow nodded. "I believe you are right. She was near starving when I found her." He sighed heavily. "I hope you find her before it is too late."

"Draw me a map," Eric commanded. "Show me where she is, and I will leave immediately."

"I will gather some foodstuffs for you to carry on your journey," Shala said quickly.

Although she was unhappy about being left behind, she consoled herself with the thought that Eric would travel faster alone. And soon, if all went well, she would see her dearest friend again. Soon, Nama would return to her home among the cliffs.

Fourteen

There was no sound to mark her passage as Nama made her way upstream in search of Garrick. When she came upon the small creek that branched off the river, she hesitated momentarily. Would he have crossed the creek, she wondered, then decided he would not have.

The animals had left a narrow trail beside the creek, and it made her passage easier. Nama had only gone a short distance when something—a mere whisper of sound—brought her up short.

Her heart jerked suddenly, then picked up speed as she searched the small clearing ahead. Sister Moon sent her silvery light cascading down upon the meadow, darkly shadowing the branches of the trees growing on three sides, yet illuminating the figure of the man who stood gazing silently into the creek where countless stars were reflected on its surface.

He had stripped away his upper garment, leaving himself naked to the waist; and his golden torso gleamed in the moonlight, his dark trousers molding his lean hips and thighs while emphasizing the length of his legs.

Nama shivered, but it was not fear that caused the reaction. At least not fear of the man before her. Perhaps, though, she *did* fear herself. Or rather, she silently amended, she feared the desire that rose unbidden as she watched him.

As though suddenly becoming aware of her presence, Garrick turned to face her; and although she could not see his features clearly, she sensed he was frowning.

Tipping his head to one side, he watched her for a long moment while her pounding heart threatened to explode from the strain.

Nama was frozen to the spot, unable to leave even though she suddenly felt threatened by him.

She was uncertain of the threat he posed, having no fear for her life; but, the urge to escape his presence was almost overwhelming.

Run! a silent voice cried.

But she, foolish girl that she was, did not heed the cry. She remained there, poised on her toes, unwilling to leave, yet afraid to stay.

"Nama!"

His voice was a command, demanding that she stay. But it was the catalyst that broke the spell and freed her frozen limbs.

Panic-stricken, with the blood pounding through her veins, she raced through the forest, intent on putting as much distance as possible between them.

Behind her, his footsteps crunched over brush and other debris as his long, powerful legs carried him swiftly forward until, suddenly, his long arm reached out and his hard fingers curled around her wrist, halting her in mid-stride and spinning her around to face him.

"Let me go!" She struggled desperately to escape. "Son of a dog! Release me!"

"Be still!" he commanded grimly.

She paid no heed, kicking at his shins with her bare feet, twisting like a mad animal to break his hold. But even as she struggled, her nostrils flared at his heady male scent. It drugged her senses with its potency, drove her to desperate fear, made her writhe futilely against him.

His huge frame dwarfed her much smaller one as he bent her backward over his arm. His voice hissed another angry command, and she twisted her head to avoid the sound.

Muttering a curse, he pressed his face nearer. Her struggles brought her lips into contact with his. Although it was only a mere brushing of flesh, the action froze her into immobility. She went cold all over, then felt fiery-hot. Time seemed to stand still, and Nama waited in breathless fear as their lips remained poised against each other.

Then, with a low growl, his mouth covered hers in an all-consuming kiss. Time was suspended for a long moment; and she could feel his heart thudding beneath the fragile cover of his skin, was aware of her own heart hammering in her throat, keeping time with his.

The heady scent was stronger now. She knew she should struggle against him, should at least attempt to break free, but something held her still, freezing her body in place as his lips softened, moving against hers . . . coaxing, persuasive, need-ful.

Nama felt goose bumps break out on her flesh; her heart picked up rhythm, beating faster and faster, sounding louder and louder until she wondered if the frail cavity of her rib cage could contain it.

His hand slid down her back, leaving behind a blazing trail along the path it had followed. When he cupped her buttocks and brought her against his lower body, she felt him move against her, stirring up feelings that threatened to choke her.

"No!" she gasped—a muffled sound, but it was enough to break the fragile link that had connected them.

His head lifted, and he stared down at her with burning need. "No?" he grated, his nostrils flaring slightly with a suggestion of proud arrogance. "You deny your body wishes my possession?" His grip tightened on her buttocks, and he pulled her harder against him as though intent on making certain she was aware of the hugeness of his desire.

"No!" she said again, recognizing the fear in her voice, the whispered plea for mercy. "You must not do this thing!" Even as she denied him, she knew her body ached for him. But she could not allow him to claim her, dared not. He was such a big man that it frightened her, especially since, if he had a gentler side, he managed to keep it well hidden. "I—I will w-work for you, Garrick, and I will t-tend your animals," she stuttered, "but—but I cannot join with you. I cannot!" Even as she uttered the words, she remembered the feel of his lips on hers, so warm, so tender.

Feeling a desperate need to escape, she tried to wedge her arms between them, but there was no need. Without prior warning, Garrick released her. Then, with body held rigid as though his displeasure was great, he stalked away from her and disappeared into the shadows, leaving her staring after him in confusion and dismay.

Garrick left her in the moonlight, his body aching with wanting her, his thoughts in turmoil.

Why does she tremble so at my touch? he questioned. Although he had bedded many women and there had been others who trembled beneath him, they had not feared him. But Nama did. And the very thought of her fear burned through him, made him want to chase it away, to scatter it to the four winds and turn that feeling into longing, to see her tremble in another way . . . possessed by him.

He knew women, knew that, given half a chance, he could turn her fear into longing. And yet, if she would not allow him close enough to caress her, then it would prove an impossible task.

"I could take her anyway," he muttered savagely, and as soon as the words were spoken, he felt shame for them. Nama had more than her share of courage, but she reacted fearfully to his advances. Perhaps she sensed his great need, sensed that he could barely control himself where she was concerned. Why did he lose control so easily? How long had these feelings been creeping upon him waiting for such an occasion as tonight to make themselves known.

God, she had been beautiful, standing in the moonlight with the stars captured in her shining ebony hair.

Drawing a deep, shuddery breath, he tried to relax his tense body.

But he could not.

Not while his blood still flowed with the heat of his desire. Not while his body still burned to bury itself in hers, to be enfolded by her sweet femininity.

"Damn the *skraeling* wench!" he muttered and in the next instant asked himself what could possibly cause her to be so afraid of him. "Am I such a monster I strike terror in the hearts of all who behold me?" he demanded of the night air and immediately knew the answer though the silent night had made no reply.

Garrick had been told many times by many women that he was a man most women would desire. So why did Nama look at him as someone to be feared. Thor's teeth! He had given the wench her freedom! Had told her she could leave if that were her wish. What else did she want? Why did she react to him with fear rather than desire?

His fists clenched and unclenched and he breathed deeply, trying again to relax his tense muscles. But he knew it was in vain. He needed a woman. Not just any woman, he realized, remembering Walks With Thunder. No. His need was for

one particular woman . . . a courageous, beautiful
woman who stood no higher than his shoulder.
He needed Nama. And he would have her, he decided. No matter how long it took.

His muscles were tight with restrained passion;
and Garrick, realizing the only way to release himself from its grasp was to tire himself out, searched
the shadows for a way to expend his energy. Finding nothing there, he looked at the silvery creek.

Gauging the depth of the clear water with expert
eyes, he stripped away his breeches and dove into
the stream, emerging in the middle of the cold
water a few moments later.

With powerful strokes, Garrick moved through
the water. Anyone who had had occasion to see
him would have known him to be an accomplished
swimmer. The water rippled turbulently around
his muscular body as he cut through the storm over
and over again, trying to ease his frustration by
tiring himself out.

Nama's troubled thoughts kept her awake long
into the night, and she opened her eyes in the
half-light before dawn to find Garrick striking
flint to spark a fire.

She watched him from beneath heavy lashes,
wondering if the easy way he held himself meant
his dark humor of the night before had left him.

When he turned to face her, she realized it had
for his lips spread in a wide smile at the sight of

her. "Good morning!" he greeted. "Did you sleep well?"

Nama, assuming the greeting was meant to be polite, replied in kind. "Good morning. Yes. I slept very well. And you?" The words had barely been uttered when she wished them unsaid. True, they were merely a greeting, but the latter question could easily have been taken for a taunt.

She felt relief that he allowed her question to pass with a mere, "As well as could be expected."

Feeling a blush color her cheeks, she scrambled from the fur-covered willows that made up her sleeping mat and set about the task of preparing their morning meal.

Desiring that this particular breakfast be memorable, Nama decided to grind some of the acorns she had previously gathered and make bread.

While she pounded the acorns into a fine powder, Walks With Thunder heated a thick, flat stone with which to bake the bread once the batter was ready.

Delving into the pack that held their supplies, Nama extracted honey and some hackberries she had saved for just such an occasion. After adding water and some ash for leavening, she beat the mixture until it was free of lumps.

"What are you doing?" Olaf asked, stopping beside her and staring curiously at the mixture.

"Making bread," she replied.

"A change will be good," he said, dipping & finger into the batter and tasting it with a frown. "At least," he amended, "it might be."

She laughed. "Wait until the batter has cooked before you decide. You will like it."

She was proved right. Both men complimented her on the bread and requested more at their next meal, promising outrageous gifts if she would comply.

Shortly after, still flushed from the compliments she had received, Nama sat astride Midnight and boldly leaned back against Garrick.

That day was much like the ones that followed with nothing memorable to set them apart from the others except Garrick's continued goodwill.

At times, though, when he was unaware that he was watched, she saw a darkness descend upon him that he obviously meant to keep hidden. But upon finding himself under observation, he would shrug away the mood and revert to the friendly, amiable person that caused her more unease than his other self ever could.

One night, several days after the incident at the creek, Nama sought solace by gathering pine branches and placing them apart from the others where she would be sheltered from their view by a thick stand of pines.

She was conscious of Garrick's eyes on her as she returned for the rolled-up fur piece that would complete her sleeping mat and waited for him to comment. He did not. Instead, he continued to converse with his brother in a low voice.

Nama was on the point of retiring when she heard Garrick approaching.

"Come with me," he said softly.

Having no thought other than compliance, Nama followed him to a secluded glade beside a fast-running stream. Somehow, it reminded her of that other night . . . the night that was never far from her thoughts.

"Why have you brought me here?" she asked, her voice sounding almost breathless.

"Because I wanted you to see it," he replied.

"It is a peaceful place," she commented, knowing words were inadequate to describe the grassy meadow dappled with silvery light. "And very beautiful."

"Mere words could never describe such beauty," he said huskily.

Finding herself in total agreement, Nama met his eyes and found herself the focus of his attention. A flush warmed her cheeks, and she lowered her lashes quickly to hide her expressive dark eyes.

"It was on such a night that we met." Garrick's voice was like a warm blanket on a cold night. "Do you remember?"

"How could I forget?" she asked.

"You were swimming in the moonlight."

"Then attacked," she said, barely controlling a shudder.

"Swim with me now," he urged. "Let me wipe away the memory of that night."

"The memory is not all bad." *Because you found me.* The last words could only be spoken in her mind; otherwise, he would think her bold.

No," he agreed, "because I found you."

Her heart jolted, and she gave a start of surprise. Had he read her thoughts? *No.* she answered her own question. *He could not have done so.*

His gaze was a soft caress. "Swim with me," he said again.

Nama nodded her head. Although he was disturbing to her in every way, she could not have refused him. Her fingers were awkward as they fumbled with the ties on her soft hide dress.

"Let me," he said quietly.

She stood before him, trembling, while he unfastened the garment and allowed it to fall at her feet. Then, wearing nothing but her bracelet, she breathed harshly, waiting for Garrick's next move, longing for his touch, wanting to know the heat of a man's passion while at the same time fearful of that knowledge.

To her extreme dismay, Garrick paid no attention to her nakedness. Instead, he disrobed and, before she caught more than a glimpse of his masculinity, arched his body and made a clean dive into the creek.

Nama knew she was courting danger by joining him but did not care. The heady excitement she felt was addictive. She wanted this moment to continue and, no matter what the outcome, could not have turned away from him.

Following Garrick's lead, Nama arched her body and dived into the water. When she surfaced, she found Garrick beside her.

His fiery hair looked copper beneath the silvery light of the moon. And his brilliant eyes sparkled with mischief. "Are you not glad you came?" he asked softly.

"Yes. I am glad."

They cavorted in the moonlight, splashing and chasing one another back and forth until Nama called out breathlessly, "Stop, stop! Allow me time to rest."

"Do you concede?" he asked, brushing wet strands of hair from her eyes.

"Yes." She smiled at him. "I concede."

"Then I will claim my prize," he said softly, his head dipping down and his lips brushing lightly against hers.

"What is this you do with the mouth?" she muttered against his lips.

"It is a kiss," he replied. "And you must not speak while our lips are together."

"Why?"

"Because it is not as effective. Have you never been kissed before?"

"No. My People know nothing of this, but my friend, Shala—" She stopped, realizing she had almost said her friend Shala had experienced such things with his brother.

"Yes?" he drawled. "What about your friend, Shala?"

"She would like it."

"And you do not?"

"No. I mean, I do like it. It creates a pleasant feeling."

"Pleasant?" He frowned down at her as though

he were displeased. "That is not the feeling I wished to convey."

"Perhaps something went wrong," Nama suggested. "Would you like to try again?"

"Indeed I would." His mouth claimed hers again. Harder this time, but only slightly so, for he was careful their bodies did not touch.

Nama felt a stirring in her belly that spread downward toward her thighs and lodged somewhere between her legs. She felt breathless, excited, wanting something more, yet unable to determine what that something was.

He lifted his head and gazed down at her. "Still only pleasant?" he inquired.

"Something else, too," she replied. "The touching of lips makes me feel . . . breathless. Like I have been running through the forest. And my heart . . . it beats so. See?" She took his hand and lifted it to her breast. Immediately, her nipples hardened and her heart picked up speed. "That is curious," she said shakily. "When you touch me there, my heart beats like thunder."

"And when I do this?" His hand caressed her breast, and it swelled against his palm. "What happens then?"

"M-my heart continues to b-beat furiously," she stuttered, easing away from him reluctantly. "Perhaps we should not continue."

"I could not stop now," he murmured softly, his breath whispering against her ear. "Not when my heart beats as fast as yours. See?" He took her hand and carried it to his chest the way she had his only moments before.

"Yes." His smooth flesh was warm beneath her hand. "Your heart does beat fast. Is that a good sign?"

"Very good," he said, nibbling at her earlobe. "We must certainly continue."

"I—I never knew ears could be so—so—" She stopped, lost for words.

"Sensitive?" he asked softly, his breath whispering against her flesh.

She nodded, unable to speak because of the lump that blocked her throat.

"Do you want me to stop?" he asked, tilting her chin to look at her closely.

Stop? Alarm widened her eyes, and she shook her head to rid him of that notion. Her action caused a smile to twitch at the corner of his lips.

"Then let us continue," he whispered.

Without another word, his lips found hers, covering them with an expertise that was hard to deny. How many women had known his touch? she wondered just before all thought gave way to pure sensation.

His mouth moved upon hers and his tongue traced the outline of her lips, causing her to shudder with exquisite longing. Then his mouth lifted, hovering agonizingly close, and she sensed a waiting quality about him but had no idea what he wanted from her.

Uttering a sigh, his lips moved upward, touched her closed eyelids gently, then her nose, before continuing their searching quest downward until they found her mouth again.

His tongue streaked out, retracing the outline of her lips, then probing at the center of her mouth, demanding entry.

Mindlessly, she opened her mouth and felt the moist warmth of his tongue sliding inside. A tightening in her loins preceded a sensual warmth that soon turned to a languorous yearning deep inside her being.

When he lifted his head again, Nama opened her eyes and stared dumbly into his watchful face. Her resistance was gone as though it had never been, her fear drained away as though it had never existed.

She felt the shock of his touch against her breast, yet she could not look away from his intent gaze, not even when he took her arm and waded toward the creek bank. When the water circled around his waist, Garrick swept her into his arms and carried her out of the water.

Her eyes were still locked with his when he placed her on the long grass and joined her there. She closed her eyes at the first touch of his hands against her breast, wanting to savor that moment, to remember it forever. He touched her at will, caressing her nipples, teasing and tantalizing until, with a groan, she slid her arms around his neck and pressed her body hard against his.

Her fingers tangled in his dark hair, trying to pull his mouth to hers again, but he resisted, driving her wild by burying his face in the side of her neck instead.

"No, Garrick!" she protested fiercely. "Kiss me! Do not tease me this way! Let me feel your lips on mine again!"

"If you feel my lips, then you will also feel my body," he said harshly.

"Then let it be so," she said through clenched teeth, "for I can stand no more. I feel as if a fire burns inside me and the flames must be quenched lest they consume me."

"So be it," he said gruffly.

With their mouths entwined, he lifted his body and fitted it over hers, parting her thighs with his own.

When he thrust within, she felt a momentary pain that was quickly replaced with quickened desire. Her mind was almost senseless as he moved against her, setting her body afire and stoking the flames with each thrust until at last, poised high on a peak, she arched against him, shuddering with the ecstasy of release, and a keening sound broke from her lips

Nama's breathing slowly quieted while she snuggled against Garrick's hard, muscular body, content to be lying in his arms.

So this is what Shala experienced. Nama told herself. *And the reason she could not leave Eric.*

The thought of Eric was quickly followed by the memory of the lie she had spoken about him. She must tell Garrick the truth about his brother and herself, must let him know his brother survived.

Nama tilted her head back, pushing lightly against his embrace. She wanted to look into his eyes, to note their expression when she told him the truth about Eric.

Immediately, he tightened his embrace. "Stay!" he said harshly. "You have nothing else to lose, woman! You have given it already."

"What do you m-mean?" she stuttered.

"You lied about your relationship with my brother," he snarled. "You never joined with him!"

How could he know, she wondered. "I was going to tell you," she whispered, feeling as though her world had suddenly fallen apart.

"When?" he demanded. "And why did you lie about it?"

"I—because I thought—"

"You thought your treatment would be better if we thought he loved you," he snapped.

She flinched away from him, feeling a sharp pain slashing through her. Garrick had reverted to the cruel stranger she had first met. He had not changed at all, had only made her believe he had done so. Had the false mask been donned just so he could satisfy his lust?

Feeling unbearably hurt, Nama turned her face away from him to hide the tears that slipped slowly down her cheeks. Unable to leave his arms, she huddled there, her heart knotted into a hard ball of misery while a feeling of despair washed over her.

She could not tell him the truth now. Not when

he had reacted so violently just because he learned
she had not joined with his brother. What would
he do if he learned she had spoke falsely of his
brother's death?

No. She could not tell him. Not now. He had
proved himself unpredictable. It must be the nature
of the Vikings, as their violence surely was, for even
Olaf was formidable when aroused. Whatever happened, they must never learn Eric had survived.

Fifteen

Three days after he began the journey, Eric reached the mountain that Black Crow had described. Although he had been blessed with clear skies since leaving the mesa, the cluster of rain clouds moving swiftly overhead told him a storm was on the way.

As Eric began his climb up the slope, the air turned sultry and the sky darkened as the clouds became heavier. The slight breeze turned into a wind blowing around him, whipping his golden hair into his eyes.

Hearing a heavy rumble of thunder, Eric brushed the hair out of his eyes and sent an anxious look toward the sky. The clouds were thicker now. And closer.

A jagged streak of lightning reached for the ground. Crack! Thunder rumbled again, and it was quickly followed by another streak of lightning.

Crack!

The wind howled around Eric, pushing at him, tearing at his clothing, slowing his progress up the mountain as though it were a living thing intent on keeping him from the girl he sought to reach.

Eventually, though, after hours of struggling against the wind, Eric saw the cave the trader had described. Elation flowed through him as he hurried forward, thoughts of the journey homeward filling his mind. it was too late to start back today. Instead, they would wait until morning. If they began their journey at first light, he should be back with Shala before another three days were over.

His searching gaze penetrated the dark, gloomy cave, and he frowned. It seemed empty, unoccupied. Why was there no fire to warm the interior? And, more importantly, where was the girl who dwelt there?

He knew this was her cave. That much was obvious from the hides and baskets that littered the floor.

Eric's frown deepened and he wondered to where Nama had disappeared.

The moon cast its pale light across the grassy meadow, outlining the couple who lay entwined beside the silvery creek, together, yet still so far apart.

Garrick was plagued with countless questions, unable to relax. it was obvious Nama had lied to him—at least in part—about her relationship with his brother, but her reasons for doing so were still not clear.

It was also obvious now why she had resisted

him for so long. Her maidenhood had been intact, proof that she had no lover before him. That fact caused him pleasure, but it was a small emotion compared to the fury he felt over the deception.

"Garrick," she murmured softly, seeming to guess the path his thoughts had taken. "Are you angry with this woman?"

Anger was a mild word that stopped far short of what he was feeling; but when he spoke, his voice was calm, showing no sign of that emotion. "Would you not feel anger toward *me* in the same circumstances, Nama?"

"This woman was afraid," she admitted hesitantly. "She was a prisoner. Has she become one again, Garrick?"

"No," he replied, softening ever so slightly. "You are free to come and go as you please." He cupped her chin, feeling her flesh warm against his palm. "Why did you lie, Nama? What exactly was your relationship with my brother?" he asked gruffly.

"We were friends."

A great relief swept over Garrick, and he tightened his arm around her. "It is enough," he said huskily, pressing a soft kiss against her cheek. "More than enough." He studied her in silent contemplation, wondering how this wild, savage land could have produced a woman of such great beauty. "You are a complete mystery to me, Nama."

"Mystery?" she questioned. "I have no knowledge of this word."

No interest either, Garrick decided, when she

raked her palm across his chest, entwining her fingers through the soft mat of curls there. Although the action caused a stirring in his lower body, Garrick refused to give in to that feeling. Instead, he covered her hand with his own and held it captive. "A mystery is a puzzle," he explained. "Something unknown."

"And this woman is a mystery?"

"You are," he muttered. "And when I am confronted with a puzzle, I feel inclined to solve it. Help me do so, Nama. Allow me to know you better. Speak of yourself, of your life before we met."

"There is not much to speak of," she murmured, stirring restlessly in his arms. "My life was simple before we met."

"But who *are* you?"

"I am Eagle Clan," she replied. "I have told you this. My People live among the cliffs of a great mesa far from here."

"Why are you here . . . living alone . . . apart from your people?"

She lowered her thick lashes, hiding her expressive eyes from him. "There is a reason," she whispered. "But I cannot say."

He frowned at her. "What about your parents? Your mother and father? A brother or sister? Surely there is someone who belongs to you."

"I have no one," she said, swallowing hard.

Realizing how painful the subject was to her, Garrick squeezed her hand gently, then spread her fingers apart, laying her palm against his chest. "You have someone now," he told her. She looked so appealingly beautiful in the moonlight that he could have stopped the tide from flowing more easily than he could have stopped his mouth from claiming hers in a long kiss.

Nama was relieved the questions had finally stopped. She had been afraid of what she might disclose, afraid of Garrick's rage should she disclose the real facts about his brother. He would find out in time, she knew. When he reached Norway, he would find his brother there, waiting for him; then he would be furious at her deception.

But she would not be there to see, would not be there to feel his anger. And surely, one day he would understand, would forgive her for keeping her knowledge to herself.

What did she know anyway? She could not be certain of Eric's fate; she knew only that when she last saw him it was his intention to return to his homeland. How could she know what had happened to him? It was obvious Garrick had not seen him or he would not have been searching for him, yet she dared ask no questions. Instead, she would hold her tongue, would lose herself in Garrick's embrace, knowing that soon she would be left alone with only memories to sustain her through the long, lonely seasons that would follow his departure for his homeland.

Intent on making as many memories as possible, Nama opened her mouth beneath his and felt the quick intrusion of his tongue delving into the moist cavern of her mouth.

Her arms tightened involuntarily and her tongue dared to touch his and she almost gasped with shock, feeling an instant stirring in her loins. Her hands slid down, stopping on his broad back, and she clutched him to her, unconsciously urging him with her soft moans.

Garrick groaned as if he were being tortured, tightening his embrace until it was almost painful. His tongue swept the dark cavern of her mouth, probing deeply, searchingly.

Nama felt deprived when his mouth left hers; but the feeling was quickly gone when his lips moved lower, his mouth opening again to cover one taut nipple while his hand moved lower, down past her navel until it pressed gently between her thighs.

"Garrick," she moaned, as his fingers delved into her most secret parts. "What are you doing?" She attempted to trap his hand within her own, but he would not allow it.

"Be still," he muttered.

She could do little else now, for her traitorous body was responding to his movements, reacting with quivering anticipation to each downward stroke.

"Take me now," she begged. "Do not make me wait."

He continued to stroke her, making no move to enter her, until her breath came in ragged gasps and every thought except her sudden, overpower-

ing need for him disappeared from Nama's mind.
Only then did he move over her, and she welcomed
the warmth of his weight. His body fused with
hers, then began to move, slowly at first, then
building in tempo until she felt a glorious explosion that was almost painful in intensity. And when
it was over, she lay beside him, basking in the
sweetness of release and wishing their time together would never end.

The sun peeped over the eastern horizon, paint-
ing the sky with glorious color as its golden rays
crept over the forest and meadowland.

Eric knelt on the ground, his dark eyes riveted
to the tracks before him, vaguely aware of the
meadowlarks that flitted from branch to branch,
chirping cheerfully, ignoring the man who had intruded on their territory.

The tracks were unmistakable to Eric. Although
unknown in this new land, they were common in
Norway. The tracks had been made by horses.

Hope surged through Eric. Dare he believe the
tracks were made by his kinsmen? It was possible
other travelers had found their way here, but more
probable that his failure to return to his ship had
generated a search for him.

Karl must have returned to Norway these many
months past as Eric had demanded he should if
he failed to return.

A smile curved Eric's lips as he looked at the
hoofprints again. Two of them, following the tribu-

tary that branched off the big muddy river, taking the same path that Eric had taken last fall.

He was almost positive he knew the horses. They would be Midnight and Thunder, and his two brothers would sit astride the great steeds, searching for their elder sibling.

He uttered a short laugh. He should not be surprised. Were he in their place, he would have done the same thing. Family ties were of the utmost importance among Vikings. They took pride in their ancestors and had a strong sense of what was due from one kinsman to another.

"What will they think of my little family?" he asked aloud, startling a nearby squirrel that had ventured close, perhaps thinking him as inanimate as the trees and shrubs of the forest.

Chattering angrily at the intruder, the squirrel scampered away, climbing up the nearest tree and hiding among the branches there.

Anxious to meet his brothers again and wondering at the same time what they had to do with Nama, Eric took up their trail. He did not worry about Nama's safety because neither were violent men; but, he thought with a smile, they would probably have availed themselves of her many charms.

Remembering the store the Eagle Clan set on virginity and the way they protected their young girls from the lust of the men around them, Eric hoped his brothers had either restrained themselves or else had been gentle while slaking the desires of their bodies. Otherwise, Eric knew, Shala was likely to lay the blame for his brothers' actions at his own feet.

Eric felt a need to hurry and quickened his stride, intent on reaching the muddy river as swiftly as possible, feeling certain he would find the longboat that had brought his kinsmen to this land there.

Sixteen

It was midafternoon when Nama first caught sight of the big, muddy river. The air was heavy and moist, almost stifling in intensity; and Nama felt a mournful oppression, a gloomy bleakness emanating from the dark, still bayous where Spanish moss and ivy-covered live oaks grew in abundance beside water sycamores.

Perhaps the bleakness did not come from the bayous, though. Perhaps it came from within her, generated by the knowledge that Garrick would soon be gone from her life.

She looked at the river, searching for the longboat that would carry him away from her, but it was nowhere to be seen. In fact, the river was so wide that the furthermost bank could barely be seen from this distance.

The horses' hooves made a dull thudding sound as they trod upon the thick moss growing in the dense forest, following the river south, traveling beside it whenever possible, detouring when they must, but always returning to the river.

It was near sunset when Garrick's steed snorted and quickened its pace. The forest

Now, for the first time...

You can find Janelle Taylor, Shannon Drake,
Rosanne Bittner, Sylvie Sommerfield, Penelope
Neri, Phoebe Conn, Bobbi Smith, and the rest of
today's most popular, bestselling authors

...All in one brand-new club!

Introducing KENSINGTON CHOICE,
the new Zebra/Pinnacle service that delivers the best
new historical romances direct to your home,
at a significant discount off the publisher's prices.

As your introduction, we invite you to accept 4 FREE BOOKS worth up to $23.96

details inside...

We've got your authors!

If you seek out the latest historical romances by today's bestselling authors, our new reader's service, KENSINGTON CHOICE, is the club for you.

KENSINGTON CHOICE is the only club where you can find authors like Janelle Taylor, Shannon Drake, Rosanne Bittner, Sylvie Sommerfield, Penelope Neri and Phoebe Conn all in one place...

...and the only service that will deliver their romances direct to your home as soon as they are published—even before they reach the bookstores.

KENSINGTON CHOICE is also the only service that will give you a substantial guaranteed discount off the publisher's prices on every one of those romances.

That's right: Every month, the Editors at Zebra and Pinnacle select four of the newest novels by our bestselling authors and rush them straight to you, even *before they reach the bookstores*. The publisher's prices for these romances range from $4.99 to $5.99—but they are always yours for the guaranteed low price of just *$3.95!*

That means you'll always save over $1.00...often as much as *$2.00*...off the publisher's prices on every new novel you get from KENSINGTON CHOICE!

All books are sent on a 10-day free examination basis, and there is no minimum number of books to buy. (A postage and handling charge of $1.50 is added to each shipment.)

As your introduction to the convenience and value of this new service, we invite you to accept

4 BOOKS FREE

The 4 books, worth up to $23.96, are our welcoming gift. You pay only $1 to help cover postage and handling.

To start your subscription to KENSINGTON CHOICE and receive your introductory package of 4 FREE romances, detach and mail the postpaid card at right *today*.

We have 4 FREE BOOKS for you as your introduction to KENSINGTON CHOICE

To get your FREE BOOKS, worth up to $23.96, mail card below.

FREE BOOK CERTIFICATE

As my introduction to your new KENSINGTON CHOICE reader's service, please send me 4 FREE historical romances (worth up to $23.96), billing me just $1 to help cover postage and handling. As a KENSINGTON CHOICE subscriber, I will then receive 4 brand-new romances to preview each month for 10 days FREE. I can return any books I decide not to keep and owe nothing. The publisher's prices for the KENSINGTON CHOICE romances range from $4.99 to $5.99, but as a subscriber I will be entitled to get them for just $3.95 per book. There is no minimum number of books to buy, and I can cancel my subscription at any time. A $1.50 postage and handling charge is added to each shipment.

Name _____

Address _____ Apt. # _____

City _____ State _____ Zip _____

Telephone (___) _____

Signature _____

(If under 18, parent or guardian must sign)

Subscription subject to acceptance

KC 0994

We have
4
FREE
Historical
Romances
for you!

Details inside!

thinned near a bend in the river, and Midnight trotted forward with an eagerness that was hard to ignore.

Had they reached their destination?

Nama's question was answered when they rounded the bend and the horse came to an immediate stop. She could feel the big stallion's muscles quivering with excitement beneath her legs.

Apprehension swept through her when Garrick slid off the animal, stepped over the gnarled trunk of a water sycamore, and strode to the edge of the water.

Nama looked out over the river, and her eyes widened with horror when they beheld the monster resting on the surface of the water.

It was a loathsome creature, one whose hideous features were enough to send the color from her cheeks. She had dreamed of such creatures in her most frightening nightmares but never thought she would encounter one while awake. it was a water serpent of monstrous proportions whose fearsome head reared high above its long body, whose glowing eyes of amber gazed scornfully across the water, seemingly unaware of their intrusion.

But was the beast really unaware? she questioned.

Every fiber of Nama's being cried out in silent terror, ordering her to run . . . to flee the monster serpent before it saw them; but she could not. Her blood had turned to ice and her limbs were frozen, unable to move.

"Aaiieeeeeee . . . !" The fearful cry came from Walks With Thunder who had sought refuge from the terrible monster by burrowing her face against Olaf's massive chest.

"What is wrong, Walks With Thunder?" he asked, wrapping his arms around her. He turned to Nama with a worried frown. "What is she afraid of?"

Nama swallowed around the lump of fear lodged in her throat. "She is—Walks With Thunder is fearful of—of the d-demon serpent," she stuttered.

"What nonsense!" Garrick growled, "There is no demon serpent. That is only our *langskip*. The vessel that brought us here."

"My eyes are not blind," Nama snapped, anger at his stupidity momentarily overcoming her fear. "Look, you!" She pointed toward the monster. "See it there! See the serpent floating on the water? It must have devoured your vessel!"

"No," Olaf said, uttering a short laugh. "It is our ship. The monster you fear is only a wooden carving created in the likeness of a serpent. Please explain that to Walks With Thunder."

The words were spoken with such sincerity that Nama had no recourse except to believe them. Even so, her voice had a slight tremble when she translated Olaf's words to the language of the People.

Although her moans ceased and her trembling lessened, Walks With Thunder would not remove her head from Olaf's chest so that she might see the truth in his words. Instead, she continued to cling to him, seeming to find solace in his arms. When had the woman's feelings for the golden-haired Viking changed? Nama wondered. She had been so wrapped up in her own emotions that her eyes had seen nothing but Garrick.

Not now, though. Not while confronted by such a monster as the one floating on the water. Nama had no wish to view the monstrous head—be it wood or otherwise—but she found she could not look away from it. That was the only reason she saw the small boat being lowered over the side of the monster boat. A flurry of movement told her the craft was being manned, that Vikings were settling into it and taking up the paddles.

What would they be like? she wondered uneasily, watching the vessel glide through the water, coming closer and closer to where they stood.

All too soon for her liking, the boat scraped gravel and one of the four men inside leapt out and clapped Garrick on the shoulder.

"Praise be to Odin!" he cried joyfully. "We were afraid the two of you would not return." His gaze swept over the two women before returning to Garrick. "You did not find the ones you searched for." The words were a statement rather than a question.

"No," Garrick replied. "But now, at least, we know their fate."

"They perished?"

"Yes."

"All of them?"

"To a man."

"How did you find out?"

"From Nama." Garrick motioned to her. "The rest of his party had already perished when Eric reached her village. He was fatally injured when she found him."

"I pray that he did not suffer long."

"He lived throughout the winter . . . several months after she found him. He lived among cliff dwellers who called themselves Eagle Clan."

"You said the woman told you?" He looked curiously at Nama.

"Yes," Garrick said shortly. "Eric taught her our language."

"Lucky for us," the big Viking said, continuing his study of Nama. "You are called Nama?"

Nama's mouth was so dry that she was afraid she could not properly form the words needed for a reply, so she settled for a nod of agreement.

The stranger took her hand in his much larger one. "I am pleased to make your acquaintance, Nama. My name is Karl."

Amazing though it was, Nama's fear of the big man evaporated and she smiled shyly at him. "I am happy to know you," she said in a formal tone.

"You must tell me about this place, Nama. I am eager to learn about your people and how they live and—"

"There will be time enough later for your questions," Garrick interrupted.

"Then we are staying awhile longer?" Karl queried.

"No. Nama goes with us to Norway."

A sudden chill swept over Nama. She would have welcomed the words had they come before she viewed the horrible wooden monster floating in the middle of the river. But the thought of traveling on such a boat sent terror streaking through her. Even the knowledge that she would be with Garrick did little to dispel that emotion.

Her gaze returned to him. It would have helped to allay her fears if he had not been so grim, if his eyes had not been so hard when they looked at her.

"I cannot go," she protested.

Ignoring her protests, he swept her up and lowered her into the boat. "Stay there," he said shortly.

Although she was afraid of the wooden monster, it was his tone rather than the fear that prompted her words. "I will not go!" she cried, standing upright, feeling the boat sway unsteadily beneath her. "You said I was no longer your captive. You promised I would remain free."

"And so you shall," he said grimly. "But in Norway."

"Son of a dog!" she spat. "May your tongue wither and die. May your—" She stopped suddenly, clapping her hand over her mouth. She must not curse him lest her words—spoken in anger—become fact.

"Sit down and stay put," he commanded, entering the boat and pulling her down beside him.

"Do not do this thing, Garrick," she begged, sending a fearful gaze at the larger vessel floating in the middle of the river. "Allow me to stay here. I have no wish to ride that monster."

"You are being stupid, woman," he snapped. "Silence your tongue."

Silence her tongue? Nama's blood boiled in her veins. She would not be called stupid. Nor would she be told to silence her tongue. She had a right to speak her mind and she would do so.

"I will not be silenced," she snapped. "Nor will I ride on that fearsome beast."

"It is not a beast. I told you it was a ship. And I will not remove the carved wooden head to convince you of that fact."

She fought against him, managing to free herself from his grasp. "Go away. Leave me here," she shouted, scrambling across the boat and throwing one leg over the side.

Strong fingers snared her wrist and pulled her back, securing her between his legs. "Be still, Nama. I will not leave you behind." He held her tightly between his powerful thighs making further movement impossible.

Realizing the impossibility of freeing herself, Nama ceased her struggles. But she was not done yet. Even though her love for Garrick was strong, her fear of the monster-boat was greater. Somehow, someway, she would escape, or she would perish in the attempt.

Fear was a hard knot in her chest as the Vikings rowed toward the distant vessel. They spoke softly among themselves, but Nama paid no heed to their conversation. Her every thought, every emotion, was centered on the long boat with the monster-head rearing high above the prow.

Dread settled over her like a dark cloud as they drew closer and closer until finally they drew alongside the boat. Then, amazing though it seemed, her fear evaporated, disappearing like morning fog beneath Father Sun's fiery gaze.

Great relief swept over her. The large vessel did not look quite as fearsome seen close up. The head—as Garrick had told her—was only an intricately carved piece of wood.

Although she could not bring herself to board the craft, she was given no choice.

Seeming to sense her hesitation, Garrick scooped her up and handed her to a man who stood with one foot poised on the boarding ladder; and before she could react, she was passed to another man, then another, until she stood firmly on the deck.

Garrick followed closely behind her, completely ignoring her presence as he began issuing orders to the watching crew. "Ready the raft," he commanded. "The horses must be brought on board swiftly. There may be some of the *skraelings* following us." He turned to a young seaman standing nearby. "Sven, take this wench to my quarters and keep her there."

The young man called Sven snared her wrists between strong fingers. "Come," he said gruffly.

She might have gone with the man called Sven had Garrick shown any sign of softening. But there was no softness in his rock-hard features, no sign of kindness in his grass-green eyes.

Twisting her arm, she wrenched it from the young seaman's grasp. "No!" she snapped. "I refuse to stay on this vessel."

Sven looked startled. Whether his surprise stemmed from her use of the Viking language or from her refusal to accompany him, Nama had no way of knowing. Nor did she care. What did concern her was Garrick's casual dismissal of her now they were aboard his vessel, coupled with his use of the word "wench" when he referred to her. Nama knew the word was used in a contemptuous manner and wondered if he had done so deliberately to show the other Vikings how small was her stature among them.

Even as the thought occurred, fear reared its ugly head again. She must make a show of strength here and now. She could not allow herself to be thought a woman of no importance. Surely Garrick could see that!

Jerking her chin higher, she glared at Sven, showing him the anger that should have been directed toward Garrick. "I said I will not go," she snarled. "Release me at once!"

A red flush crept up Sven's neck and he looked at his captain, who was silently watching the altercation. "The wench refuses to go, sir. How much authority do I have?"

"Whatever it takes," Garrick rasped, his brilliant green eyes dark with anger.

Sven reacted swiftly, stooping low before Nama knew his intention and wrapping his fingers around her calves. Before she could utter a protest, she found herself slung across his shoulders and carried away.

They were already inside the large tent when

Nama regained her wits. By then it was too late. The young man dumped her on the bed and reached for a long length of rope coiled beside it.

"Release me!" she cried, kicking out with her feet while he wrapped the rope around one of the four upright posts that stood at each corner, then fastened it to her wrist. "Garrick!" she screamed at the top of her lungs. "I will not be bound this way again. Make him stop. Make him release me."

Grimly, she kicked out, striking the young Viking over and over again, her blows landing with dull thuds against his body. But he seemed not to notice her puny struggles, continuing his efforts without pause until each wrist was firmly secured to the posts on each side of her head and her ankles were bound to the posts at the lower end.

When he had finished, he stood over her, breathing hard from his efforts; and Nama knew that, spread-eagled the way she was, there was no way she could stop him should he decide to slake his lust with her.

Even as the thought occurred, she realized he did not look lustful. Instead, he looked confused, perhaps even concerned.

Concerned? she questioned. Could he really be concerned? If he were, then perhaps she could use that to her advantage.

Sweeping her lashes down to cover her expressive eyes, she allowed her lips to tremble fearfully. It was easy to accomplish, for that emotion was present, although not as strong as the burning anger she felt at being bound hand and foot, completely at the mercy of whoever should pass her way.

How could Garrick do such a thing to her? Granted, it was the young Viking who had bound her to the posts, but it was Garrick who was ultimately responsible for the situation.

She hated him. Hated him! And she would never forgive him for this day.

Feeling the sting of tears at the thought of his cruelty, she lifted her lashes and allowed the young Viking who towered over her to see them. "Please," she murmured, hating herself for begging yet knowing there was no other way to gain her release. "Allow me to go free."

"I cannot," he said gruffly, his expression softening. "But you need not worry. Garrick is a kind man. He will do you no harm."

Nama's anger burned stronger, but she would not allow it to show. Instead, she widened her eyes so that her angry tears would not go unnoticed. She added a tremble to her lips and spoke again. "The ropes are too tight," she whispered. "They are cutting my wrists. Could you loosen them?"

Instead of doing so, he bent to check them, pushing a finger between her flesh and the rope. "They are loose enough," he said gruffly. "The ropes will not leave marks on your flesh."

"But they are painful, Sven," she argued, unwilling to accept that she could not sway him. "If you would only loosen them the tiniest bit then—"

"I—I cannot," he interrupted swiftly, a red flush

rising up his neck and staining his cheeks. "I will come back later. After we have set sail."

That would be too late, she realized. She must convince him to release her. "You must help me, Sven. You must—" She broke off, realizing further protest would prove useless, for the young seaman had already left the tent and she was completely alone.

Seventeen

Garrick became aware of the approaching storm while the horses were being loaded on the *langskip*. Although the sky overhead was clear, dark clouds were gathering in the distance.

"Looks like rain." Olaf's voice came from somewhere close behind him.

"More like a storm," Garrick said, studying the clouds anxiously. "Look how dark they are." Although the heavy clouds were located northwest of them, they were approaching fast.

"We should be able to outrun it," Olaf said.

"I pray you are right," Garrick said gruffly. "But those are rapid-moving clouds."

He had no worry about the safety of the ship that had been built to his own specifications. It was a hundred and ten feet long from the tip of the prow to the stern. The keel was shaped from a single piece of oak from which the stem and stern rose in elegant and sharply profiled curves. Designed for both rowing and sailing, the ship boasted twenty oar-holes on each side.

Garrick turned to search the deck with a trained eye. The brawny crew that had been readying the vessel for its journey home had done their work well. He saw no reason to delay their departure.

No sooner did he make his decision, then the wind gusted, whipping a lock of hair across Garrick's face. Impatiently, he pushed it aside.

"Where is Nama?" Olaf asked.

"Sven took her to my quarters."

"Will she stay there?"

Garrick's smile was grim. "She has no other choice." He knew he spoke the truth. Sven had been told to keep her there and, whatever happened, he would do exactly that.

"Perhaps the two women would feel safer together," Olaf suggested.

Garrick had no doubt of that, but Nama might gain strength from Walks With Thunder's presence and he dared not risk that. He could not delay his departure to search for her should she leave the ship.

Garrick frowned darkly at his brother. "Just see they are kept apart."

"That is not like you, Garrick," Olaf persisted. "I thought you cared for Nama. Was I wrong?"

Garrick looked at the clouds again. They were closer now. "I have no intention of explaining my reasons," he said shortly.

"If you have no objection, I would like to see Nama," Olaf said quietly.

"What purpose would that serve?" Garrick asked, eying his brother severely.

Crack! Thud! Bump!

The *langskip* suddenly shuddered beneath a series of hard blows, then lurched to one side.

"Thor's teeth!" Garrick shouted. "What in the devil hit us?"

Olaf lurched to the side rail and bent over it with Garrick only a step behind. The two men stared at the swirling water only a few feet below them. It was muddy and swollen, filled with foam and swirling objects that continually bumped against the side of the ship.

Bump, crack, thud!

Several logs struck the boat, one after the other in quick succession. Whole trees floated toward them, uprooted by the storm.

Even as Garrick watched, one of the trees—a giant oak—struck the side of the boat with such force that he lost his footing and slid across the plank deck.

Immediately, Garrick righted himself.

Cupping his hands around his mouth so his voice would carry over the noise the floating objects made as they struck the ship, he gave the order to depart. "Hoist the sails!"

Even as he shouted the command, he saw a wall of water coming around the bend and reached quickly, curling his hand around the railing. Just in time. The heavy water struck the boat with a fearful blow, causing Garrick to lose his balance again. Then the angry wave swept over the deck, carrying loose barrels and boxes alike—along with those hapless beings who happened to be caught off guard—into the river's watery embrace.

Garrick, having been forewarned, was one of the

lucky ones. His grip was too tight, his hold too strong to be pulled loose from the railing. Others were not as lucky, he knew, having heard their fearful cries as they were washed overboard.

The *langskip*, having dipped sideways as the wave struck, quickly righted itself.

The river swelled angrily around them, surging against the wooden siding, slapping against the planks; but the ship, designed to ride calm in the angriest of seas, continued to bob gently upon its furious waters.

"Search the water for survivors!" Garrick shouted, even as he knew there could be none there. The current was too strong for anyone to stay afloat. Whoever—or whatever—the storm had cast into its muddy waters would likely stay there forever.

Garrick searched for his brother, who had disappeared. Had he gone overboard with that first wave? Even as panic washed over him, he saw the big, blond Viking striding toward him, his boots thumping across the plank deck.

"Walks With Thunder is bruised but otherwise unhurt," Olaf said, explaining his disappearance. "Have you checked Nama?"

Fear spread anew within Garrick, but this time the fear was for Nama's well-being. He cursed himself for forgetting about her, even while he told himself the ship must come first.

"Sven is with her," Garrick said, his gaze sliding toward the tent where she was confined. He felt a small measure of relief when he saw it was still intact. "He will keep her safe."

"Sven is midship with the horses," Olaf announced, turning abruptly away from his brother. "Since you obviously care little for the woman's safety, I will make her my concern." Without waiting for a reply, he strode to the tent and disappeared inside.

Garrick would have followed his brother had the wind not begun to howl, flattening his clothing against his body, shrieking through the rigging and billowing the sails to their fullest, and reminding him of his duty as ship's captain.

The ship began to move slowly downstream amidst the sound of thunder cracking across the heavens and jagged streaks of lightning that struck the earth one after the other, seeming to reach with deadly fingers for the ship that sought so desperately to escape.

Garrick alternately watched the rigging on the sails and kept an eye on the tent until Olaf reappeared. Then, feeling satisfied that Nama had not suffered unduly, he turned his full attention to maneuvering around the obstacles floating on the river.

Although dark clouds in the north told Eric it was raining there, the sky overhead was clear, the sun warm against his skin.

He felt a sense of breathless anticipation as he climbed the mountain that stood between him and the river. What would he find when he reached the top? he wondered.

Yesterday morning he had abandoned the trail he followed after determining the riders were using the river as a guide. And, since they were journeying in a southeasterly direction, it was obvious they were returning from whence they had come.

And Eric knew that location. It was the big, muddy river that flowed into the ocean.

Sweat beaded Eric's forehead and his breath came in short bursts as he topped the rise and stopped to rest. Spread out below him was a sheltered valley, lush with a verdant growth of trees and bushes. Sunlight sparkled on the wide river that lay like a silver band in the middle of the valley. As he had suspected, a *langskip* floated on the water. And if he were not mistaken it bore the colors of his brother Garrick.

Excitement quickened his blood as he gazed upon it. Soon he would see his brother.

He started forward, slipping and sliding down the slope toward the river, eager to see Garrick again.

Suddenly he skidded to a halt. No! his mind protested.

He saw the wall of water coming around the bend . . . saw it strike the *langskip*. The long ship shuddered beneath the blow then quickly righted itself.

Although the distance was too great and he could not see movement on the boat, he saw the sails rising above the vessel and knew, without a doubt, that he was already too late.

His brother was leaving for Norway. And there was no way Eric could reach him in time, no way to stop the longboat from leaving.

And what of Nama, he wondered suddenly.

Was she aboard the vessel, too?

Nama was furious, absolutely seething with anger. Something had struck the boat with enough force to toss things around inside her prison—indeed, one of those items had struck her forehead with enough force to break the skin—and Garrick cared nothing for her safety. Had he done so, he would surely have come to her. Instead, Olaf had looked in for a brief moment, then quickly disappeared again.

She would not allow the hurt she felt to surface. Nama could not do so and remain strong. Instead, she hardened her heart against Garrick, whipped her emotions into a frenzy and kept them there by promising herself there would come a time when he no longer held the upper hand. When that time came, she would avenge herself on him.

She would bind him, spread-eagled on the ground; then she would burn him with blazing sticks, would skin him alive with her knife, would—

Tears sprang to her eyes as she thought of him in torment and she blinked hard, trying to dry her eyes. Why should she care what he suffered? she asked herself. He cared nothing for her. He could not care and treat her in such a manner.

She sniffed and turned her head sideways, attempting to use the sodden bedding to wipe away all trace of her tears, but they continued to fall despite her efforts to control them.

Her misery was so acute that it was almost a physical pain, but she was determined to keep it hidden. Garrick would probably be gratified to see her tears.

That thought only served to make her weep harder. She was unaware of another presence until she heard a man's voice. "Do not weep, little one."

She turned to see Sven standing above her. His blue eyes were kind as they met hers. "Are your tears caused by fear?" he asked gruffly.

She sniffed and looked at him through misty eyes. "How long must I stay bound this way?" she asked plaintively.

"Would you give your promise you will not escape?"

She nodded her head eagerly. She would promise anything to gain her freedom.

"I fear I cannot trust you," he sighed.

Nama gazed at him in feigned confusion. "Surely you do not think I would speak falsely, Sven!" By using his given name she hoped to generate an intimacy that would win him over. "Even if I wanted, I could not swim to the shore. The distance is far too great."

He hesitated, and she quickly pressed her advantage. "Please, Sven," she coaxed, looking up at him through thick lashes. "You would not regret my release. I promise you." She licked her dry lips and heard him catch his breath.

Smiling inwardly, she repeated the action. Sven desired her. That much was obvious. If she could play on that desire, then perhaps she could gain her release. "The bedding is soaked," she whispered. "And it chills my flesh."

"I will change the bedding," he blurted out, obviously eager to please.

Bending over a sea chest, he opened the lid and delved through it for a moment. When he rose again, he held a large piece of material in his hands.

Nama waited impatiently for him to unfasten her bindings; but, to her consternation, Sven lifted her body and pulled the bedding from beneath her. The dry bedding was spread in a like manner; and when the chore was finished, Sven left her alone again.

Furious that there was nothing she could do to free herself, Nama's unreleased anger exhausted her and she fell immediately into a deep sleep.

Time passed swiftly as Garrick and his crew tried to outrun the storm.

Guiding the longboat through the muddy river took every bit of Garrick's attention, leaving him no time to worry about the girl still confined to his quarters.

The storm followed them all the way to the ocean, and its fury never lessened.

Garrick thought the storm was not unlike a living entity whose only thought was to drive the intruders from its land.

It was a busy time for Garrick, who worked beside his crew until finally they were floating safely on the ocean. Only then did he have time to take a head count. It was then he discovered five of his men had been lost overboard.

Garrick felt the loss of each man and mourned their passing, knowing he would have to take the news of their deaths back to their families, who waited for them in Norway.

Finally, Garrick had time for other considerations. With the memory of death still hovering around him, he sought comfort in the land of the living.

He strode across the plank deck, his body eager for the pleasure awaiting him inside his tent, his mind already attuned to her presence.

Pushing aside the entrance flap, he sought the girl who would provide his release from tension, and his eyes widened with surprise.

She lay on his bed, spread-eagled between the bedposts, awaiting his pleasure.

Eighteen

A delicious warmth covered Nama, seeping into her flesh and spreading slowly throughout her body. She felt a wet moistness behind her ear and heard a soft moan.

She wondered vaguely who made the sound, wondered fleetingly why she felt no alarm. But as quickly as the thought occurred, she knew the answer.

The moan caused her no alarm because the sound was not an eruption of pain. Instead, it was caused by extreme pleasure, such as Nama herself was experiencing at this very moment.

A warm wetness enclosed her nipple, and she felt a curious pulling sensation that caused a spreading heat in her lower body.

Opening sleep-dazed eyes, Nama stared in surprise at the man who suckled at her breast.

Garrick! He had finally come to her! But it was obvious releasing her was not on his mind, because her hands were still restrained and so were her feet.

A surge of fury swept over her. "Stop that," she hissed, bucking beneath his body as she tried in vain to throw him off. "You cannot erase your misdeeds in this manner."

With her nipple held firmly in his mouth, Garrick tilted his head and met her gaze. She thought she detected laughter in his eyes and cold, black rage threatened to swamp her.

How dare he treat her so!

His lips tightened around the nipple, and Nama cursed her traitorous body for betraying her while she glared at Garrick.

There was no doubt he was all man. Even with her nipple in his mouth, he was dangerous-looking and powerful, from his brilliant green eyes to the hard muscled lines of his body.

She hated him for what he was doing to her, but how could she stop him?

"You would do well to stop tormenting me," she snapped. "Else you will come to regret this day."

He released the nipple and moved over her. "It is not my intention to torment you," he said gruffly. "I have other things in mind."

Raising himself on his hands, he moved higher until his mouth hovered inches above hers. She waited breathlessly for his next move, her heart thumping like a frightened rabbit caught in a trap.

Garrick's lips curled in a smile, and he kissed the tip of her nose, then traced the curve of her lips with his tongue. When she parted her lips to protest again, his tongue darted into the moist cavern of her mouth and probed the wet darkness there.

Although Nama tried hard to curb the feelings he generated, she was unsuccessful in her attempts. Her skin puckered with goose bumps and her hardened nipples were rigid with desire while her whole body tingled and felt tautly alive.

Suddenly he released her and stood up beside the bed. His brilliant eyes never left her as he removed his clothing and carelessly tossed it aside.

"No," she pleaded, unwilling to allow his possession while she was in such a vulnerable state. "Do not take me this way, Garrick. Release me from these bonds."

"You must first make me a promise," he said huskily.

"A promise?"

"That you will make no attempt to flee."

"I cannot," she moaned. "I have no wish to travel to your land. Do not ask it of me."

"I do ask it."

"I cannot," she said again.

"Then remain my captive."

"I will never forgive you if you do this," she said, blinking her eyes to keep the tears at bay. "Someday you will regret your actions."

His green eyes darkened, resembling a stormy sea. "It is not my wish to deny you anything, Nama," he said softly. "But you must promise me. Say the words that will gain you release."

"I promise," she whispered, tears brimming over and spilling down her cheeks.

His expression showed his relief as he reached for the ropes and unfastened them, kissing each tethered member as he did as though to ease any pain she might have suffered there. Then, with a low growl, he joined her on the bed, covered her body with his own, and clamped his teeth over her right earlobe.

Although she shuddered beneath his touch, Nama was still angry with him. That fact was responsible for her actions as she bucked beneath him, trying to throw him off even though she knew that was an impossibility.

Releasing her earlobe, he licked at the sensitive skin beneath, then moved downward, nuzzling her throat, tracing his tongue across the soft flesh, and leaving a trail of fire in his wake.

Desire flared like molten heat in her loins, and her throaty moans would not be held back any longer.

The sounds seemed to fan his desire for her flesh as he continued to move down her body until he reached the mound of her breasts. His lips scorched her with their heat; his teeth worried her throbbing, swollen nipple, while his tongue laved it.

Nama cried out with longing as white hot flashes of passion seared through her. His hand slid lower, caressing the soft mound of hair between her thighs; his mouth continued to work its magic on her nipples.

Nama's breath came quickly, unevenly as she sought to control her emotions. Yet that was impossible, she found, especially with his hand nestled so firmly between her legs, his long fingers evoking pleasures that caused her to twitch and thresh beneath his touch.

The combination of his mouth on her breast and his fingers working their magic was too much to bear. Nama arched against his body, trying to find release from her torment.

His mouth released her breast and moved down the softness of her belly and paused near the lush, sable pelt that glistened between her legs.

What was he about? she wondered wildly, staring down at his fiery curls.

As though goaded beyond belief, Garrick gripped her taut bottom tightly and fitted his mouth against her sensitive feminine core.

Nama quivered beneath him as his tongue laved her most secret place, stroking the moist velvet there, continuing its arousal until her whole body exploded into a million tiny fragments.

Having gained her release, Nama lay limply on the bed, trying to control her quickened breath. But Garrick was not finished with her yet. He raised himself above her, fitting his body over hers. Then, while she stared in wide-eyed amazement, he plunged into her.

Immediately, the fires that Nama had thought were quenched ignited again. His lips muffled her cries of pleasure as he began to move, thrusting his rod deeper and deeper, quickening his pace with each backward stroke. Nama abandoned herself to him completely as she met each thrust with one of her own, climbing higher and higher until she exploded with the joy of release.

* * *

Several days later Nama stood near the ship's rail watching the gulls circle the ship. A frown marred her forehead, reflecting her troubled mind. Garrick had told her their journey was nearly over and she wondered what fate awaited her in the land of giants.

Nama could have been happier under different circumstances. She would not have been so fearful if she thought Garrick really cared for her. But he did not. Although he came to her at night, seeking pleasure from her body, his heart remained his own.

"Why do you look so sad," asked a deep male voice from beside her.

Nama knew without looking who had spoken. She would recognize Sven's voice anywhere. He had become her constant companion, a fact which seemed to displease Garrick. It was for that reason she encouraged the young seaman.

"Would you not be sad if you had been taken from your homeland against your will?" she asked.

His blue eyes admired her. "Yes," he conceded. "I imagine I would. But I am told you are not going to Norway as a slave, Nama. It is said you are a free woman."

"What good is freedom in a strange land?" she asked despondently. "I have little knowledge of your ways. I do not know what is expected of me when we arrive."

"I imagine you will be a concubine," Sven said gently.

"I am a concubine? The word is unfamiliar to my ears. What does it mean?"

"Well . . ." His face flushed and he looked embarrassed. "You know. Concubine. Garrick's woman. His wench."

There was that word again. *Wench.* "Concubine means the same as wench?" she inquired.

"Not exactly. Wench can apply to other women, too. Those other than concubines."

"Then explain *concubine.*"

"It is a woman who belongs to a man."

"Like his mate. They belong to each other for life?" Perhaps there was no need to fear the future after all.

Sven frowned heavily. "No. Not for life. Just for as long as he wants her."

Wants her, wants her, wants her. The words echoed in her mind, over and over again. What happened when he no longer wanted her? she wondered.

"Then a concubine is a woman who pleasures *every* man," she said, forcing the words past the lump that had formed in her throat.

"No. Not that either." He looked away from her as though he could no longer hold her gaze. "A concubine only pleasures those her master chooses."

"Then a concubine is a man's possession." Her voice was hard, her lips tight.

"Yes." He glanced nervously over her shoulder,

seeming to search for someone. "Perhaps Garrick should be the one to explain."

"You are doing well," she said, hiding her anger and stretching her lips into a wide smile. "Continue, please, with your explanation. Does a Viking have more than one concubine?"

"Of course," he said quickly. "A Viking may have as many concubines as he can afford. I think Garrick owns six." His eyes narrowed thoughtfully. "But that number may be wrong. I think he may have given Thorvauld two of them just before we sailed."

"What about you, Sven? Do you have any of these . . . concubines?" she asked, determined to speak despite her rising anger.

"No," he said softly. "I have never met a woman that I wished to own. Not until now." Although he kept his distance, his voice was a soft caress. "I thought after awhile . . . when Garrick is no longer interested, then perhaps . . . if he would consider it . . . would you mind . . ." His voice trailed away, leaving several sentences uncompleted.

But Nama knew what he suggested. He wanted to own her, to possess her as Garrick had done. Why not? she asked herself, ignoring the pain in her knotted heart. If anyone owned her, then why not this young seaman who had already proved himself kind.

"Nama!"

Nama jerked her head around to see Garrick scowling darkly at them. Curling his hand, he mo-

tioned her toward him, but she resisted, edging
sideways toward Sven, vowing in that moment
never to hasten to his side the moment he beckoned.

She would never forgive him for what he had
made of her. *A whore.* A Viking word, yet whatever
name such a woman was called, she was the same
in any land . . . a woman whose fate was sealed,
who would be given to any man who desired her
body.

No. She would *never* forgive Garrick for what he
had made of her.

Never.

Garrick stood at the prow and studied the sea
around him. It moved continuously, creating hills
and valleys, its color never the same.

Sometimes it was the dark green of a dense forest, while other times the green would become brilliant like new spring grass. Just when he thought
he knew its color, it would change, would deepen
from blue to green, then change to a sparkling,
iridescent silver before changing back to blue
again.

Whatever its color, though, Garrick loved the
sea. When his thoughts were troubled, as they were
now, he yearned for the sea, longed for it as
though it were a beloved woman that gave him
comfort when it was needed.

The feel of the spray against his face gave him
peace. The low hum of the wind among the rig-

ging, the snapping of the sails as the boat pressed forward was music to his ears. And yet, at this moment, he found no peace in that sound. His confrontation with Nama was too recent, the memory too strong for him to find release from this anger that consumed him.

Why had she rejected his embrace? he wondered. Why had she avoided his touch as though it were a plague?

Try as he would, he could not find the answer.

Neither could he find peace.

He told himself he did not care. Told himself he would not suffer without her. She was only a woman, after all, and the world was full of those who could please him more.

But in his heart of hearts he did not believe that. And one small corner of his mind told him there was no other like the woman from the Eagle Clan.

But even so, he would not allow her to treat him so. He was master, and she was . . . what? Slave? No! He had promised her freedom, yet it was a freedom that would be limited, could be nothing else. Should he make her his concubine? His lifelong mate?

Garrick realized then that he would allow Nama to be whatever she wanted, to fill whatever role she decided on as long as she remained beside him.

Anything else was unthinkable.

Whatever else happened, she was his; and that would never change.

He would see to that.

Nineteen

They arrived in Norway shortly before nightfall. Nama's first impression was of jagged rocks thrusting from the sea. When they drew nearer she could see craggy bluffs and sheer cliffs, but there was no sign of forests in this stark, desolate land, not one single tree to lend it beauty.

Garrick steered the ship into one of the many canals that opened to the ocean, while the crew furled the sails, tied them, and stored them away.

Nama was aware of the countless number of people who raced toward the canal, apparently intent on welcoming the newcomers.

The sight of so many people, most of them standing a head taller than she, caused Nama's heart to jerk with fear. If pleading with Garrick would have altered the situation, then she would have done so. But it would change nothing. Therefore, she must accept her circumstances, must make the best of a bad bargain.

She flashed Garrick a look of bitter hatred, but he did not see. His attention was focused on the dock. She heard the sound of wood scraping against wood as the vessel bumped against the quay; then Sven leapt over the side, taking a rope with him.

After securing the ship to the dock, Sven turned to greet the crowd that surged around him.

"What was the new land like?" a beefy man asked, clapping Sven on the shoulder.

"Did you find Eric?" asked another man.

"Did you fight with the *skraelings?*" The question came from a small boy who had somehow worked his way to the front. "Were they fierce, Sven? How many did you slay?"

"We saw the *skraelings.*" Sven laughed, tousling the boy's blond curls. "But we did not fight them. As to what they are like . . . look there!" He pointed to Nama. "We brought two of them back with us."

Nama shrank back as the boy fixed her with an intense gaze. As she did, an arm circled her waist and she twisted around to find Garrick standing behind her. Her muscles tightened and her body stiffened, but he seemed not to notice her reaction.

"What do you think of my home?" Garrick drawled, smiling down at her.

"I hate it!" she snapped, pulling away from his embrace. "Never have I seen such an ugly, desolate place." The insults were barbed, designed to make him hurt.

His body tensed. "Nevertheless, you will remain here for the rest of your days." Catching her wrist in one hand, he unfastened her bracelet.

Wondering why he had taken it, Nama watched

him leap over the side of the vessel and join Sven on the quay.

A bitter cold despair settled over Nama, spreading through her like a physical pain; and she turned away, unable to look upon the laughing crowd.

Walks With Thunder joined her. "You are a foolish girl, Nama," the woman said sternly in the language of the People. "You would do well to speak pleasantly to Garrick instead of using him to sharpen your tongue. Can you not see he holds your future in his hands?"

"My eyes are not blind," Nama replied sharply, using the same tongue. "Of course I can see."

"Then why do you deliberately anger him?"

Nama swallowed around the lump in her throat. "He is the reason for my pain, Walks With Thunder. He slakes his lust on my body, yet he cares nothing for my feelings."

"Who told you he must care?" Walks With Thunder asked gently. "Garrick is no different from any other man. Did you think he was?"

"Yes," Nama admitted. "I did think so."

"Then you were wrong," Walks With Thunder said. "You must change your ways, Nama; otherwise, you will never find happiness in this land. Or any other," she added. "A woman must bow to her man's wishes, whatever they are."

"What are the two of you talking about?" Karl asked, stopping beside the two women. Without waiting for a reply, he went on. "What do you think of Norway? Is it not beautiful?"

Nama opened her mouth to repeat her previous words about its ugliness, then closed it again. Like Garrick, Karl did not want to hear such things. To him, the land was beautiful.

"The brothers are eager to greet their family." Nama recognized Sven's voice and felt surprise that he had boarded the vessel again. "They said we were to bring the women," he told Karl. "Brynna will be waiting impatiently for them."

Brynna? The name was unfamiliar to Nama. Did it belong to a man or a woman?

Nama turned to see Garrick and Olaf climbing into a square contraption that was pulled by a horse. "They ignore their prisoners since they are back among their own people," she said scornfully.

Karl frowned at her. "Of what prisoners do you speak, Nama?"

Her gaze was sharp, knowing. "Of Walks With Thunder and myself? Who else is prisoner here?"

"There are no prisoners on this vessel," he said gruffly.

"Then what would you call us?" she questioned. "I did not ask to come here."

"Walks With Thunder seems content enough."

Hearing her name upon the Viking's lips, Walks With Thunder turned to him with a question in her eyes. When Nama told her what the Viking had said, she smiled slightly. "I, too, have fear. Who would not when faced with a strange land and such giants as these? But the fear is small. And the eagerness to explore is great. I wish to know how these people survive in a land without forests."

"You will find out soon enough," Nama commented sharply. "Look!" She pointed at the people toiling in the fields while another, larger man, obviously a Norseman, watched over them. "My eyes tell me those people are the workers in this land; and if they were content in their living, they would not need someone to make them labor in the fields."

Turning to Karl, she spoke in his language. "Are those people slaves?"

He shifted uncomfortably. "Yes. They are slaves, captured during raids. But there is no need to feel sorry for them. If they had captured one of us in battle, then the roles would have been reversed. It would be Norsemen working the fields with one of them overseeing the work." He shrugged his wide shoulders. "It is the way of life, Nama. He who is stronger enjoys the plunder of battle. Now, come along. Garrick will expect to see the two of you when he meets with his family in the big hall." The last was said with a tug on her arm that brought her toward the unloading platform.

There was no time for further conversation as they disembarked from the ship and climbed up on one of the square conveyances. Karl told her it was a carriage. Pulled by a black horse, it carried them swiftly uphill toward a large building comprised of earth, stones, and turf, the like of which she had never seen before.

"That building houses the *jarl* and his family,"

Karl explained, seeming to sense her curiosity. "The walls are thick to keep out the cold."

As they topped a rise, Nama realized she had been wrong when she'd said there were no forests in this land. The forests were there, only hidden from the sea by the hills.

Her narrowed gaze swept over the dwellings that were scattered over the meadows. All of them had low, thick walls and roofs whose layers of turf had grown into a solid, grassy mass so that they looked like little hillocks. Children roamed the roofs at will, some of them accompanied by their dogs.

The horses pulled the carriage through stone gates that seemed to be the only entrance to the dwelling where Garrick's family lived, and once inside; the horses were drawn to a halt before the wide steps leading to the doorway.

"Make way!" Karl shouted to the watching crowd, most of whom were as fair as Nama and Walks With Thunder were dark. The people continued to surge around the carriage, their excited voices drowning out Karl's.

Seeming to sense the futility of shouting, Karl leapt from the carriage and faced the crowd with widespread arms. And, as though compelled by that alone, they parted to make a path for the newcomers.

Karl took the lead, with Nama following closely behind him; Walks With Thunder was third in line, leaving Sven to take up the rear. He used that position to push them along when their footsteps faltered.

Mounting the steps, Karl pushed open the door, then waited for Nama to enter before him. Her heart beat fast with trepidation, but she had no choice except to go on.

"Garrick has bade me welcome you both to the Nordstrom home," Karl said formally.

Nama was struck by the shadowy darkness of the room which was lighted by several tall, thick candles positioned high on the walls.

Why were there no windows? she wondered, remembering her own home high among the cliffs which had many windows to allow the warmth of the sun inside.

Impatiently, Karl shoved her forward, hurrying her across the room to another one that was much larger than the first. Nama guessed, by its size, that it was used for communal purposes.

The room was long and narrow with raised earthen side-floors that were cushioned and covered with draperies. Stone slabs were used as foundation for the decoratively carved roof-posts.

Although Nama was intensely curious about her surroundings, her fear of the unknown took precedence

The babble of voices was all around them, and Nama found herself the object of curiosity. She recognized the Nordstrom brothers across the room, saw they were engaged in conversation with another man who, even without his great size, would have dominated the hall.

"The jarl," Karl said, apparently noticing her

fascination with the man. "Fergus Nordstrom, father to Garrick and Olaf."

And Eric. she added mentally. "You called him a jarl," she said, studying the dark-haired, barrel-chested man. She could easily see the family resemblance. "What is a *jarl?*"

"The headman around here. He owns all the lands . . . as far as the eye can see. He is like a chief or shaman."

"The chief does not own the lands," she replied. "Nor does the shaman. The land is there for every living thing to enjoy."

"Here, they belong to the jarl. As do the people who live on them." He pushed her toward the jarl and his two sons. "He will want to see you."

"Does he consider himself my owner?" she inquired.

"No. At least, I think not. Garrick is responsible for you, but his house is on his father's land, so perhaps . . ." His voice trailed away uncertainly, yet his footsteps did not falter. Perhaps they even hurried somewhat in his eagerness to be rid of his charges.

"Who is the woman?" Nama eyed the middle-aged woman who sat on a high cushioned seat. The amber gown she wore contrasted sharply with the hair coiled on either side of her head.

"She is Gilda Nordstrom, Garrick's mother." There was no more time for questions as they traversed the long hall where polished weapons hung from hooks on every wall. All too soon they stood before the jarl and his companions.

Nama met his eyes and lifted her chin defiantly, refusing to show submission even in the face of her fear.

"What have we here?" the jarl asked in a great booming voice. Cupping Nama's chin in one large palm, he studied her with deep intensity.

"This is Nama," Garrick said, stepping forward to stand beside her. "She is from the new land. Her people call themselves Eagle Clan."

"Eagle Clan, hmmmm? How odd. Is she yours?"

"Yes. She is mine."

"How did you come by this beauty, Garrick?"

"By right of conquest," Garrick replied, throwing her a cold, tight smile that sent a chill dancing across her flesh.

"Conquest, eh? Will she be put up for sale?" his father asked.

"If she is, then I offer two cows." The voice belonged to a man wearing a purple mantle.

"Two cows and two pigs!" bellowed a voice from across the room.

Nama could not control the fear that trembled through her as the men bargained for her in much the same manner she would have bargained with the traders who came to her village.

She kept her eyes lowered, unable to meet Garrick's eyes, fearing what she would see there.

"You will have to wait, gentlemen," Garrick said shortly. "She is not for sale at this time. Perhaps, though, at a later time that would be a consideration."

His father roared with laughter. "You obviously have not finished sampling her wares, eh?"

"What could you possibly want with such a creature, Garrick?" The dark-haired woman who had spoken curled her fingers around his arm possessively. Her brown eyes swept Nama from head to toe, and her nostrils flared with obvious distaste. "She is dirty and ill-kempt and might even be carrying a disease upon her person or, Odin forbid, even head lice." She gave a delicate shudder as though saying the word aloud might infect her.

Nama's head jerked up, and she glared at the woman who had spoken, then at the man who had allowed the insult without the slightest reprimand. Instead, he watched her closely for some reaction, obviously wondering if she would retaliate.

He could wait forever, she decided, for she would not dignify the verbal attack with words.

Deciding she would not break her silence, he uncurled the other woman's fingers and said, "She is not dirty, Carlotta. Only her clothing. Yours would be, too, had you spent a month aboard ship with only one gown. And I can assure you she is not diseased."

"How can you be certain?" the woman asked plaintively.

"This discussion is ended," Garrick said shortly.

"Of course, love," Carlotta murmured. "Whatever you say. I will leave you to your business and await your pleasure in your longhouse." Having made her prior claim on Garrick known to his newest prize, she strolled casually away from them and disappeared into the crowd.

Nama seethed inwardly. She had been publicly humiliated by the woman who was obviously one of Garrick's many concubines.

I will leave you to your business and await your pleasure in your longhouse.

The words stabbed Nama as they had been meant to do, having been uttered with the express purpose of reminding the crowd of her status among them, while her actions were designed solely to show Garrick's new possession that she was less than nothing . . . a mere captive, while Carlotta herself was the favored one.

He was welcome to her, Nama told herself.

Head lice!

Nama's lips tightened grimly at the remembered insult. Nothing would have suited her better at the moment than to be able to give Garrick something vile . . . be it head lice or the black plague that she had heard the Vikings discuss on the long voyage.

Suddenly a voice intruded on Nama's thoughts. "What would you have me do with her, Garrick? Surely she will be more trouble than she is worth." The woman who had spoken was Garrick's mother, Gilda Nordstrom.

"How so, Mother?" he asked, sending her an obviously fond smile. "She is stronger than she looks and can, in most cases, take care of herself." He turned glinting eyes on Nama, and she suspected he was laughing at her. "Perhaps she would do well in the kitchen among the other slaves."

Slaves! The word wounded Nama. She had already suspected that was to be her fate, even though Garrick had claimed she would be a free woman.

Although she was crying inside, Nama knew her face would be devoid of emotion; but it took all her effort to keep it so.

Lifting her chin a degree higher, she met the older woman's eyes and waited for instructions.

"How odd, Garrick," the woman exclaimed. "She seems to have understood what you said."

"She understands, Mother," Garrick said. "The reason is still to be explained. It is the way I came to know of my brother's death."

Gilda Nordstrom's face seemed to crumple, but she quickly regained control. "You must tell us all about it now." She climbed the step and took her seat beside the jarl, then motioned to someone in the crowd. "Hilda! Show the women their sleeping quarters; then take them to the kitchen and see they are well trained in their duties. I will speak with you later about them."

"Mother," Garrick began, his gaze flickering between Nama and his parent. "I have to tell you that—"

"I am ready, Garrick," she interrupted. "I wish to know everything you can tell me about the fate of my oldest son."

His face softened, and he sat at her feet, taking her hand in his as he began the tale.

"Come with me," a stout, gray-haired woman said, urging both Nama and Walks With Thunder away from the others.

"We have been given over to this woman," Nama told Walks With Thunder, who was looking confused.

Without a backward glance at the man who had betrayed her, Nama followed the Norse woman from the long hall, leaving the Nordstrom family and their multitude of friends behind.

The room where they were taken was similar to the one they had so recently left, but far less inviting. Like the main room, it was long and narrow with raised earthen side-floors.

Hilda pointed to the raised portion. "You will sleep there," she said gruffly. "Blankets are kept in the chests." Hilda eyed them sternly. "You will both do well here if you tend to your work and keep your mouths shut. Now, come along with me and I will show you the kitchen."

"Is she angry with us?" Walks With Thunder asked, speaking the only language she could converse in comfortably—the tongue of the People.

Nama shrugged her shoulders. How could she know what the other woman was feeling when she did not say? She could not offer words of comfort to Walks With Thunder, not when she was feeling such bitter, cold despair herself, not when her miserable heart was crying out for solace, aching for a man who would only cause her torment.

That knowledge twisted and turned inside her, causing a suffocating tightness in her throat. She was a woman facing the harsh realities of loneliness, and she cursed the day she had ever met Garrick Nordstrom.

Twenty

There was silence in the long hall as Garrick told his parents all he knew of their eldest son's death. His expression softened as he stroked his mother's hand. "According to Nama, Eric did not suffer unduly, Mother, and it should give you comfort to know he was not alone during the last days he spent on this earth. The pain he suffered must have been greatly eased by her presence."

"Yes. It would seem so," she replied softly. "And for that the woman must be commended. We owe her a great debt for what she has done." Her expression became puzzled as she studied him, and Garrick had the feeling she could see his innermost thoughts. "Do you not agree, Garrick?"

"Yes, Mother," he replied. "I am in complete agreement. We do owe her."

"Why then has she been given over to servitude?" she asked sharply.

Trapped beneath her censuring eyes, Garrick felt like a child caught in a mischievous prank. Anger at himself for feeling that way was responsible for the flush that warmed his cheeks. That knowledge alone made his voice cold when he spoke to his mother. "The woman is mine, Mother! I saved her life many times over."

"And that makes it yours? She receives poor payment for services rendered," Gilda Nordstrom snapped. "She should have better than the servants' quarters."

"Garrick has no need to explain himself, woman!" Fergus growled.

"My father is right," Garrick said. "I need not explain; but if I do not, then your conscience will be sure to trouble you."

"And yours will not?"

"No, it was never my intention to leave Nama in the servants' quarters. Only a means of teaching her the wisdom of conforming to our ways."

"I see." Gilda considered his words. "Then she is being punished for some misdeed?"

"Not punished exactly."

"Then what?"

"He has answered your question sufficiently, woman!" the jarl roared. "Now leave your son be. The wench is of no interest to me. She belongs to Garrick and he may do as he pleases with her." Although his voice was harsh, his wife remained fearless in the face of his wrath.

Ignoring her, the jarl focused his attention on Garrick. "I would hear more of this new land. What did you find there? What treasures abound in the land that Lief Ericson spoke so highly of?"

"The land itself is a treasure," Garrick replied, focusing his attention on the jarl, eager to escape his mother's questions.

"How so?"

"It is a land of sunshine with plenty of rain. The land abounds with forests and green meadows, and we found grapes growing without aid from human hands."

"Grapes? Growing wild?"

"Yes," Garrick said with a smile. "They grow in such abundance that a man could quickly gather enough to make wine for his entire household . . . indeed, for all who occupy his lands." Garrick had known that would get his father's attention, for everyone knew the jarl's liking for wine. "And there were creatures there the like of which I have never before encountered in all my travels."

"Grass-eaters?"

"Yes. Many of them. They would be a good source of meat. A never-ending supply." Garrick went on to describe the animals he had seen in the new world: The buffalo, the beaver, the antelope, the elk, the cougar, the prairie dog, and the moose.

Realizing he held his audience enthralled, Garrick described the great horned owl with its feathery "horns," told them of the colorful turkeys and of the soaring bald eagle with its magnificent white head-plumage and neck-ruff, that had such an enormous wingspan while in flight. He told of squirrels and rabbits and other animals too numerous to name and of the fishes that occupied the rivers and lakes in that faraway land.

"And gold?" the jarl asked eagerly. "Did you find gold?"

"We had no time to look," Garrick explained. "But there is a blue stone there the *skraelings* seem to prize highly." Garrick pulled Nama's bracelet from his pouch and held it toward his father.

The jarl took the bracelet and examined it thoroughly. "Very pretty," he commented. "How did you come by this?"

"It belongs to Nama."

"Ummm." The old jarl's eyes glinted, and his lips curled slightly. "What of their weapons, Garrick."

"Crude. Constructed of wood and stone."

"Axes?"

"A similar weapon. But it is crafted from stone."

"Bows and arrows?"

"Yes. And they are skilled marksmen."

"Even so, they would have no chance against Viking warriors."

"That is so," Garrick replied. "No chance at all." He wondered why he suddenly felt as though he had betrayed a friend. He owed no loyalty to the natives of that faraway land. None whatsoever.

"Several Viking ships could sail up that muddy river and, with veritable ease, conquer whole tribes. There would be none strong enough to stop them," Garrick stated.

A vision rose in his mind of painted warriors falling beneath his blade, but imposed over that was a vision of Nama, her expression one of horror as she watched him slay her people.

"Must you speak of plunder, Fergus? Now? When our sons have only just arrived?" Gilda

Nordstrom asked plaintively. "I have heard nothing from my youngest son yet." She looked toward Olaf, who was deep in conversation with a woman.

"Do not interfere with what does not concern you, woman," Fergus snapped.

"How can you say it does not concern me when I have already lost one son to that faraway land?"

Garrick was, as always, disturbed by his parents' argument. "There will be time enough later to make plans regarding the new land," he said. "At the moment I am too weary to contemplate such an event. I only wish to retire to my longhouse."

He was on the verge of telling his mother to send Nama to his chambers when he remembered Carlotta would be waiting for him. By Odin, the woman was presumptuous. He might have preferred the company of the German beauty Karin or the more exotic Lupe, whom he had brought from a distant island. Or Helga, his Finnish concubine, might have been the object of his desire. How could Carlotta know what he himself had not yet determined.

Had not determined? Even as the thought surfaced, he knew it was not so. He had made his decision. He wanted Nama. But first, there was Carlotta to be dealt with. And it would not hurt Nama to wait awhile. Perhaps the waiting would even do her good, would make her eager for his attention.

"Ale!" the jarl shouted. "Bring us ale. My sons are home again, and there is need of celebration!"

A tankard of ale was shoved into Garrick's hand, and he raised it high as his father proposed a toast.

"To my sons, Garrick and Olaf," he shouted. "And to the new land that we will soon conquer."

"To Garrick!" The men shouted as they raised their tankards of ale. "To Olaf! To the new lands!"

Gilda Nordstrom stepped down from the raised seat; and, as though a signal had been given, several richly dressed women left their places and followed her from the room, for when the men were bent on celebration, it was time for the ladies to retire.

Nama spent a restless night, waking early the next morning with a pounding headache. Having no wish to draw attention to herself, she tried to ignore the pain, hoping it would ease after she had assuaged her hunger.

"Which one of you is called Nama?" asked the young woman nearest them as she braided her blond hair.

"That is my name," Nama replied.

"And your companion is Walks With Thunder?"

"Yes."

"Will you be working in the kitchens?"

"Yes," Nama said again.

"I work there, too. My name is Mary." She looked curiously at Nama, then her eyes moved to Walks With Thunder. "They say you are *skraelings*. Is that true? Are you savages?"

"No more than the men who captured us," Nama said shortly.

"Garrick and Olaf?" Mary's look was curious.

"Yes," she answered, even though she knew she should not have included Olaf, for he had been nothing but kind to her since the day they'd met.

"They say Eric taught you to speak our language."

"Yes. You have been correctly informed."

Mary smiled at her. "I was one of Eric's concubines," she said softly.

"And now you are a slave? Did Eric do this to you?"

"No," Mary said grimly. "Someone else is responsible for my change of status in this household."

Before Nama could ask the meaning of her words, Hilda appeared in the doorway. "Hurry along now, girls. Cook will be furious if you are late."

The six other girls who occupied the sleeping chamber hurried toward the door, and Nama followed Mary while Walks With Thunder trailed along behind them.

The kitchen was even larger than it had appeared to Nama the night before. Perhaps it only seemed that way, though, she thought, her gaze taking in the workers bustling around the room, each occupied with her own particular task.

She wondered how long they had been there, guessed it had been awhile because the air was permeated by the smell of savory stew bubbling in the iron cauldron hanging above the central hearth.

Following Mary's lead, Nama took a bowl and spoon from a long table and motioned to Walks With Thunder to do the same. After their bowls were filled with stew, the two women seated themselves on the long bench and filled their stomachs.

The food did not ease her headache as Nama had hoped and, by midmorning, the pain in her temples had left her pale and drawn. She was feeling light-headed when Hilda told her she must go to the dungeons.

"Dungeons?" she questioned, staring at the woman who had shoved a tankard of ale into her trembling hands. "What is a dungeon? And where will I find it?"

The woman's faded blue eyes regarded Nama with surprise. "You have never seen a dungeon?" Her lips twisted in a grimace. "Then it is time you did so, since you must know what Cook is threatening you with when you do not obey her quickly enough." She turned to a golden-haired lad who was busy washing pots. "Gunther. Show Nama the way to the dungeons."

"Come along then," Gunther said cheerfully, obviously glad to be relieved of his duties even if it were only for a short while.

Gunther was only a youth, standing no more than an inch taller than Nama. Feeling unthreatened by him, she followed the lad from the hot kitchen into the great room where she had been brought before the jarl the day before. Although there were several people sleeping on the cushioned side-floors, there were none she recognized.

She wondered fleetingly where Garrick had slept, then forced thoughts of him from her mind. He had made her position clear, and she would not waste energy crying over him when that same energy could be put to better use.

Gunther opened a door set into a far wall. It led to a long, narrow passage that ended with another door. Nama's heart beat fast with trepidation as the lad pushed open the heavy wooden door wide enough to allow them through.

Nama stared down the narrow stone steps that were barely visible in the dim light cast by a single thick candle set high on one wall.

A scurrying sound somewhere nearby sent alarm streaking through her. "What was that?" she whispered.

"Only rats," he said in a matter-of-fact voice.

"Rats!" She could hear the tremble in her voice. Then, as a furry body brushed her unclad foot, she uttered a terrified shriek.

"Who goes there?" shouted a harsh, male voice from below. "Identify yourself!"

"Just me—Gunther," called the lad.

"Oh," came the reply. "The German lad. What are you about up there?"

"Hilda sent me to show one of the new girls the dungeons. We brought a tankard of ale."

The guard, a heavy-set, gray-haired individual, stepped into the light where he could be seen.

"Give me the ale and show her around. Just stay away from the first two doors. The men behind them have been kept away from skirts so long they might kick the doors down to get at her."

Nama felt a quiver of fear. What kind of men had the strength to do such a thing? She shoved the tankard of ale at the guard, who pinned her with his sharp gaze. "New here, are you? Scared, too! No need to be. Just do what they tell you and you should be fine." He raised the tankard to his lips and poured ale down his throat. Then, with a lusty belch, he turned to her again. "You go ahead and look at the prisoners if you want. Just keep clear of the door."

Fear for her surroundings silenced her tongue for a moment, but it was that same fear that caused her to force words beyond the lump in her throat. "I have s-seen enough," she whispered. "Can we n-not l-leave here now?"

A squeaking sound and the knowledge that the place was infested with rats sent her gaze searching for the creatures. Her gaze skittered here and there, up and down, until a movement near a small, barred window set about five feet above the dungeon floor caught her attention and she focused on it. Although the room beyond the bars was shadowy at best, she could see a face pressed close against the window, could even see the blazing eyes that fastened on her.

Despite the guard's admonishment to stay away from the door, she found herself stepping closer to it, her limbs seeming to move of their own accord.

"Who you got in there?" Gunther asked the guard.

"Patrick Douglass," the guard replied. "He earned a month's stay this time. And more even unless he repents and asks for favor from the jarl."

"Aye," Douglass said, his voice hoarse and scratchy as though he were ill. "I am here for a while, lad, for it is not my way to beg pardon for saying what I think."

"No," the guard agreed, with something like admiration in his voice. "It is not your way." He tilted the tankard of ale again and emptied it down his throat. "Too bad," he said, staring morosely into the empty vessel. "There was little enough of it." He handed the tankard to Nama. "Tell Cook it was not even enough to warm my bones. Have her send more next time."

"We can but try," Gunther said. "Little good it may do. Come on, Nama." Her name rolled easily off his tongue. "If we delay too long, we may find ourselves occupying one of those cells."

Nama needed no further urging. She followed him out of the dungeon and hurried up the steps, eager to be away from the dark, damp place. But the memory of Patrick Douglass' pale face stayed with her. "Why did they lock him away?" she asked.

"Because he has too much pride for a slave," was the reply. "He never learned to do what he was told without answering back."

So slaves were not supposed to have feelings, Nama thought resentfully as she followed the boy

back to the kitchen. Until now she had had no real
knowledge of slaves except what she had heard
from the traders. She had barely escaped from the
Desert Clan, who would have enslaved her just as
surely as these Vikings had done.

Although Gunther delivered the guard's mes-
sage, asking for more ale, the cook only laughed,
giving the request no consideration at all.

Resuming her work at the long table, Nama tried
to put thoughts of the dungeon and Patrick
Douglass out of her mind as she peeled vegetables.
But he would not be so easily dismissed. She was
still lost in thought when she became aware of eyes
on her.

She looked up and saw Garrick.

Nama had no idea how long he had been standing there and, furthermore, she did not care. She
had nothing to say to the man who was responsible
for sending her to this place of insufferable
heat . . . this place the Vikings called *kitchen*,
where the harsh voice of Cook could be heard
above all else, constantly issuing orders and promising punishment to those hapless beings that did
not hurry with their tasks.

Nama herself had not yet been pinned with
those piercing eyes, nor had she been struck by
the big wooden spoon that landed often enough
on others; but she felt certain that was only because
Cook worked on the other side of the large room
and had not yet noticed her awkwardness in com-
pleting her tasks.

Nama's lips tightened in a thin line, and she

cursed the day she had met Garrick. He was the cause of her discomfort. It was his fault that she was here in this awful place.

Crossing the large room toward her, he brushed past all the other occupants as though they did not exist. When he stopped beside her, his large body blotted out the rest of the room.

"What do you think of my home, Nama?" he asked, his brilliant green eyes holding hers.

"The kitchen is hot," she snapped. "Have you never noticed?"

"No. I never come here much."

"No. You would not."

"And the rest of my home?" he asked. "What do you think of it?"

"The dungeon is damp and cold."

"It was designed to be that way." He frowned down at her, obviously disconcerted by her answers. "What were you doing in the dungeon?"

"I was sent there with ale for the guard."

"I see." His expression became wary. "What do you think of the rest of my home?"

"I have seen nothing except the kitchen and the dungeon; therefore, I have no opinion."

"You could see more if you wished," he said softly, cupping her jaw in one rough palm and tilting her face upward so she would have to look at him. "Why do you continue to resist me?"

"Release me!" she hissed. "The others are watching us."

"I care nothing about them," he replied. "Just say the word and you need never work here again."

"Not as long as you find favor with me," she said. "But when that time is past, what happens then, Garrick? Will you send me back to these same kitchens or will you give me to your men in payment for their services?"

"What are you talking about?" he asked angrily. "Who put such ideas into your head?"

"Then that is not your usual practice?"

"Of course not!" he roared.

Nama was aware of a hush in the kitchen and knew everyone was listening to them; and yet, she could not still her tongue. "Did you not give Thorvauld two of your concubines before you sailed?" she pressed.

"Someone has been filling your head with nonsense, woman," he blustered. "Tell me who it was."

"Nonsense?" she asked coldly, her eyes blazing defiance at him. "Then you did not give Thorvauld the women?"

"I will not stand here and be questioned in such a manner," he snarled, gripping her upper shoulders tightly as though he intended to shake her hard. "By Odin, woman, you will cease these questions."

"Very well," she said. "I will ask no more."

His gaze swept over her, taking in every detail of her appearance. "That brown woolen shift you wear is drab," he said, his voice still harsh. "It does nothing for your tanned skin."

"The other workers are dressed in the same manner."

"Yes. But—" He broke off, leaving the words unsaid. Instead, he gazed at her for a long, thoughtful moment. "How long will you hold onto your anger, Nama?"

"How long will you keep me here, my lord?" The words were said mockingly.

"Someone has already begun your training," he said, commenting on the way she had addressed him.

"The kitchen master is an eager teacher."

"Indeed." Garrick's fingers tightened on her flesh as he narrowed his gaze on the man who, next to the cook, ruled the kitchen. Then he looked at her again, seeming to search her soul. "Do you wish to be relieved of your duties here?"

"What other duties would replace these?"

"They would be of a more personal nature."

Realizing he was still angry with her and could not be speaking of his own personal needs, Nama felt she knew the path his thoughts traveled. She had already learned of the women kept to service the warriors, and her face paled at the thought she might soon join their ranks. "Do I have a choice?" she asked huskily.

He stiffened, and his hands dropped to his sides. "Of course. You may remain here if that is your wish."

"Then please allow me to do so, my lord." The title was tacked on in her hope to appease him.

"Very well. At least for the moment. We will speak again when I return."

Return? Apprehension streaked through her. Where was he going? And for how long?

Her mouth opened to give voice to the questions, then quickly snapped shut again as she realized the way her words would surely be received.

Garrick remained beside her for a long, silent moment. Then, apparently deciding she had no more to say on the subject, he spun on his heels and left her standing in the middle of the kitchen, wishing she had given in and begged him to take her out of here. Yet another part of her was glad that she had stood her ground and refused him that satisfaction.

Twenty-one

Garrick's troubled thoughts were the source of his restlessness as he joined the other men readying for a hunt. Since he was unwilling for his companions to know his mental state, he forced a jovial camaraderie and feigned an eagerness to begin the hunt.

Olaf was the only man among them who suspected his brother's eagerness was false, and he voiced his thoughts when they found themselves alone for a brief time.

"You seem troubled, Brother. Do you worry about leaving the woman from the Eagle Clan behind?"

"Of course not," Garrick said shortly. "She is of no import."

"Then why do you continue to punish her?"

"I am not punishing her."

"Why send her to the kitchens then?"

Garrick's brows drew into a deep scowl. "The reason does not matter." He glared fiercely at Olaf. "And you need not pity her. She likes the kitchens."

"Nonsense! No one in their right mind likes the

kitchens. It is a hot, dreary place filled with people whose sweat makes their clothes cling to their bodies. Why would anyone want to spend time in such a place?"

"You forget she was bred in a hot, arid land," Garrick reminded. "Did our bodies not drip with sweat when we crossed the vast desert land very close to where we found her? She was grown in such an environment and chooses to remain there."

"Nonsense," Olaf said again.

"Be silent," Garrick snarled, remembering the way she had looked at him the last time he had seen her—as though he were something that had crawled from beneath a rock. What had he done to deserve such treatment? he asked himself.

Nothing! he replied mentally. The wench had probably never before heard of such a thing as gratitude.

"Leave me be," he said in a cold voice. "Speak no more of the woman if it is your wish for us to remain friends as well as brothers." He turned away from Olaf, shutting away the expression on the other man's face, wishing he could shut away the memory of the woman from the Eagle Clan as easily.

But he could not do so. Try as he would, he could not forget the way she had looked when he had first seen her, swimming naked beneath the moonlight, her copper-colored breasts floating just above the surface of the water. Just the thought tightened his groin and stirred his manhood.

Why could his mind not control that member? he wondered. And why did his heart ache as though squeezed in a giant fist just because she looked at him with such loathing?

It was not lust that drove him. Had it been, he would have slaked his desire on Carlotta last night instead of sending her from his bedchamber.

No. It was definitely not lust that drove him. Any one of his concubines would have been eager to offer herself to him. Instead, he yearned for a woman who refused him.

By Odin's blood, he would not allow her to treat him so callously! The moment he returned from his hunt, he would send for her. He would demand an explanation, would, if necessary, even reveal his feelings for her.

Even as that thought occurred, Garrick rejected it. How could he reveal his feelings when the wench obviously cared nothing for him? He knew her feelings all too well. She had made them clear in the kitchen while a crowd of people watched his humiliation.

Remembering the silence that had filled the kitchen as he shouted at her, Garrick seethed with anger. He should not have allowed her to argue. He should have demanded she be punished. The kitchen master would have taken over and lashed her back to shreds had Garrick only given the word. But he could not. Just the thought of her tender flesh cut and bleeding was more than he could bear.

Dammit! Did the woman not know he was

sought after by many women? Was he not the best warrior, the best hunter, and was he not endowed with great wealth?

Yes. A thousand times yes! And, if he knew kitchen gossip, by the time he returned, she would be well aware of that fact. Well aware, too, that he could have any maiden he chose. That alone should make her aware of the honor bestowed upon her.

Becoming aware that, in his introspection, he had kept himself apart from the others too long, he called out, his voice booming through the large room. "Will the lot of you hurry? Think you the beasts will all be waiting patiently for the kill?"

The jovial teasing spun Olaf around; and when he saw his brother's expression, his shoulders lifted and a smile spread across his face. "I wager there will be more pelts on my belt when we return than on yours, Garrick."

"What do you wager, little brother?"

"Two spring calves," Olaf said promptly, pushing wide the big door.

"Done," Garrick shouted, flinging his arm around his brother's shoulder and striding forward eagerly. "And you can add two more of those calves if my hides total twice your own."

"You agree to take my calves, but you have not said what will be my prize should you lose the wager," Olaf complained.

"That is because you will be the one to lose."

"Nevertheless," Olaf said dryly. "I would know what you do not intend me to win."

Garrick's smile spread even wider. "Look at this one." He included the other men in the circle in the joke. "Would you just look at my little brother? He expects to have more hides than I possess when we return from the hunt."

Karl joined in the teasing. "It would be a kindness to allow him to win this once, Garrick."

"No, no, I cannot," Garrick said, waving a casual hand dismissingly. "After all, I have my reputation to think of. It must be maintained at all costs."

"Nevertheless," Karl said, "he should know what you put up on the wager. Every man should know what he almost won in a contest."

Olaf's face was flushed from all the teasing, but Garrick took no notice of it. After all, he reasoned, Olaf was used to teasing. It had long been his lot in life, due to the fact that he was the younger brother and would rather tend a sheep than hunt one.

"Very well," Garrick agreed. "I will agree to whatever he thinks the prize should be."

Something flickered in Olaf's eyes, making Garrick feel he would not like what he was going to say.

He was right.

"Two spring calves to Garrick should he win." Olaf met his brother's look with a long one of his own. "And, two more if his skins total twice mine."

"And what price do you claim should you win?" Karl asked.

The answer came quickly. "Two nights alone with the *skraeling* wench should my brother lose the wager."

"You may have all the nights with her you desire," Garrick said shortly. "The *skraeling* wench belongs to you."

"I speak of Nama, woman of the Eagle Clan," Olaf said softly. "She will be my prize."

Garrick sucked in a sharp breath. "No."

"Is it possible you think you may not win this time?"

"Nama will not be put up for barter." Garrick's jaw was clenched, and he glared at the man who had suggested such a thing. "And, if you suggest anything of the kind again, little brother, you are likely to feel my fists against your flesh."

"Desist, Garrick," Olaf urged, reaching out and squeezing his older sibling's shoulder. "I spoke only in jest. I have no desire to bed your wench. My words were meant to reward you for your teasing."

Garrick, realizing Olaf spoke the truth by the clear look in his eyes, breathed deeply of the fresh air and forced himself to relax. But, even though Olaf had explained, the enjoyment Garrick had been feeling, the jolly camaraderie, had gone from him. His mind had turned again to the woman who occupied so much of his thoughts. The very thought of another man possessing her had angered him beyond reason. And he was angry at himself for feeling that way.

Although Nama found the work in the kitchen hard, she was strong and did not suffer unduly because of it. And, as the days passed, her willingness to lend a hand wherever it was needed fostered respect and most extended their hands in friendship. The girl Carlotta was the one exception.

Carlotta, with her dark hair and flashing eyes, seemed to hold a privileged position among the household. She did less work and more gossiping than any of the others and seemed less fearful of repercussions. Although Nama wondered why that was so, she spent little time considering the matter. Not until Carlotta turned her attention to the woman from the Eagle Clan.

That particular morning, the third one since their arrival in Norway, Nama had been working on her assigned tasks for several hours when Carlotta sauntered in.

Nama was bent over the long wooden table scraping peels off vegetables, lost in thoughts of days gone by, of her mother and life among the rocks when she was still a woman of the Eagle Clan.

Suddenly, Elspeth, the maid working beside Nama, clutched her forearm and spoke in a shrill, envious voice. "Coor, now, would you look at Carlotta! Ain't she grand? See how she's all decked out in feathers fine enough to wear to the queen's ball."

Although most of the words made no sense to Nama—for who, or what, was a queen?—the use of the words "fine" and "feathers" in regard to apparel brought memories of the turkey-feather blan-

ets her people were so adept at making and sent
wave of homesickness shivering through her as
well as a curiosity to see the garment spoken of
with such eagerness.

Nama looked at the girl who stopped beside her
o show off her new gown, her uppermost feeling
one of puzzlement. Carlotta did not wear feathers.
nstead she wore a gown colored the same shade
s the cardinals that flew among the branches of
he trees back home.

Carlotta was conspicuous in the extreme since
ll the other servants wore woolen shifts like the
one Nama wore. Most of them were garments that
ad been faded long ago to an indiscernible color
hat closely resembled mud.

The woman had paused beside Nama, and it was
obvious she waited for a comment on her finery.

"It is a very pretty garment," Nama said.

"*Very pretty* are not the words to describe such a
reation," Carlotta said, her lips curling into a sat-
sfied smile. "It is a *beautiful* gown." She eyed
Nama with something like triumph and tossed her
uxurious ebony hair. "And I will leave the giver
o remain a mystery to everyone," she purred in
thick, honeyed, Spanish accent.

After helping herself to fresh-baked honey-and-
poppyseed bread that had been left to cool on a
nearby tray, she spun on her heels and sauntered
cross the hot room, her trim bottom swaying with
provocative exaggeration as though she wished to
all attention to that part of her anatomy.

"Hummph!" the cook snorted. "Thinks she's

too good for the likes of us!" She wiped her brow
with a floury hand and slumped down on a nearby
stool. "Guess if I had half a chance I might do
the same as Carlotta. But the chance for things like
that is long past for me." She looked down at her
wide girth. "My cooking has seen to that."

"What does she mean?" Nama whispered to
Elspeth.

Elspeth tossed her a quick smile. "She means
she has lost her chance for exchanging pleasure
for an easy way of life."

"Exchanging pleasure?"

Elspeth's smile widened. "You really are an innocent. Carlotta is a concubine. The gown was
given in exchange for favors. It was Carlotta's payment for giving pleasure to her master. And that
is the reason she comes and goes as she pleases
while the rest of us must endure the heat of the
kitchen."

"But she does work here." The words were no
sooner uttered then Nama remembered the way
Carlotta would come into the kitchen and settle
herself down on a stool—something that was strictly
forbidden—peel a couple of vegetables while she
talked with the workers, and then suddenly, as
though becoming tired—or bored—with the task,
would leave the kitchen. "At least," she corrected,
"I thought she worked here."

"She only comes when her master is away and
does not need her services."

"So a concubine is really only a servant . . . like
us?" Nama asked.

"A glorified servant, but a servant nevertheless,"
replied Elspeth.

"A sex-slave," said Jasmine bitterly.

Nama threw a curious look at Jasmine. It was
obvious from her sallow, bruised face that the girl
had been ill-used.

Mary, conscious of Nama's look, gripped her
forearm and whispered, "She has been mistreated
by the warriors."

Sudden fear streaked through Nama, and she
quickly looked away from the girl. "Will she be
sent to them again?"

"More than likely," Mary said. "She displeased
her master, and he desires her no longer."

Nama tried to speak, but the words refused to
move around the knot in her throat. Garrick had
threatened her with such punishment, and she had
taunted him. Should she find him quickly and beg
his forgiveness? But how could she when she had
no idea where he was? Carlotta would know, but
Nama could not bring herself to ask the girl.

Just the thought of Garrick bedding the woman
made her angry enough to claw his eyes out.

He had avoided her since they chanced to meet
in the kitchens the morning after they had arrived,
and he had probably been looking for his lady love
then and been distracted from his search when he
saw Nama.

Rage boiled through her veins, sending her fear
into hiding. He was welcome to the bitch, Nama
thought viciously. She had no trouble applying that
word to Carlotta even though it was not in use

among her own people. The word had been be
yond her knowledge until she arrived in Norway
but she found it suitable for describing the dark
haired concubine. Nama only wished there was
one equal to it that she could apply to Garrick.

But she could not find one. Her language was
not designed for such usage, and she had not
learned enough of his to know a word that best
described the way she thought of him at that mo
ment.

Even as her mind boiled with rage, her heart
cried out in torment. Garrick! How could you do
this to me? You might just as well have clutched
my heart and torn it from my body!

Realizing that Elspeth wanted to speak more of
Carlotta and knowing she could not stand to hear
the details, Nama closed her mind to the conversation, as she had been taught to do in times of
trouble. She made her senses aware, instead, of
the flurry of movement around her as each person
hurried to complete their assigned tasks so they
might finish in time to enjoy what little sunshine
was available to them.

But Nama had no need to hurry with her tasks
for she had not yet been allowed to feel the sun
against her skin and she was beginning to wonder
if she ever would again.

That thought caused her intense pain. What reason did she have for continuing this stifled existence? she asked herself.

None, came the silent answer. And yet, did she
have the courage to end her life?

She thought not.

It seemed that, whatever the future held, she was bound to face it. Even though her cowardly heart screamed out a protest, she must continue this life and make of it whatever she could.

But, she told herself, she would not live her life as a slave, subject to a man's whims. As Garrick would soon discover. Somehow she would find a way out of the situation she was in. And she would make Garrick sorry they had ever met.

Twenty-two

Nama spent a restless night, tossing and turning on the unfamiliar bed, feeling almost suffocated by the stale air in the bedchamber. Her troubled night caused her to oversleep, a fact she was totally unaware of until Walks With Thunder returned to the bedchamber.

"Wake up, Nama!" cried the woman from the Desert Clan, shaking Nama urgently.

"Why?" Nama asked, blinking sleep-fogged eyes at the other woman. "Is something wrong?"

"How can I know when I cannot understand these people?" Walks With Thunder asked. "I only know they are excited about something!"

"Why does it concern you?" Nama asked, rubbing her weary eyes to clear them of sleep. Slowly, she became aware that the bedchamber was empty. "Did I oversleep? Is Cook angry with me?"

"Yes, you overslept. But Cook is still unaware of your absence. She is too excited to notice."

"Excited?"

"Yes. She speaks in a loud angry voice and strikes anyone who comes near with her big wooden spoon. Yet the anger is only a pretense."

"Pretense? How do you know that?"

"Because of the smile in her eyes."

"She has a smile?" Nama tried to imagine the gruff cook with a smile in her eyes but found it impossible.

"Yes. A smile. She is happy about something. I know because she even smiled at me. Me! Walks With Thunder, who always brings a frown to her face. And Cook is not the only one who smiles. Everyone in the kitchen is smiling."

Since coming to Norway, Nama and the woman from the Desert Clan had become as close as two women could possibly be. And, from their many conversations, Nama knew Walks With Thunder was not accustomed to smiling faces, especially smiles that were directed at her. Although she was a beautiful woman and many men had desired her, she had not been the recipient of their smiles, only their lust.

Walks With Thunder spoke little of her joining time with Gray Wolf, said only that he was a cruel man and she had been happy to find him dead. Perhaps, Nama reasoned, that was the reason the woman felt drawn to Olaf. He had shown nothing but tenderness to her since the first day they had met.

"You should have asked Mary or Elspeth what was happening," Nama scolded. "They would have told you."

"I know such a few words of their language," Walks With Thunder said. "And when I try to use the words I have learned, they laugh at me."

"Mary would not laugh."

"Mary was not in the kitchen. She is working in another part of the house. Come." She tugged at Nama's arm impatiently. "You waste time with questions. I must know if the excitement is caused by the returning hunters."

Throwing back the covers, Nama scrambled off the bed and snatched up her shift. Perhaps the men *were* returning from the hunt. That would certainly be a source of excitement in the kitchen for, if the hunt were successful, there would be food to prepare and ale to be fetched from the cellar.

Happiness flowed through Nama at the thought of seeing Garrick again. Perhaps there would be time to bathe and wash her hair before he saw her. Probably not—there would be so much to do that she had little hope of stealing a few moments for herself. If only there were more hands to do the chores. Perhaps Carlotta would lend a hand and—

Nama paused in the act of shoving her hands through the armholes of her shift. She had entirely forgotten about Garrick's relationship with Carlotta. If the hunters were returning, the woman would most certainly not be coming to the kitchen to offer any help. Instead, she would be waiting for Garrick in his bedchamber.

"Hurry!" Walks With Thunder urged. "Why are you taking so long to dress?"

Seething with anger at the thought of Carlotta in Garrick's bed, Nama shoved her arms into the shift and yanked it down over her body. Her lips were tight as she washed herself and combed her hair. But even a fire dies when it is no longer fueled, as did her anger. It began to subside as surely as grains of sand upon a beach, slowly carried away by the ebbing tide until there was nothing left but a growing excitement at the thought of seeing Garrick again.

When the two women reached the kitchen, Nama realized Walks With Thunder had not been imagining things. Something unusual *was* happening. There was an unmistakable air of excitement among the servants, and yes! Cook *did* have a smile in her eyes when she turned to chastise Nama for being late.

"You would pick this morning to sleep late, you lazy girl!" she cried, waving the large wooden spoon in a threatening manner. "There is so much to do and not enough hands to do it. Well, never mind. You have finally come to help. And that help will be much appreciated. You have certainly proved yourself willing enough to do your share in the past."

Nama's eyes widened as she stared at the woman. Had she really uttered those words of praise?

"Be off with you now," Cook snapped. "Gunther has been sent to help the hunters carry the meat. You will have to do his chores. Fetch the milk and be quick about it. There is baking to be done." She pressed her hands against the side of her head, leaving splotches of flour there, and cried. "So much to do and so little time."

Nama was still unsure what was happening and,

although Walks With Thunder had resumed scrubbing vegetables at the long table, she waited anxiously for Nama to discover the source of the excitement.

"What is happening?" Nama asked Elspeth.

"Have you not heard?" Elspeth asked in surprise. "The Lady Brynna, who has been visiting in Novgorod, returned last night. And Thorvauld brought news of the hunting party. It was a huge success. The hunters are bringing so much meat home they require additional help to carry it." Her eyes shone with excitement. "There will be a double celebration tonight. One to welcome Lady Brynna home and the other to honor the hunters. And, best of all, the servants will celebrate, too. I can hardly wait until tonight!"

"The servants will celebrate?" Nama wondered how that was possible. "Who will wait on the tables and carry food and ale to the big hall?" she asked.

"We will take turns," Elspeth replied, throwing a quick look over Nama's shoulder. "Shhhh! Cook is watching us. You must hasten to do her bidding."

A hurried glance told Nama that Cook was headed her way. Nama quickly fled from the room, making her way down the long corridor until she reached the great hall. Moments later she pushed the front door open and stepped outside.

Although the air was cool, the sunshine was warm against her bare arms and Nama breathed deeply of the fresh air, feeling grateful to Cook

for being allowed to do so for the first time since
her arrival.

Realizing she must show her gratitude by com-
pleting the chore as quickly as possible, Nama hurried down the wide steps, then skidded to a sudden
stop. She had only just realized that although she
had been told to fetch the milk, Cook had failed
to tell her where to go.

What should she do? Nama wondered frantically,
unwilling to return and ask directions of the
woman, fearing that she would never again be sent
on such a chore. Gunther had told her the milk
came from the barn. But where was the barn?

There were many buildings, some of them resembling the longhouse that was home to the
Nordstrom family. Nama guessed they housed the
families of the Norsemen who seemed to be always
about.

But where was the barn?

Could it be one of the smaller buildings beyond
the longhouses? Deciding it must be, she set off
at a brisk pace toward them. She had only gone a
short distance when she heard someone call her
name.

"Nama! Stop a moment."

Recognizing Sven's voice, Nama turned quickly
to greet him. "Sven! How good to see you!"

His smile was quick. "And I am glad to see you,
Nama. Where have you been keeping yourself? I
have watched for you constantly but never had occasion to see you before today."

She grimaced wryly. "My chores have kept me

in the kitchens. This is the first time I have been allowed outside. And if I do not hurry, it will probably be the last," she added grimly. "Please tell me where the barn is. I must fetch the milk for Cook."

"I will do better than that," he said, gripping her forearm. "I will take you there."

"I am grateful, Sven. I thought you would have gone with the others."

"I would have except for my foot," Sven said.

"Something is wrong with your foot?" she asked with concern, noticing for the first time that he was limping.

"My clumsiness caused it," he admitted with a flush. "I stumbled and pierced the flesh with my sword. The wound is not bad," he hurried to explain when she expressed concern. "But it was decided I should allow it time to heal instead of going on the hunt."

"Perhaps you should just show me the barn instead of accompanying me there."

"Would you deprive me of even that small pleasure?" he asked plaintively.

She laughed up at him. "It is a pleasure to walk with me?"

"Yes," he said gruffly, his eyes admiring her. "It *is* a pleasure, Nama."

Feeling as though she were being observed, Nama looked away from Sven and found a group of women watching them. The women, who numbered three, were speaking together in low tones while focusing their attention on Nama and Sven.

"Who are those women?" Nama asked curiously.

"They are Garrick's concubines," he replied, following the direction of her gaze. "Have you not had occasion to meet them?"

"No. Only Carlotta."

"Would you like to make their acquaintance?"

"No," she said abruptly. "There is no time. I must hurry and take the milk to Cook before she becomes angry with me."

"Very well. But you must allow me to introduce you when you have more time."

Seeing the women had taken the lilt out of her step and cast gloom over an otherwise happy occasion. Nama told herself it was only because she felt so ugly beside them with her shapeless brown shift and bare feet while they were dressed in silk gowns and slippers. But in her heart she knew that was not the only reason.

They were Garrick's concubines . . . his women. And they, like Carlotta, were allowed to share his bed while Nama occupied the servants' quarters.

When she returned to the kitchen, she laughed and joked with the other women, hoping to keep her depression from them, but Walks With Thunder seemed to sense her innermost thoughts and spoke to her when she had the chance.

"You think of Garrick, do you not? What worries you, Nama? Is it Carlotta? You need not worry about that woman. She poses no threat to your position."

"What position is that?" Nama asked shortly. "One of scullery maid?" She used the language of the Norsemen as well as their own tongue, since the language of the People did not contain the word *scullery*. "It is not a position to be desired among the Vikings. Carlotta would be the last to covet my position here."

"It is not your position in the kitchen I speak of, but your position with Garrick."

"The less said about him the better," Nama said, wishing she could make her voice sound more certain, wishing her heart did not feel like a shriveled-up knot in her chest.

"Do not take this attitude, Nama," the woman said softly. "If you would allow Garrick to know your innermost feelings, you would surely be rewarded."

"With a new dress? Like Carlotta!" Nama slammed the vegetable she was peeling down on the big table and felt a blush staining her cheeks as several heads turned in her direction.

"Careful," Walks With Thunder urged. "Do you wish others to guess your feelings?"

"No," Nama said in a small voice. "I have no wish for them to know." She looked at the woman from the Desert Clan. "I must thank you, Walks With Thunder, for your concern. Although our people are enemies, you have been a good friend to me. I hope you know that friendship is returned."

Walks With Thunder nodded her dark head. "I know. But it makes me happy to be told."

Realizing they had become the target for many eyes, including Cook's, the two girls fell silent and attended to their work.

Nama chided herself for being a foolish girl with foolish dreams that had no chance of coming true. She would fare better if she forgot the flame-haired Viking who was responsible for bringing her here. She must realize that he was beyond her reach.

And so her thoughts went, one moment chiding her for being foolish, the next calling Garrick every vile name she could think of. She was taking her anger out on the pots she washed—another of Gunther's chores that had been assigned to her—when someone spoke her name.

Looking up inquiringly, she recognized the woman who had addressed her as Gilda Nordstrom's personal maid.

"You are to go to my lady," the woman said.

"Garrick's mother?"

"Lady Gilda Nordstrom," the woman corrected firmly. "And, Nama, you will address her as *My Lady*."

What could the lady of the house want with her? Nama wondered. Had she done something wrong? Something so bad that Cook sent her to the other woman rather than deal out the punishment herself?

"Hurry and wash yourself before you go," the maid commanded. "And straighten your clothing." She eyed Nama's shift as though she found it offensive. "Do you have nothing else to wear?"

"No," Nama replied in a small voice, wondering why she needed other clothing if she were to be chastised. Sudden fear swept through her as another thought occurred. Perhaps her punishment would be dealt with the lash and they did not want her blood staining the shift she wore.

Nama was trembling with fear and wondering what she had done to warrant punishment when she entered the large room where Gilda Nordstrom worked at a loom.

"You sent for me?" Nama inquired, bobbing her knees the way she had been taught.

"Yes, dear," the woman said in a kindly voice as she dipped her regal head in a nod. "Come closer. My daughter Brynna wishes to make your acquaintance."

Nama looked at the only other occupant of the room, a girl with flaming red hair worn loose about her shoulders.

"I am pleased to meet you," Brynna said, rising to her feet and holding out a hand.

Nama, unsure of what was expected of her, settled on a quick curtsy. The action brought a smile to the girl's lips and her hand fell to her side. "There is no need for formality," she murmured, resuming her seat.

Nama continued to stand politely, relief flowing through her that she was not to be punished for some misdeed and wondering why Brynna had expressed a desire to meet her.

"Brynna and I usually spend this time together with our weaving," Gilda Nordstrom said, "but somehow, this morning . . . well, my thoughts keep turning to—"

Brynna quickly interrupted her parent. "Mother

is trying to tell you that we have been passing the morning by wondering about my brother Eric and his last . . . days." The last word was spoken with a tremble. "I understand those days were spent with you, Nama, and wondered if you would mind talking about him."

So that was it, Nama thought. They had no intention of punishing her for some misdeed. They only wanted to know more about Eric . . . and his supposed death. Meeting Brynna's brilliant blue eyes, Nama recognized the pain the girl was feeling and wished she could tell the girl the truth. But she could not. If they knew Eric lived, they would surely punish her for misleading them.

No. She must continue on the path she had already taken. They thought Eric was dead, and they must continue to believe that.

"What do you wish to know?" Nama asked, keeping her gaze lowered.

Before Brynna could answer, Lady Gilda spoke up. "Everything. And, Nama, your pretense of servility does not fool me. Your spirit has not yet been broken." Nama's eyes widened with surprise. How had the woman known? Gilda Nordstrom smiled at her. "I know what you are feeling. I was brought here against my will, too. And, try as he will, Fergus has yet to break my spirit. Now, sit down my dear and begin your tale." She pointed to a nearby couch that was covered with the soft material they called *velvet*. "Sit over there, dear. You should find it comfortable enough."

"Oh no!" Nama said quickly. "I have been forbidden to sit in your presence."

"Oh, I know," the woman replied, waving a careless hand as though the order were of no consequence. "In normal circumstances that is how it should be. At least while there are others present. But I gather your story will not be short, and you would soon tire if you were kept standing there. No. I insist. You must be seated."

"Go on, Nama," Brynna laughed. "Mother is used to getting her way."

Reluctantly, Nama seated herself on the soft velvet material, feeling as though, at any moment, Hilda would come storming into the room and demand that she be punished for doing so.

"Now, begin," Brynna demanded. "When did you meet Eric?"

"He came to us during the long cold," Nama began, forming the words slowly so none would be misunderstood. "It was late, and Father Sun was seeking his rest for the night when—"

"Father Sun?" Brynna inquired. "You speak as though you believe the sun is a living entity."

"Shush, Brynna," Gilda Nordstrom admonished. "Allow the child to continue."

"I apologize," Brynna said. "But you must speak to me another time about your people and their ways."

"Yes, yes, Brynna. Another time," Gilda said impatiently. "Proceed, my dear."

And so Nama did, repeating the story she had already told Garrick; but this time her memory was

orely taxed, for these women were interested in
details. How long did Eric lie abed with his injuries? How was his appetite? What were his thoughts
about her people? Did he ever speak of his home?
Of his family?

Nama answered the questions to the best of her
ability, yet always reversing her role with Shala's.
And finally the questions ended and the women
fell silent, each lost in their own thoughts about
Eric.

Finally, Nama cleared her throat to break the
silence. "Will there be anything else, My Lady?"
she questioned.

"Yes," Brynna spoke up before her mother
could answer. "You have told me about my
brother, Nama. Now please tell us something
about yourself."

"M-myself?" Nama stuttered, her eyes flashing
quickly to the other girl. Why had Brynna made
such a request?

Twenty-three

"Yes," Brynna said firmly. "I wish to know more about you. You have already told us your home was a cave. Do all of the people in your land occupy caves?"

"Oh, no." Nama hastened to explain. "Only me. I was an outcast, made that way because—" She broke off and dropped her eyes, realizing she should feel shame, as Shala had, for being cast out of her clan. But she did not feel shame. Could not. In fact, when faced with almost the same situation, Nama had fled the clan.

No! She could not feel shame. Would not even make a pretense of doing so.

"Why, Nama?" Brynna asked. "Why were you made an outcast?"

"Yes, my dear," urged Lady Gilda. "Please continue."

Nama needed no further urging, for it was obvious these women were interested. Her eyes flashed indignantly when she said, "The clan shaman cast me out for refusing to join with him."

"Oh, dear," said Gilda. "And you had to live in a cave to survive?" Nama nodded her head. "Was there no one who could help you? What about your family? Your mother?"

"My mother could not help. She was bound by clan law."

"Women are usually bound by some law or another," Lady Gilda said shortly.

"Laws created by men," Brynna muttered. "Continue, please. You were cast out by your clan . . ."

"Yes. The Eagle Clan."

"Is there a reason behind the name?" Brynna asked.

A reason? Nama thought for a long moment, then said, "We have always been called Eagle Clan. We were given that name by Mockingbird when we first came to the fourth world."

"A bird gave your people your name?" Brynna laughed gaily. "How quaint."

"Brynna!" Lady Gilda said sharply. "Cease your teasing. Never make fun of anyone's religion."

"Religion?" Brynna looked surprised. "I am sorry, Nama. I had no idea you were speaking of your religion. Please tell us more."

Nama swallowed hard around the lump in her throat, telling herself it was foolish to be hurt by Brynna's laughter. "Cook will be wanting me," she muttered, hoping she would be allowed to leave.

"Oh, Nama," Brynna said with distress. "Please accept my heartfelt apology. I meant no offense."

Realizing the girl really meant the words she spoke, Nama resigned herself to remaining with them. Actually, she found it no hardship, for she liked both the Lady Gilda and her daughter Brynna.

"Yes, Nama," Lady Gilda said. "Please go on. Tell us more about your people. How long have they occupied your land."

Nama settled back on the couch and folded her hands in her lap. "Since the beginning of time."

"Then start there," Brynna said, bubbling with curiosity. "Tell us everything you know about your people."

Searching for a way to begin her story, Nama decided to start where the elders of her clan did when they told the tale. "In the beginning there was the Creator."

"You speak of our Christian God?"

"There is but one true God," Nama said. "We call *Him* Tawa. He rules over a domain of endless space and time and His power is stronger than even that of Father Sun, who is responsible for the light that heals, the light that warms our bodies throughout the day and nourishes our crops when Mother Earth sends them bursting from her good soil."

"What a colorful description of the sun," Gilda exclaimed. "Why do you refer to it as Father?"

"Because he is the source of all life. Without him, the crops would wither in the field."

"You speak of crops. What do you plant?"

"Corn, squash, and beans."

"Are all the people farmers?"

"No. Many clans never stay long enough in one

place to plant crops. Instead, they are wandering people who follow the buffalo."

"Garrick spoke of the creature—a great, hairy beast the natives depend on for their existence."

"That is true." Nama explained how the plains tribes could not survive without the buffalo. They used the tough skin for their dwellings and sleeping mats, how they used every part of the animal, wasting none of it. She told of the clan shaman who donned the buffalo hide during ceremonies and called upon the spirit of the great beast for strength.

"Then they worship the buffalo?" asked Brynna.

"Worship?" questioned Nama, never having heard the word before.

"Yes," Brynna said. "Do they believe the beast is a god with godly powers?"

"No," Nama replied. "All the clans know there is only one Creator. But there are many people who occupy Mother Earth, and Tawa cannot always see all their needs. That is why we call upon the Spirits for intervention."

Brynna was completely absorbed in the tale. "Your Tawa sounds very much like our Christian God."

"I know nothing of your god," Nama said.

"Surely Eric told you something about our beliefs," his mother said. "It was my understanding that he lived with you for several months."

Nama was unsure how to answer. She knew that Eric had spoken of his ancient gods to Shala, but had he spoken of the one they called Christian

God as well? She had no way of knowing. She had claimed a relationship with Eric that was false, and now she was trapped by the lie.

She studied the looks on their faces. Both Gilda Nordstrom and Brynna spoke kindly to her, but would that kindness continue if she told them of her deception? If she admitted that it was her friend Shala and not herself who had saved Eric's life, then captured his heart, what kind of punishment would she receive at the hands of these Vikings?

She feared it would be too severe to withstand.

Their questions about Eric set her own mind to wondering what had happened to him. She had thought he would be in his homeland, but he had not returned.

Where was he? Black Crow had spoken with them after Eric had rescued Shala from the Wolf Clan. Nama had thought their destination would be the longboat. But it must not have been so.

If only she could tell these women that he had not perished. But she dared not. The lie had been spoken, and she dare not deny her words.

Suddenly realizing she was the focus of both mother and daughter's attention, a flush crept up her cheeks. "My mind wandered for a moment," she said apologetically. "You asked me a question?"

"Did Eric not live with you for several months and did he not speak of his God?"

"Yes. He lived with me during the whole of the long cold, the season you call winter. But he spoke only of the old gods to me. The ones he referred to as ancient gods."

"That is strange," Brynna said. "I would think in his last days he would—" Tears filled her eyes, and she choked back a sob, apparently unable to continue.

"That has been Mother's greatest worry, that one of her children would not be able to seek forgiveness for their misdeeds before departing from this world," Brynna said.

"I am sure Eric would have done so," Nama said, wanting to take away the woman's grief. "He often went alone among the rocks and stayed there at length. He never told me why, but it could very well have been for that purpose." The Spirits would surely approve of her words even though they might be false. After all, they were spoken to ease another's pain.

"Tell us more of your people, Nama," said Brynna, obviously intent on diverting her mother's thoughts from her oldest son.

"I—well—" She floundered, wondering where she had stopped the tale, then decided to begin at the beginning again. "In the beginning there was Tawa. He created the stars and planets of the universe to give dimension and substance to his realm. Then, when that was done, he placed the ant and insect creatures deep within the earth.

"But the creatures proved unworthy. They fought among themselves and did not understand the meaning of life, so Tawa sent his emissary, the Spider Grandmother, to show the creatures the way

to a new world where they might live in the way
he wanted."

"Our world," Brynna breathed.

"No," Nama denied. "Not our world. The Spider Grandmother led the creatures up from their
old world to the new one Tawa had created for
them closer to the surface of the Earth. And, as
they emerged, a miraculous thing happened."

Realizing she had their complete attention, she
spoke in hushed tones, as the old ones did when
they told the story to the children of the clan.
"The creatures found their bodies were changing.
Many had the form of bears; some had become
wolves, while others were rabbits."

"And some people?" Brynna asked.

"No. At that time there were no people. Only
furry animals of one kind or another. And still
they were unsatisfied. They fell to fighting and
killing among themselves and refused to understand the meaning of life. Since this was not what
Tawa wanted of his creation, he sent Spider Grandmother to them once again.

"Gathering all the creatures about her, she led
them upward to a third world where some of them
changed into people. They were told to plant their
corn and live with peace, friendship, and rever-
ence, toward the Spirits and, above all, toward
Tawa, as they had twice before been instructed."

"And did it work this time?" Brynna asked. "Is
this the third world of which you speak?"

Nama shook her head. "No. It only worked for
a short time."

"They began fighting among themselves again?"

"Yes. For among the people were sorcerers who began leading them away from the original teachings until most of the people spent all their time gambling, stealing, or fighting and none of it working or practicing the rituals they had been taught. The rest of the people continued to work and make offerings of prayer sticks and sing the songs that were necessary to leading a good life. All this Tawa saw, and when he sent the Spider Grandmother to them again, it was with instructions to bring out of the third world only the people of good heart who understood the meaning of life. So it was done. Spider Grandmother led the chosen people upward toward a small opening at the top of the third world and through the hole—which we call a *sipapu*—to the surface of the Earth. As they emerged, Mockingbird sat by Spider Grandmother and divided them into clans—Eagle, Desert, Wolf, Round Hoof, Buffalo, and all the other clans of the world—sending each in its own direction to follow life as Tawa had prescribed among the plains, rivers, and forests he had created for them."

"What an interesting story!" Gilda exclaimed. "Thank you, my dear, for the telling of it."

Taking her words for a dismissal, Nama rose from her seat, preparing to take her leave of the two women, but it seemed the Lady Brynna had other intentions.

"Stay awhile yet," Brynna urged, then, turning

to her mother, she said, "Mother, something has just occurred to me."

"And what is that?" Lady Gilda asked.

"I would like to have Nama for my maid."

"Very well, dear. But we must ask Garrick."

Brynna's brilliant blue eyes glowed with mischief. "He would not dare refuse my request."

Twenty-four

But Garrick did refuse.

Having returned ahead of the others eager to see Nama again, he had entered the courtyard just in time to see Sven and Nama huddled together deep in conversation. As he watched, Nama laughed at something Sven had said; and when Garrick realized it was the first time he had ever seen her laugh, a slow anger began to burn deep within him. If he stepped forward now, he wondered, would the smile leave her face, would he again see the anger burn deep within her eyes?

He was almost certain he would.

Finding himself unable to watch her happiness fade away, he spun on his heels and strode rapidly across the courtyard to his longhouse. He stayed there for the rest of the day, his thoughts restless, his body demanding release. Although Carlotta or any one of his other concubines would readily come if they were called, eager to see to his every wish, he stayed alone, stoking the fires of his anger until they burned so hot they could hardly be contained.

When his mother learned of his presence in his

longhouse, she sent for him. Taking the summons as urgent, he entered the family home and sought her out.

"Garrick," Gilda Nordstrom exclaimed when he entered the room where she was weaving. "How was the hunt?"

"Successful," he said curtly. "As you must already know. Your maid said you urgently required my attention."

"Have you no greeting for me, Garrick?" came a voice from behind him.

Garrick spun on his heels and faced the girl who had remained silent in the corner until now. "Brynna! I had no idea you were back!" He wrapped his arms around her and gave her a squeeze, then held her away from him. "You have grown."

She gave a husky laugh and struck him lightly on the shoulder. "You always say that," she accused.

"It happens to be true," he said, measuring her with his eyes. "By Thor, you have grown. You are no longer a child, Brynna."

"I wish I were," she said flatly.

"Why, Brynna? Have you no wish to become mistress of your own home?"

"Not when the master of that home is Angus Thorvauld!" she snapped.

"Thorvauld?" he questioned, raising one eyebrow. "Surely Father has not already promised you to him?"

"He has. And I will have none of him, Garrick.

I mean it. If Father insists on this marriage, then I will do something rash."

"Everything you do is rash," he commented dryly.

"This will be even rasher," she promised. "I will run away. I will become an outcast," she cried, folding her arms over her chest and glaring at him.

"An outcast?"

"Yes. Nama was an outcast, yet she survived alone."

He frowned at her. "You have been speaking to Nama?"

"Yes. And that is why I had Mother send for you," she said earnestly. "Nama did a great service for this family and should not be left in the kitchens to work."

"Nama is none of your business," he said curtly.

"She is the business of this entire family," Brynna protested. "She saved Eric's life."

"We only have her word for that," he said.

"You doubt her story?" his mother asked with raised eyebrows.

"Not that she knew him, for that much is undeniable, but her relationship with him is suspect."

"In what way?" questioned Gilda.

"She said they were lovers."

Comprehension suddenly dawned on his mother's face. "And you have proof they were not." It was not a question, but a statement.

He gave an abrupt nod. "I have proof."

"Whatever they were to each other she obviously cared for him," Gilda Nordstrom said.

"Wait a minute," Brynna snapped. "What kind of proof do you have, Garrick? Did you ravish her?"

"Brynna!" Gilda's shocked exclamation rang out. "Do not speak of such things in this house."

"Is the speaking of it more shocking than the fact?" Brynna demanded. "You have not answered my question, Garrick."

"That is none of your business, Little Sister. And you are too young to speak of such things, much less know about them."

"But not too young to be handed over to Angus, who will surely do the same thing to me."

"No!" her mother exclaimed. "He would not."

"He had better not," Garrick said, "Or he will answer to me on the battlefield."

"The battlefield." She gave an unladylike snort. "You think the battlefield solves all problems. Well, it does not. And even if you met him on the battlefield and killed him, what good would that do me? I would already have suffered the indignity of rape."

"I will speak to Father about the marriage," Garrick said gruffly. "You are much too young to wed." He sighed wearily. "Now if that is all . . ."

"No," Brynna said smartly. "The problem of Nama has not yet been solved."

"Nama is not a problem," he said grimly, turning on his heels and heading for the door.

"But Garrick," she cried, "You have not heard me out. I want her for a maid."

Her words did not halt his progress. He gripped

the doorknob and, pulling the door open, stalked
through and slammed it hard behind him.

Upon leaving the Nordstrom women, Nama resumed her duties in the kitchen. Around midday
she chanced to look up and see a middle-aged
woman enter the room. Nama felt an idle curiosity
about the woman's identity, but it was only fleeting,
forgotten the moment Elspeth, who had been talking about her childhood, put a question to Nama.

"Do you have family, Nama?" she asked.

"A mother," Nama replied wistfully.

"Do you think she knows what happened to you?"

"She does not," Nama replied. "She believes I
have perished."

"Does she—" Elspeth broke off suddenly, staring
at a point just beyond Nama's left shoulder.

Nama turned to find the middle-aged woman
behind her.

"Are you called Nama?" she inquired.

Nama nodded her head, wondering if Brynna
had sent for her again. "Yes. That is what I am
called."

"Then you are to come with me."

Obviously expecting no questions, the gray-
haired woman turned and strode quickly away.
Nama could do nothing except hurry after her.

Instead of going to the back of the house, they
crossed the great hall and went through the front
door. Nama had, of necessity, to run because the
woman's legs were much longer than her own.

They crossed the courtyard and went past several longhouses similar to the one they had left, except smaller in size. At the last one, the woman stopped and knocked at the door.

"Enter," said a gruff voice from inside the room.

Nama knew who had spoken and, even though the woman pushed open the door, Nama's feet would not carry her forward, would not budge, even though her heart cried out for her to run . . . to hurry into Garrick's arms.

Impatient with Nama for delaying, the woman pushed her forward into the room then closed the door behind her with a sharp thud.

Nama's gaze flickered around the room that appeared to be empty. Then she saw him. Garrick's large frame stood immobile beside the fireplace.

"Come here," he said in that familiar gravelly voice that she remembered so well.

Her heart fluttered wildly as she licked lips that had suddenly gone dry. And her voice, when she spoke, sounded strained. "You sent for me?"

"Yes." His green eyes traveled over her drab shift with something like distaste. "That garment is not attractive on you, Nama."

The insult was like a slap in the face. It stung. "I agree," she replied stiffly, thinking of his concubines in their lovely silken gowns. "Yet I must wear it or go naked."

"It is not my wish for others to see you naked," he said, his eyes caressing her. "Nor is it my wish for you to continue wearing such an ugly garment."

"That is a problem."

"Yet it is a problem that can easily be solved," he said. "I will have other garments made for you."

"Does it really matter what a *thrall* wears?" She deliberately emphasized the word the Norsemen used for their slaves.

He went absolutely still, and his gaze narrowed slightly, boring into her. She knew he resented her words, yet she had spoken only the truth.

"You need not remain a *thrall*, Nama. If you choose, you could share my longhouse with me." He waved a careless hand at his surroundings. "Would you not like that?"

"And what would you demand of me should I accept your kind offer?"

"Only that you look upon me with favor and cease this verbal taunting."

"So little? You do not wish to join with me again?" she taunted.

"Would it be so bad if I did?" He answered the question with one of his own. "You cannot say you do not find pleasure in my embrace."

"Things change," she said abruptly, lying through her teeth.

"Not this."

"Yes."

"No. Come here," he beckoned. "Allow me to prove it."

She wet her lips and sucked in a sharp breath, stepping back at the same time to avoid his embrace.

But he would not allow her to escape. Reaching out, his right hand closed over her left forearm and pulled her closer, into the circle of his arms. "You are not immune to me, Nama. I can feel how your body responds to mine."

She pushed against him but found herself held firm.

"No," he breathed against her cheek. "Stay."

Despite herself, her body gave in to his demands. She melted against him, felt her nipples tauten as they pressed against his firm male chest; and the weakness of her knees made her stay there, held firmly against him.

She remembered the nights beneath the Anasazi moon when he had possessed her with his body, and she felt a longing so great to be held that way again that it became an ache in her heart.

Oh, Great Creator! How could she turn from him when she wanted him so?

Why should you? her heart asked. Why not take what he has to offer? Why not create a storehouse of memories to last you in the days to come. Yes, why not?

He seemed to feel the moment when she allowed herself to let go. His arms tightened around her back and brought her harder against him, and his lips met hers in a long kiss that was both tender and possessive.

When his mouth lifted from hers, he pushed aside the shoulder of her garment and pressed his mouth against it, pushing it farther aside and running his lips down toward her breast. She arched closer to him, wanting his mouth on her breast as she had felt it once before.

The fabric was in the way. She struggled to remove it, but they were too closely entwined.

He moved to help her, fumbled at the fastenings, and released the first one when suddenly, without warning, the door was shoved open.

"Thor's teeth!" The exclamation was spewed into the air around them as Garrick looked up to see his brother standing in the doorway, transfixed by the sight of them together.

"Sorry," Olaf muttered, his cheeks flushing with color. "I was unaware that you were—that you had—" He backed away toward the door behind them. "You can go ahead with what you were doing. I will just—just—"

"Stay!" Nama cried, disentangling herself from Garrick's embrace, then turning to the man who held her by the wrist. "If you are finished with me, then I will return to the kitchens where I belong."

"Nonsense!" he snapped. "You have no business in the kitchen."

"Then why was I sent there?" she demanded.

His lips tightened. "Then go there if you are so inclined. I have no wish to detain you when you have such important things—like peeling vegetables—waiting for you."

Realizing he was furious with her, she hurried from the room while Olaf was there to stand between her and the fury of the man who had stolen her heart.

Twenty-five

Nama's heart beat wildly with remembered passion as she hurried across the courtyard, intent on putting as much distance between herself and Garrick as she could in the least possible time.

She could feel the warmth in her cheeks and knew they must be flushed with the weight of her embarrassment. Another moment and she would have been naked!

Her spirit guide must have sent Olaf into that room. She was so flustered that she kept her head lowered, unwilling for others to see her shame; otherwise, she would have seen the woman coming toward her.

But she did not. She had no idea until hard fingers curled around her forearm and brought her to an abrupt halt. Nama looked up to see Carlotta, the last person she would have wished to see at that moment.

"You have been with Garrick!" the dark-haired woman hissed, her talon-like fingers digging into Nama's flesh. "You are a fool. He cares nothing for you."

Nama's chin jerked up and she met the other

woman's accusing glare. "Then why did he send for me?" Nama challenged.

"He did not," Carlotta denied. "You went to him. Why? Did you hope to be taken off kitchen duties?" A smile spread across her face, but it was not a nice smile. "It did not work, did it? That is why you were running. You were disappointed because Garrick rejected you."

"Think what you like," Nama said, attempting to pry the other woman's fingers from her arm. "Release me!" she demanded. "Otherwise you will answer to Garrick."

Carlotta's laughter rang out across the courtyard, and her eyes flashed with spite. "Are you threatening me? Trying to make me believe you would complain to him about me?" She pushed her head closer, and Nama could feel her harsh breath against her face. "What would you say to him, little woman from the Eagles? Would you say Carlotta does not like you? He already knows that. Would you say Carlotta has threatened you? He would not be surprised, nor would he care." Her fingers uncurled, and she threw Nama's arm away from her as though she found the touch of her skin vile. "I will allow you to leave now," she said calmly. "Run away, little bird. Run. Fly to the great house and hide yourself away in the kitchen. But remember this: Should you pose any threat to me . . . should you ever get in my way . . . I *know* where to find you."

Laughing loudly, Carlotta went on her way, leaving Nama staring after her, wondering just how

far the woman would go if she felt her position
with Garrick was threatened. She must be out of
her mind, Nama told herself. Why does she see
me as a threat? Does she treat Garrick's *other* concubines in the same manner?

The questions were still whirling in Nama's
mind when she entered the kitchen. Then, suddenly, there was no time to worry about Carlotta,
for the moment Nama entered the room, Cook appeared beside her, holding two heavy platters of
honey-and-sesame-seed bread.

"Take these to the great hall," Cook said gruffly.
"Position them around the table, then hurry back
here." She turned away from Nama, muttering,
"There is so much to do and so little time left!
Why do they keep dragging my help away?"

Feeling guilty for having been called away, Nama
hurried with the task, placing each platter as Cook
had directed then scurrying back to the kitchen.

Cook spied her the moment she entered.
"Here," she said, shoving a heavy platter at
Nama, who had barely time to grasp it before an-
other—equally heavy—one was shoved at her. "Put
those sweetmeats on the sideboard," she muttered.
"Elspeth can serve them later."

"The sideboard?" Nama questioned, never having heard of its existence before now.

"Yes, the sideboard," Cook growled. When
Nama continued to stare at her, she explained.
"The long table near the wall. The tarts are al-
ready there."

The tarts, Nama thought, hurrying from the

room. She would recognize the sideboard because the tarts were already there. The platters were so heavy that Nama feared she would drop them. What would Cook do if she returned to the kitchen and told her the sweetmeats were spoiled? she wondered, hurrying through the passage toward the great room.

She heaved a sigh of relief when the platters rested safely on the sideboard next to the platters of tarts, then hurried back to the kitchen again.

When Cook saw her enter the room, she threw her hands up in the air and exclaimed, "No one cares that we have so little help! No one! Off with you, girl. Lady Brynna has sent for you."

Nama felt she should apologize to Cook for leaving the kitchen again, but feared the woman's reaction.

Wondering what Brynna could possibly want with her, Nama hurried to the other girl's bed-chamber.

When she entered the room, she found Brynna waiting beside the huge four-poster bed examining several brightly colored gowns that had been placed on the coverlet.

"Do come in," Brynna called, when she saw Nama hovering near the doorway. "Tell me, Nama. Which of these gowns do you prefer?"

Wondering if Garrick had actually consented to her being Brynna's personal maid and hoping it was so, Nama examined the gowns closely. One of the gowns was fashioned from a bright-blue fabric that was the exact shade of Brynna's brilliant eyes and Nama quickly told her so.

"Forget the color of my eyes." Brynna picked up the nearest gown and held it against Nama's body. "What do you think of this scarlet gown?" she asked.

Nama looked down at the garment that was so dazzling against her own coppery skin. It was beautiful. But on Brynna, with her fiery curls, well . . .

Realizing Brynna waited for her reply, Nama said hesitantly. "It is very beautiful, Brynna. But if you do not like the blue one, then perhaps the green garment would suit your coloring better." Nama was no authority on gowns. How could she be when she had worn nothing but rabbit skins until coming here? But she must answer, because Brynna obviously desired her opinion. "Yes," she affirmed. "I believe you should choose either the blue or green gown. They most definitely suit your coloring better than the red one does."

"Yes, yes," Brynna said impatiently. "But do *you* like the red one?"

Nama turned her attention back to the red gown. "Yes," she murmured. "Who would not like such a gown? The color is very beautiful. I have seen that very same color on the cardinals that inhabit the forests near my home." She stroked her hand across the silky material. "And the material," she went on. "It is so soft. It would cover your body in such a way that every woman at the celebration would envy you its possession."

"Or you," Brynna muttered.

Nama sent her a puzzled look.

"The red gown is yours," Brynna explained.

"Mine?" Nama gasped, eying the beautiful gown, hardly daring to believe what her ears had heard.

"Yes, yours," Brynna repeated. "I am giving it to you."

"But where would I wear it?" Nama protested. "It is too beautiful to be worn in the kitchen."

"You will stay out of the kitchen in the future," Brynna said grimly. "From this moment on, you will be my personal companion."

"Companion?" Nama questioned breathlessly. "Not your personal maid?"

"No. Companion. And if anyone dare object, they will feel the lash of my tongue."

"Garrick will object."

"No. Garrick came to me awhile ago and told me to take you out of the kitchen. He said you were to be given a gown and were to attend the celebration as a guest."

"Why?" Nama asked suspiciously.

"Oh, I imagine he has his own reasons," Brynna said, her lips curling in a secret smile. "Now . . . we must hurry." She tossed the gown over a chair. "There is so much to do if we are to be ready in time for the celebration. We must bathe and wash our hair and—"

"Should we not decide what you are going to wear?" Nama interrupted.

"Oh, no." Brynna waved a casual hand of dismissal. "That was decided long ago. I knew there would be a celebration when I returned, so I had a special gown designed. Look." She picked up a satin gown of mottled green that made Nama think of a forest and held it against herself. "What do you think?" she asked. "Is not this fabric unique?" Brynna whirled around, allowing the material to swirl around her, delighted with her selection. "Have you ever seen colors blended this way?" she asked.

"It is lovely," Nama agreed; and although she thought her own gown more beautiful, she would have cut out her own tongue before admitting it. "The dark and light greens in the garment remind me of the forests back home."

"I thought of a forest when I saw the fabric," Brynna admitted. "To me, it represents the freedom and infinite peace of my very own special forest."

"Your own special forest?" Nama questioned.

"Yes. It is a special place to me, located only a short distance from here. Close enough for a young girl to enter and hide herself away from others."

Hide herself away from others. Why had Brynna felt the need to hide herself away? Nama wondered.

"I miss the forests," Nama murmured wistfully. "There is much peace to be found there. I would like to see yours sometimes . . . if that would be allowed."

"And you shall," Brynna said. "When there is more time, I will show you my secret place."

"Secret place?"

"Yes. It is located deep in the forest . . . a little rock house that no one remembers—if they ever knew of its existence. I used to hide there from Father and my brothers when I was younger. They never once discovered my hiding place. Never came near my little house."

"Is it hidden so well then?"

Brynna laughed gaily. "Very well. The trees grow so close together that the horses cannot pass between them. And, to my knowledge, nobody has ever cared enough about that section of the forest to explore it on foot. Except me. And I have not been there in years," she added wistfully.

"It sounds very peaceful," Nama remarked, wishing she could go there, could experience its solitude. But she could not. She was not free to go anywhere she wanted, could only do as her masters commanded. She was no longer a free woman and must, of necessity, bow to the will of others.

But the time would come, she promised herself, when she would be free again.

All she had to do was wait and watch, and the time would surely come.

Garrick, seated in his tub of bath water, knew he must make a decision soon. Since he had returned from the new land he had not visited his concubines. He knew the servants—as well as his women—must be wondering about it. But he had felt no desire for anyone except Nama.

Remembering the happiness on her face when

she had laughed with Sven, he felt anger surge anew. Why did she save her smiles for Sven? Garrick wondered.

He remembered the night on the *langskip* when he had found her tied to the bedposts. Their bodies had been so attuned to one another, as though they had been created with the thought of making the two one.

What nonsense! And yet, was it really? He had never thought a woman could become so important to him. Had always thought he could control his emotions. But, despite his efforts to stay heartfree, the wench had gotten under his skin. Now he must either bed the woman or send her away from him so that she would not continue to mar his relationship with his other women; otherwise, his manhood would be suspect.

His lips curled into a smile as that thought entered his mind. Surely keeping four concubines satisfied was enough proof that he was a man.

But your concubines are not satisfied, a small voice reminded. *You have not sent for any of them since your return. Nor have you even spoken to them.* That was a fact which Olaf had brought to his attention earlier in the day.

Olaf!

"May he be hauled away in Odin's chariot!" Garrick muttered aloud.

The big lout would stumble in at the most inconvenient times. If he had not come then, Garrick would surely have had Nama in his bed. Of course he could have made her stay anyway, but he had still been smarting from the accusation that he had ravished her.

Ravished her!

"By Thor, Brynna's bottom needs warming properly for that suggestion."

A sudden thought occurred that gave Garrick pause. Had Nama told his sister she had been ravished? He sat straighter in the tub and glared at the door. She could not have done so. But how could he know for sure?

"Blast it!" he shouted. "They are two of a kind."

The great room wore a festive air, lit by a multitude of thick candles that cast a myriad of flickering lights against the ceiling and walls.

Nama, wearing the satin gown that showed off her skin to perfection, sat next to Garrick at the long table. It felt strange to be served, especially when the servers were people she had worked beside and who had since become her friends.

Even now Elspeth hovered beside her holding a platter of sweetmeats and urging her to try each one in a low whisper.

"My belly is already too full, Elspeth," Nama whispered. "I cannot eat another morsel."

"I could eat them if I were seated where you are," Elspeth muttered in a low voice. "I say take all that is offered and then some. Uh, oh," she added. "Lord Fergus is looking this way. Best if I be moving along." She moved swiftly to Garrick's side and offered the platter, but he waved it away impatiently.

"No, thank you, Elspeth," he said. "I have had enough food."

"Ale then, my lord?" she asked.

"Yes," he agreed, looking at his empty silver-rimmed drinking horn. "I could use some more ale."

As soon as his drinking horn was filled, he rose to his feet and held it aloft. "I propose a toast," he said, in a voice loud enough to carry around the great room. "A toast," he repeated. "To Nama, Woman of the Eagle Clan!"

Although puzzled, the men rose to the occasion, raising their drinking horns and shouting, "To Nama! Woman of the Eagle Clan!"

"May she be fruitful and bless me with many children!" Garrick said loudly.

Nama felt a warm flush coloring her cheeks. Why had Garrick chosen this way to announce his intentions? If anyone there had wondered about her status among them, their questions had been answered by his toast.

Had he intended to shame her?

She searched his expression, trying to find an answer to her question. But he would not allow her to see any emotion there. Even so, his brilliant eyes glittered with possession.

Having learned the role of a concubine and knowing that, under Viking law, any children she bore him would be considered bastards unless he chose to legalize them, Nama became more and more certain that Garrick meant others to know her position in the household.

That knowledge stabbed at her with the fierceness of a knife. The pain was so intense that tears stung her eyes and she lowered her lashes, unwilling for others to see her anguish.

"To Nama!" the guests shouted. "May she be fruitful!"

Holding their drinking horns aloft, the men poured the ale down their throats.

Servants rushed around the table with buckets of ale to refill the drinking horns the moment they were emptied and the toasts continued—as did the drinking.

Garrick was toasted. The jarl was toasted, and so was his wife. Lady Brynna was toasted; the future children were toasted; then Nama was toasted again. The cook was toasted, and the hunters were toasted, as well as the men who had carried the meat home. And then, when no other voice rang out, when no other toasts were proposed, Garrick still cried out for more ale. And when his silver-rimmed drinking horn was filled, he raised it high and toasted the servant who carried the ale.

And throughout the festivities, Nama sat silent and wounded, blinking back tears of pain. Occasionally she would glance up at Garrick and wonder how a man could drink so much ale and still show no effect. Several men had already succumbed to the drink, barely making it to the sideboards before falling asleep.

As time passed, Garrick became quiet, his gaze

never leaving her. He reminded her of a hawk just before it swooped on a rabbit— continually circling in the sky, yet swooping closer and closer, readying itself for that final, downward plunge that would see its victim caught beneath its claws.

Was he, like the hawk, savoring her fear?

Suddenly Lady Gilda rose from the table and motioned to Brynna, who did the same. When she realized they were leaving the room, Nama would have followed them had Garrick allowed her to do so. But the moment she rose, he snagged her wrist and pulled her back down.

"You will remain here with my other concubines," he ordered.

Nama flicked a quick glance at the women who sat on the other side of the table. They seemed unaffected by his mood. Were they used to it? Nama wondered.

Her nerves were stretched to the breaking point as the celebration continued. She had begun to wonder if the night would ever end. She tried to ignore Garrick, but he would not allow it. Even now, he was raising his hand, beckoning her closer. Knowing she must obey or be publicly humiliated, Nama leaned closer to him.

"Come here, wench," he growled. "Seat yourself on my lap."

His lap? In front of the others? Next he would have her gown around her ankles. She shook her head, refusing to allow herself to be demeaned while others were watching.

His brilliant green eyes darkened when she refused him, but he said not a word. Instead, he raised his hand and looked straight at Carlotta, obviously sending the invitation her way.

With a pleased smile, Carlotta left her place and threw herself onto his lap, wrapping her arms around his neck. Her eyes gleamed with malice and triumph as she met Nama's gaze.

The tears she had managed to keep at bay suddenly overflowed, rippling down her cheeks in silvery streams, and Nama stared at him with wounded eyes. How could Garrick humiliate her in such a manner? And after making certain the others knew she had joined the ranks of concubine!

Pushing away from the table, Nama rose to her feet. She refused to stay there any longer. Garrick could do what he wished, but she was leaving the great room now!

Surprisingly, Garrick did nothing to stop her.

Twenty-six

Finding herself unable to sleep in the unfamiliar room located next to Brynna's bedchamber, Nama stared up into the darkness and formulated a plan of escape. But where could she go in this strange land?

Suddenly she remembered Brynna's abandoned house that was hidden deep in the woods. The words Brynna had spoken surfaced in Nama's mind. *The trees grow so close together that the horses cannot pass between them.*

Yes! That was the answer. She would go there and stay. Then she would never have to see Garrick caressing his other women again.

Realizing Walks With Thunder would worry if she left without a word, Nama slipped from her room and hurried down the hallway leading to the servants' quarters. Upon finding the kitchen door open, she slipped inside and found several loaves of bread. Shoving two of them inside a coarsely woven bag, Nama added several large wedges of cheese and secured the opening with heavy cord. Then, after slinging it across her shoulders, she hurried on her way.

Walks With Thunder woke when Nama entered the room. Opening startled eyes, she jerked upright and exclaimed, "What is wrong, Nama? Why are you here? I thought you would be with the Lady Brynna!"

"Shhh!" Nama whispered, tossing the woman's shift to her. "Don your garment swiftly. When we are alone, you will be told everything."

Nearby, Elspeth stirred in her sleep. Fearing the woman would waken, Nama tiptoed quietly out of the room and waited for her friend in the hallway. A moment later, she was joined by the woman from the Desert Clan.

"Why are you here so early?" Walks With Thunder asked. "Has something happened?"

"I am going away," Nama announced.

"Away? Where?"

"To a secret place that no one knows about."

"You could only know of such a place if you were told," the woman said briskly. "So someone else knows."

"The Lady Brynna knows. But if she remembers telling me about it she will not give me away."

"How can you know that?"

"Lady Brynna has become my friend. She would never betray my trust."

"I would like to go with you," Walks With Thunder said.

"You?" Nama looked at her in surprise. "But why? I thought you were happy here? What about Olaf?"

"Olaf has no interest in me," Walks With Thunder said, her voice revealing her pain. "I saw him at the celebration with Jasmine in his arms."

"Jasmine? Oh, Walks With Thunder. I am sorry. I know how you feel, though. When I last saw Garrick, he was holding Carlotta in his arms."

Moisture glittered in Walks With Thunder's eyes. "Olaf has sought me out many times of late, and I thought it was only a matter of time before he would speak to me about joining with him." Tears overflowed and slid down her cheeks.

"They are alike, Garrick and Olaf," Nama said harshly. "But then, they are brothers. Let us hurry away from here."

"What about food, Nama?" Walks With Thunder asked.

"I thought of that. I took bread and cheese from the kitchen."

"Cook will beat us!" Walks With Thunder exclaimed.

"She cannot," Nama reminded. "We are leaving this place. But we must go quickly. Before we are found out."

Nama hurried from the longhouse with the other woman only a few steps behind. There was no sign of life around the other buildings. . . . All was silent.

From her vantage point, Nama could see the blue of the ocean in the distance and knew there would be no escape in that direction.

"Look," whispered Walks With Thunder, tugging at her arm. "The forests are that way." She pointed to the north.

"Yes. That is the forest Brynna spoke of. And the fjord lies to the south," Nama muttered, sparing only a brief glance for the narrow channel, knowing there would be boats there, knowing as well that two women alone could never raise the sails, much less guide a longboat through the fjord to the ocean. They had no recourse except to seek refuge in the forest.

"What about the dwellings located between us and the forest?" Walks With Thunder asked. "There are so many of them. Someone may see us running toward the trees and alert the others."

Nama had already seen the small houses that occasionally dotted the landscape between the great house and the forest. "The crops in the corn fields will afford us some cover." She turned to the other woman. "You can still return undetected if you should so desire."

"No," Walks With Thunder replied. "Since Olaf has no interest in me, they would surely give me over to some other man. Once before, my own people gave me to a harsh master. It is not my wish to suffer that fate again." There was a deep sadness in her eyes. "I never thought Olaf would treat me so." She drew a shuddery breath. "It hurts more when the heart becomes attached."

Yes. It hurts more, Nama silently agreed. Then, trying to ignore the pain that was firmly lodged in her chest, she said, "We must hurry away before anyone discovers we have gone."

Fear dogged their footsteps as they raced toward the forest, but their flight went uninterrupted.

And when they entered the safety of the thickly growing trees, Nama breathed a sigh of relief.

They traveled swiftly through the forest, stopping only for short periods of time to rest, and by late afternoon they were both weary to the point of exhaustion. They had stopped beside a narrow stream to rest and refresh themselves when suddenly a sound brought Nama to her feet.

Cra-a-ck!

Fearfully, Nama whirled to face the danger and saw a deer, emerging from a thicket of pines, headed for the river.

Relief swept through her, and she laughed aloud. "It is only a deer," she whispered.

Nama chided herself for being such a coward. The deer was a timid animal, nothing to cause such fear. She measured the antlers with her eyes. It was a fine buck. A large one. Her mouth watered at the thought of fresh meat cooked to a fine turn.

As though sensing her thoughts, the animal turned its head to stare at her with large brown eyes. Then, seeming to judge her to be no danger, it went to the river and stopped between two mossy ledges of rock where it lowered its head to drink.

If only she had her spear, Nama thought. She would move ever so carefully, curling her fingers tightly around it and pierce the animal in a vital spot.

As though sensing her thoughts, the buck jerked its head upright. It stared at her for a long moment, then bounded up the bank, its white tail disappearing in the brush.

Releasing a disappointed sigh, Nama sank down beside the swiftly flowing water. Her belly growled with hunger but she knew she dared not assuage the craving. Not when the food she had brought must last two people until more could be found. She drew up her knees and dropped her head on them. She was wasting time, but they needed to rest.

The forest around them was filled with sounds. Frogs croaked along the river bank and birds twittered, flying from branch to branch, making cracking sounds that—

Birds did not make cracking sounds by lighting on branches. It was not birds she heard. It was a human sound, as though boots were crunching across twigs and leaves.

Someone was approaching!

Scrambling to her feet, Nama ushered Walks With Thunder behind the nearest tree . . . just in time.

An old man suddenly emerged from the forest and bent to fill his water container from the creek. When he stood up, he groaned and held a hand to his lower back.

A full beard, streaked heavily with gray, covered his face, and that same gray could be found in his sandy-colored hair. He looked toward the tree where they were hiding and spoke in a gravelly voice. "You might as well show yourself, girlie. I know you are there."

Motioning Walks With Thunder to remain hidden, Nama stepped from behind the tree into full view. "How did you know?" she asked.

"I could smell you," he said. "Never known an animal who smelled of perfume."

Of course, she thought. She still wore the scent Brynna had put on her the night before. She should have known better.

"What are you doing here?" the old man asked, studying her with a penetrating gaze. "Are you hiding from somebody?"

"Suppose I am?"

He shrugged his shoulders. "Matters little to me. Are you hungry?"

She nodded her head, thinking of her last meal the night before. Although the table had been heavily laden, she had been too miserable to eat much.

"Then tell the other one to come on out. I got plenty of food at home for the three of us."

Walks With Thunder, having learned enough of the Viking language to know she had been discovered, left her hiding place and joined them.

"Is your house nearby?" Nama asked, studying the old man closely, wondering how far he could be trusted.

"Only a short walk," he replied.

"Do you live alone?"

He nodded his grizzled head. "You got objections to that?"

"Of course not." Nama decided they might as well accompany him and partake of his food. Their presence had already been revealed and perhaps, while they ate, she could convince him to hold his tongue about them. "We will accompany you."

"Thought you might," he said gruffly. "Come along then."

They traveled only a short distance before they reached the rock house where the old man lived. It was then that Nama realized Brynna's secret house was already occupied.

"Stew should be ready," the old man said, shoving the door open and nodding toward the iron pot hanging over a hook in the fireplace. "Set yourselves down and rest while I dish up."

"Allow me to do that," Nama said quickly.

"Help yourself," the old man said. "Nobody ever accused me of being overly fond of woman's work."

"What are you called," Nama asked as she busied herself with the cooking pot.

"Mick O'Halloran," the old man replied. "How about yourselves?"

Nama knew there was no need in hiding their identity. If the Vikings came looking for them, there were no others around who fit their descriptions. "I am Nama, Woman of the Eagle Clan," she said. "And my companion is Walks With Thunder."

His gaze examined them thoughtfully. "Thought as much," he said finally.

"You have heard of us?" Nama paused in the act of dishing up, waiting for his reply.

"Everybody hereabouts has heard of the two

women the Nordstrom brothers brought home
with them."

Nama's look was measured. "We cannot allow
ourselves to be captured again, Mick O'Halloran.
We were not born to live as slaves to these Vikings,
nor to any other man."

"Guess not," he said laconically. "Neither were
most of the other slaves around here. Most were
born free. Lived as freemen until the Vikings plun-
dered our homes and took us prisoner. Same goes
for me."

"You are a slave to the Vikings?"

"Not now. There was a time when I was."

"How did you come to be free?" Nama asked.

"Did a good turn for old Fergus, and this was
his reward."

"This?" She waved a hand around her. "The
house and your freedom?"

"The house and what he called freedom. Yes."

"You said 'called freedom.' Does that mean you
are not really free?"

"Is a man free when he cannot go where he
wishes?"

"You are guarded?"

"No. But it is my wish to return home. Fergus
will not allow that."

"Why? If he does not wish you to serve him,
why does he keep you here?"

"Fergus does not trust easily. I have been here
so long that I know the ways of the Vikings. He
knows I could go to his enemies and lead them

here, that I could point out their most vulnerable places." His blue eyes were sad.

"Would you do that?"

"I have many friends here that would suffer in a raid. I would not like to see that happen." He shrugged his shoulders. "But Fergus . . . he would not take the chance. He worries that my anger would erupt if I were among my own again." His gaze turned inward. "He should know better. I've been here for fifty years now. I have no kin left in England. The few friends I have are here in Norway."

"Then why do you wish to leave?"

"It is my greatest wish to die in my homeland, to be buried beside my mother and father."

A face appeared in Nama's memory, partially hidden by the bars that kept him prisoner, and a plan began to take form in her mind. "Mick O'Halloran, if you had a boat, could you find your way across the great salt water?"

He smiled. "Could a baby find its mother's teat? Yes. I could find my way home, but I cannot sail a longship by myself."

"How many people would it take?"

He was thoughtful for a long moment. Then, "Depends on how big the vessel was. What do you have in mind, lass?"

"There must be others who want to leave this place . . . who seek freedom at any price."

"Yes, I suppose there are. But I have lived in this cottage these last ten years now, and my friends are all old like me."

"I have become acquainted with a young man who would like to be free," she said, her mind on Gunther. "He says there are others like him who would be eager to escape from this place."

"His name?"

Although Nama felt she could trust the old man, she had no intention of divulging Gunther's name. If he were questioned, he could not speak what he did not know. "His name is of no consequence," she replied. "Time enough to know it when we have left this accursed place behind."

The old man's lips twitched slightly as though he were amused, but his expression remained solemn. "You have a plan for leaving here?"

"Yes," she agreed, handing a bowl of stew to Walks With Thunder, who carried it to the old man. "We will speak of it after we have eaten."

Filling the other two bowls, she handed one to the other woman, then followed her to the table and seated herself. "You are a good cook," she pronounced after tasting the stew.

"I've had enough practice," he growled. "I am curious about this plan of yours. Does it include stealing a longboat?"

"We could not leave this place without one."

"How would you go about it? The longboats are not left unguarded."

"A woman can do much that a man cannot," she replied with a smile, thinking of the many times the guards had eyed her with pleasure even while she was dressed in her crude garments. Surely, dressed in one of the gowns that had been made for her, she could keep the guard distracted long enough so he could be taken unawares.

"You are right," he said, "if the women were not sought after by the jarl and his sons. But if they were, if the women you are speaking of are yourselves, the women would not have a chance to work their wiles. They would be taken prisoner on sight."

"Yes." Nama looked through the open door. How long had they been gone? Was there time to return to the great house and cover their escape?

"We have been gone too long already," Walks With Thunder said, guessing the path her thoughts had taken. "They will be searching for us now."

"Perhaps. But then again, maybe not. They do not expect me in the kitchen, and I could say I went walking and took you with me."

"They would not believe us."

"Let me think," Nama said, her thoughts in turmoil. "Perhaps we could enter the great house without being seen. We could say we were there all the time."

"If they are looking for us, then every passage will have been searched."

"We must take the chance," Nama said. "What else can we do, Walks With Thunder? They will search the house and surrounding buildings, then widen that search until eventually they cover the entire forest."

"They will surely do that," Mick replied. "There is no place you can safely hide. Even if there were, winter will soon be here; and you would freeze to death caught in the open."

"We must make plans for our escape," Nama said. "Then we must return to the great house before they learn we are missing."

Twenty-seven

It was already too late.

Garrick had slept late that morning. When he finally woke and pushed himself to his elbows, his head throbbed so furiously that he thought it must be Thor trying to pound some sense into the lovesick mortal's head with his enormous hammer.

After calling for some headache powders to ease his pain, he sent his maid to fetch Nama. After all, he reasoned, it was her fault he had consumed so much ale the night before. And now that his body needed soothing, it was her duty to attend it.

But when the woman returned, she was alone.

Garrick waited for an explanation, then exploded in fury. "Odin's blood, woman!" he shouted at the cringing messenger. "What do you mean?"

"She c-cannot be found, my lord," the woman stuttered, backing away from the bed where he had been reclining. "We have gone through the great house, leaving no place unsearched. But she is not there. She has disappeared."

"A woman cannot disappear."

"She gives every appearance of having done so, my lord."

"Bring me my trousers," he shouted, climbing from the bed and swaying dizzily, uncaring of his nakedness. "Hurry, woman." He meant to find Nama if he had to tear the place apart stone by stone.

When his trousers were in his hand, he pushed his feet into the legs of the garment and pulled them up around his hips. Then he took the shirt from the woman hovering fearfully nearby.

"Bring me my boots," he snapped, "and quit hovering like that. No, I can get them myself. Just get out of my sight. Leave me alone."

The woman needed no further urging. She bobbed her knees in a curtsy and scuttled out of the room as quickly as possible.

Fear warred with anger as Garrick pulled on his boots and hurried out the front door. He called the guards to him, ordering an immediate search of the surrounding buildings. When that search revealed nothing, he expanded the search until they finally reached the stables.

Upon entering, he found Peter, the stable boy, busy currying Midnight. He looked up at Garrick's entrance.

"Good day to you, my lord," he said, touching his cap respectfully with his forefinger. "Were you needing the stallion?"

"Are you alone here?" Garrick demanded, ignoring the stable boy's question. He sent his searching gaze around the stables, probing the shadowy areas, peering into each stall, hoping to find some sign of the woman he was looking for.

"Yes, my lord," Peter replied uneasily.

Garrick's gaze sharpened. Was the lad trying to hide something? "How long have you been here?" he growled.

"Since early morn."

"Nevertheless, we will search the stables." Garrick issued quick orders, but the search revealed nothing, gave no clues to the whereabouts of the two women.

Garrick's scowl deepened. "Saddle the stallion," he ordered. "Have him ready on my return."

He had no sooner stepped outside the building when Olaf joined him. "No luck?" he questioned.

"No," Garrick replied. "We will have to widen the search."

Olaf sighed. "Today of all days! We were supposed to address the assembly at Kaupang today."

"We cannot go until the women are found," Garrick said curtly. He gave the order to cover the docks and search the town. "She must be hiding somewhere," he muttered.

And wherever she was, he would find her, he added to himself.

Father Sun hovered high overhead by the time Nama and Walks With Thunder reached the river where they had seen the deer. They were wading through the water when Nama discovered they were being observed.

It was Gunther, standing beside the river with a pole in his hand. His lips curled in a smile as he watched them approach. "I thought the two of you would have given the master more of a chase," he commented idly. "But here you are, practically falling into his lap."

It was obvious he knew they had run away. That meant everyone in the house knew, Nama realized. They would have to change their plans. She looked at the fishing pole Gunther held.

"What are you doing?" she asked.

He explained the art of fishing with a pole and line, then showed them the stringer of fish held captive by a line and a stout stick.

Nama stared at it as an idea began to form.

"What would you take for the fish and the pole?" she asked.

"What do you have to trade?" he asked.

"Nothing right now," she said.

"I thought so." He started to walk away, fish and pole in hand.

"Wait," Nama cried. "If you give it to me now and keep your mouth shut about who caught the fish, then you will be richer by two gold pieces."

"Where are you going to get the gold with you locked up in the dungeon?"

The mere mention of the cold, damp dungeons made Nama shudder inwardly. "If you give me the fish, there will be no need of dungeons."

"Are you going to claim you've been fishing all the while?" A smile quirked his mouth. "It just might work." His gaze sharpened. "Can you really get the gold?"

"If you want it," she said. "I am sure Garrick has plenty."

"You think he will just hand it over?"

"Perhaps not. But I can easily lay my hands on it while he sleeps."

"What if I say no and tell him what you been up to?" Gunther asked.

"Then you would not have the gold."

"And you would be in the dungeon."

"Yes. That is true. You can keep the fish and give up the gold and leave us to the dungeon if you wish. But what would you gain for having done so?"

"The master might give me gold for telling him what you said."

"Do you really think so?" She raised a dark brow. "Do you know anyone else who was given gold for doing what was expected of them?" She had to convince him or they would surely find themselves whipped for attempting escape. "Besides. The gold might not be your only reward."

"What does that mean?"

"I have a plan to leave here."

"Leave Norway?"

"Yes."

"What makes you think it will work any better than your last one?"

"Because it is a much better plan," she said mysteriously. "And there are others already included. Men who wish to see the last of this place."

"Men?" He looked at her in surprise. "They could find their way to England."

"They could find their way anywhere."

He thought about that for a minute. "I guess nothing would be lost if I just keep my mouth shut and wait awhile," he said finally. "Gold will surely never find its way into my pocket any other way. And if we should make it back to England—well, I got me a grandma there that will welcome me home. The Vikings killed the rest of my folks when they raided the town." He held the stringer of fish toward her, but when she reached for it, he pulled it back. "What guarantee do I have you will honor the bargain?"

"You could always tell your master I attempted to bribe you."

"Yes, I could." His eyes flashed suddenly. "Here." He stretched his arm out and handed her the stringer of fish that were already gasping for lack of water. "You can have them. Just remember who gets the gold. And the trip to England if it comes to that."

"Thank you," she said softly. "You will get your reward."

Suddenly, they heard the sound of distant barking, and Gunther looked toward the great house. "It sounds like you'd better be ready to do some explaining," he cried. "Just leave me out of it." He waded into the water and disappeared into the wooded area on the other side.

Nama, with fast-beating heart, handed the pole to Walks With Thunder. "Carry it in the same manner that Gunther was holding it," she instructed, waiting only until the other woman had slung it over her right shoulder.

Then, feeling as though she were going to her doom, she walked slowly toward the hill where the great house was located.

"I am afraid," Walks With Thunder said, her voice quivering slightly.

"Only a fool would not be," Nama said, striving to control her own trembling. "But if we are careful, we can make them believe us."

Suddenly the dogs emerged from the fields and headed straight for the two girls. Nama held the fish higher, as though she were fearful the dogs would spoil the catch; but in truth, she wanted to make sure the riders saw the stringer of fish.

She stared doubtfully at the dogs as they drew closer, but a quick whistle made them stop just short of the two women. The lead dogs dropped to their bellies, their pink tongues hanging out, their eyes never leaving their prey.

Recognizing Garrick in the lead, Nama waited until he had reined up beside her then pretended indignation. "Why have you set the dogs on me, Garrick?" she complained loudly. "Have you lost your senses?"

"What are you doing here?" he growled, dismounting with fluid grace and glaring at her with his brilliant eyes.

"Fishing," she replied, hoping her voice sounded calm.

"Why?" he asked, staring at the stringer of fish

as though he found them offensive. "Do the fish in the river taste better than those supplied by the servants?"

"Fish always taste better when they are caught by oneself," Nama replied, holding the stringer of fish higher and smiling as though she were proud of them. "Look!" she exclaimed. "There is enough for both our suppers."

"Give the fish to Karl," he said harshly. "You will ride home with me."

Nama was conscious of his palm beneath her breast as they rode to the great house. When they reached the stables, he left the stallion with Peter and dragged her to his longhouse. No sooner had the door closed behind them, then he began to throw questions at her. "Why did you leave without telling anyone? And if you wanted to go fishing, why did you not say so?"

She arched a fine brow. "I left early because that is when the fish bite." She hoped that was true. "I was unaware that I must first ask permission."

"Where did you get the fishing pole and the stringer?"

"From a lad who works in the kitchen." She pressed herself against him and moistened her mouth, aware that he was watching. "Why are you making such a fuss over nothing, Garrick?"

"You will do nothing of the kind again, Nama."

She moved away from him. "So I am still a prisoner?" she questioned, trying to keep her distress from showing. If she were not allowed away from the house she would be unable to put her plan into action.

"You were never a prisoner," he said coldly. "But there are reasons why you cannot be allowed to leave the great house."

"What reasons?"

"We will not speak of them at the moment," he replied, his gaze sweeping over her shift. His lips tightened. "I have already told you that I do not like that thing you are wearing. Why have you not thrown it away?"

"Is it your wish for me to wear the red silk gown to the river, my lord? It would surely be spoiled."

"Then I will have others made," he snarled. "But if you wear that garment one more time, I will rip it apart!"

"Very well," she said coldly, realizing she was wasting time and there was no way of getting gold from this room today. She would have to put Peter off.

"Nama," he sighed, taking her into his arms. "What am I going to do with you? You cannot run wild here as you did in your own land. There are many men who might seek to harm you."

"I can take care of myself," she snapped, wishing her body would not betray her mind as it was doing. Wishing she did not want to press closer to him, that she did not want to feel his flesh against hers, his mouth upon hers.

"Not against such men as these," he said, his palm smoothing down her long, dark hair. "They are hard men, Nama. Fighting men."

"Like you!" she said shortly, fighting the constriction in her throat.

"Like me," he admitted, his gaze softening slightly. "We live in a harsh environment here in Norway, my sweet. We must be hard men to survive the rigors of our society." His arms tightened around her. "But there are times when we can afford to be softer, Nama. Times like now, when we are alone in my chambers and my body wishes to be joined with yours." She made a protesting little move in his arms that only served to tighten his embrace. Then, gently, he tilted her chin upward and lowered his mouth until it brushed against hers in a soothing, controlled kiss that left her wanting more.

Confusion mingled with desire. Whatever she had expected from Garrick, it had not been this exquisite tenderness. She waited with bated breath for him to continue.

"You have much to learn, my sweet," he said, as she continued to stare at him with growing passion.

She swallowed around the lump in her throat. "Then teach me," she said hoarsely. "Teach me now, Garrick."

His mouth quirked ever so slightly as though he were amused by her acquiescence, and she felt a curious hurt that he should laugh at her expense. She moved in the circle of his arms, pressing her hands against his chest in a silent request to be released, but he ignored the action and lowered his mouth ever so slightly until it hovered above her own.

Yet, still, he did not make that final movement that would allow his mouth to cover hers. Instead, he continued to watch her, his green eyes glittering avidly, as though he knew how badly she wanted to feel his lips against hers and was holding back that moment, intent on punishing her for some misdemeanor.

"Let me go," she husked, blinking back the moisture that sprang to her eyes.

"Never!" he whispered fiercely.

She watched the sensuous curve of his mouth as it lowered toward hers. A flash of exquisite sweetness seared through her at the first touch of his lips. Her mouth parted slightly, and he laid claim to that warm, moist cavern as his hands moved down to the small of her back and arched her against him.

Remembering the amused quirk of his mouth, Nama tried to hold back her response, but she might just as well have tried to hold back the tide for all the good it did her. Her arms slid around his neck, her fingers twining in his bright hair as he increased the passion of his kiss and she answered it with her own.

Finally, almost reluctantly, his lips left hers and he stared down at her with eyes that burned with fiery passion. Her heart was pounding faster than its normal rate, and an inner trembling was making it hard to stand on her feet. Her fingers moved without will to his broad chest, and she fumbled with the fastening on his upper garment, feeling the quickened pace of his heartbeat beneath her palm as she did so. A tremulous thrill grew inside her. He wanted her as badly as she desired him.

"Love me," she whispered, her voice thick with emotion.

He shook his head negatively. "No, my dear, I fear I cannot."

"Cannot?" Her fingers stilled against him. "Why?"

"There are things that wait for my attention."

She felt stunned. "What things?" she asked, her mind reeling. What had he been about anyway if it had not been his intention to join with her? Anger began to overcome her. He was responsible for the growing heat in her loins.

"Many things of import," he said, his gaze still locked with hers as though he knew the way she was feeling and felt complete satisfaction for having been responsible for it.

Then, while she stared at him in confusion, he set her aside. "Sweet Nama, we will continue when I return from Kaupang."

Then he left her, and her anger was stirred into a burning flame. It was a flame that burned brighter with each passing moment, but she would not allow its fury to overcome her good sense.

She was alone in Garrick's bedchamber, and the gold that she had promised Gunther was practically in her hands. Nama crossed to the big chest in the corner; but before she could open it, the door was flung wide open and Carlotta stood facing her.

"What are you doing here?" she demanded, her eyes glinting with hatred.

"Garrick brought me here," Nama flung at the other woman, angered at the intrusion.

"Garrick is gone," Carlotta retorted.

"He will return," Nama said, curbing her impatience to be away. If the woman would leave the room, the gold could still be hers.

"When he does return, then he will find me here," Carlotta said, throwing herself on the bed.

Realizing the other woman had no intention of leaving while her rival was in the room, Nama knew she had no choice except to leave herself.

Nama would not allow her anger to show as she left the room and closed the door behind her. But as the day progressed, the anger that had been stirred to life last night and stoked by the events at noon became a flame that burned brighter as the day progressed until that night, having been fed for many hours, it finally erupted.

Twenty-eight

Nama's thoughts whirled furiously as she hurried across the courtyard, devising and discarding plans for releasing Patrick Douglass from the dungeon.

What if he refuses to help? a silent voice questioned.

The thought slowed her pace. She had never even considered that possibility before, and had just imagined that anyone confined as he was in such a horrible place would be willing to do anything to gain his freedom.

But perhaps that was not so, for if memory served her right, the guard had said all he must do to shorten his time there was beg his lord's pardon and ask for favor.

And he had refused!

Patrick Douglass must be a proud man, not easily subdued . . . therefore, despite his pale features, a strong man.

That thought caused hope to flare anew. Such a man was exactly what she needed. He would have the strength to see them through whatever dangers lay ahead of them.

Spirit guide, she cried silently, *Show me the way to release Patrick Douglass from his prison.* Remembering Garrick would only be away for two nights, she added, *And please hurry.*

She was passing between two of the longhouses, paying little attention to her surroundings, when she heard a whisper of sound just before hard fingers curled around her forearm and pulled her into the shadows.

Remembering her confrontation with Carlotta, her cowardly heart jerked with fear. Relief swept over her when she recognized Gunther. "I was—"

"Quiet!" he hissed, his gaze going past her as though he suspected danger lurked nearby. "Come behind the building. Nobody will see us there."

"Is that necessary?" she asked, following him. "Would anyone think it unusual to find us talking together?"

"They might if Garrick realizes the gold is gone and suspects you stole it." After determining they were hidden from view, he turned to face her with outstretched hand. "Give it to me."

"I had no time to search, but—"

"Why not?" he interrupted angrily, his hand falling to his side. "You were still in Garrick's longhouse when he left. You had time to search." He glared at her. "If you think you can—"

"Calm down," she said shortly. "Carlotta came in before I had time to search."

His shoulders drooped suddenly. "Carlotta. I might have known. I saw her go in, but I hoped she stayed away from his bedchamber until you had time to look for the gold." His lips thinned into a straight line, and he glared at her. "You owe me that gold, Nama. I did you a favor, and you owe me."

"You spend too much time thinking about gold," she snapped. "What good is gold here? We need to concentrate on more important things. Like leaving this accursed place."

"I want that gold," Gunther said grimly. "I want to feel it in my pocket when Garrick discovers your plans and throws you in the dungeon."

Nama could hardly believe the lad before her was the same one she had met just a few short days ago. Gone was the carefree youth he had presented to those around him, and in his place was this wild-eyed boy who continued to harangue her about two pieces of gold.

"You will have the gold," Nama said grimly. She had finally taken control of her life again and she had no intention of allowing this boy to interfere in any way. She must convince him to keep silent, to allow her time to complete her plans. "You will have the gold," she repeated. "But you need not keep it in your pocket, Gunther. You will go with us to England. To the woman you call *grandma*. But please, help me find a way to release Patrick Douglass."

Nama had no idea if her words of reassurance about the gold had calmed him or if it had been her reference to his grandma and England. Nor did she care. The only thing that did matter was that when he spoke again he was no longer angry.

"It could be dangerous."

"I know," she told him. "That is the reason I need your help."

"What do you have in mind?" he asked.

"I must speak with Patrick Douglass before we make further plans," she said. "And to do that, the guard must be otherwise occupied."

He frowned at her. "Why is it necessary to talk to him before we get him out?"

"Suppose he refuses to help?" she inquired. "There is no need to release him if he refuses."

Nama felt a sudden stab of guilt as she remembered the pale face pressed against the window, but instantly rejected that guilt. His confinement was none of her doing. And it would be hard enough to escape this place without complicating matters. Releasing a prisoner from the dungeon could alert the guards to their escape sooner; and if they must escape without his help, then Patrick Douglass would have to remain where he was.

"I thought you already had all this worked out," Gunther complained. "But you have done nothing at all. Have you even made plans to obtain a long-boat? We are going to need one, you know."

"I have already thought about that," she said. "I plan on wearing my red-silk gown when we leave this place."

"A red-silk gown?" He smacked his head with his palm. "Is that the whole of your plan? Just to wear the gown? How will that get us a vessel?"

"It will divert the guard so Patrick Douglass can steal up behind him and—"

"Whamo!" he said, smacking his right fist into his left palm. A smile spread across his face. "Do you really think the gown will divert him."

"The gown and myself," she assured him, remembering how Garrick and the other men at the feast had eyed the enormous amount of bosom left exposed when she had worn the gown to the feast.

"It might work," he said, sweeping his gaze over her body, seeming to be surprised at what he saw. "Knowing the guards, I suppose it will. What about food for the trip?" He looked at a small building close by, then added, "I could take care of the food if you can get me the keys to the storehouse."

"Where are they?"

"Cook has them. She keeps them by her all the time."

Nama grimaced. That might prove difficult. "I will do my best to get them," she said. "Now, about Patrick Douglass. Does that same guard stay there all the time?"

"No. They change at regular intervals."

"Would it be possible to speak to Patrick during the changing of the guards?"

"No. The new guard goes down there before the old one comes up."

"The guard sometimes sleeps," she said slowly, wondering if she could catch him sleeping and speak to Patrick without his knowledge.

"So do the prisoners," Gunther commented, apparently reading her mind. "And you might wake the guard while trying to wake Patrick. It seems to me the only chance you've got of talking to him without anybody listening is to knock him out."

"No!" she said with alarm. "That would alert the guards, allow them to know something was happening. Besides, I would never be allowed to enter the dungeon carrying anything strong enough to subdue a guard."

"I meant knock him out with something else," Gunther whispered conspiratorially. "Like sleeping powders. Put some in his ale."

"Sleeping powders?" Nama's eyes widened. "You know where there is such a thing?"

"Sure," he said, cramming his hands into his pockets and leaning back against the wall. He actually seemed to be enjoying himself now. "Cook keeps the drugs locked up in the kitchen."

Cook again. She would be a most formidable opponent. "I will think of something," she said. "Some way to acquire some of the sleeping powder."

"Good. And the sooner the better." He smiled widely at her. "You know, this thing might really work. And, Nama, if we really escape, you can forget about the gold. Seeing my grandma again will be reward enough. When do you plan on seeing Patrick?"

"Tonight," she replied. "And if he agrees, then you must carry word to the old man in the forest. He will meet us tomorrow night at the fjord."

"The old man? Mick O'Halloran?"

"Yes. He will show us the way to your land." *And also mine.* she added silently.

* * *

In a large hall in Kaupang, Fergus Nordstrom addressed an assembly of jarls, each of them interested in learning more about the new land from those who had already been there.

"My sons tell me grapes grow wild there," he said in his great booming voice that was loud enough to reach every corner of the large room. "They grow in such abundance that a man who settled there would no longer have to import his wine. He could make his own."

"What about gold?" inquired the nearest man.

"There might be gold, but—"

"We saw no gold," Garrick interrupted his parent.

"Did you look for gold?" asked Othere.

"No," Garrick admitted. "We did not. Other matters concerned us more. We went in search of our brother."

"Tell them about the blue stones, Garrick," Fergus urged. "Show them the bracelet the woman wore."

"What about the women?" Othere demanded while the bracelet was being handed around. "You say the natives are dangerous, yet you captured two of their women and lost not a man on the journey."

"We lost no men, yet the previous expedition lost six," Garrick reminded. "One of those lost was my brother." He looked out over the assembly. "All of you knew Eric Nordstrom. No other could equal him on the battlefield, and yet, he never returned."

The bracelet had made its rounds among the men until it reached Othere. "The stone is quite unusual," he said, turning it over to study it closer.

"Unusual, yes," Garrick agreed. "But not gold."

"No. But its value is yet to be determined," Othere said slowly. "Perhaps we should show it around the marketplace and see what the merchants would offer."

"The bracelet is not for sale," Garrick said shortly.

"You need not sell it," Othere told him. "You need only to determine its value."

Garrick had no intention of showing the bracelet around the trade grounds. Not now at least. For some reason he felt the need to hurry and return home, to see Nama again and assure himself that all was as it should be. But he had a duty to his fellow Norsemen and he must perform that duty to the best of his ability.

"The land is rich," he told them. "There are many animals and plenty of sunshine and rain to grow healthy crops. But there are great dangers as well. The natives are cunning. They attacked us many times; and, without the speed of our horses which carried us quickly away, we would surely have been killed."

"But you did have the horses," Othere pointed out. "And you did escape."

"Yes. We did," Garrick agreed. "But how many horses could you carry on your ships? My ship was long, and yet my horses were without food for several days before we landed."

"Is it possible you wish to keep the land to yourself?" Othere asked suddenly.

"Of course not," Garrick said with irritation. "I have no intention of ever traveling that way again. Why should I? What good are blue stones when we must journey so far to find them? My family has become wealthy by trading goods of Norway. Our walrus ivory is much sought after, as are our walrus and seal-hide ship-ropes. We breed reindeer for trade, and animal skins are easily come by and much in demand among the people in other lands. All these things are acquired without danger to us."

"When have Norsemen ever been concerned about the dangers involved in settling a new land?" asked Othere. "Was your brother Eric concerned?" He answered his own question. "No, he was not. And neither was Leif Ericson. Otherwise, this new land would still be undiscovered."

"Has your taste for battle suddenly deserted you, Garrick?" taunted Thorolf, who was seated beside Othere.

"If you wish to test my skills, then I will gladly oblige you on the battlefield tomorrow," Garrick said grimly.

The man quickly subsided, for Garrick's skill on the battlefield was known by all and had been equaled by none save his brother Eric.

Garrick knew he had done all he could in Kaupang. If the Norsemen chose to invade the new land, then they would. Nothing he could say would make a difference in their decision. He could only hope that Nama would believe that.

When Nama went to Brynna's bedchamber, she found her sprawled across the bed, her face pale and strained.

"What is wrong, Brynna?" Nama asked, hurrying across the room. "Are you ill?"

"Oh, Nama," Brynna said, opening her eyes to a mere slit. "I am so glad to see you. My maid, Jasmine, has gone to the village, and I have the most pounding headache. Would you go ask Cook for something to ease the pain?"

Nama hurried to the kitchen and approached the cook who was busy kneading dough. "Brynna is ill," Nama blurted out. "She needs something to ease her head."

"A headache?" Cook inquired, rubbing her hands together to rid them of dough. "Poor dear. She has been under such strain since finding out about Eric." She lowered her voice. "The master really should allow her more time. But that is just like a man. He wants what he wants. And right now, he wants her to wed that man."

"What man?"

"You have not heard?" Cook inquired. "The poor dear feels so bad about having to wed Angus Thorvauld. No wonder she stays awake until the wee hours. And no getting out of the marriage either. Garrick spoke to his lordship and was put in his place. The lands have got to be had is the way old Fergus is thinking."

"Lands?" Nama had no idea what the cook was talking about.

"Of course the lands!" the cook snapped. "Old Fergus has an eye on Angus Thorvauld's lands. But no matter how much he covets them, the Lady Brynna should not be sacrificed." She fastened her eagle eye on Nama. "But then, who am I to say what old Fergus can do with his own daughter?"

Nama wondered if the cook expected a reply. Obviously not, she decided when the woman suddenly spun around and hurried to a tall cabinet positioned in the corner of the room.

Unfastening a large key from those hanging from a ring at her waist, she opened the cabinet and extracted a bottle, frowned at it, then extracted another one.

"Take both of these," she said, turning to face Nama again. "This one is headache powders." She handed the small bottle to Nama. "And this other one will make her sleep. But be careful with it. Use just a small amount . . . only a pinch. Too much would be dangerous." Her brows drew into a heavy frown. "Maybe I should—"

"I have knowledge of this powder," Nama said quickly, unwilling to give up the small bottle now that she held it in her hands. "I will administer it carefully, and only if Brynna so desires."

"Very well," Cook agreed. "But as soon as you are done, return the bottles to me."

Nama hurried down the narrow passage leading

to Brynna's bedchamber, her mind already searching for something to hold some of the white powder that she so badly needed.

Brynna lay still on the bed, and for a moment Nama thought she might be sleeping. Then she spoke.

"Were you able to get the powders?"

"Yes," Nama said quickly. She poured a glass of water and carried it to the bedside. "Cook sent the headache powders and she also sent something to make you sleep."

"It does," Brynna agreed. "But give me the headache powder now, Nama. And leave the other bottle here. I might have need of it later."

Nama was delighted to obey. She would have to inform Cook of Brynna's wishes or the woman would surely wonder about the powders. She sat with Brynna until her headache eased enough for her to fall into a deep sleep. Then Nama returned to the kitchen where she informed Cook of Brynna's decision to keep the medicine with her.

Although she looked for Walks With Thunder, she was nowhere about. Nama supposed she had been sent on an errand and determined to seek her out after she had spoken with Patrick Douglass.

That night, after the household was silent, Nama crept to the kitchen and filled a tankard with ale, then added a pinch of the white powder, keeping in mind Cook's warnings about its effect. Then, she made her way to the dungeon.

The shadows seemed even darker than before

and the guard's voice harsher, making Nama wonder if she had made a mistake going there.

"Who goes there?" the guard demanded.

Instead of identifying herself, she called, "I have b-brought you ale." Silently, she cursed her trembling voice.

"Ale?" the guard questioned. "Well then, come on down." He watched her as she descended the stairs. "What a good girl you are," he said, his lips suddenly stretching into a wide smile. "I have trouble staying awake this late at night."

"It is a pity you are required to stand guard here," she said, making her voice sympathetic as she handed the tankard of ale to him. "Is it really necessary? Those iron bars look strong enough to keep any prisoner behind them." She moved closer to the barred door of Patrick's cell.

"And so it is," the guard agreed, eagerly lifting the tankard to his mouth. He took a long swallow then said, "Those doors are solid enough. Thick, too. They are strong enough to withstand the strength of six men. Only a key can open those doors. This key." He patted a large key fastened to his belt.

"Are you sure?" she asked, gripping the bars with her hands as though testing their strength when in reality she hoped to waken the prisoner within.

"I am that," he said, raising the tankard again to finish the ale. When he had done so, he gave a loud belch. "Good stuff," he grunted. "And I thank you kindly for bringing it."

Since he showed no sign of being affected by the drink, Nama wondered if she had given him enough of the powders. Perhaps her pinches were not as large as Cook's pinches were.

"What are you doing up so late?" the guard asked abruptly.

Fearing his questions and feeling certain she had not put enough powder in his drink, she moved away from the cell and put a foot on the stairs that would take her out of his reach. "I had to fetch headache powders for the Lady Brynna," she replied, making it appear she had only recently done so. "Cook told me to bring the ale," she lied smoothly.

"That was nice of the old bird," he commented. "She deserves my thanks for sending the ale. Nobody else thinks of me. Very few even know I exist." He expelled a long sigh and sank down into the chair that was placed near the wall. "They send me down here with orders to guard the prisoners and then forget about me." He sighed again and scratched his shaggy head. "Cook has more sympathy for her fellow man than I would ever have thought. Beneath that hefty bosom lies a heart of gold." His dark eyes pinned Nama. "You be sure and tell her how much the ale was appreciated. No!" he said suddenly. "it would be more polite for me to tell her myself."

"Oh, no!" Nama exclaimed, fear surging through her. "She would not expect that. You must not!"

"And why not?" His eyes narrowed suspiciously.

"Well, it is just . . . maybe she does not want others to know she has a sympathetic streak. After all they might think to take advantage of her."

"You could be right," he agreed. "And I guess that would make her think twice about sending more ale to me."

"Yes," she said quickly. "It certainly would."

"Hmmmm. Then you tell the old dear for me."

"I will."

He uttered another sigh and leaned back in his chair. "Run along with you now," he said kindly. "And many thanks for bringing the ale."

Nama backed up the stairs, keeping her eyes on the guard, whose eyelids drooped lower and lower until they finally closed. She stood there for a long moment, afraid to move until he began to snore. Then she crept quietly down the stairs again and crossed the small room to the first cell door.

"Patrick," she whispered, "Are you awake?"

"That I am," he answered quickly. "What are you about, lass? Did you drug the guard?"

"Yes."

"Then get his key and unlock the door. And be quick about it!"

"Not yet," she said.

"When then?"

"Tomorrow night. Maybe."

He uttered a curse. "Why wait? If you are going to set me free, then why not now?"

"First, plans must be made. And promises given."

"Speak if you must then. But my mind would rest easier if I were already out of here."

"Where would you go?" she inquired. "What would you do?"

He remained silent for a long moment, and she realized he must be considering her question. Then, he spoke again. "Nowhere on this godforsaken island."

"Then we will have need of a longboat. And food. And someone who can navigate the vessel."

"My desire to be free must have clouded my mind," he growled. "Speak, girl. Tell me your plan."

She wasted no time in doing so.

"It might just work," he rasped when she had ceased speaking. "How many men have you already recruited?'

"Only you and the old man and Gunther."

His snort of contempt was explosive, leaving no doubt in her mind what he thought of her other recruits. "We need more men," he snarled. "The plan has no chance of working without a crew."

"I stand ready to help," came a voice from the next cell.

"And me," said another farther down the way.

"That makes three men, one old man, a boy, and a woman," Patrick said. "Still not enough." He remained silent, then said, "Can you go to the town?"

"If I cannot, then Gunther could."

"Good. Get word to three men there." He gave her the names. "They might be interested since you already have a longboat and supplies. Do you think you can get word to me after you speak to them?"

"No. We dare not risk it. To come here again might make the guard wonder. And we cannot take the chance that he might refuse the drink tomorrow night."

"Then we must rely on you."

The guard snorted suddenly and Nama spun around, fearing he had already wakened. But his eyes were still closed, and he resumed his snoring. Nevertheless, Nama felt the drug might already be wearing off.

Patrick Douglass must have been of the same mind, for he spoke urgently. "Away with you, lass. If the guard wakes and finds you here, all will be lost!"

Nama needed no further urging. She hurried up the stairs and went straight to the servants' quarters to speak with Walks With Thunder, but the woman was not on her pallet.

"Who is there?" inquired Elspeth, rubbing her sleepy eyes.

"Nama," she said, identifying herself. "I am looking for Walks With Thunder."

"She is no longer here," Elspeth replied. "I thought you would have known."

"Where is she?"

"In Olaf's longhouse. He asked her to be his wife. All the servants are talking about her good fortune. How is it you did not know?"

"I have been kept busy today and had no time to see her," Nama replied.

Realizing she could not count on Walks With Thunder's help now, Nama retired to her bedchamber, intent on getting as much sleep as she could before morning came.

Twenty-nine

Nama had barely settled down on her bed when she heard the squeak of her door opening. A flicker of apprehension swept over her.

Who sought her out so late at night?

Her heart began a steady thud as she pushed herself to her elbows, readying herself for flight if it became necessary.

"N-Nama?" a trembling voice questioned.

The words alone were enough to identify the speaker, for who but Walks With Thunder would know the language of the People?

"I am here," Nama said gravely.

"Would you allow me to enter?"

"Friends need not ask permission."

"Neither do friends keep secrets from one another," replied Walks With Thunder, pushing the door wide enough to allow her body entry.

"Some things do not need explaining," Nama said sadly. "Your love for Olaf is one of those things."

"And I do love him," the woman said, quickly crossing the room to the bed. "My heart was dead until Olaf found me. He has made me live again."

"I know," Nama replied, thinking about her own foolish heart. "Do not concern yourself, Walks With Thunder. I—"

"Desert Flower," the woman quickly corrected. "Olaf has thrown away the name of Walks With Thunder and has given me back my first name." Her voice trembled when she added, "He called me his little Desert Flower. He truly loves me."

"Of course he does," Nama replied, trying to control her own envy.

"He has not even joined with me," the woman who had been called Walks With Thunder said. "He said we would wait until the marriage took place." She groped for Nama's hand. "He must mean what he says. If he only wanted to join with me, he would not wait to take my body, would he?"

Nama realized the woman was unable to accept that a man like Olaf could so easily love her. "No, he would not," she said firmly. "Put thoughts of that nature out of your mind. Be happy, Walks—" She broke off and quickly corrected, "—Desert Flower."

"I am," Desert Flower cried. "But it seems wrong for me to find happiness when you cannot."

"It is not everyone's destiny to find happiness with a mate," Nama told her friend with a heavy sigh.

"You would not consider staying here?"

"No," Nama replied heavily. "I cannot."

"Your answer is not unexpected," Desert Flower said. "I would have gone with you if Olaf had not spoken out. But he has, and now I could never bring myself to leave him."

She placed her palm on Nama's cheek in a soft caress. "May the spirits watch over you in your journey home. Goodbye, friend."

Moisture filled Nama's eyes. "Goodbye, Desert Flower."

The woman's bare feet slapped against the cold stone floor as she crossed the room and slipped through the doorway, then eased the door closed behind her, leaving Nama in darkness again.

Nama felt surprise to feel moisture sliding down her face. *Tears?* she questioned, wiping them away with the back of her hand. This was no time for tears. Instead, she should be rejoicing.

"It *is* a time for rejoicing," she muttered. "Walks With Thunder has become Desert Flower."

Nama knew she need not worry about the other woman's future. Not when it was in the hands of a man like Olaf Nordstrom. So why was her heart a tight knot of pain? she wondered. Why did it ache with such intensity?

Not because of Desert Flower, she suddenly realized. No. It was because Nama herself had hoped to find such happiness with Olaf's brother Garrick.

Garrick, her heart cried, *why could you not love me?*

Hurt was a thick knot in her throat, and her eyes slowly filled again; but she could not give way to her pain, could not allow herself the relief of tears.

A knock on the door startled her, and she slid from the bed and hurried across the room. She pulled the door open, expecting to find Desert Flower again. Instead, she found Brynna Nordstrom.

"Nama," the girl said. "I heard your door open and knew you must be awake. May I come in?"

"Of course," Nama replied, holding the door wider so that Brynna could enter. "Is something wrong?" she questioned. "if you are unable to sleep, then we could use some of the sleeping powders."

"Yes," Brynna sighed. "I do not like using the powders, but neither do I like staying awake all night."

"Perhaps if you stayed with me awhile . . . if you spoke of what troubles you so . . ." Had she been too presumptuous? Nama wondered.

"You would not mind if I stayed awhile?"

"Of course not," Nama said firmly.

Although she realized how badly she needed sleep so her mind would be clear for what lay ahead, Nama felt drawn to this girl who had been nothing but kind to her.

"Stay the night if you like," she urged. "My bed is soft. And wide," she added. "It will easily accommodate two people."

Brynna, needing no further urging, curled up on Nama's bed. "Which side do you want?" she asked.

"It matters little," Nama said, amazed the girl had even asked the question.

"Then you take the front side," Brynna said, scooting across the bed to make room for Nama.

Hesitantly, Nama resumed her position on the bed. Brynna was silent for a while, then she spoke. "Are you in love with Garrick, Nama?"

Whatever Nama had expected, it had not been that. She thought about how to answer and then decided to be truthful. "Yes."

"I thought so. Do you mind that he has other women?"

"Yes. Would you mind?"

"I have no idea," Brynna replied. "But I think if I loved a man that . . . yes!" Her voice became firm. "I would mind."

If I loved a man. The words echoed in Nama's mind. Was that what troubled Brynna. That she must soon wed a man that she did not care for? "Brynna?"

"Hmmmm?"

"They say in the kitchen that you are soon to wed."

For a moment there was silence and Nama wondered if she should have kept silent. Then Brynna spoke. "Yes, that is true. Father has promised me to Angus Thorvauld."

The bitterness in her voice told Nama the other girl did not favor the marriage. "The marriage is unacceptable to you?"

"Yes. Completely unacceptable."

"Then you must not join with him."

"What can I do, Nama? Father wants this marriage. He will force it on me whatever my wishes." Her voice trembled and she sniffed, obviously near tears. "Father does not see his cruelty. Angus has

little patience, particularly for women. Angus will
not allow for my innocence but will take me ruthlessly." Her voice became wild. "I told Garrick Angus would ravish me, if necessary, but he paid no
heed. Eric would not have allowed this to happen.
If he were in Garrick's shoes he would have
thought of some way to save me."

"You must not allow yourself to be used in such
a manner," Nama said, feeling the other girl's pain
and fear.

"What can I do?" Brynna cried.

"Run away." Nama advised. "That is what I did
when the shaman wanted me to wed Standing
Wolf. He was a cruel man who had already gone
through several wives," she added harshly. "I
would not be another."

"You ran away from your people? That is how
you came to be alone when Garrick found you?"
Brynna took Nama's hand. "How did you ever find
the courage to go alone?"

"I did not leave the clan alone," Nama replied.
"I could not have done so when I am such a coward."

"A coward?" Brynna laughed shakily. "Would
that I could be such a coward, Nama. You are the
bravest woman I have ever known."

"No. I am a coward. Had not Shala consented
to travel with me then I could never have found
the courage to leave."

"Shala?"

"Did I not speak of her before? She was a true
friend. She was an outcast, living alone until she

found Eric. She came to me then and asked for help moving him to her cave. He was heavy, such a big man, as Garrick and Olaf are. And he required so much food while he recovered from the broken leg he had suffered in his fall. But Shala had been alone long enough to know how to hunt. She was able to supply him with enough food until he was well and able to—'' Nama broke off suddenly, aware of Brynna's still, almost breathless state, aware too of how much she had revealed. But perhaps the damage could yet be mended. Perhaps—

"Then it was Shala," Brynna's voice came out of the silence. The bed squeaked as she raised up on her elbows; and although the room was in darkness, Nama could feel the other girl's gaze. "Not you, but your friend Shala who found my brother. It was she who loved him. Who cared for him. Why did you say otherwise?" she questioned. "Why did you say you found him, Nama?" Without waiting for an answer, she went on. "I thought it was unusual that you could speak so calmly of his death, that there was no emotion in your voice. It was because you did not love him. Shala did. You were only a friend, someone not truly involved with him."

Realizing there was no use denying Brynna's words, Nama said, "Yes. It was Shala who loved him."

"Why did you say it was you?" Brynna questioned.

"Because I thought Garrick would be grateful and treat me with kindness." She had to make Brynna understand. "I was afraid, Brynna. Your brothers are so big, and I was alone with them. I did not mean to mislead them about Eric. They mistook my words, thought he was dead, and I allowed them to—" Nama broke off, uttering a gasp of horror as she realized what she had disclosed.

"You lied!" Brynna accused in a shocked voice. "Nama, you lied about Eric's death!" She removed her hand from Nama's.

Tears welled into Nama's eyes and she began to sob quietly, pushing her face into her hands. "Yes," she whispered. "My tongue did not speak the truth."

"He lives?"

"Yes, he lives."

Brynna scrambled off the bed and stood trembling beside it. "I cannot believe it," she cried. "Eric is alive! Oh, I must tell Mother. I must tell Father and Garrick and Olaf. Eric is alive!" She danced around the room, whirling madly for a moment in her excitement. "We must—" Suddenly she broke off and stared at Nama. "Nama," she said in a subdued voice. "Do not take on so. It is a time for rejoicing."

"You forgive me?"

"Of course I forgive you," the other girl said, putting her arms around Nama. "Did you not think I would? Is that why you are crying?"

"Garrick will not forgive me so easily," Nama said.

"He might be angry," Brynna conceded. "Probably even furious. After all, it means returning to your land to fetch my brother. But he will soon forget his fury, I think. Perhaps though, it would be best if you stay out of his way for a while."

That was putting it mildly, Nama thought. "What will become of me?" she questioned.

"Become of you?" Brynna asked. "You will stay here with me."

"And when you have gone?"

"The wedding!" Brynna said. "In my excitement I had forgotten about the wedding." She thought for a long moment, then said, "I will not marry Angus. I will appeal to Eric, and he will put a stop to it."

"When is the marriage planned?"

"Next month," Brynna said forlornly. "Eric cannot help me. There is no time to go there and bring him back."

Nama spoke before she thought. "You could go to him, Brynna."

"Go to Eric?" Brynna questioned. "You mean take a ship and travel to your land?" She was obviously excited at the thought. "But where could I find a crew willing to take me there?"

"Would you really consider it if you did have a crew?" Nama asked breathlessly.

"I most certainly would," Brynna said emphatically.

"I have a solution. But first, I must have your promise to keep my secret."

"You have it."

So Nama told her of the plans already in progress. Brynna listened breathlessly, added her own ideas, and extracted a promise from Nama there would be no bloodshed—a promise quickly given. Then the women began to revise the old plan.

Thirty

The sun was high overhead by the time the Nordstrom men reached their home. Although he was impatient to see Nama, Garrick forced himself to wait, telling himself that he would see her in due time. There were other matters that must, of necessity, claim his attention first. Things that should have been done long ago.

He dreaded the moments ahead, knowing they would be awkward, perhaps even painful to some. As a result, his stride was not as bold, not as confident as usual, when he entered the longhouse given over to Karin, the oldest of his concubines, and informed her of his intention to marry soon.

"Will your marriage affect our relationship, my lord?" she asked softly, her delicate skin flushing as she peeked at him from beneath thick lashes.

"Yes, it will, Karin. It is for that reason I have sought you out before speaking to the woman involved." He shifted uncomfortably. How did you tell a woman you had been so intimate with that you no longer desired her? And how would it make her feel? Would she burst into tears? Garrick expected that reaction and hated the very thought of a tearful, distraught woman. "You may stay here if that is your wish, Karin. Or you may return to your home. Either way, you will have enough gold to assure you of a comfortable future."

Her gaze shifted to the window as though she could not bear to look at him any longer. "Then you have no further use for me?" she whispered.

"No," he said abruptly, hating the conversation, wanting not to be here, wishing he could leave before realization struck and her tears began to flow. Yet he could not act in such a cowardly way.

There was no sign of tears when Karin's gaze swept back to him. And, to his utmost consternation, she actually smiled. "Then will you arrange for my return home?"

Whatever Garrick had expected, it had certainly not been this calm acceptance. A sting of betrayal struck him. Realizing she was still waiting for an answer, he replied, "Yes, of course, Karin. Just let me know when you are ready to leave."

"Tomorrow," she said.

His copper-colored eyebrows swept up in surprise. "Can you really be ready so soon?"

Her expression was one of amusement. "I have been ready since you returned from abroad, my lord. I realized one day this would happen."

"How could you possibly know when I did not?"

"Perhaps I know you better than you know yourself."

"Please explain."

"It is not in your nature to commit less than your whole heart."

Commit his heart? Yes, he silently admitted. It was definitely committed.

"Do the other women also know my heart has been taken?" he asked dryly.

"Yes. They know."

"And will they accept my marriage as easily as you have?"

Instead of answering his question, she chose to explain, perhaps thinking to save his feelings. "Griselda has often spoken lovingly of her home, my lord. Her family is poor and your generosity well known. She will not trouble you with tears. And Lupe . . . well, she has spoken many times of her plans should you ever tire of her. Again, your generosity will help her achieve those plans."

"Carlotta?" he inquired.

"Carlotta is Carlotta. She does not confide in others." She shrugged her shoulders. "Who can say what Carlotta will do?"

Garrick found out soon enough. Carlotta ranted and raved and cursed the day he was born, swearing she would not allow him to share a life with the *skraeling* bitch.

"You have no say in the matter," Garrick said shortly. "You have been offered gold for services rendered although that was not necessary. Take the gold and leave voluntarily, Carlotta, or find yourself sold in the slave market."

"Sold as a slave?" she gasped, her face becoming ashen. "You would really do that to me?"

"I will do whatever is necessary," he said coldly. "The choice is yours to make."

"There is no choice," she said shortly. "I will take the gold you offer. But I would rather stay here in my longhouse."

"That option is no longer open to you," he said curtly.

"But you said it was," she cried, clutching his forearm with talon-like fingers.

"That was before you made threats against Nama," he said coldly, uncurling her fingers one by one. "I cannot forget those. And I will not have my wife tormented by you."

"Why do you marry her? She brings you no fortune, no lands."

"I have no need of those things," he said harshly. "Now, do you go voluntarily?"

Carlotta silently turned away from him. "Yes, and I will do it today, my lord."

"A wise decision," he said, turning on his heels and striding from the room.

After making arrangements for Carlotta's departure, Garrick returned to his longhouse and poured himself a glass of mead, feeling a need to wash the sour taste his confrontation with Carlotta had left in his mouth.

"Do you require anything, my lord?"

Garrick turned to see his maid, Matilda, standing in the doorway. "Not right now," he said.

He slumped down on a nearby settee and waited for the mead to relax his tense muscles. But for some reason, that did not occur. He looked around the room, noting the paintings hanging from the wall, each chosen by himself with an eye to making his home as pleasing to the eye as was possible.

But the room had a lonely feel to it.

It took him a moment to realize what was lacking. It was Nama.

Nama. Woman of the Eagle Clan.

She was such a little bit of a thing; but somehow she had crept beneath his defenses, had found her way into that cold, knotted organ that passed for his heart. How had this happened? he questioned. At what moment in time had she become so necessary to his happiness?

Uncurling his long legs, he leaned forward and restlessly stirred the coals in the fireplace, watching them spit and spark as he did so. How like those coals of fire their relationship had become . . . steadily glowing one moment, sparking to flame the next.

Garrick felt an urgent need to see her, to have her speak her feelings aloud. She was not immune to his charms, he knew. She was guileless, unable to hide the way she felt when they made love. There was no doubt in his mind that she cared for him, so why did she continue to shy away each time he came near?

Perhaps she was only waiting for him to speak out, to make his intentions clear. Well, she need not wait any longer.

"Matilda!" he roared.

She came immediately, as though she were hovering just outside the door waiting for his call.

"Send word to Nama that I require her company for the evening meal. I want her dressed as befitting her status as my future wife. That part is not to be disclosed," he added, "only attended to."

"Right away, my lord."

"No." He stopped her from leaving. "Stay a moment longer. We have a meal to plan. It must be perfect. Two candles on the table, placed just so. A bottle of wine and some cheese and . . . bread. We must have bread and meat."

The woman turned to leave, but Garrick immediately called her back. "Sweetmeats, too, Matilda," he said. "Several kinds. Perhaps some spice cakes and . . . oh, yes, those little poppyseed cakes."

"Yes, my lord," the woman said, her lips twitching slightly. "And will there be anything else?"

Just Nama, he thought as he shook his head at the woman. Just my woman from the Eagle Clan.

A thrill of frightened anticipation swept over Nama as she made her way to Garrick's longhouse that evening. She had been caught unprepared by his unexpected arrival but, vowing not to be deterred, had quickly revised their plans to include his presence.

Nama had bathed carefully, allowing Brynna to

dab a small amount of perfume behind her ears
and in the valley between her breasts, and she had
dressed carefully in one of Brynna's nicest gowns.
Fashioned from the finest cloth—pure Byzantine
silk—the gown dipped low, barely covering her nipples, which left her feeling exposed. The turquoise
silk had been gathered beneath her breasts then
allowed to fall in a straight line to her ankles, effectively hiding her lower body unless she moved.
Then, the fabric clung to her body, molding and
caressing her hips in a manner that had turned
heads as she crossed the great room where the others waited for the evening meal.

Nama was conscious of the exquisitely crafted
silver filigree bracelet she wore on her left wrist.
She had been assured that Garrick was completely
unaware of the bracelet's dual purpose since
Brynna had acquired it in Novgorod while he was
gone.

Finding herself at the door of Garrick's longhouse, Nama knocked hesitantly. Heavy footsteps
sounded from within, and the door was suddenly
flung open.

Garrick stood before her.

She had never before seen him dressed in such
splendor. A green-silk shirt with billowing sleeves
gathered close around the wrists was tucked into
tight black trousers that molded his hips and
clung to the firm mound of his manhood.

Nama was unaware that she was staring until
he reached out, curled his fingers around her

forearm, and pulled her inside, shutting the door firmly behind him.

Then, blushing furiously, she stood before him, wondering if it would be as easy as she had thought to leave him.

"You are lovely," he said huskily, pulling her into his embrace and pressing a soft kiss against her cheek.

"It is the gown," she replied. "Brynna's gown. It would look good on anyone."

"Soon there will be no need to wear my sister's gowns," he said gruffly. "When I was in Kaupang I engaged a seamstress. She should arrive tomorrow. She will make all the gowns you desire."

"Did she make the gowns for your concubines?" she asked.

"No. It was another woman," he said, setting her aside and crossing the room so that he might look into his bedchamber. Apparently satisfied with what he saw, he turned back with a grin. "Are you hungry?" he asked. When she gave a nod, he went on. "Good. Matilda has our meal ready and waiting."

"In the bedchamber?" she asked hesitantly.

"Yes," he replied softly. "In the bedchamber."

Their last meal together was all that Nama could have wished. The candlelight cast flickering shadows across Garrick's angular features, making him appear dangerous, almost sinister. She chided herself for allowing her imagination to roam unchecked.

Garrick was not some unknown malevolent

spirit. He was the same man who had caressed her in the most intimate manner possible, the same man who had shown her such exquisite pleasure when they had joined together aboard the long-boat.

Why did he seem so fearsome now? she wondered. Was it because she knew he would react in a violent manner when he discovered her missing? The very thought of his reaction caused goose bumps to break out on her arms, and she shivered with fear.

"Are you cold?" Garrick asked, noticing the re-action.

"Yes, my lord. Would you stir up the fire?"

"Of course," he said.

While his back was turned, Nama pressed the catch on the filigree bracelet, opening a secret compartment, and shook some of the white pow-der contained inside into Garrick's silver-rimmed goblet

After stirring the mixture with her finger, she quickly added more wine to cover any taste of the powder. She had barely finished when he put the poker aside and took her in his arms.

"Wait, my lord," she whispered. "I have poured wine to relax you."

"I am relaxed enough," he growled, claiming her lips with a hard kiss.

When he lifted his head, she spoke in a breathy whisper. "We must not rush this moment, my lord. We must savor it for a while. I have poured you a drink so we could toast each other."

"That requires two drinks," he said, "unless you wish to share mine."

She hastened to pour another and handed him his goblet. "To us," she murmured, raising her glass toward the ceiling.

"To us," he repeated, draining the goblet quickly.

Nama's heart thumped loudly as he reached for her. Her garments quickly disappeared, as did his, and then he joined her on the bed, covering her lips with his own.

Nama wound her arms around his neck and returned his kiss fervently, knowing that he would soon be fast asleep.

He sighed as his lips left hers. "I am more tired than I realized," he said gruffly.

"Then sleep for a while," she said softly, smoothing his brow with the tip of her forefinger. "There will be time for loving later."

His lips curled into a smile, and he yawned widely. "I have been waiting for a chance to speak with you alone and now all I can think of is sleep."

"You are overtired from your journey," she whispered, keeping her voice low to encourage drowsiness. "You may rest, my lord, knowing that I will be here when you wake."

Expelling a sigh, he closed his eyes and settled down comfortably.

Nama waited until his even breathing told her he was asleep, then she delved into the chest in the corner until she found a length of silk rope.

Realizing she had little time to finish what she had started, she bound his feet to the bedposts. When that was done, she attended to his right hand, wrapping the rope around it and tying it off to the bedpost.

She was tugging at the rope to test its strength when his eyelids lifted and he stared at her. "What are you doing?" he asked, tugging at his bound hands.

"Binding you, my lord," she replied with a smile. "Just the way I was bound on your vessel."

He smiled at her, obviously believing she was playing some kind of game with him. "And do you intend to make love to me, to retaliate in kind?"

"Yes." She tugged at the rope binding his other wrist. Like the other one, it held firm, unyielding.

"You need not do this, you know," he said huskily. "I can think of nothing more pleasurable than having you make love to me."

She allowed her gaze to roam freely over his nakedness, admiring the broadness of his chest, the muscular shoulders and his slender hips, knowing it would be the last time she would ever see him.

But she intended to make it memorable, to store up memories to last a lifetime. As they must, since she would be returning to the land of her birth.

Leaning over him, she flicked her tongue across the flat male nipples, one after the other, taking pleasure from the way he sucked in his breath at her first touch.

Realizing she had started too low, she moved higher and outlined his lips with her tongue. His groan brought her immense satisfaction.

She closed her mouth over his earlobe and nipped it with her teeth.

"Ouch," he said, but a quick look told her there was a smile on his lips.

She bit him again, harder this time.

"That hurt," he complained.

"Good," she whispered softly, inserting her tongue in his ear.

Garrick sucked in a sharp breath, and Nama realized something had happened to his lower body. His maleness was hard against her leg. She restrained a smile and turned to the other ear, inserting the tip of her tongue.

He strained against the ropes, breathing heavily. "Release me, Nama," he begged, writhing on the bed. "I want to touch you."

"No," she said. "I am not yet finished."

She ran her tongue down his neck, licking and biting his flesh and tweaking his nipples as she went. She could actually feel his heart thumping inside his chest and found a sense of satisfaction at that.

Closing her mouth over his left nipple, she laved it with her tongue while her right hand sought the rigid staff that stood erect. As her fingers closed around the silken flesh, Garrick uttered another deep groan.

Feeling encouraged by his reaction, Nama stroked him gently while all the time she moved down his body with her tongue, dipping the tip into his navel and twisting it back and forth before continuing lower . . . down the hardness of his belly toward the hard throbbing flesh of his staff.

"Stop it, Nama," he growled. "Allow me freedom, woman! I want to hold you in my arms. I want—"

He broke off with another groan when her lips found the softness between his thighs. She nipped the delicate skin there, stroking her tongue up his long staff until her lips closed around it.

"Odin's blood, woman!" he choked. "Stop this torture."

But she would not. She continued to stroke him until he was near explosion. Only then did she raise herself above him to insert his staff into her hot feminine core. Then she rode him, faster and faster, each stroke building in strength until they both reached their peak and found their release in an eruption so powerful that the bed actually moved several feet across the floor.

Nama lay atop him then, quivering, drained. She had not expected to be so affected herself, and that she was left her saddened. And angry.

Garrick had stolen her heart, had taken everything she had to give without giving anything of himself in return.

"Release me, Nama," he said huskily. "Release me now."

"No."

"Release me, woman, or you shall rue this day!"

"Your threats do not disturb me, my lord," she said, leaving the bed and gathering up her clothing.

"I make no threats," he rasped harshly, his voice becoming louder. "You may consider it a promise."

"Neither do your promises disturb me. Why should they? You can do nothing trussed up the way you are. And by the time you are released, I will be far out of your reach."

"Nama," he roared. "Turn me—"

He never finished what he was saying, because, fearing he would be heard, she snatched up a cloth and stuffed it into his mouth. "Now close your eyes and sleep, my lord."

"Mmmpphhh, mmmpphhh." Although he could not speak around the rag, it was not for want of trying. And all the while his eyes promised retribution.

She looked at him sorrowfully. "We could have been happy, Garrick," she said.

A growl came out of his throat as he tried to work the rag out of his mouth while his brilliant eyes gazed—no! pleaded—with her.

Somehow, she did not take pleasure in knowing that he was pleading. Instead, the knowledge disturbed her. "If only things had been different," she said. "If only you had cared."

"Mmmpphhh!" he said as she placed a soft kiss on his cheek, then finished dressing herself.

* * *

Nama wondered, as she left him there if she would ever get over the pain of leaving him.

She believed she would not.

Thirty-one

Garrick's heartbeat thundered in his ears as he fought desperately to free himself, bucking and twisting and writhing on the bed. But all his efforts were in vain.

He cursed himself for a fool! She must be gloating over how easily he had been overcome, how trusting he had been. He should have been suspicious of her acquiescence, of her apparent eagerness to be in his arms.

Damn her! She was capable of the foulest treachery. And yet, even knowing that, his foolish heart, that twisted, gnarled organ that was so vital to life, was afraid for her.

I will be out of your reach. Out of your reach. Your reach. Your reach, your reach.

The words echoed over and over in his mind. What had she meant by that? he wondered. Where could she possibly go in this land that was so unfamiliar to her where he could not reach her?

Nowhere.

But she had seemed so certain, so sure of herself. She had obviously thought the whole thing out, most certainly had a plan of some kind.

But what? he wondered. She could do nothing alone . . . could go nowhere without help of some kind.

His heart gave a sudden jerk of fear. Had she obtained help from someone? It was a distinct possibility. But whom? Who would dare risk his wrath by helping her escape?

Realizing he must find her quickly, before harm could befall, he renewed his efforts to free himself.

He bucked and jerked and yanked at his wrists, feeling the warm spurt of blood as his skin was abraded, but the bonds held tight.

He was making enough noise to alert anyone nearby. But he had dismissed the maid and was now alone in his longhouse.

Even as that thought occurred, he heard a thump beyond the door. His pulse raced with sudden hope. Had Nama returned?

"Mmmpphhh!" he said, cursing the rag that made it impossible for him to shout. If it were Nama in the other room, then she knew his circumstances. But if it were his maid returning for some unknown reason—

"Mmmpphhh!" he said again, staring at the door with burning eyes.

Creak!

The sound was unmistakable now. Someone *was*

out there. If only it were Nama having second thoughts about leaving.

"Mmmpphhh!" he uttered to remind her he was still waiting to be released.

Suddenly the door to the bedchamber was shoved open a crack; but, although candlelight streamed across the room, it did not reach the bed, which remained in shadows.

"Garrick," a deep voice whispered. "Are you asleep?"

It was not Nama, but Olaf who had entered the longhouse.

"Mmmpphhh!" Garrick groaned, bucking his body until the bed trembled. "Mmmpphhh!"

"What?" Olaf asked. "What did you say, Garrick?"

"Mmmpphhh!" If Garrick could have spoken, Olaf would have felt the lash of his tongue. Yet he just stood there, his gaze never once seeking out the bed where Garrick was confined.

Why did the lummox stand so hesitantly on the threshold? And why did he keep his eyes averted from the bed?

Garrick bucked and jerked, his body rising upward and falling with such force that the bed trembled and bounced. "Mmmpphhh!" he said.

"Sorry, Garrick," Olaf muttered, jerking his head back. And, to Garrick's utter astonishment, his brother pulled the door toward him, obviously intending to shut it and leave Garrick the way he was.

Garrick vowed in that moment to strangle his

brother the very moment he gained his freedom.
"Mmmpphhh!" he howled. "Mmmpphhh!"

He jerked his body upward again, letting it fall
with enough force to scoot the bed at least three
inches from its original position.

Immediately, the door was shoved open
again . . . a mere crack just large enough to allow
Olaf's head to enter the darkened room. "Garrick?" he whispered, his gaze still carefully averted
from the bed. "Garrick? Are you all right?"

"Mmmpphhh!" Garrick moaned, rolling his eyes
at his brother and bucking his body again until the
bed moved another two inches.

Hesitantly, as though unsure how his actions
would be received, Olaf shoved the door wider,
allowing the beam of candlelight to fall across the
bed.

"Mmmpphhh!" Garrick growled.

Olaf looked at the bed, and his eyes grew round
with surprise. "Garrick!" Olaf exclaimed, hurrying toward the bed. "What happened to you?"

Garrick rolled his eyes at his brother and said
again, "Mmmpphhh!"

"How did you get this way?" Olaf asked, working at the rope that bound Garrick's wrist to the
right bedpost. "Did Nama do this to you? By
Odin's blood, you look funny, spread out that
way." A rumble started deep in Olaf's chest, and
Garrick glared angrily at his brother. If he dared
to laugh—

One look at Garrick's grim expression sent
Olaf's laughter into hiding.

Suddenly Garrick's wrist was free, and he yanked the rag out of his mouth and uttered a stream of curses that even sent his brother's eyebrows shooting upward.

"Lummox!" Garrick finally declared. "Where have you been?"

"In my bedchamber," Olaf said, stepping back to eye his brother resentfully. "There is no need to call me names, Garrick. I came as soon as I knew something was wrong."

"Knew something was wrong?" Garrick questioned quickly. "How could you know?"

"Desert Flower told me. She was obviously upset about something but refused to tell me what she was concerned about. As soon as I learned the reason, I came directly here to warn you."

"Are you going to tell me what she said," Garrick asked impatiently, "or must I guess?"

"From the looks of you, I expect you already know."

"Thor's blood, Olaf! Would I be asking you if I already knew what was going on?"

"Nama told you nothing?"

"Only that she would be out of my reach by the time I was released."

"And so she shall if her plan works."

"And that plan is . . ."

"Nama has devised a plan for leaving Norway."

"Alone?"

"No. She plans on releasing Patrick Douglass from the dungeon. I started to go there first, but since your longhouse is next to mine it seemed more practical to come here on the way. I thought you might have convinced her to stay with you." His look was rueful. "And the way that bed kept bouncing so hard, I thought surely—" He flushed and broke off suddenly. "It sounded as though you and Nama had settled your differences."

All the time Olaf had been speaking, Garrick had been donning his garments. He could not waste a moment. He was not sure how long she had been gone; but if he hurried, he might be able to stop her from releasing the prisoners.

It was already too late for that. Nama had again drugged the guard's ale and used his key to release Patrick, Lacey, and another man whose name she had yet to be told. Immediately upon his release, Patrick had relieved the guard of his sword and knife, handing the latter to Lacey with instructions to use it only if necessary.

Lacey quickly objected. "The guard should be permanently silenced," he growled.

"He can do us no harm," Patrick growled, sparing a momentary glance for the sleeping guard. "Not tied up the way he is."

"Neither can a dead man," Lacey snarled.

"Leaving him dead could get us hanged if they catch up to us," Patrick declared, rounding on the other man. "Up to now we have only been thorns in their sides, but that would change if they found the guard dead." His expression hardened. "And Lacey," he added softly, "I am in charge here. If you have different ideas, then you can forget them right now."

Fear coiled inside of Nama, tightening her stomach into a knot as she hurried up the stairs leading from the cold, damp dungeon. She had not allowed herself to think about the men whose help she had enlisted. But now she must. And she was suddenly uncertain about what she was doing.

These were hard men. Like Garrick and his brothers. And they, like the Vikings, were both tall, broad, and powerful. She must have lost her mind! How could she hope to control such men?

As though knowing the path her thoughts had taken, Patrick sent her a quick glance. "Be not concerned," he urged softly. "There will be no trouble. I will personally guarantee that."

Nama gave an inward sigh of relief, feeling again as she had done before. Patrick could be trusted to keep his word, and he was strong enough to keep the others in line.

They had, of necessity, to cross the great hall, where warriors had sought their sleep upon the raised earthen side-floors. Feeling as though her heart were lodged in her throat, Nama crept across the room headed for the outer door, fearing at any given moment a cry would give away their presence. Finally, they were outside the great house and running toward the back of the building.

Nama saw Brynna step from behind the stables at the same moment that Patrick spied her. He stopped immediately, muttering curses beneath his breath as he wrapped his fingers around her forearm.

"Release me!" Brynna demanded angrily, reaching for the sword that was sheathed at her side.

"I cannot," he growled, pinning her with a hard gaze. "What are you about, running around in the middle of the night?"

"The same thing as you, fool!" she spat, glaring at him with rage. "I am going with you!"

Realizing she had not explained the change of plans to Patrick, Nama hurried to remedy that error.

Although Patrick was not overjoyed at the news, he held his silence, something that Mick O'Halloran refused to do when he joined them behind the inn near the pier. "The Lady Brynna should not be here," he complained. "She could spoil what little chance we have to escape this heathen place. They might have allowed us to leave without her, but with her along they are sure to come after us."

"Maybe we will be long gone before they know," Lacey said, eying Brynna with an inscrutable expression that made Nama uneasy. "Maybe the lady will bring us good luck. If we are caught, we could use her for barter."

"You are fools if you think they would not give chase," Brynna said. "With or without me. The plan requires a *langskip,* and not one of the men in my family would allow a vessel to escape them without going after it. Anyway, if I had not come, who would have outfitted the ship? We need food and water for the journey. What better way to load the supplies than have the guards do it for us?"

"They did not question the reason for loading the supplies?" Nama asked.

"Why should they?" Brynna replied. "Why should they suspect the daughter of the jarl of stealing a vessel?"

"She is right," Patrick said, pinning Mick with his hard gaze. "None suspected her. If you have no stomach for this, then go back to your home in the forest."

"Who would navigate for you?" Mick asked.

Patrick smiled at him. "I could find my way home blindfolded. Go back home, old man."

Nama interrupted. "If you are having doubts, please go home, Mick O'Halloran."

"No. I will stay with the rest of you." He sighed. "What have I to lose anyway? My life will soon come to an end. What does it matter if I die in bed or at the end of a blade?"

"No one is going to die," Brynna said quickly. "Is that understood by all? There is to be no bloodshed."

"What would you have us do if we are confronted by armed men when we try to board the vessel?" Lacey demanded. "Should we ask them real nice to step aside and allow us to make off with one of the jarl's longboats?"

"There will be no bloodshed," Brynna snapped.

"If anyone has a different opinion, then now is the time to say so.

"I say so," Lacey snarled.

Brynna stepped around the building, obviously planning to alert the guards to their presence, but Lacey's hands had already streaked out, his arms binding hers against her side while his right palm covered her mouth, muffling her cries as he dragged her back into the shadows.

"Here now," said Mick, whose old voice trembled. "Let the lass go."

"Loose her," commanded Patrick, the tip of his sword coming to rest at the base of Lacey's neck in a most threatening manner.

"What if she—" Lacey broke off as the blade dug into his flesh.

"Now," Patrick ordered grimly.

Lacey's breathing was harsh as he shoved Brynna toward Patrick. "The whole thing is on your head then," he snarled. "If we find ourselves hanging by our necks, then you know who to blame."

Brynna shivered and rubbed her upper arms. They were red from the pressure Lacey had applied to her flesh.

"Are you all right, Lady Brynna?" Patrick asked.

"Yes." Brynna summoned up a weak smile. "If we have any hope of carrying out our plan, then we must act quickly."

Nama quietly agreed with the other girl. Too much time had passed. Already, Garrick might have found a way out of his bonds. He could be searching for her even now.

And she was afraid of what he would do if he found her.

Thirty-two

Nama's knuckles were white as she tightened her grip on the ship's rail, her gaze searching the area around the pier for movement. But there was none. Nothing to cause her alarm. Nothing to tell her they had been discovered in their flight.

It had been easy . . . so easy.

Brynna had approached the guard and kept him distracted while Patrick Douglass positioned himself behind the man. A well-placed blow delivered by Patrick's fist had knocked the man senseless. He had crumpled to the ground, unaware of the others who quickly scrambled aboard the chosen vessel.

Silently, the men had taken up the oars. Lacey, Mick, and Gunther had manned one side of the longboat while Patrick and the other prisoner had taken positions on the opposite side.

Now the *langskip* moved silently across the water headed for the mouth of the fjord. At the pace they were traveling, they would soon reach the open sea.

With the guards out of the way and the longboat theirs, Nama found herself with time enough to consider her actions. Had she made a terrible mistake? she wondered.

The thought of never seeing Garrick again was almost more than she could bear. Yet how could she have shared him with his other women?

Oh, Garrick. Nama cried. Why could you not love me? Could you not see how my heart was breaking? Or was it only that you saw and did not care?

She swallowed around the pain in her heart and bowed her head, mourning the loss of her beloved.

Garrick sucked in a sharp breath when he saw the guard sprawled on the ground near the quay. His narrowed gaze swept over the longboats fastened to the long, narrow dock. He did not need to count them to see that one was missing. That much was obvious at a glance. There should have been five vessels at anchor. Instead, there were only four.

It was obvious that Patrick Douglass and the other escaped prisoners had taken to the open sea. The certainty that Nama must be with them sent fear streaking through Garrick.

"Odin's blood," he growled harshly. "I will see the lot of them boiled in oil if they disturb one hair on that woman's head!"

Suddenly Karl cried out. "Look there!" He pointed up the fjord. "In the shadows of the cliff."

Garrick strained his eyes and could just make out a large, moving shape.

"They are out the mouth of the fjord, not yet on the open sea!" Karl exclaimed.

"Man *The Defiant*," shouted Garrick, moving his arm in a wide sweep, urging the warriors who awaited his command to move onto the *langskip*. Every man among them knew the larger vessel the prisoners had stolen could never outrun the smaller longboat.

Leaping over the side, Garrick hurried to the stern, leaving the steering to the capable hands of Karl. He was unwilling to allow *The Argyle* out of his sight, afraid it would disappear into the fog that was only a short distance away and never be seen again.

"Man the oars," he shouted. "And unfurl the sails. We must catch that boat before she reaches the fog."

Garrick's heart thundered within his chest, beating in rhythm with the brawny crew as they bent forward, dipped the oars into the water and pulled back, bent and pulled, muscles straining with the effort expended to send the longboat along as fast as possible. And the vessel responded the way it was designed to respond. The boat cut smoothly through the water like a serpent, closing the distance between *The Defiant* and the larger vessel that had already left the fjord.

Garrick swallowed around the knot in his throat, realizing suddenly that the vessel that carried Nama away from him should have been easier to see now that it was no longer in the shadows of the cliff.

But it was not.

The wind gusted, whipping his hair around his face, obscuring his vision, and he pushed it away quickly, casting an anxious glance at the clouds that were quickly rolling in. Panic swept over him like wildfire, stabbing into his heart, that vital organ where pain had become firmly lodged, held there by the knowledge of Nama's betrayal.

He tried to tell himself it did not matter, but his heart would not listen. It continued to ache, to shrivel into itself until it was only a hard core of pain.

Garrick leaned forward, hoping to decrease wind resistance even while his mind told him they were still moving at a brisk pace. But even that pace seemed too slow.

"Row, men, row!" he shouted. "Put your backs into it. Move *The Defiant* along!"

They must overtake the other vessel, for the thought of losing Nama was more than he could bear.

The vessel that carried Nama and her companions had barely reached the mouth of the fjord when Wind Woman decided to make her anger known. She howled and moaned, tossing the longboat about as if it were no more than a leaf caught in a strong current after the spring thaw.

Realizing they dared not go on, Nama lurched across the deck to where Brynna stood, her feet braced apart, her golden hair flying around her head as though it had a life of its own.

Clutching Brynna's arm, Nama shouted to make herself heard. "Wind Woman is angry. We cannot continue. We must turn back."

"No." Brynna replied, her voice barely audible before it was swept away by the force of the storm.

"We must," Nama cried, fear stabbing at her. "If we continue, we will surely die!"

"I have weathered worse than this," Brynna shouted. "Hold on to the railing, else you may be flung into the sea."

Mindlessly, Nama clutched the railing and gripped it tightly. Not a moment too soon, either, for the ship plunged forward suddenly, reaching into the angry swells of the open sea.

The waves rose to mammoth heights, crashing into the longboat with so much power that Nama wondered how long the frail craft could withstand the battering.

"Help us, Blessed Star People," she cried, lifting her face toward the heavens.

But even as she beseeched them for assistance, she realized they could not come to her aid. They were probably not even aware of her predicament since most of the earth had become hidden from their view by Cloud Man, who had donned his heaviest cloak.

Nama watched anxiously as Cloud Man drifted closer and closer to Sister Moon, reaching for her with feathery fingers that seemed intent on obliterating her silvery face.

She realized that, if that happened, they would be lost. Without the pale light sent down by Sister Moon, the occupants of the longboat would be left in complete darkness, unable to navigate the large body of water that seemed intent on taking their lives.

But wait! Wind Woman had ceased her eternal wailing. Her breath had become gentle, almost nonexistent. Did that mean she no longer objected to their leaving?

"Unfurl the sails!" Patrick Douglass commanded.

"Have you lost your senses, man?" Mick O'Halloran asked. "If the wind picks up again, as it surely will, the sails would be ripped apart."

"We have no choice," Patrick growled. "Look down the fjord. We have company."

Nama's gaze followed Mick's, and she gave a start of surprise when she saw another longboat cutting through the water toward them.

"Unfurl those sails," Patrick said again.

The women hurried to help the old man, but the task that had gone so smoothly when Nama had arrived in Norway seemed awkward and clumsy now. And while they worked, the other longboat drew steadily closer.

"We will never make it," shouted the old man. "How can we expect to outrun them when they have ten times the manpower?"

"We cannot give up," shouted Patrick. "Heft those sails."

Nama's fingers fumbled as she tried to hurry

with the unfamiliar task while her heart thumped furiously in her chest.

"Hurry!" Patrick shouted. "They are almost on us!"

Even as he shouted the warning, it was already too late. Wood ground against wood as the boats collided. Vikings swarmed like locusts over the side of the smaller vessel onto the larger one that contained only a handful of people.

The men were quickly overcome by sheer numbers without a drop of blood having been spilt. Garrick's hard gaze pinned on Nama, who had sought refuge at the farthest point on the ship, the railing on the opposite side. He was halfway to her when Brynna suddenly flung herself into his path.

He stopped suddenly, a look of confusion covering his mask of anger. "Brynna?" he questioned. "They abducted you? By Thor they will—"

"No," she shouted, spreading her feet and glaring at him. "They carry no blame for my presence aboard this vessel."

"Then how? Why are you here?"

"I am with them. I stole the vessel, not them. I loaded it with supplies. If any is to blame then, it is I."

"You go against your own flesh and blood."

"As you did, Garrick, when you turned your back on me."

"I did nothing of the kind."

"You did. And I will not accept Angus Thorvauld for a husband."

"So you sought help from these cutthroats. Do you expect them to sway Father?"

"No, I expect Eric to sway him."

"Eric is dead."

"No," she cried. "He lives!" She pointed to Nama. "Ask her if you do not believe me. Eric is alive and well. He lives on the same mesa where the Eagle Clan dwells."

Again, Garrick pinned Nama with his gaze, and she flinched before the accusation she saw there. He started toward her and she backed away, sliding her hand loosely along the side railing.

Suddenly, without warning, Wind Woman became angry again. She howled and moaned, flinging spray against the vessel, obscuring Nama's vision. Knowing Garrick was fast approaching, she released the rail and wiped the water out of her eyes.

While she was in that vulnerable state, the bow of the longboat dipped suddenly, sliding into the valley of two giant waves. Nama was caught off guard; her feet slid out from under her, and as the boat surged upward, she was slammed against the railing with such force that the wood splintered.

She screamed, blinded by the spray that flooded the boat, swept toward the center, then pulled toward the railing again, striking it with such force that it cracked beneath her weight.

With unsteady legs, she tried to haul herself upright, using the rail for support, unaware of its weakness.

"Take my hand," Garrick shouted, stretching it toward her.

But Nama could not. The memory of his anger was too strong, too near the surface of her mind. She moved backward, trying to elude him.

Again the bow lifted, then plunged down into the valley between the waves. Nama grabbed for the railing, but there was nothing to save her from plunging over the side into the maelstrom of madness that waited below.

Garrick saw Nama fall into the ocean, and his heart gave a crazy lurch of fear, knowing it would take a miracle to save her now. But he could do no less than try, for life without her would not be worth living. He tied a rope around his waist as he searched the waves for her, knowing she would probably surface again and he would have to be ready at that moment.

"There!" Brynna shouted, pointing at a particularly large wave. "See! There she is!"

Garrick did see her, but only for a brief moment. Then the rough sea swallowed her again, dragging her under to what would surely be her watery grave.

Garrick dove into the water, uncaring that his life might be forfeited, his only thought to save the girl who had stolen his heart.

But the ocean was so big, so vast, and the swells so high that, even though he searched the water around him, his arms remained empty.

Refusing to give up, Garrick sucked in a huge gulp of air and went under again to renew his search. He stayed there, sweeping the water with outstretched hands until his lungs burned from lack of air.

God help me! his mind screamed as a red haze began to form behind his eyes.

Realizing he must have air if he had any hope of finding Nama, he struggled upward, bursting from the water and gulping at the life-giving air. *Nama!* his mind screamed. Where are you?

He looked at the longboat, riding the waves so near to hand, and saw Patrick pointing behind him. Spinning around, Garrick caught a glimpse of a white face before it went under again.

Frantically, he swam that way, his powerful shoulder muscles fighting the pull of the current as he sought to reach the woman who had captured his heart. A wave surged upward as he felt something brush his arm, saw the tangle of dark hair wrapping around his wrist.

But even as he reached for her, he began to slide into the valley created by the rising waves. Desperately, he clutched at the hair sliding away from him, wrapped his fingers in it, and pulled her closer.

Kicking his feet, he launched himself closer to her, grabbed her wrist as they slid into the trough and were quickly submerged by the waves washing over them.

His heart exulted with gladness.

Never mind that danger was all around them,

that they were both on the point of drowning. And never mind that the waves were swelling higher with each passing moment.

No. Never mind. The only thing that really mattered was the reality of Nama, clutched tightly against his chest. And if their days on this earth were over, then they would go to that great beyond together.

Together, as they were meant to be.

Garrick allowed his body to relax, knowing it was useless to continue to fight the current and content in the knowledge that Nama was held fast in his arms.

Suddenly, he felt a tug at his waist, remembered the rope fastened there, and realized the other Vikings were bent on pulling them out of the ocean.

Hope flared anew and, without releasing his precious bundle, he kicked his feet, helping the crew all he could in their efforts to save them.

Thirty-three

Nama lay among the rumpled bedclothes, feeling replete in the aftermath of Garrick's loving.

It had been two weeks since she had attempted to leave him and not a day had passed since then that she had failed to murmur a prayer of thanks to the guiding spirits for sending Garrick after her.

We were both so near death, she thought, and it was all so unnecessary. If I had listened to my heart, I would never have tried to leave him.

Tears misted her eyes as she remembered the way she had regained consciousness and found him bending over her, speaking of his love for all to hear. It was still hard to believe in that love. And hard to believe she had been forgiven for deceiving him about Eric.

The Spirits must surely have guided her footsteps when she left her mountain and crossed that desert. They must have known she and Garrick were meant for each other.

"What are you thinking about, love?" Garrick whispered tenderly, his breath soft against her ear.

Smiling at him with misty eyes, "I was just remembering how we met." She spoke her thoughts aloud.

"Do you believe your Spirits guided me as well?" Garrick asked with a smile. "After all, if I had not been in that place at that time, I would not have found you."

"Yes," she said, "The Spirits sent you to me."

"Nonsense," he laughed. "They had no hand in my destination. I found you because I decided to go for a walk beside the river."

"But you were at the river," she argued.

"Because it was the way my brother had gone before me," he explained. "No, my love. I am afraid your Spirits cannot take credit for that."

"Believe what you will," she said, eying him sternly. "But I know how you came to be where you were. You were led there by another hand."

"That of big brother Eric," Garrick said stubbornly.

She grew silent as he mentioned his brother again. "Are you certain you have forgiven me for deceiving you about your brother?"

"Eric?" he questioned, raising his coppery brows. "Yes, my love. You are forgiven. How could I begrudge you when I almost lost you? You have explained your reasons." He uttered a heavy sigh. "But it does mean another long journey."

"He may not wish to return with you. Have you considered that?"

"Not return to his home?" he questioned. "What nonsense! Of course he will return with us."

"His heart is no longer his own," she reminded. "He has given it to Shala."

"If she is anything like you, he will not leave her behind."

"She will not come." The words fell between them like stones.

"Not come?" he asked. "Why would she not come? You said she loves him."

"Eric means more to her than anyone else . . . except possibly her babe," she amended.

"She has a child?" He frowned at her. "You did not tell me that."

"Because the child was not born when last I saw her."

"And the child's father?"

"Eric."

"So he has a child, does he?" A wide grin spread across his face. "It is hard to think of Eric as a father," he mused.

"And yourself, Garrick?" she questioned softly. "Do you have trouble thinking of yourself as a father?"

"I never considered it before."

"You had better do so," Nama whispered softly.

He sucked in a sharp breath and his eyes rounded with surprise. "Are you—does that mean—are we—"

"We are going to be parents," she explained since he could not find the words to finish his question. "Do you mind very much?"

"Mind? Of course not!" He squeezed her tightly,

then looked alarmed. "Are you all right? Did I hurt you? Do you need anything?" he rambled.

"Yes. I am all right." She laughed, answering his first question. "And no, you did not hurt me, and again no, I need nothing." She gazed up at him with sparkling eyes. "Are you happy, Garrick?"

"A family of my own. My heart is too full for words."

"Then perhaps you can see how your brother feels about leaving Shala behind."

"But there would be no need to," he argued. "Shala and the baby will come with him."

"She is afraid of your gods, Garrick. She will not come here."

"Our gods? They are only a myth, Nama. We no longer believe in their power."

"Yet I have heard you call upon them." Her eyes were wide with confusion.

"You misunderstand, Nama. I speak to the ancient gods, Thor and Odin, as I would speak to friends. When I am angry I call out their names. But when there is fear in my heart, when I am in pain, I call upon the one true God: The Christian God that created the heavens and all creatures great and small. It was to Him I prayed when you were close to death. And it was He who answered my prayer."

"Shala did not know," Nama muttered. "How could she when Eric continually called out to the ancient gods?"

"Then you must tell her," Garrick said, leaning up on one elbow.

"Then you intend taking me with you?" Her heart beat faster at the thought.

"Of course," he said, tightening his arms around her. "I could never leave without you. I need you beside me."

"To speak for you?"

"That, among other reasons," he said, tracing the curve of her lips with his tongue, causing goose bumps to break out on her arms.

She shivered and nestled her head into the curve of his shoulder. "I am glad you need me, Garrick. Do you think Olaf will travel with us?"

"I imagine so."

"When will we go?"

"My, you are full of questions," he teased.

"But I wish to know," she pouted. "When will we go?"

"Soon after Brynna's wedding."

Nama became still, a fact that he seemed unaware of. "So your father still insists on the wedding, even though Brynna has no wish to marry Angus."

"Yes, he does insist. And, perhaps it is for the best. That little escapade two weeks ago proved that Brynna needs a strong guiding hand. Angus can provide that." He tightened his arms around Nama, apparently unaware of her growing anger. "Now, go to sleep, love. Do not trouble yourself about my sister."

Nama lay in the bed beside him, her thoughts raced. He was not an innocent girl who was being forced to join with a man she had reason to fear.

After Garrick was sleeping soundly, Nama sought Brynna out in her bedchamber. The two girls whispered together for a while, making plans for the future.

"Garrick will be angry with you for helping me," Brynna muttered when the plans were made to their satisfaction.

Nama shrugged her shoulders. "My husband has been angry with me before and I have no doubt will become so again."

"Nevertheless, Garrick may suspect you."

Again, Nama shrugged. "If there are questions asked of me, then my answers will be truthful. But you will be too far away to be caught by the time that occurs."

"You are not afraid of him?"

Nama smiled a secret smile. "I have ceased to fear him," she replied, then told her secret in the language of the People.

Brynna's eyes widened. "Did you say you were with child?" she asked, obviously wondering if she had misunderstood the words that Nama had been teaching her for the last two weeks.

"Yes," Nama affirmed. "That is so."

"The babe will be here before I return," Brynna said wistfully.

"Never mind," Nama replied. "There will be other children. Come now." She wrapped her fingers around a heavy statue that rested on a table. "It is growing late, Brynna. We should hurry."

The two women left the bedchamber and hurried down the dark hall leading to the dungeon.

Before Brynna opened the door, she cautioned Nama to remain where the guard could not see her.

A few moments later Nama heard the sound of the guard's voice. "Who goes there?" he asked gruffly.

Nama heard Brynna reply. "It is only I, the Lady Brynna."

"Lady Brynna!" the guard exclaimed. "I never thought it was you, lass. I was sure it was the other one. Garrick's woman."

Nama crept silently down the stairwell, stopping at the curve and peeping around. She could see the guard scratching his grizzled head. "I would never have suspected the wench of drugging me. Well, I got me orders now. No ale while on duty. And a sad thing it is, too."

Nama felt relief that Brynna's part in the escapade had been kept secret; otherwise the guard would not have been so relaxed.

"Here I am rambling on like this, and you have come here for a particular reason," he went on. "Now, what can I do for you, my lady?"

"I would like to speak with Patrick Douglass," Brynna said.

"Well, now, my lady . . ." He seemed embarrassed. "I've got orders about that."

"Oh," Brynna said, coming down the stairs and standing near the cell to keep the guard's back to the steps. "What are those orders?"

"They said nobody was to go near the prisoners. They've got plans for them."

Nama clutched the heavy statue tightly, hoping she could strike the guard hard enough, but not so hard that she would do permanent injury to him.

She was vaguely aware of Brynna's loud, complaining voice, but Nama tuned the words out as she crept quietly down the stairs.

Slowly . . . slowly . . . just one more step and she would be situated just above the guard's head.

Nama raised the statue high and saw Brynna's gaze caught by the movement, knew by the way the guard suddenly tensed that he had been alerted.

He began to turn and Nama struck, bringing the statue down to meet the guard's head. She heard a dull thud as ivory met flesh and saw him crumple to the floor.

Then Nama stood there, staring at the guard she had felled, unable to make a sound, unable to move a muscle as Brynna snatched up the guard's keys and released the prisoners.

Patrick's gaze immediately found the guard, and he knelt beside him and took his wrist between finger and thumb. "His pulse is steady," he said, meeting Nama's eyes. "You have done him no real harm."

"He has no idea you were involved, Nama," Brynna said softly. "Return to your bedchamber. Stay there with Garrick. No one need ever know the part you played in all this."

The two women embraced each other, then Brynna hurried off toward the town and beyond . . . to the docks where a longship was anchored, still carrying the supplies they had loaded two weeks before, since it had been decided that Karl would use the vessel on another journey that would take place the day after tomorrow.

It appeared Garrick had not changed position since Nama had left him; but the moment she crawled into bed beside him, he uttered a sigh and reached for her, drawing her close against him.

Nama lay awake long into the night, thinking of Brynna and praying she would be all right.

There was no doubt in Nama's mind about her actions. She could have done nothing else. Brynna had a right to live her life as she chose, with whomever she chose. And she did not choose to join with Angus Thorvauld.

Nama herself had refused to accept a man she feared and had faced many hardships. But if she had it all to do over again, she would make the same choice.

Because she had left her people, she had found Garrick. The Spirits had guided Nama to her love, and perhaps, they would also help Brynna.

And Brynna had something that Nama had not had.

She had Patrick Douglass beside her.

Remembering the way Patrick had looked at Brynna, Nama felt certain he would stand between Brynna and danger. He was a strong man. Powerful. And he would look after the young Viking woman until the day she found the man of her dreams.

The man who stood guard near the quay, un-suspecting of another attack, was easily overcome. He was quickly trussed up, bound hand and foot and gagged with a rag shoved into his mouth to keep him from sounding the alarm.

Soon the *langskip,* already stocked with goods for a long trip, slid smoothly out of the fjord and into the open sea.

And on a great mesa in a faraway land another Viking waited . . . knowing that one day another *langskip* would sail up the big muddy river that fed into the ocean.

That is another story though, soon to be told.

TODAY'S HOTTEST READS
ARE TOMORROW'S SUPERSTARS

VICTORY'S WOMAN (4484, $4.50)
by Gretchen Genet
Andrew—the carefree soldier who sought glory on the battlefield, and returned a shattered man . . . Niall—the legandary frontiersman and a former Shawnee captive, tormented by his past . . . Roger—the troubled youth, who would rise up to claim a shocking legacy . . . and Clarice—the passionate beauty bound by one man, and hopelessly in love with another. Set against the backdrop of the American revolution, three men fight for their heritage—and one woman is destined to change all their lives forever!

FORBIDDEN (4488, $4.99)
by Jo Beverley
While fleeing from her brothers, who are attempting to sell her into a loveless marriage, Serena Riverton accepts a carriage ride from a stranger—who is the handsomest man she has ever seen. Lord Middlethorpe, himself, is actually contemplating marriage to a dull daughter of the aristocracy, when he encounters the breathtaking Serena. She arouses him as no woman ever has. And after a night of thrilling intimacy—a forbidden liaison—Serena must choose between a lady's place and a woman's passion!

WINDS OF DESTINY (4489, $4.99)
by Victoria Thompson
Becky Tate is a half-breed outcast—branded by her Comanche heritage. Then she meets a rugged stranger who awakens her heart to the magic and mystery of passion. Hiding a desperate past, Texas Ranger Clint Masterson has ridden into cattle country to bring peace to a divided land. But a greater battle rages inside him when he dares to desire the beautiful Becky!

WILDEST HEART (4456, $4.99)
by Virginia Brown
Maggie Malone had come to cattle country to forge her future as a healer. Now she was faced by Devon Conrad, an outlaw wounded body and soul by his shadowy past . . . whose eyes blazed with fury even as his burning caress sent her spiraling with desire. They came together in a Texas town about to explode in sin and scandal. Danger was their destiny—and there was nothing they wouldn't dare for love!

Available wherever paperbacks are sold, or order direct from the Publisher. Send cover price plus 50¢ per copy for mailing and handling to Penguin USA, P.O. Box 999, c/o Dept. 17109, Bergenfield, NJ 07621. Residents of New York and Tennessee must include sales tax. DO NOT SEND CASH.